FIREWEED

AN AMERICAN SAGA

Nellie Buxton Picken

Kenmore, WA

Northwest Corner books, an imprint of Epicenter Press Inc., publishes reprints of out of print titles about the Pacific Northwest.
For more information, visit www.EpicenterPress.com

Published by arrangement with Epicenter Press, Inc.

Cover design by Aubrey White

ISBN: 978-1-941890-18-9 (Paperback)
ISBN: 978-1-941890-17-2 (Ebook)

Library of Congress Control Number: 2018955684

Printed in the United States of America

In loving memory
Robert Lyons Picken, Sr. (1891-1967)
and
Robert Lyons Picken, Jr. (1916-1988)

Contents

I.

Lifestyle, Okanogan Valley

1.

A Father and Son Management

As soon as he heard the rattle and jerk of the paper carrier's Ford truck, Ed McLaren jumped from the leather chair he had been waiting in and walked outside for the newspaper just delivered to the tin cylinder on the post at the end of the driveway. McLaren, cattleman for fifty years, retrieved the *Spokesman-Review* and stood with it in his hand as he surveyed the breaking day in the Okanogan Valley of Washington State.

The mid-June sunshine was already glittering on the sharp, snow-capped peaks of the Cascade Range to the west. This morning even the white clouds in the ultramarine sky had distinct edges.

When Ed stepped outside in the Okanogan country he became companion to the whole natural world. In one sweeping glance, he had an unobstructed view of two mountain ranges with forested slopes; flat-topped alluvial benches, some covered with irrigated apple orchards, and some with a shaggy rug of wild sunflowers, purple lupine, and sagebrush; and the long stretch of bottomland. The Okanogan River, which meanders out of Osoyoos Lake at the Canadian border, bisects the bottomland. The river can be traced to its confluence with the Columbia River by the corridor of cottonwoods and bushes on the banks, the only greenery in what might appear to strangers as a dry and barren trough.

Ed's house was situated halfway along the river course. He owned the sixty acres of land that sloped down to the river behind his house. Across the river rose the palisade of Whitestone Mountain, precipitous, striated sedimentary rock, down which a lovelorn Indian maiden might have hurtled herself with great dramatic effect.

The water-grade highway that ran a hundred yards in front of Ed's house had been first an Indian trail, then the ready-made roadway for trappers visiting Fort Okanogan, established in 1811 at the confluence of the rivers. The next travelers were miners in the 1880s, hurrying up the Okanogan trail to the gold strike in the Cariboo country. Now the highway, running north and south, links the towns from Oroville to Brewster, the traffic consisting of hay trucks, truckloads of cattle and apples for market, and tourists' cars.

The Okanogan National Forest, above the benches on both sides of the river, is a vast area of pine, fir, and tamarack trees, interspersed with groves of quaking aspen that turn a shimmering gold in the fall. Hidden in the forest are small valleys watered by streams: Cecile Creek, Sarsepkin, Bonaparte, Antwyne, Scotch Creek, Salmon Creek, and more. In these valleys are the cattle ranches. From mid-June to September cattle graze on the bunchgrass, pine grass, and pea vine in the national forest. The timber is also a hideaway for deer, bear, cougars, bobcats, and rattlesnakes. Of the forest birds, magpies and crows are most numerous.

In addition to the valleys and streams, the forest offers the riches of Conconully, Osoyoos, and Lost lakes, and a dozen more small, concealed lakes. They are popular vacation spots, where fishermen can catch rainbow trout varying in size from ten ounces to six pounds.

A QUARTER-MILE BEYOND Ed's house stood a sign: "WELCOME TO BONAPARTE POP. 515."

The citizens of Bonaparte provided services to valley inhabitants within a radius of thirty miles. They ran the bank, stores, clothing shops, pharmacies, movie theater, and cattle auction, as well as the U.S. Forest Service office and the post office.

The town was named for Mount Bonaparte, largest among the scoured rock monsters of the Okanogan Highlands, the old, rounded mountains to the east. Bonaparte, with an elevation of more than seven thousand feet, asserts its authority over Phoebe Mountain, Spur, Strawberry, Buckhorn, Hull, Ruby, Buck, and all the others in the range.

As he stood in the driveway, Ed noted fog on the face of Mount Bonaparte. Bill was there with cows and late calves. Ed suspected that he should have helped drive the herd to the mountain range despite the protests of his son and his wife. Bill had no feeling for how cows were uneasy in fog.

Eleanor, Ed's wife, had told him the night before, "I don't care when you get up, but I am not cooking breakfast until seven. Bill said he doesn't need you; they can get an earlier start if they don't have to wait for you."

Bill and his family lived ten miles up the highway on the river at what was still called the Johnston place after the first owner. The Lazy Ear corrals and feed lots had been at the Johnston place since Ed bought the homestead forty years ago; he had discovered that Eleanor could not endure the proximity of the cow business—the bulls riding the cows, the uninhibited pissing and shitting. Fortunately, Bill's wife, who had grown up around livestock, seemed oblivious to the activities that bothered Eleanor.

Ed lingered a moment. One old tom cougar, who lived in the middle of the shale and was getting stiff for overtaking wild deer, might try to sneak up on a calf. But trust Bill to have the .30-30 saddle carbine handy if necessary—sometimes even when it was not necessary. Ed turned his attention from the range and walked into the house.

Throughout his adult life Ed had lived in what was now pointed out as the "First House in Bonaparte." As a bachelor homesteader he had knocked together the first version from government sawmill scrap lumber. When he married he hammered on an extra room and pantry; later, sleeping quarters for his two boys. When his daughter was born he paid a carpenter to add another bedroom. Eleanor construed as stubbornness Ed's attachment to the work of his own hands. Even though comparative prosperity now made a new house possible, Eleanor had been forced to settle for a remodeled one with an electric range and refrigerator.

The piecemeal dwelling had been unified by the addition of a low porch on three sides of the house. Landscaped in front with heavy sod, and in back with a windbreak of Jonathan apple trees, the home was comfortable, and even picturesque from the road. The lawn was watered by overflow from the irrigation ditch every ten days. When the boys had lived at home, Eleanor had made them mow the lawn regularly, but now that they were in homes of their own, the grass grew eight to ten inches high before Ed hired a neighbor boy to cut it with a mulcher. Letting the grass grow was not negligence; Ed liked high grass. He was also proud of Eleanor's flower garden. Whenever he had the lawn chopped, he told the boy to cultivate the flower garden, too. Eleanor grew prize-winning gladioli and roses.

SETTLED AT THE dining table in the ell, Ed scanned the front page of the newspaper to which he had subscribed for as long as it had been delivered in the valley. Eleanor had twenty minutes to make good her promise of breakfast by seven. In the kitchen, she was plunking the frying pan on the burner and filling the coffeepot at the sink with brisk efficiency. In a moment he smelled and heard bacon frying and coffee percolating.

The newspaper featured a picture of, and an interview with, Ezra Taft Benson, the Utah Mormon whom President Eisenhower had appointed secretary of agriculture. The secretary, Ed knew, would be guest speaker at the National Cattleman's Association annual meeting at Denver. He had felt the impulse to attend one more national conference, but when he had spoken to Bill about their making the trip together, his son showed little interest.

Prognosticators said that the cattlemen's conclave this year, 1954, would be more controversial than any in history. Some Western cattlemen, not long in the business and not so enamored of the rugged individualist traditions of the National Cattleman's Association, had formed an organization to push the cause of price supports on cattle.

"Sure, price supports would give the market a boost," the Old Line growled, "and for a while everything will be rosy. But what of the effect of a guaranteed profit in the business of cattle raising? More cattle! Cattle numbers are already at an all-time high—ninety million."

"You have to be big or go under," Bill declared.

His father answered consistently, "You don't want more cattle than you can feed yourself. Start buying feed, and you start buying your tombstone. One hard winter will clear out flimsy operators. Never let your supply of hay run out."

Even now, cattle foraging on inadequate grassland were starving until their bones stuck out. Men new to the stock business had counted too heavily for feed on small acreages of river meadow bought at enormous figures. People were installing expensive sprinkler systems on meadow pastures to make them more productive. Bill, too, was wrangling for automatic sprinklers at the Johnston place.

"You want sprinklers on the meadow because they're stylish, but they're unnecessary to our layout," Ed maintained.

Office of Price Stabilization administrator Michael V. DiSalle, days before his departure, had blandly told the Associated Press, "We most emphatically do not intend to remove price controls from beef and cattle. On the contrary, new enforcement measures are under study."

DiSalle was gone. Ezra Taft Benson was the new man for the new chapter in progress. The lid was off the price of beef. Benson, in the front-page article this morning, announced his intention to reduce governmental control of agriculture.

Ed turned to the inside pages of the *Review* to look for propaganda for the Wilderness Bill, but found none. He noticed with satisfaction a small report: "A House-Senate conference committee yesterday approved $13,000,000 for range improvements on the national forests, plus a $170,000 increase for range resource administration and $90,000 for revegetation."

On page five, "Regional News," his eye caught a young man's face, with Indian eyes, calmly looking at him from the newsprint. The caption read: "Delbert Gaston, Conconully, Okanogan County, announced his candidacy for U.S. Congressman from the Fifth District at a Republican caucus meeting in the Jim Hill Hotel in Omak on Monday."

The accompanying article said: "Gaston, member of the state legislature for two terms, makes his bid with the support of Okanogan County Republican progressives who favor modernization of public land laws. He will speak to the Okanogan County Cattleman's Association on Friday, June 18, at the annual meet in Omak."

Ed's chest tightened; his vision blurred. Analix Westmore Gaston's son, with whom Ed had avoided direct acquaintance for thirty-five years, was facing him.

ELEANOR, SMALL AND angular, clad in the day's full armor of fresh cotton housedress and apron, entered from the kitchen with the coffeepot. She looked over Ed's shoulder at the paper.

"Who's that?"

"Fellow running for congressman. Grandson of Old Man Westmore."

"Mort won't want him. You know what people will say."

"What will they say?"

"At least quarter-breed Injun."

"Doesn't make much difference these days—never did except to people like your brother."

"I've never understood why you always took up for the Westmores—squaw man and his brood."

"I don't want any coffee."

"Ha! Scared because your hands tremble lately. Your body isn't iron anymore."

She filled her own cup, placed the pot on a trivet, and made a second trip to the kitchen for bacon and eggs. When they finished eating, Eleanor began clearing the dishes.

Ed went to his bedroom to pick up his Stetson from the dresser. Like many Okanogan cattlemen, he constantly wore a hat as protection from wind, rain, and sun for his bald head.

Eleanor followed him to the porch.

"Here's your jacket. You left it on your chair. I put a sandwich in the pocket."

"Don't need a jacket. It's summer."

"Still June."

Grateful for the sandwich but unable to admit it, he accepted the garment. The only emotion he and Eleanor felt free to express verbally to one another was irritation. They communicated by third party. At times, Ed said to Bill, "Your mother doesn't give a damn about me. Lives in a world of her own. All she cares about are her blood relatives."

"For not giving a damn, she's fed you and kept you clean a long time," Bill replied.

Eleanor's favorite remark to Bill was, "Your father could show more consideration."

"Oh, he looks out for you," Bill would assure her.

"Where are you going this time?" Eleanor asked her husband.

"I'll be in the pickup most of the day."

"Remember I've asked Bill and Susan to dinner. Try and get home on time for once. You stayed out till dark last night."

"Stayed out till dark most of my life, haven't I?"

"For your age, you do an awful lot of running around."

She ignored his snort. "If you're bound to go someplace, why don't you find Bill and remind him about dinner? He takes after his father in forgetting time."

Ed backed the half-ton pickup from the garage and drove in second gear through town. He shifted into high on Number 7, North.

Although Ed had sidestepped sharing his plans with Eleanor, he had a definite program of activity for the day. He had been in haste to escape the darts of his wife's tongue. Seeing the picture of the young quarter-breed Indian, Delbert Gaston, in the *Spokesman-Review* had aroused an agony that had never been reflected anywhere in its true proportions. Ed had willed himself to think of other things for thirty-five years.

His first stop was at his leased lands on the national forest. He must begin studying leases and deeds he held. He parked his pickup at one side of the trail in case any vehicle wanted past, hiked a quarter-mile, and ensconced himself on a stump to survey the terrain. He recalled that he had left home without taking his morning dose of medicine that Doc Crothers had prescribed a few days before. The physician's words had given immediacy to the question of how long Ed could continue to manage his properties and business actively. Recently Ed had experienced a dizzy spell as he had stalked away from an altercation with Bill.

Bill, at the Johnston place corral, had been gunning calves through the routine of branding with the use of a holding device, a contraption he called a "cradle."

Ed's lifelong procedure, learned from Carr Westmore, was to assign a husky boy to throw a calf to the ground. One boy sat on the animal to hold it down while another whipped a rope about the neck and hind legs for the few seconds needed to apply the hot brand. The simple method of body contact caused minimal pain and fright to the calf.

Bill's use of the cradle—an authoritarian, impersonal tool—made Ed bark out the cowman's precept, "Take it easy!"

Bill, who was extracting a red-hot brand from the fire, asked, "What's a matter?"

"Gettin' rough, aren't you?" Ed challenged his son. "I don't like that cradle."

Bill shrugged.

"With this rig we're doin' a hundred in a couple hours. We gotta get done. These critters shoulda been on the range a week ago. You said so yourself."

Bill, thirty-nine years old, was a husky fellow who had been adept with stock from childhood. His handsome face, shining with sweat from the brand fire, showed that he was fed too well by his women—his wife and his mother.

"I don't like that electric prod you're usin', either," Ed added.

Hugo Salk, who was using the prod to herd calves one by one through the chute, shared the old man's doubts. Throughout the Second World War, while the boys were away, Hugo had been Ed's right hand.

"I never seen such jumpin' and caterwaulin'. You got 'em scared before they get near the brand. You oughta tell Bill, Ed. They're gonna break some necks and ribs."

"You tell me to manage, Dad, so *let* me!" Bill interrupted.

"We'll back off, Hugo," Ed decided with effort. "You go ahead and run things, Bill. I'll count—if you still do that in your operation."

He took the grease pencil from the top of the corral fence post, clamped his mouth shut, and stood ready to tally. As he recorded steers and females by fives on the plank, he willed his anger away.

A jobber named Oldern owned and operated the cradle. With ruthless firmness, Oldern clamped each calf between curved metal bars while Bill applied the brand and cut off the testicles. When a terror-stricken animal thrashed about excessively, the jobber sometimes reopened the jaws and made adjustments.

Oldern's response was too slow for one hapless baby bull. At the animal's bawl of anguish, Oldern manipulated the levers. When the iron jaws finally gaped open, the bull lay still. Bill carried it to the grass outside the corral.

Ed stared at the inanimate object. Wide-open eyes had turned to stone. Rebuke had echoed in its final cry over the meadow: the anger of young life denied fruition. An hour ago the calf had frolicked and sucked. Soon, the mother, as her udder swelled, would low mournfully from the herd. Let Bill explain to her, "All the men who make big bucks use cradles to speed operations."

Flinging away the tally pencil, Ed strode to his pickup.

"Where you goin'?" Bill called.

"I'm not hangin' around here. Nobody can tell you a damn thing!"

Bill had the grace to walk over to his father.

"Cool off! One calf, thirty dollars. We can take the loss of a few head and come out with a profit."

"You go to the Hot Place!"

Ed jammed his foot on the gas pedal and sped away, leaving a trail of blue exhaust.

A MILE ALONG the road, he was forced to stop the pickup. His heart was pounding in a way it had never done before. A sharp pain was running the length of his arm.

When his heart slowed, Ed restarted the truck. The pain persisted enough to make him stop in town to see Doc Crothers. Doc had served in the army throughout the war; he had also learned to drink in the army. Some people preferred to take their aches and pains to the abstinent new doctor in town, but Ed had never seen Doc Crothers inebriated. Anyhow, he could confide in a man with a few open, human troubles of his own.

"What do you think it was, Doc?"

"Can't say for sure. Ever had a spell like this before?"

"I got dizzy once after a bronc threw me off before local option."

Doc laughed.

"Wish I'd seen it! You're O.K. now, likely, but I'm going to subject you to the indignities of physical examination. Take off your clothes and put on this gown."

After a blood pressure test, a prick in the end of his finger, and an electrocardiogram, Ed waited for the diagnosis.

"You've got to expect symptoms when you reach seventy, Ed," Doc began. "Your heart isn't thirty years old anymore."

"Did I have a heart attack?"

"Not an actual heart attack, but it seems like you had some anginal pain."

"Should I forget the whole thing? I was kinda mad at Bill just before it happened."

Doc Crothers paused, shifted in his seat, and looked Ed in the eye.

"I'm not the lying type, Ed. You wouldn't appreciate any soft soap. Telling it straight, I'd say from the looks of your EKG, you ought to make out a will."

"Holy mackinaw! How much time have I got?"

"Oh, nothing definite as that! You'll probably live another twenty years. But you wouldn't like to get caught short. What I mean is you better make your plans for the long haul for your family. Stops feuding later."

"I get the message. Anything I have to be careful about?"

"Yep. Almost everything connected with the cow business. You can ride, but no lassoing steers. Get your rest. If you feel a pain like the one you had today coming on, put one of these tablets under your tongue and let it dissolve. Keep the bottle handy. And here's some high-quality syrup for your blood pressure. Better hide it from Eleanor. She'll look at the alcohol content on the label and throw it out."

Ed put the bottle of tablets in the glove compartment of the pickup. He probably would never need them. He stashed the syrup in the bottom drawer of his bureau. Eleanor found it the first time she put in a supply of clean socks and underwear. She forced him to explain to her what it was.

"No surprise to me your blood pressure is up," she said, "the way you traipse around, acting like a kid."

She left the bottle where it lay and went to the kitchen for a tablespoon.

"I suppose you've been swigging it. Did you notice the label says one tablespoon at a time?"

ED, SITTING ON the stump, deliberated over the future of his estate. He had never been as sure as Eleanor of Bill's ability to manage the Lazy Ear, but Bill, the only one of their children at Bonaparte, was the logical candidate. The older boy, Sam, was a professor of agronomy at Iowa State College of Agriculture. Leila, their daughter, was married to a Whitman County wheat farmer who was in partnership with his father.

If Bill was to take charge, written applications should be made for transfer of the leases on Forest Service and Bureau of Land Management grazing lands.

What Ed saw around him worried him. Since 1905 he had grazed cattle here among the fir, pine, tamarack, and spruce, on the forest floor carpeted with native grasses. He knew that when permits were passed from one family member to another, the government agencies were showing an increased inclination to reduce the number of animal units allowed on a given range. By assuming the lease, Bill would face the risk of a cut in the cattle herd.

At one time, the bunchgrass here had grown knee-high and rippled like water in the wind. The timbered area had been like an open park with young, well-spaced trees. But the trees had become mature, then old, and finally, diseased. And the increasing amount of underbrush, protected against burning by Forest Service policy, kept livestock from access to the grass.

On his own property, Ed sold his mature trees to Biles-Coleman Lumber Company and cleared and burned the underbrush so that grass could flourish. He had the best private range in the country; his cows were the sleekest and fattest.

When asked for his secrets, he responded, "Secrets, hell! I study range management journals. Your cow crop is as good as the grass it eats! For grass to grow, you have to get rid of the old timber and underbrush, or nature will take care of the whole problem of dead wood with one fire that will burn from natural barrier to natural barrier over the whole forest. Question of time is all it is. Forest Service land is a tinderbox. The policy of no brush-burning has to be changed."

Bill tried to downplay his father's controversial opinion. "Lots of folks think you have to go easy on that controlled brush-burning. You just make the Forest Service sore when you argue with them, and you get everybody in dutch."

"Oh, I know it," Ed said bitterly. "I got nobody on my side but the facts. Forest Service land is stagnating."

At the moment Ed had no one to talk back to him. He walked to a spring that he had enlarged by blasting it out with dynamite several years ago. He had installed a trough as a watering place for his cattle, carefully dividing it with a log to prevent stock from climbing in and hurting themselves or fouling up the water. Ed took a tin cup from a post and dipped it into the cold water that was fit to drink for human beings as well as cows.

A quarter-mile below, Ed spied Bill and noted with satisfaction that he was at work on the barbwire fence that divided the McLaren lease land from the Caliente place on the south. Ed and Bill had agreed that the old fence needed a fourth strand of wire. One thing to be said for Bill was that as soon as he finished one job he began another. He had been up since four herding the cows and calves to the range, and now he was making them secure. A large spool of barbwire, threaded on a spindle crowbar, was loaded on the bed of Bill's truck. Ed could hear Bill's hammer ringing as he pounded staples into fence posts.

When Ed saw that Bill had company, he bristled; it looked like the Caliente girl, wearing blue Levi's. A cayuse was grazing nearby with the reins dropped over its ears. It was difficult for Ed to believe that the girl was there to help—no Caliente ever helped keep up a fence—but when Bill moved the truck forward, the girl guided the wire along the ground as it unrolled from the spool

Her father, Old Man Caliente, would shamelessly parade lumpjaws fit only for canning at the Bonaparte auction. As soon as it was legally possible, he took his sons from school to work on the ranch. But the sons, one by one, ran away to follow the rodeos. Caliente refused to join the Cattleman's Association or even to vote for fair legislation such as branding laws. He abused his livestock and moved onto the range too early in the spring. Just as he trampled the grass, he trampled everything else.

Ed had heard gossip that the girl with Bill, the only girl in the family, had managed to stay in school through the twelfth grade. Mrs. Caliente—who had once been a plump, giggly girl employed in the Bonaparte tavern, but who now looked considerably harder—had come to town for the first time in ten years and withdrawn money from the family bank account to buy her daughter a high school graduation dress. But the girl had not attended the evening exercises. People said that Old Man Caliente had sent her to round up strays on graduation day and that she got lost in the hills and was out all night.

She still had not gone about her business when Ed finished eating the sandwich that Eleanor had put in his jacket pocket. He would have delivered the reminder about dinner if Bill had been alone.

He hiked back to his pickup and continued to a tract of his own deeded timberland on the far side of the mountain. Here, too, the trees—Douglas fir and white pine—had attained their full growth, the top branches flattened out and the bark turned yellow. He would offer the timber to Biles-Coleman, and after they logged it, he would burn the stumps and fallen timber and reseed the grass.

2.

Transfer of Responsibility

Evening fog was rising in the hills when Ed conceded that it was time to go home—time to announce a change in management of the Lazy Ear, his spread. It would come as no surprise. Eleanor had intuitively invited dinner guests for the occasion.

The sun had edged deeply southwest, but despite his lateness, Ed stopped the pickup when he glimpsed a conical canvas tent. It was of the mail-order variety used by the Okanogan Indians as a substitute for a traditional deerhide tepee. Who was ignoring his "No Trespassing" signs posted at intervals along the fence?

Mary Twetas, whom he had known since he came west, pulled herself cumbersomely to her feet from beside a dead fire. Roots spilled from her lap.

"Hi, Ed. What you doing out this way?"

"Hi, Mary. What you doing on this creek?"

"Peelin' speetlum roots. You want some?"

She proffered the contents of her cupped hands.

"Got plenty?"

"Sure. Good crop this year. Dug two days; just peelin' today."

He took off his Stetson, and she filled it with dirty but dry roots.

"Thanks. I like speetlum flavor. Good for stew. Maybe my wife will make some."

"How you like our camp? We cleaned out the spring. Your cows didn't do it any good."

"My cows have to drink in my creek."

"Oh, sure. They don't bother us. Them cows are real good about stayin' away from camp even when we aren't here."

Ed did not press the point of proprietorship. Indians, unlike paleface hunters, knew a cow from a deer and preferred the deer to eat.

"Ever use speetlum brew?" Mary asked.

"Never used speetlum for medicine, just for seasoning like onions. I used to work for Old Man Westmore. His wife was Okanogan. She said speetlum brew was good for everything. Think it'd be good for a pain running up the arm?"

"You got pain in your arm, Ed? You take this right home and have your woman boil you up a real strong brew. It's better 'n all the store medicine put together."

ED EASED THE pickup into the garage after sundown. Eleanor would be cross. As he entered the front door, she was bringing a rib roast to the dining table in the ell. Bill and Susan were already seated at the table.

"You been waiting on me?" he asked.

"We just about didn't," Eleanor said. "We were dishing up without you. Wash, but don't use the sink in the kitchen."

Ed held out his hatful of roots.

"What's that stuff?"

"Speetlum roots. You know, those pink sandroses."

"I guess it is at that. Where'd you get it? Dig it while we waited for you to appear?"

"Mary Twetas gave 'em to me. Remember her?"

"No."

"Second wife, widow now, of old Chief Ohotkolin. Lived in the shack on our meadow. You ought to remember. She's with a gang on the river place. This is speetlum harvest time."

"I remember her," Bill said genially. "By golly, Dad! You out late with that gal? She was a terror when I was a kid."

"She sure isn't now. Her teeth are all broken in front. She's fat. Sits in the dirt. But she's friendly."

Susan affected bright interest. "I always wondered how they cook their roots."

Eleanor could not forego an opportunity to share her knowledge of recipes, even Indian. "Use it in stews, or boil it plain and put sugar and milk on it," she said. "But I never would cook it."

Susan said to her father-in-law, "Give me a bite. I've always wanted to know what it tastes like."

"Hadn't it better be washed?" Ed demurred.

"Oh, don't bother. I read someplace that people eat a square yard of dirt in a lifetime."

She selected a root from Ed's hand and nibbled.

"Want a bite, Bill?" she asked.

"Naw. I know what it tastes like—nothin'. "

"Indians swear it's the best medicine there is," Ed declared.

"I don't believe it," said Eleanor.

Ed carried his gift to the back porch and dumped it out of his hat onto the wooden bench that was the catchall for tin cans, limp vegetables, and empty bottles. After the roots withered, Eleanor would toss them on the compost pile.

Ed went to the bathroom to wash his hands, then returned to the dining area, where Bill and Susan were helping themselves to meat and potatoes. Eleanor was bringing dinner rolls from the kitchen.

"These've probably turned to rock," she fumed. "I kept them in the warming oven for two hours!"

Ed switched on the chandelier above the table.

"Don't turn that on!" Eleanor said. "It blinds everybody."

Ed sat down, but he left the light on as a signal to Eleanor that there were limits to her supervisory powers.

If there was any recompense for enduring Eleanor's sharp tongue and maternal zeal, it was the menu of roasted standing rib, browned potatoes, gravy, rolls, jam, and pickles. For this special occasion, she had even fussed with an olive and celery plate and tomato aspic.

"This is sure an old-fashioned spread," said Bill, complimenting his mother.

"Save some room for huckleberry pie," Eleanor bridled.

Susan admired the centerpiece. "Your Peace rose is beautiful, Mother. Could I have a slip?"

"Take that one home with you. Put it under a jar by the irrigation ditch, and the roots will sprout right away."

Ed noticed that Eleanor had permitted Susan the honor of setting the table: Eleanor always lumped the fork with the knife and spoon at the right of each plate, but his fork was on the left of the plate, Susan-style. He quietly corrected his place setting.

Eleanor had been the first schoolteacher in Bonaparte, but despite the refinements of an education at Whitman Academy at Walla Walla, her ways had become nearly as countrified as Ed's over the years. Early-day pioneers felt that elegant manners were useless against the vicissitudes of cold and hunger. For democracy's sake, even the intelligentsia chose to appear no better educated than their neighbors. When Ed had served in the legislature in the teen years of the century, he had learned to discard the formally correct speech he had been admonished to use at the Presbyterian academy in Iowa. He avoided creating prejudice against good facts by stating them in four-bit words.

Bill and Susan, second-generation pioneers, were graduates of Washington State College. They now, as a married pair, belonged to the Fifty Couples Dance Club, used cosmopolitan slang, and eschewed "done" in the third person singular.

Susan and Eleanor treated each other with the over-politeness of women who were required to get along, but who set each other's nerves on edge. Susan was the daughter of Hal Buck, who owned the ranch next to the Johnston place. She would inherit her father's estate, a fact that tempered Eleanor's behavior. Ed knew that Eleanor hated Susan's smoking at the table, but that she would say nothing about it tonight.

While Eleanor was cutting the huckleberry pie in the kitchen, Susan offered cigarettes from her case to Bill and Ed. Bill took one. Ed shook his head. "Nope. Thanks. When I smoked, I rolled my own."

"Good night! The dark ages!"

Ed wondered what Eleanor would say if she knew Susan last week had charged two hundred dollars worth of beer and wine to the McLaren joint account at Blackwell's. Ed had questioned Bill about the amount.

"That musta been for the barbecue we gave for the Fifty Couples before the dance at Okanogan," Bill had explained.

"The hell with that kind of expense! I'd better fix it so you and Susan pay your bills separately!"

ELEANOR BROUGHT IN the huckleberry pie, still warm in the pan and cut into segments. Ignoring the smoke, she said, "You're next to the dish cabinet, Susan. Let's use the hand-painted plates from the middle shelf below. I'll get the coffee."

Susan snuffed out her cigarette, rummaged in the cabinet for the plates, and put them at Eleanor's place. After circling the table with the coffeepot in hand to fill the cups, Eleanor reseated herself and skillfully dispensed neat portions of midnight blue fruit between delicate golden crusts.

"How do you make pies so perfect! My huckleberry pies always run!" Susan exclaimed.

"Use just a little more flour," Eleanor advised. "My sister Ada painted the roses on these dessert plates for a wedding present to your father and me," she said. "Aren't they beautiful?"

"I like the pie on 'em better 'n the decorations," Bill said. "How about giving me my second piece right now?"

Eleanor beamed and put on a full quarter of pie.

"You want double too, Ed?" Eleanor asked. The triumph of her dinner had softened her tongue.

"I guess not. Don't care much for sweets."

Susan lit a second cigarette when she had finished her pie and pulled her coffee cup close.

"Lovely meal, Mother," she said warmly. "You went to a lot of trouble."

"Just the same old thing," Eleanor disclaimed.

"What kept you besides Indians?" asked Eleanor, now that she could concentrate on secondary business.

"Went to see the forest lease on Bonaparte. Full of undergrowth. We can't keep those cattle in there long, Bill. Can't run half as many as fifteen years ago. No burning! Forest Service has a bear by the tail and can't let go."

"Now don't go off on one of your tangents tonight!" Eleanor interrupted sharply. "Bill and Susan didn't come here to listen to a sermon."

"Dammit, they better listen! If Bill wants to stay in the cattle business, he better worry about land brushing up all over the West!"

"My dad says everybody's behind you," Susan hastened to intervene.

"Yeah, behind me. A long ways behind me."

Eleanor attempted a diversion.

"How was your arm today? You've been holding that hand up in the air to ease it for days."

Pain tracked up Ed's forearm as she spoke. He resented the invasion of his privacy. "What about my arm?"

Father and son adjourned to the living room, which was comfortably furnished with leather davenport and chairs. The women removed the last of the dishes from the table and attacked the disarray in the kitchen.

Everyone knew that if Ed had anything significant to impart, it would be after the dishes were done and all were assembled.

Bill eased off his boots and sprawled on the davenport. Ed, who always sat at his black leather chair after dinner, took the *American Cattle Producer* from the stand at his right and switched the floor lamp one notch brighter.

"Saw you workin' on the fence today. We needed that other strand."

"Yeah."

"Saw you had company, too."

"What you mean? I didn't have any company."

"Some girl in pants. Figured it was a Caliente."

"It was. Kitty. That wasn't company. She was out riding. Stayed awhile to help get the wire unrolled. She didn't have any gloves. I loaned her a pair from the bed of the puddlejumper and told her to keep 'em."

"First Caliente I ever knew to want to help with the fence."

"Ain't it the truth! Kitty swears she is going to run away like her brothers. They never have nothin'. She had a hell of a row with her old man last night. Had to gentle her a bit."

"You gotta give her credit, but I don't know what else you can do."

"Promised her I'd get her a date to the Saturday night dance if she didn't run away."

"You'd be heading her for trouble. Her old man scares off anybody that goes to the house."

"Yeah, you're right," Bill mumbled as his cigarette ashes showered on his chest. "Dammit."

"God, you're messy!" Ed grunted. "Your ma's so clean about everything, but she never could toilet train you."

ELEANOR AND SUSAN, having made the kitchen ready for morning, came into the living room.

"You're hogging the whole davenport," Susan told Bill. "Shove over, or sit up."

"Heck, I was just getting comfortable," Bill said as he shifted grudgingly.

"After all, he's been up since four o'clock," Eleanor said.

Susan refrained from saying that she had also been up since the same hour.

"Mom, how about the cherries? They ripe yet? I was figuring on a handful."

"After all that supper, you still want cherries!" Susan said in disgust.

Eleanor jumped to her feet. "I have some Rainiers ripening in the cellar for jam. They make good jam if you pick them green."

Although there was now a full cement basement under the house, Eleanor still called below stairs "the cellar."

"Don't go down those steps and back again for Bill, Mother! He doesn't need any cherries. He's getting fat. He's eaten too much already."

"I don't see what makes you think he'll get fat," Eleanor said. "He isn't a bit fat."

"He's beefy," Ed pronounced.

Bill changed the subject. "When you want to start selling dry cows? I took a couple to the auction yesterday. You weren't around to say yes or no."

"That's all right, I guess. You mean those two heifers by the spring on the Anderson place? Lost their calves. No sense keeping 'em. What did you do with the check?"

"Still got it in my pocket. You want it deposited?"

"You might as well keep it for incidentals," Ed said.

"It makes me mad!" said Eleanor suddenly. "Bill has to ask about every detail."

"We gotta watch every move," Ed said. "The market could go to the bottom this year the way it did in '52. What would we do if we come up against a hard winter and a cost-price squeeze?"

"Hell, Dad, I oughta let you have it! All this talk, and I'm on handouts. I got nothing to lose so far."

"Don't act cute. You know damn well everything that's going on. What do you think I was doing up on the forest lease today? I'm turning the forest permit over to you, and they're gonna cut the animal units in half. They always make their cuts at the time of transfer. What will you do for extra hay next winter? Rain was scarcest this May than it's been in years. Isn't much of a hay crop."

"Fellow can get all the hay he needs at Malott for thirty-five dollars. Lots of people are beginning to think it doesn't even pay to put up hay anymore."

"Nobody can afford to buy hay when you need it. You can't rely on its being cheap, or even on being able to get it."

"Bill's never had a chance to manage by himself," Eleanor interjected. "He should have a right to do things by himself to prove that he can. You and I should go somewhere and let Bill take over. Lots of people leave the place to their children."

ED'S HAND WAS called. He was ready with his conclusions and a program of action more drastic than anyone imagined. He had never mentioned his heart spell and did not intend to. As head of the house, he spoke the verdict: "I'm sick of being crowded all the time. I've decided what we're gonna do. Doc tells me I may live another twenty years; and I don't want twenty more years of this. So your mother and I are gonna deed all the property over. Bill will have to assume mortgages to buy Sam and Leila out. He'll be in debt for years."

Eleanor made the first noise. "Thank God!"

"You may not be thanking God for long. Wait till Bill finds out how hard it is to maintain a margin of profit."

"I'm willing to take a chance," Bill said as he sat upright. He had expected at most to be admitted to one-fourth partnership.

"What we'll do," Ed continued, "is your mother and I will go to visit Sam and Leila. We'll take papers for them to sign. I'm not giving anything to one of my kids without the others knowing they'll have their share."

"Fair enough," Bill said.

Ed liked the way his son spoke. Underneath his spoiled layers, Bill was a man.

"I know Sam and Leila will rejoice," Eleanor said with hands clasped together, her eyes glowing. "They have their own interests that keep them from ever wanting to run this place. Besides, when we go to Iowa to see Sam, your father should look up his brother and sister. It was a terrible, heartless thing when he didn't go to his own mother's funeral! What your sister must think of me!"

"If I show up in Boone, it'll scare the pants off my little brother for fear I want some share in Ma's farm."

"We don't need to stay with him and your sister," Eleanor said. "We'll be at Sam's. Sam can drive us to Boone some Sunday. It's only twenty miles from

Ames. I looked it up on the map."

"You've been wanting to go on a trip. Now's your chance," Ed said, glad to have the business over. He stirred in his chair to signal that the meeting was adjourned. He turned his attention to the *American Cattle Producer*.

Eleanor, Susan, and Bill retired to the dining table to discuss the revelation over some more coffee.

"I notice how he is putting all the deeds and leases in a cardboard box," Ed heard Eleanor say. "He's getting everything together for the lawyer."

Ed's head fell to one side. He dozed. He had been crowded enough for one day.

He woke to the stir of Susan's and Bill's departure and roused himself. "Say, Bill! I've been meaning to check with you. You going to Omak on Friday?"

"To the Cattleman's meeting? I guess so, if you are. I don't get much out of it, though."

"O.K. See you there. Drive down in our own cars. Then we can both come home when we want to. I might drive up to see Carlquist's grass trials on the field trip."

"I'm going, too," Susan announced. "At least to part of it. We've formed the Okanogan County Cow Belles. The men will have to take the ladies to the banquet. Want to come along, Mother?"

"Heaven forbid!"

Ed's blinking eyes fell to the cherries in Bill's hands. Eleanor had gone to the basement after all. Her youngest son took home everything he came for.

"You were certainly no company," Eleanor said as the car left the drive. "You better wake up enough to go to bed now."

"Yeah, you're right."

He heaved himself to his feet and started toward the bathroom. Then he turned back to her as he thought of some thing else he wanted to mention.

"The timber on the mountain has to come down. I'm going to see Biles-Coleman in a couple days and ask them to cruise it and make a bid."

"Hunh! I don't know if that's a good idea. I hear the price of timber is low. Besides, isn't Bill supposed to handle things like that now?"

"Not quite yet," Ed was short. "If we don't sell that section quick, it'll start to rot and be no good for lumber."

They slept in adjoining bedrooms, a practice that had developed gradually over the years. Eleanor used to retire early while Ed stayed up to read, but she complained that when he did come to bed, he always turned on the light and made a racket that woke her up. So Eleanor had never remarked when Ed began to sleep in what had been the boys' bedroom. Once a week she provided fresh sheets for him and left them loose at the bottom so that his toes would not be cramped.

Sometimes he missed her animal warmth, but he never mentioned it.

MOVING ON A direct course, Ed went next morning to the United States Forest Service office downtown. The agency was housed in a plain white box on a concrete foundation. The official nature of the structure was indicated by a large United States flag fluttering on a strong, high pole. Two windows were positioned with perfect symmetry on either side of the front door. The entry step was covered by a portico of shingles held up by two four-by-fours.

Inside at a rolltop desk sat a young man in khaki—Jim Thorsen, forest ranger and graduate of the Yale University School of Forestry.

"Good morning, Ed. Have a chair."

"Thanks. Have some business this morning."

Ed liked the ranger as an individual; he was intelligent and knowledgeable about his work.

Jim went to the thirty-cup aluminum coffee maker and drew cups for Ed and himself.

"Something particular on your mind?"

"Matter of fact, there is. Put our cows and calves on the range yesterday. Went up to look things over. The underbrush is so thick up there you can't ride a horse through it."

Jim sighed. "We've been over this ground before, Ed. I can't give you permission to burn."

"That isn't natural. Fire is part of the cycle. It gets rid of bugs, weak trees, and undergrowth."

The boy in khaki shook his head.

"The service has a policy of stopping all fires."

"I know your line. Overgrazing opened the forest floor to brush. But don't forget who started the Forest Service. Cattlemen wanting protection of the range. One thing I want to mention. When the underbrush got thick, all the Indians did was burn off the forest floor and the grass came up."

"But the trees were often burned, too. Trees are necessary for preservation of the watershed. They conserve moisture."

"I don't agree. Trees transpire a lot of water into the air. Maybe they do prevent soil erosion, but a good stand of grass will do the same thing. You'll get a good stand of grass if you kill out the rank underbrush by setting a fire when ground and atmospheric conditions are right. There isn't much danger of a spreading fire. A fire will hardly bum on the flats in the forenoon."

"Yes, but the forests are hilly. Get one of those brush fires on a hillside, and you have a fierce blaze. On the north slope, fire may not bum hard, but bum the south slope and the fire is hot enough to kill. Burning in the forenoon may be all right, but what if it goes into afternoon? There may be suitable burning days, but they're hard to pick. Let the wind come up, and you've got a crown fire."

"How about standing there and watching it? That's what I've always done on my own land."

"You fellows on your own land may have time to stand there and tend the fire, but it costs too much for the Forest Service to hire crews. It costs about thirty-five cents to burn the same land that the Service can protect adequately for three to four cents under the present protection methods."

Ed finished his coffee. He carried his cup to the sink.

"You stop all fires on the forest, and the U.S. Forest Service will be holding a bear's tail and won't dare let go. You'll have a fire hazard everywhere like a tinderbox. Nothing will stop dry brush fires once they get started. The fires blaze up to the crown of the forest and burn to natural barriers."

"Sorry, Ed. When it gets down to cases, a ranger only reflects policy; he doesn't make it."

"You should see my grass stand right next to your forest land."

Jim Larsen laughed ruefully, "I've seen it. Maybe you should have burned the whole damn mountain. But don't you ever dare to say I said so."

"I know the position you're in. Shouldn't spout off to you. Made myself forget what I really came for."

"Ask me any favor except to hand you a box of matches, and I'll try to oblige."

"Need some blanks to fill out. Bill and I have talked it over, and we've decided it's time to have the permits on the federal lands changed into his name."

"I guess it's inevitable, Ed. You want the range kept in the family. Have to warn you, though. In Spokane they may cut the animal units."

"Yeah. It's happened. But we do need to get organized."

The ranger opened a desk drawer and selected the required forms.

"You and Bill both have to sign the application. Probably they'll send out cruisers before the transfer."

Ed spent Thursday describing his Forest Service leases on blank lines. He drove to the Johnston place to leave the completed forms in Susan's care.

Next week he would take care of the Taylor grazing lands at the Bureau of Land Management offices.

3.
Bill and Susan

No more primary human relationship exists than that among the young people who grow up on neighboring ranches in the Okanogan Valley. Bill and Susan shared such a relationship long before their marriage.

Part of a close-knit group of youths, they ice-skated on Aeneas, Whitestone, and Spectacle lakes. They skied on the hills in the open farm fields. Sometimes they walked back up; or, on a lucky day, someone with a team of horses and a sled would give them a ride up the hill. When skating or skiing, they usually built a bonfire for keeping warm and for roasting apples or potatoes. They fished in the lakes and in the mountain creeks and carried frying pans to cook and eat the trout before going home.

The young people learned dance steps from one another at the Grange and Odd Fellows halls of Ellisforde, Wauconda, Molson, and Tunk Valley and at Maple Hall, west of Riverside. The New Year's Eve dance took place at Loomis. Those who went to college came home to the extended family for Thanksgiving and St. Patrick's Day reunions.

Social events, whatever the season, reflected the boundless energy of young animals who lived outdoors.

Susan first knew she was Bill's girl when he and his big brother Sam brought their Christmas present sleds to school. At recess, Sam and Bill allowed everyone a tum at coasting down the steep hill behind the schoolhouse. All the boys zipped down fearlessly, lying on their stomachs. The girls, who were afraid to guide, took their turns kneeling behind Sam or Bill and clutching the side rails of the sled. They squealed in terror at the speed of the Flexible Flyer with steel runners.

Not Susan!

"Why don't you let me go down by myself?" Susan asked Bill.

"A Flexible Flyer goes mighty fast," Bill warned.

Susan grabbed the sled from Bill and did a running belly flop at the top of the hill. She coasted as far as the boys did.

As she lugged the sled up, her cheeks glowed bright red. Her stocking cap had fallen off, and around her head was the blazing glory of bright yellow hair.

"Can I do it one more time, Bill?"

"Sure."

"How come she gets so many turns?" the sixth-grade boys without sleds yelled. "It's somebody else's turn."

"She's my girl," Bill announced.

Everyone accepted his words, even Susan.

IN HIGH SCHOOL, they slouched together through the tedium of English, French, algebra, and biology. Susan wrote most of the themes, with the result that Bill in all his life never learned to spell. But he did display occasional flashes of scholastic aptitude when the biology teacher asked questions "to make them think."

Mr. Barden, a master of science who had taken the only employment available to him during the Depression, tried to spark interest in a roomful of pupils yawning over the extensor and flexor muscles.

"Why don't you get as tired on a hike up and down hills as on a hike on a flat stretch of road? Susan, what is your guess?"

Bill, to cover Susan's embarrassed silence, spoke up: "You use two different sets of muscles for walking up and down hill. You divide the tiredness among more muscles."

"Right, Bill! I wish you'd start to study. You could get an A as easily as your brother did if you'd try."

"Billy, you're as smart as Sam, just like Mr. Barden said," Susan said after class. "But you're always goofing off. Don't act stupid to be the opposite of your brother."

Bill played the oaf for the first two years of high school as he moved in the shadow of his brother, who earned straight A's, was high point man in basketball, pitcher for the baseball team, and quarterback for football, in addition to holder of the county record for the hundred-yard dash.

After Sam graduated and left for Washington State College, Bill improved. He felt somehow promoted and more necessary to his father on the ranch. He no longer disappeared after school.

Besides, Susan cautioned, "If our grades aren't good enough, we'll never get into Pullman. You're going to be taller and heavier than Sam. You could get on the varsity football team, I bet."

Bill ruminated; his grades moved up to B's.

Bill and Susan each knew what the other looked like at the worst. Grimy and sweaty, they were indistinguishable as male and female—tall Bill and tall Susan—in Levi's and cotton flannel shirts, helping in the haying, carrying salt to range cattle on horseback, cutting fallen trees off trails, riding fence to find breaks, herding cattle from brush, hammering on broken-down corrals.

At the end of work, before supper, they hightailed to their respective homes to pick up their bathing suits. Bill drove his jalopy to Susan's; then they headed for Spectacle Lake. Before they joined the crowd of Bonaparte young people yelling, joking, and splashing on the beach, they swam across the lake and back. They developed physiques that made them king and queen of the Senior Prom.

Sometimes Bill, when at the height of his conceit as football or baseball star, strutted down the hall in the company of a swarm of adoring sophomore and junior girls instead of Susan.

On such days, Susan went outside at noon behind the school with one of the Pein boys and smoked cigarettes. She blew her breath in Bill's face at the door of the chemistry lab.

"Susan! Smoking cuts your wind!"

"I'm not in training for football, hero," she retorted.

When Matt Pein asked her to a dance at Oroville, she went with him, but only once. Bill retaliated by treating her like a mangy mutt for a month.

In college Susan was a recognized adjunct to the star football player. Bill majored in animal husbandry, doing well enough on familiar ground. Susan tried to enroll in animal husbandry, too, but was shooed to the department of home economics.

Despite Bill and Susan's constant companionship, she retained her technical virtue for longer than she was given credit. In her senior year, her sorority reprimanded her in a chapter meeting for allowing Bill to neck with her in her bed. She moved off campus, and Bill unwound his muscles without intrusion in her apartment.

"What's the difference?" Bill reasoned. "We're gonna get married as soon as we're through school."

Susan gave in with lingering doubt. She had never had much chance to look for another mate. Sometimes she was envious of Cathy Hall, who wallowed in infatuation and persuaded the whole sorority to kneel before the picture of her current beloved and chant his sacred name: "Dan Jones! Dan Jones! Salaam!"

When she asked herself, "What would my life be like without Bill in it?" she came eventually to the conclusion that she could imagine no such life.

Susan and Bill had been married eighteen years. Their "seven-month baby" was now a college student demanding his own jalopy.

As they drove home to the Johnston place after Dad McLaren's announcement that he was deeding the property to them, they were jubilant.

"Wow! You're the manager in charge of accounts! You can buy and sell!" Susan gloried in the possibilities.

"I'm gonna update operations right off the bat," Bill said. "I've already got a list of machinery."

They went to bed at once. Next morning began at five o'clock.

Bill left to work on the fence after breakfast. Glenna and Deanna, in high school, and Tom, the oldest, home from his freshman year at Washington State, faded away to Osoyoos Lake, where the young crowd would be gamboling in the first freedom of summer vacation. Bill, who remembered how he had been shackled to chores as an adolescent, was inclined to be lenient with his children. But as soon as haying started, he would impress Tom into service.

The family lived in a white house shaped like an apple box. It had been the McLaren wedding present to a young couple in obvious need of immediate housing. It was less than half the size of either the red barn or the vehicle shed, but had sufficed for years, providing sleeping space and a table set out with an ample food supply.

The old Johnston place, too drafty for a year-round dwelling, still stood on the premises and served as a bunkhouse for hired hands whenever there were any.

Depressed by the sight of the raided breakfast table, Susan went to the stove for an extra cup of coffee. She lighted a cigarette and stood at the sink as she drank and smoked.

The euphoria of the night before had vanished. She should whip through the housework, make a noon sandwich for Bill, and join him.

"To heck with that!" she decided. "Kitty Caliente can help with the fence some more. He's such a big shot to her."

Lately she had been growing impatient with Bill's sympathy for Kitty's troubles. Considering it a joke, he had told Susan that he had spent one night with Kitty.

"I was holed up at the England place. It was dark, and I still hadn't found the calves. I went into the shack, built a fire in the stove, and opened a can of pork and beans. Dad always keeps those places stocked with tin can rations. Hugo eats most of them.

"Dumped the beans in a frying pan and was lookin' in the cupboards for some crackers when I heard something hitting the door. I unlatched the hook and looked into the dark. Here was this kid shivering, holding a cayuse by the reins.

" 'Hello!' I said. 'What you doin' out here this time of night?'

" 'Lost, I guess,' she says. 'Mind if I put my horse in your shed? She's hot. Can she have some water?'

"I saw it was that Caliente kid, scared to death. I told her, 'Sure. Only you can't water a horse while it's hot. Come in and have some pork and beans first.'

"That kid ate all my pork and beans; had to open another can for myself. I went out and watered her horse for her and tied it in the shed.

"When I came back inside, she was bawlin', not makin' noise, but she certainly was unhappy.

"I asked her, 'What's a matter?' She said it was her graduation night and her Old Man had made her go out and hunt strays. She couldn't go home 'til she found 'em all. She hadn't found any.

"I put my arms around her and let her cry."

Susan sniffed. "I bet you did! 'And all night long you held her in your arms, just to keep her from the foggy, foggy dew.' "

"That's about it," Bill admitted. "Anything wrong?"

"Not if that's exactly how it happened. Of course you both slept in your clothes, or are there blankets up there?"

"What kind of a heel do you think I am?" Bill countered.

"You know as well as I do."

It seemed to Susan that all her life she had been a flunky, doing what Bill told her to do, ignoring how he sopped up adulation from females. Now, with the entire responsibility for the Lazy Ear falling on their shoulders, the course of her life would never change. The next thirty-nine years would be exactly like the past thirty-nine.

Since joining the Fifty Couples Club, an outgrowth of increased prosperity in the community, Susan had begun to covet the higher quality of life in other households. When Hank and Lurline Lodge had bought an old-timer's spread on Pine Creek, the first thing they did was build a seven-room home designed by an architect to blend with the natural setting. Lurline, a vague doll-like creature, had never ridden a horse, let alone herded a cow, before coming to the Okanogan. Hank was minimally equipped for the new life he had entered, having been a buyer for fifteen years for Swift and Company, meat packers. He pretended to melt into the lifestyle of the region, but he brought a city smoothness that was lacking in Bill and other men in the Fifty Couples. Hank knew, at the start, the proper clothing for the sales ring and the range, but he lacked respect for certain traditions. He proclaimed himself an innovator of the cow business.

"I can't understand why all you fellows break your backs putting up a ton of hay per critter when you can buy all you need for thirty-five dollars a ton. You can buy hay for less than you can put it up."

Sitting in the kitchen, Bill had chuckled at his visitor's heresy. "Try saying that in front of my Old Man."

"Don't you guys ever do anything different from the Old Man?" Hank asked.

The question rankled. She and Bill, nearly forty, were still obeying Mother and Dad McLaren and Susan's parents, Mama and Papa Buck.

Financial independence was seldom given to the younger generation on the Old Man's ranch. Ed McLaren doled out various sums of money after cattle sales. The Bill McLarens bought their clothes and other necessities with cash, as long as it lasted, then charged to the Lazy Ear accounts. Old Ed paid the bills after close scrutiny. No Okanogan ranch was expected to pay much money for a food supply. The spread slaughtered a beef as necessary and stored it in a rented freezer locker in town. The women grew and canned vegetables and fruit. The young people milked a dairy cow before and after school.

Susan was filled with turmoil that she could not completely understand. Six thousand acres of range and meadow land were to be deeded to Bill and herself without so much as having to pay the closing costs. Five thousand acres of Forest Service and Bureau of Land Management land would go into their names as leaseholders.

The stickler was that they were assuming two hundred thousand dollars of debt, which must be paid over a long period of time from the annual income of the Lazy Ear. Her mind fastened on "thirty years."

Nothing in her life had been free of the overhang of a huge debt for land. Her father was land poor; her husband would be land poor. All yearly profits would be invested in calves that would become cows and steers for sale. Thirty years ahead of rising at five o'clock, cooking meals, washing dishes, running errands to town for more wire or nails, and having her hair done at Millie's Salon—the only luxury in her life.

She brightened at the thought of perhaps getting a new hairdo, then a sudden insight flashed in her mind. What she really wanted was for someone to recognize her as a woman. She was going along to Omak tomorrow with Bill, to attend the meeting of the Cow Belles. At the banquet, she could present a new Susan to the world, not Susan McLaren, née Buck; but "Susanne," a more glamorous, interesting person altogether! She would make someone say, "I didn't know you had it in you!"

SHE PICKED UP the phone to dial Millie's Hair Salon in downtown Bonaparte. Millie's eyes would pop with joy at the amount of money she would earn. Permanent, dye job, cut! Manicure with silver nails!

Bill had signed the back of the check from the sale of the two dry cows and had given it to Susan to cash. This time it would not all go for boot socks and candy bars.

Susan tried several times before she could get the line. At length Millie trilled, "Good morning! Salon!"

"Millie! Do you have a boyfriend on the string? Your line was busy for half an hour!"

"Isn't it a fright! Don't tell me, I know. The Cow Belles are attending the Cattleman's annual banquet tomorrow night, and you want the works!"

"Oh, that's right! You'll be busy. You can't give me a perm tomorrow, but how about a hair style and color?"

"No can do tomorrow. If you could come to town today, I might be able to work you in."

"Can you take me in an hour? I absolutely need a color."

"Since when? Your hair is nice enough!"

"I want it to look like buttercups," Susan was firm. "My hair used to be the color of buttercups. It's bunchgrass now."

"Come on, then," Millie said good-naturedly. "I'll try to mix some buttercup paint."

Susan waited fifteen minutes while Millie finished a customer. She took a *Vogue* magazine from the rack. As she leafed through the pictures of beanpole models in high-fashion gowns, she thought of how she could have been a model, given a different environment. She was not only tall, but lean and firm from riding and lifting. But Susan suddenly stopped daydreaming with the stark realization that she didn't even have a dinner dress to wear to the banquet. She found herself staring at a photo of one tall model who stood with a hip thrust forward to show off a black and white sheath dress, suited only to a perfect figure. Large squares of white alternated with large squares of black. The caption underneath read, "Sophistication supreme from Leonine at $300."

The model was smiling disdainfully as though to say, "Okanogan County is thousands of miles away, where the Cow Belles go to banquets with their husbands. I dare you to try to look like me!"

Susan laid the magazine aside when Millie called her to the station.

"Are you sure you want a color, Susan?"

"Not sure, but I'm going to have one anyhow."

Millie shook her head but proceeded. Under the dryer, Susan could scarcely wait. When Millie combed her out, she studied herself in the mirror.

"Not too brassy," Millie judged. "I didn't have to bleach you. Your hair is light enough to take a blonde dye."

"Looks like the good old days," Susan decided cheerfully.

"What's Bill going to say?" Millie asked.

"He'll never notice. I might make someone else notice, I hope."

"Susan, are you going through the change? You and I are only honest-to-God thirty-nine."

Millie and Susan had attended grade school and high school together and were in a closer-than-family tie.

"I am going through something weird—don't know if it's the change. But what I need is a change! When I was a kid once I had a wild idea of running away to New York to be a model."

"That I can understand," Millie said. "Remember when I ran away from home to be a movie star? All the further I got was to beauty school in Spokane, and then back here. Married Joe and been supporting him ever since. We don't get far, do we?"

"I think I'll wear war paint and powder tomorrow," Susan said.

She had paid her bill, but instead of leaving so that the next ranch wife could be beautified, Susan picked up the issue of *Vogue* and leafed through the pages to the black and white sheath on the blonde model. "Come here, Millie! I'd like to look exactly like this at the banquet."

Millie studied the glossy photo.

"The print is strange, but the style isn't anything. Just a couple seams and a few darts. A person could make that in an hour or two. Must be some material to make it cost three hundred dollars! 'Damask,' it says. What's damask?"

"A tablecloth! Take a white tablecloth, cut it into squares and dye half of them black! Dad's sister sent me a damask tablecloth for a wedding present eighteen years ago. We've never used it once. I think I left it at Mother's. I'll go take a look. But don't you ever dare tell Mother what became of that tablecloth!"

"You nut!" Millie giggled with her. "Try it! All it would take is a package of Rit. Be sure to use vinegar."

"I'm afraid it's hard to tell what will become of that tablecloth, but I'll have fun."

When she stopped at her parents' house, she felt lucky to find no one home. She went to what had been her girlhood bedroom and lifted the lid of her hope chest, which had been supplied by her mother and ignored by Susan. The banquetsize damask tablecloth, in glistening, silken splendor, lay on top. Before her mother could appear, Susan seized the fabric and hastened back to her car.

SHE STOPPED FOR black dye and black and white No. 60 thread at Blackwell's. Although she seldom used it anymore, Susan had a sewing machine. In college, as a home economics major, she had been instructed in how to cut out a pattern. If Bill and the kids stayed out of the house for six hours—and they usually did—-she would have time to manufacture a glamorous creation before tomorrow night.

When Dad McLaren came over to the Johnston place at six o'clock, Susan greeted him cheerfully but distractedly. She had black and white squares of cloth laid out on the table. "Got time for a cup of coffee, Dad?"

"No thanks. Almost suppertime."

"Which reminds me, I haven't started anything to eat around here. Bill and the kids will be in any minute; better get a hustle on."

"What you doin' with those squares of cloth?"

"Believe it or not, I'm trying to make myself a dress to wear to the banquet tomorrow."

"Glad you joined the Cow Belles. Sorry Eleanor won't."

"Mother's not much of a joiner, is she?"

"When she was your age, maybe she was. She still goes to the Garden Club."

Susan scooped her project into a bundle to clear the table. Her father-in-law laid down a manila envelope.

"This has papers in it for Bill to sign. Application for transfer of our rangeland on the forest."

"I understand how important they are."

"Have Bill look them over and sign 'em. He might as well mail 'em. Probably the answer will come to my address."

"YOU GOT YOUR hair done, Mom!" was all the comment that Susan heard from the family at dinnertime.

It had required more time than she had anticipated to cut the tablecloth, dye half the squares, and then rejoin all the segments. She had hidden the dress, still unfinished. She told Bill she had decided not to waste the whole day tomorrow at Omak. If he would go in the truck in the morning, she would take the car and meet him at the hotel before the banquet.

Bill's interest that evening centered on the papers Dad had left.

4.

At the Cattleman's Meeting

As Ed drove south along the Okanogan River highway to the Cattleman's meeting at Omak, his eye accepted unconsciously the roadside towns, the apple orchards, and the foothills, devoid of all vegetation except sage and bunchgrass, still showing a tinge of green from the new growth. The curves and planes of the mountain ranges on the skyline were uncomplicated and sure as though their creator had wished to make a blunt statement of strength.

Because he wasted nothing, least of all time, Ed drove at the speed limit to his destination, but his spirit was in no hurry. He was telling himself he would have had more sense if he had stayed home. In his day, Ed had been the archangel of the Cattleman's Association. As a charter member he was still chairman of the honorary advisory board, a position he regarded as "on the shelf."

The annual session would be one more turn in the perpetual cycle of men squabbling openly and covertly to wrest land, the basic source of income, from one another. The state legislature had recently enacted a law that combined the former state land departments into one new Department of Natural Resources, with an accompanying shift of power supposedly to improve administration. Ed had heard that Delbert Gaston had been behind the Shefelman bill that created the department; what he would say at the meeting would be worth hearing.

Throughout fifty years of membership in the association, Ed declared at intervals, "Aw, I'm quittin," but it was the idle threat of a piqued lover. Each year when the policies were formulated, he was compelled to state his opinions of the resolutions, especially any pertaining to government subsidies or price supports.

Ed railed, "Nowadays you kids have prosperity. You don't remember the Depression much. Everything is supported by subsidies that keep prices up. You don't consider the results of supports."

Bill argued, "Mort says you got to have a floor someplace. Most old guys like you turn thumbs down on supports; but a few of 'em—including some who've made a real killing—see the government supports on everything but livestock. There might be some sense to havin' supports on cattle, just to keep from losing out to all the price-supported industries."

"You quote your Uncle Mort one more time, and you can go work for him!"

The admiration that Eleanor and Bill showed for Mort's wealth rankled Ed's soul. "I coulda made a million, too, by stealin' Injun land with whiskey and horses," he snarled.

Ed had once been extolled in the *American Cattle Producer* in the fervid language of the trade journal. The editor, who traveled a thousand miles to interview him, reported: "Ed McLaren's life is deeply rooted in the Okanogan Valley. He has been a cattleman since the turn of the century, a true representative of the Westerner whose name is in history."

But Ed overheard Bill remark to his mother, "See in this magazine, where Dad has been sounding off about what a great guy he was forty years ago?"

Eleanor responded, "It hasn't been easy living with a man forever in some wrangle or fight."

SUCH DIFFERENCES, HOWEVER were kept private. Ed today would sit beside his son to show family solidarity, companionship in the congenial operation of a cattle ranch. Leaders at cattlemen's meetings often spoke of the father and son tie—"This heritage of freedom that we pass on to our sons."

In moments of cynicism it seemed to Ed that Bill mainly wanted freedom from his Old Man's stinginess and antique caution. In the postwar years, it was taking all of Ed's knowledge of management to show a profit. Flimsy operators were going bankrupt buying hay they should have put up for themselves in preceding summers. In spite of record production and farm prices at a hundred and five percent of parity, taxes and expenses of operation were overburdening the cattle industry. Ed sold timber to pay current expenses; other men without reserves were facing disaster in a cost-price squeeze.

Knowing the size of his father's bank account, Bill was amused, "Why worry so much? Come a hard winter, you can get emergency relief grain from the government. Everybody else does when he needs it."

IN OMAK, ED parked in the lot behind the Jim Hill Hotel, named for James J. Hill, the railroad tycoon who built the Great Northern Railway into the Okanogan country. As Ed locked the cab, he noticed a hammer lying loose in the bed of the pickup.

"Dammit!" Ed muttered.

He recalled that Bill had used the pickup yesterday afternoon. Ed climbed into the open pickup bed for the hammer, unlocked the cab door and placed the tool inside. Bill left tools lying everywhere, unmindful that their loss added to the over head.

"Most people won't steal another man's tools," Bill would defend himself.

"There's always one cheapskate who will," his father retorted.

THE BANQUET HALL of the hotel was furnished for the morning session with rows of folding chairs that stayed empty until the last minute before the call to order. Men whose legs were accustomed to the space of outdoors lingered in the lobby and doorways. Yesterday the powdery dirt of the cow trails had covered the Okanogan County cattlemen. Today their bodies were scrubbed, and Levi's and workshirts had been exchanged for newly cleaned whipcord pants and jackets. The swarthy faces, which did not lose one season's tan before another started, wore the sheen of recent shaving.

Although now reduced in height from the six feet three inches he had reached when he came west as a youth, Ed could look over the heads of the majority of the assemblage. The only other concession to the aging process appeared on his face, where a few dry, red patches remained—scars of skin cancers the Doc had removed. "Too much sun," Doc had explained. Other cattlemen who had spent a lifetime outside showed the same scars.

Ed appeared as hardy as the rocky hills through which he had ridden horseback for fifty years. He weighed a hundred and seventy pounds, as any cattleman could estimate, and moved like a mountain lion indigenous to the Okanogan highlands. His arrival signaled a general movement toward the abhorred chairs.

"Sit with us, Ed."

"Thanks, but I got Bill spotted. Better sit with him. See he's saving me a place."

"Bill was tellin' me you and the missus might take a trip East next month."

"Blabbermouth kid!" Ed joked.

From the chair beside him, Bill removed the jacket that he had used to hold a place for his father. He winked at his friends and scolded in a loud whisper, "Sit down! Quit holdin' up the parade!"

The meeting began with the flag salute, the reading of minutes, and the usual rigmarole of jokes from the chair.

"Most of us from more 'n fifty miles away drove in yesterday and took rooms here at the hotel so as to be on hand bright and early this morning. When I came downstairs for breakfast, I met an old-timer in the lobby. He said he arrived so late all the rooms were rented and he had to sleep in a chair by the cigar stand. I said, 'You're welcome to go up to my room and take a bath or anything.' He says, 'Thanks, but I took my bath before I come.'"

Despite a surface jocularity, Ed felt a crosscurrent of animosity in the room. He glanced at the program.

"Lieu Lands."

The Honorable Delbert Gaston of the state legislature would discuss "procedures to be adopted by the State Department of Natural Resources in regard to disposition of land recently transferred by the federal government to the states."

Ed took the roll with his eyes of the tough old men who held most of the land of the county, the largest county in the state. With them he had carried on his friendships and waged his wars. Some of these pioneers had yielded active management of their property to their children and indulged themselves in fishing trips to the lakes and automobile trips to Spokane or Seattle. Some of the men wore comfort slippers to the meeting. Newcomers, more eager to appear like cattlemen, wore broad brimmed Stetsons and high-heeled riding boots.

A former governor of Wyoming, owner of a widely publicized cattle spread, gave the keynote speech. Ed automatically took his small notebook from his vest pocket and jotted down the main points:

"Attack problem from the basis of consuming surpluses. Retain free competitive philosophy. Proper role for govt. that when we send money around the world in foreign aid, we recommend that we send surplus food products. American taxpayer cannot afford to hold welfare umbrella over the world. We have to compete with subsidized grain and labor. Learn marketing to increase consumption of own products. When we take subsidies, we accept govt. control."

When the governor finished, the cattlemen rose to their feet in what was termed in the paper the next day "a standing ovation," instead of "chance for a stretch."

The program chairman closed the session by saying that the governor, not at present a candidate for any office, would be mingling at the social hour before the evening banquet, "and don't hesitate to go up and shake his hand. He is one of the cattlemen's best friends on the national scene."

After a ten-minute intermission, the presiding officer called order again and asked for new business. A recent purchaser of a cattle spread stood up to speak:

"I got a problem. When I took over Marv Tilton's ranch, the government cut the grazing permit in half, so I bought meadow at top price. Come to find out, it won't feed my calf crop. I've put in an irrigation system from the creek, and I keep the sprinklers going all the time, but the hay is being eaten faster 'n it can grow. I need range land from someplace quick. Will it do any good to make a trip to Olympia and ask for a crack at some of this new land? That's what I came to find out."

"Not unless you're somebody's brother-in-law," a voice called from the rear. Laughter exploded like igniting sagebrush.

The chairman banged the gavel.

"You may find partial answer to your question in the talk we'll hear in a few minutes. Before we come to it, let's take care of other business."

Legislative committee members reported on brand inspection, meat inspection, multiple use of the national forests, and tariffs on Latin American beef.

"Now I'm turning the meeting back to the program chairman," the president said.

"Del has been a member of land committees for four years in the legislature," the program chairman began, introducing the speaker. "He worked for the passage of the Shefelman bill, which created the new department."

Gaston acknowledged the applause which showed more friendliness than common courtesy required. The cattlemen knew him as a "dam good cowpoke," like all the Westmore tribe. His mother was Analix Westmore Gaston. The discerning eye could see his heritage from both his English grandfather, Carr Westmore, one of the original white settlers of the valley, and from his grandmother, daughter of Chief White Stone Mountain of the Okanogans. The young man's skin was dark, but scarcely more so than the other weather-beaten faces in the room. He was tall, lean, and muscular; his face expressed intelligence, good humor, and good will.

Ed knew and called everyone among the assembled group by first name— except the young politician with black eyes and high cheekbones. Ed noted that the Honorable Del Gaston's left ear drooped lazily in a manner identical to his own ear. In a cattle herd, such a droop would imply animals of the same bloodline.

"I'll be glad to answer general questions, but I can't presume to deal with personal problems," the speaker prefaced his remarks. "I have no authority to tell anyone that he will be able to have a certain piece of land in a given time. I can only explain some of the background of the current transfers of federal to state lands—transfer of lieu lands, as it's called.

"The Act of Congress commonly called the Organic Act provides that sections 16 and 36 of each township of the state be set aside for the purpose of providing support of the common schools.

"At the time the grants should have been delivered, when the territory became a state in 1889, large acreages of sections 16 and 36 had already been appropriated to other uses—they were homesteaded or placed with the federal reservations. The state was authorized to take indemnity lieu tracts to replace the acreage loss. Much of the land has been delivered, but not all of it. About 150,000 acres remain to be selected and granted. When this land changes hands, theoretically it will become available for lease from the State for grazing purposes.

"I asked an executive of the federal Bureau of Land Management a short time ago why this land was being delivered so slowly. His reply was, 'It hasn't been delivered because the state hasn't asked for it.'

"That's one story. You fellows tell me another."

Even though transfer of land from one landlord to another might affect some of his own leases, Ed felt like laughing over what was probably going through the mind of his brother-in law, Morton Clements, a few rows toward the front. As Ed anticipated, Mort rose to bid for the preservation of his own privileges.

"Naturally it comes to mind—what happens to us who have leases on federal lands? We leased Taylor grazing land under section 15 when it became available in 1934. If the state takes its lieu lands out of our Taylor grazing lands, we stand to lose our leases from the federal government."

The speaker paused a moment to reflect before answering.

"Mr. Clements, no doubt you would like to continue discussion of the matter that you first brought up as a visitor at a legislative committee meeting in Olympia. You recall that the committee told you that all new state lands, when they come up for sale or lease, will be subject to preference rights on the part of the present holder. Right now the agreement is to give the holder of such land a five-year preference."

"That don't satisfy me," Mort said. "There shouldn't be any time frame."

"Hell, Mort," Hal Buck rapped out, "What harm's it gonna do you to have to outbid somebody for a lease for a change?"

The roomful of men guffawed.

"Mort's workin' on his second million," someone whispered audibly.

"Nobody expects you to volunteer yourself out of any lease, Mr. Clements," Del Gaston assured him. "But we have to remember that some men are deep in debt because they bought into the business at wartime prices. They should have an opportunity if possible to lease grazing land. They haven't accumulated enough capital to buy several thousand acres even if they become available."

Mort Clements remained standing. He was a short, darkskinned, black-haired man, an ugly version of his sister Eleanor, Ed's wife. A smile twisted Mort's mouth. "There is another possibility for getting land that we all know. The federal government has adopted a policy for terminating all reservations and letting Indians live with the general population. There are more 'n a million acres on the Colville Indian Reservation that could be sold to the federal government. The Flatheads in Montana and the Klamaths in Oregon have taken their payments. Why not the Colvilles?

"The Colvilles are squatting out there poor as Catholic priests. They're sick and they're drunk and they're lazy. They don't do a damn thing but wait for their monthly per capita payment and drink it all up.

"I understand, Gaston, that you have considerable Indian blood. How do you stand on tribal termination?"

Del Gaston paused an even longer time than before.

"As you say, Mr. Clements, I have Indian blood. My mother is half Okanogan and half English. Although neither I nor any member of my family have ever lived on the reservation, we are enrolled members of the Colville tribe. My mother has close ties of friendship with the people on the reservation, her neighbors across the river. They are all members of St. Mary's parish."

"If you don't get any services, then you ought to be in favor of a cash settlement," Mort stated. "All the nonreservation Indians ought to get together and support the termination bill."

"I had not intended to go into tribal termination at this time," Del Gaston said. "I have been asked to talk to the Colville tribes on the Fourth of July at the encampment. At that time I plan to express my personal feelings."

"I'm not gonna be in Omak on the Fourth of July," Mort said. "I'd like your statement now; creates a big difference whether you are willing to make wasted range and forest land available to the general public. Cattlemen need to know your stand before they support you for any office."

Del Gaston stepped down from the podium and stood on the level of the audience. "I agree that the matter is of primary concern to this group. Also, I grant that many of the Indians who do not live on the reservation are eager for a cash settlement that they can use to buy new homes or cars, invest in business, further their education, or indulge in pleasures.

"The Department of Interior is in favor of the Colville Termination Bill; but before it can become law, a favorable vote of the majority of adult members of the tribe is required.

"A primary weakness exists even in the title 'Colville Termination Bill.' Andrew Colville was a white man, a member of the Hudson's Bay Company, who traded with the Indians at Kettle Falls in the early 1800s. On the reservation named for this white man are Nespelems, Okanogans, San Poils, Methows, Lakes, and Nez Perce. From the time of the establishment of the reservation in 1872, they have resented being lumped as one autonomous body under a chief appointed by white men. Chief Moses, who became chief by executive order, was always in a false position over peoples who had their own hereditary chiefs. My great-grandfather, Chief White Stone Mountain, never accepted or conceded to any dictates of Moses, whose home was far south on the Columbia. How can I, only one-quarter degree Indian, speak for what people on the Colville Reservation should do?

"Perhaps half those who reside off the reservation are in favor of termination; but those who live there are against termination and have no desire for change. They are happy where they are. Many are elderly and have a lifetime aversion to being moved about by white men who want their land—a hunters' and fishers' paradise, abundant with lakes, rivers, streams, and wildlife.

"I know there are white people, in their customary pattern, who feel they are entitled to the 826,000 acres of commercial timber resources owned by the Confederated Tribes.

"But let me assure you, Mr. Clements, that I am not about to cede their forest rights away. As a candidate for a federal office, I want to listen to the People—*N'Chi-lix-czin*—to determine how I should vote for them in Congress.

"There is much promotion of the idea that the Indian must now be assimilated into the white culture, but I know one thing from personal observation. The goal of the red man has never been and never will be integration with the white race."

Del Gaston ceased talking and stared at Mort Clements.

Mort, whose face had turned livid, snarled, "You still haven't answered my question."

He sat down with a thump.

ED DECIDED THAT he had nothing to contribute. As he walked out, he was joined at the door by Sven Linstrom, who had also been a bachelor homesteader years back. They went together to the parking lot.

Sven exhibited a flask left over from moonshining days.

"Have a nip."

"Sure."

"Hot in there."

"Not all the thermometer's fault."

"Yeah. Mort's."

Bill found them.

"You feeling all right, Dad? Never saw you walk out on a fight before."

"I'm sick Mort makes me sick—always has."

A caucus formed around Sven's bottle.

"It wasn't fair for Mort to bring up tribal termination," Hal Buck opened. "The subject was lieu lands."

"Trust Mort to go after what he wants," Marv Tilton, who had sold out, chuckled. "Those lieu lands won't amount to much—isolated parcels of scrub land that nobody's ever wanted. The hay land's on the reservation."

"What do you think about Gaston, Ed?" Sven asked. "You for him?"

"If I was for him, I'd help more by keeping my mouth shut than if I came out in the open on his side. The old sonsabitches would favor anybody else they can scare up, to get under my skin."

"Mort hates the Westmores, don't he?" Frank Beeman recalled. "He couldn't beat'em out of their Injun rights in early days. Remember that, Ed? You were a kid in the legislature and helped the Westmores fight him."

"I guess so."

He remembered acutely. As the son of Analix Westmore stood before the cattlemen, Ed's mind had interchanged the present with the past. He was a young buckaroo riding the strawberry roan of the public land issues. He had found it necessary to quit the room to relieve himself of the sight of the smart young man with his Injun way of meeting Mort's assault.

Clayton Brunswick, retired political writer for a coast paper, and now editor of the *Bonaparte Times*, decreed: "Gaston would be a congressman in a million. He's a comer. Remember I said so! Taxpayers from a sparsely settled region may at last have a part in national affairs. He's well-informed; has practical experience in the state government. His people, from all I've heard, kept the livestock industry going through the hard winters in the 1880s when people learned to put up hay."

"He's exactly right," Ed thought.

Del Gaston's grandfather, Old Man Westmore, had set the example of putting up a hay crop—a ton of hay for each animal—for the months that deep snow covered the bunchgrass on the range. Old Man Westmore was the hero of the Okanogan legend.

Sven and Ed joined the group going to see the results of soil conservation grass trials on Carlquist's mountain at Oroville. Bill mumbled, "Other plans. I'll meet you before the evening banquet. Susan is coming down for it."

A continuous cool wind blew over the five pastures on the mountain top. Across the nearby Canadian line loomed Old Mount Chopaka, one of the Indian braves turned to stone. H.W. Carlquist, given the honor of leading the tour by the Soil Conservation Service, stooped down and plucked a stalk of intermediate wheat grass.

"Take a chaw, everybody," he said as he bit into the stalk. "See if a cow will like that better than rye grass. You gotta starve a cow before it'll eat rye grass.

"You can't wheat farm on this land, but it makes first rate grazing wheatgrass."

"You fertilize?" Ed asked.

"Yep. Government pays fifty percent of the cost of the seed on unfertilized land and seventy percent on fertilized."

The cars and pickups drove from pasture to pasture across the fields.

"I put in five pounds of sweet clover; nothing like it for putting nitrogen back into the soil," Carlquist said.

They surveyed stands of alfalfa and wheat grass, alfalfa and smooth brome, alfalfa and Sherman big blue grass.

"Intermediate wheat grass will come out from under the snow," Mr. Carlquist said.

He recommended alta fescue, orchard grass, fertilized crested wheat grass, and Canadian smooth brome, as well as bulbous blue grass, each grown on the two thousand acres of marginal wheat converted to productive use.

As Carlquist pulled up hybrid orchard grass and displayed its big root system, Ed remarked to Sven, "Bill ought to have come along to see this. All he thinks about is more farm machinery. Know damn well he's drinkin' in the bar with the International Harvester man."

Carlquist and the soil conservation men carried on a discussion of the comparative virtues of Canadian smooth brome and Manchar brome.

"You fellows have lots of Manchar and want us to say it's as good as Canadian; but my cows won't eat Manchar after it goes dormant. It won't stool out," Carlquist told the soil conservation men.

"It's your party," said Mike Medford, the government man, and he stood back

"You're always talking about classes of soil," Sven remarked. "What's this land?"

"Most of it's Class IV," the expert answered. "Good land for pasture and hay; you can cultivate it for wheat one year in six. There's some Class II here, too. Good land with minor physical limitations—slope, slight erosion."

The party decided that they had been scholars long enough, piled into their conveyances, and took their way individually down the highway to Omak headquarters. Everyone had become thirsty and looked forward to the ensuing "reception."

THAT EVENING, SUSAN hung her coat at the entrance to the banquet hall. She posted herself and waited. Bill would find her in time. The whole mezzanine swarmed with cattlemen and their wives, and there were long queues at the temporary bar.

"What a stunning dress, Susan!" Betsey Clements, wife of Mort Clements, exclaimed.

Susan nodded her thanks. If Betsey, who bought her clothes everywhere in the world, called a dress "stunning" it was!

Bill and her father-in-law came toward her together.

"How do I look?" she challenged her husband triumphantly.

Bill pondered. "My God! You look like a Holstein. What's a dairy cow doing at a beef cattle shindig?"

"For that you pay, buster!" Susan promised. "Like a cold drink?" Dad McLaren asked.

"No thanks! The line is a mile long."

She walked ahead of Bill and Dad McLaren, who wanted to stroll from group to group. She moved into the banquet room, in which long tables were set with shiny dishes and silverware. She leaned against the wall and thrust out a gaunt hip the way the *Vogue* model did.

Within five minutes the Truway buyer, who had come to the meeting by himself, entered and approached her. He held out his hand.

"I'm Judd Thacker. I came to get acquainted with the Okanogan people, and thought I'd start with the best-looking woman here. I'm from Seattle. Don't get over the mountains often."

Ordinarily Susan would have said to a cattle buyer, "Howdy. I'm Susan McLaren. My husband and his dad, who have cattle to sell, are who you need to meet. They'll be along in a minute."

Instead, she said, "I've only been to Seattle twice in my life. I wish I lived in a big city. I'm Susanne McLaren."

"People aren't coming to the table very fast. You haven't stood here long, or I would have noticed. Do you think we have time to go downstairs to the bar for a cocktail before the crowd settles?"

"I'd love to," said Susanne.

THEY TRAVERSED THE length of the mezzanine without meeting anyone to divert their course and went down the stairs and into the darkness of the bar on the lower level. The patronage had all progressed upstairs; no one else was in the room.

"They won't start serving dinner for another twenty minutes," Susanne said as she chose a seat in a booth.

"What will you have, Susanne?"

"I think a daiquiri."

"All right. Sweets to the sweet."

Susan recoiled inwardly. "'Sweets to the sweet!' What a fool!" she thought.

A harried waitress at last appeared to take their order. She swiftly brought two daiquiris.

"I hope you don't mind if I leave you. I have to go upstairs to help serve," she apologized. "At least thirty more are coming to the banquet than sent in reservations."

"Run along. We should be up there, too," Judd told her. "Now if this has to be quick, let's get down to basics. Tell me about yourself."

"Tell me about yourself" was not in Bill's repertoire. He had never once asked Susan to "tell about herself."

Judd Thacker had used sure bait. By the time she finished the daiquiri, a drink she had never ordered before, Susan had decided that Judd would understand a woman's needs.

They hastened up the stairs to the banquet like two kids who had been playing hooky.

People were now seated at all the tables. As they went their separate ways, Judd whispered, "You didn't give me your phone number!"

"Where've you been?" an annoyed Bill asked.

Susan told herself, "I proved I am no Holstein cow." She glowed with a satisfaction that took her through the rest of the banquet, including the long presentation of awards and the endless speeches about the disaster of low tariff threats, boxweed, and freight rates versus the cost of selling in the rings.

5.

The Old Man Leaves Town

The League of Women Voters of Okanogan County began the campaign season with a collective love affair. Delbert Gaston, a remote personality, somewhat taboo in the older generation because of his quarter-degree Indian blood, fascinated the second generation wives. Feminine volunteers finagled for memberships on publicity, hostess, and ways and means committees in the Fifth District congressional primary. The romantic appeal of Gaston was more a factor in his latest candidacy than it had been in his previous forthright campaigns for the state legislature. In those campaigns he had been elected by prosaic masculine confidence in his reliability, common sense, and commensurate assets. His wife, Mary, a grade school teacher at Oroville, was never in evidence in campaign headquarters in downtown Bonaparte. She was enjoying the summer months with her children in the hills, and was no damper to the enthusiasm of the League of Women Voters, whose members raptly introduced Delbert Gaston as the great-grandson of Chief White Stone Mountain, and also of Arthur Westmore, aristocratic British cattleman.

Gaston's trail proceeded from coffee party to barbecue. A woman reporter from Spokane was assigned to his entourage. In a feature story, she noted his dark, smiling eyes, and quoted his answer to "What is your favorite color necktie?"

"Something red and black, I suppose."

Ed McLaren, reading the interview, was revolted. He threw the *Spokesman-Review* to the floor. Journalistic tomfoolishness! "By Thalia Miller." A woman writer!

In Ed's view, the candidate should be answering questions on multiple use of the public domain versus setting aside of wilderness areas for exclusive use of sportsmen. What had been published two days ago, written by the *Review's* masculine political editor, had been more acceptable. The male writer had quoted Gaston as favoring the current nationwide move to establish a special commission to investigate the five hundred existing national land laws. Here was the subject to be developed! The prospect of an impartial investigative commission should allow the party to stay together through the primary, the political editor said. Gaston's approach to the issues the long way round would allow the various interest groups to present their viewpoints. The stockmen, the sports enthusiasts, the wildlife conservationists, the lumbermen, the mining men, the bureaucrats, the young people starting on a shoestring—all could agree that equitable distribution of benefits should begin with a search for facts. All should see the advantage of being able to express themselves before a commission—but not on the subject of attractive neckties that went well with a man's eye color!

Ed noted the omission of one interest group from the editor's list: the old cattlemen with accumulated capital. Mort Clements and his outfit would be after the young man's scalp. No one in their camp would be allowed to challenge Forest Service grazing permits held since 1902.

Gaston's statement, quoted by a knowledgeable editor, exactly expressed Ed's opinion: "Speaking in a cattle community, I feel free to say I favor the cattlemen as leaders in the movement toward modernization of the public land laws. The cattlemen have studied the need for years. They were instigators of the Taylor Grazing Act, by which the government now administers 142 million acres of land, mostly in the Western states."

Leaving for Eleanor the chore in which she delighted in an exasperated way, picking up abused newspaper pages, Ed started on foot for town when it was near mailtime. His head sweated at the band of his hat, but he was used to it.

On Main Street, Hal Buck hailed him. For the fifteen minutes before the mail would be distributed, Ed and Hal adjourned as usual to the cafe and ordered coffee.

"Been to any powwows for the Injun candidate?" Hal asked.

"Not me."

"What's a matter with you? I went to a barbecue at Loomis the other day. Lot of people there."

"Seemed like from the paper, it must have been mostly women."

"Know what you mean. Holy mackerel! That dame reporter can make anybody look like a jackass."

"Clayton Brunswick wrote the other day about multiple use of the public lands. He's onto issues."

"People may be afraid of public land issues," Buck suggested.

"The government wasn't always afraid of the cattleman's use of the range," Ed rejoined. "Heck, I was one of the people getting the Forest Service into this country."

"Got yourself the best grazing land, too. Forest Service and Taylor Act both. You gonna give it up to some punk kid?"

"Whether I like it or not, I'm gonna have to give it up, at least to my son Bill. He and his mother are crowding. What I want written into the record is that cattlemen have been first to want protection of the range."

"That's Gaston's line," Buck observed. "He can be idealistic because he knows he can't get the nomination as long as Horan wants to stay in Congress."

"Sure. But he's doing some good—talking about issues. Time'll come that Horan retires."

"Horan didn't even come home to campaign this summer," Buck said. "He knows he's a shoo-in. He probably wants Gaston to try his wings."

"That's about it," Ed agreed. "I expect Gaston's arguing because he's taken more than he likes from Mort over the Shefelman bill that they put through in the state legislature."

Buck nodded agreement. "If the boy's trying to make sense about use of the public domain, he should know there are some who appreciate it. You got a lot of old dope he could use."

"Maybe. Maybe not."

"Remember all that stuff we put together for the hearings in '47?"

"Whaddya mean 'we'? I did the digging; you called the meetings."

"I admit you're the scholar, Ed. But I organize."

Ed snorted.

Hal was a past president of the Cattleman's Association too, but Ed wondered where his vote would go. From experience in '47 and other times, Ed knew that Buck sang a different tune in every camp; he talked to hear himself talk. He rose impatiently from the booth while Hal still had coffee left in his cup. Ed had sugared and creamed his own coffee and let the whole mess grow cold without taking a swallow.

Halfway home, Ed realized that he had forgotten to pick up the mail. He turned back to town in the dust of noon.

The post office adjoined the general store. As he entered, he had his usual impression of indigent townspeople who shifted uneasily at the entrance of a man who had lived in Bonaparte since Year One and who owned a great deal of land. He accepted their resentment of him.

He knew they often said behind his back, "Old birds who come here in the early days have more 'n us who've had to get along after the country filled up."

Ed would have liked to remind these people darting sullen glances his way that the old-timers of the present had dragged the roads of Okanogan County, dug the irrigation ditches, wrestled the calves, planted the orchards, and taken the lean years with the fat.

ELEANOR, DEADLY ENEMY of thrips with her spraygun in hand, was inspecting the specimens in her flower garden when Ed reached home. He knew she also had been watching the road from town and wondering what was taking him so long to get home. When he held out the letters from Sam and Leila, she moved quickly from the rows of red, yellow, white, pink, and orange blooms, and walked with him toward the house. She placed the spraygun on the porch, took a pen knife from her apron pocket, and slit open the envelopes. From the expression of her face, Ed knew that the letters contained happy responses to the news that Eleanor had already written.

"Sam and Leila both want us to come to visit while the weather is still good."

She handed the letters to Ed. As he read them, Ed felt that it would indeed be a relief to leave Bonaparte for the summer. The weather would be just as hot in Walla Walla, Washington, and Boone, Iowa, as it was in Bonaparte; but in absence, there would be another kind of respite. In the Fifth District, it would be next to impossible to sidestep the political conniving that would surround the candidacy of Delbert Gaston. Before Ed, like a high rock wall on which the shale had started to roar and slide, hung a panorama from the past which prevented his taking an active part in the campaign.

"Since you're here, and it's about noon, I'll fix a sandwich," Eleanor said as she went through the front screen door. "It'll be ready in five minutes. Don't wander off."

IN THE LIVING room after lunch, Ed opened the deep bottom drawer of his desk. He pulled out the wad of material that he had admitted to Hal Buck he possessed. It had been gathered for the congressional investigation of the Forest Service; a hearing had been scheduled in Okanogan County. The actual result had been a miscarriage. His angry impulse in 1947 had been to throw the mass of papers into the trash burner, but common sense had impelled him to jam them instead into his desk. Looking backward on the anticlimactic events, Ed bitterly recalled his arduous labors of compilation. The research had served no purpose, yet it was still "the dope."

He arranged in numerical order the pages of the original draft of his prepared, but never presented, testimony, and straightened the rumpled comers. He fingered a research pamphlet: "U.S. Department of Agriculture Forest Service Bulletin No. 62. Gifford Pinchot, Forester. Grazing on the Public Lands. Extracts from the Report of the Public Lands Commission, 1905."

Perhaps Del Gaston already had all the information that Ed McLaren had; on the other hand, the young man could scarcely have the bulletin published in 1905.

Anyone who proposed a specific program used knowledge of others.

Final platforms were the aggregate of facts and arguments passed from hand to hand and mind to mind. Final success was determined by the willingness to cooperate. Progressive legislation was the outgrowth of long stories of previous defeats. Ed's collection was ammunition for a victory yet to be won. Anything on which a person had spent so much time and energy should have some value. Perhaps it might even have some value in the 1954 congressional primary. As Hal had initially mentioned the material, Ed decided he would risk a consultation the next time an opportunity presented itself. Hal was always dropping in for a sample of Eleanor's cooking, preferring it to Mrs. Buck's.

In due course, Hal called at lunchtime.

"Sit down for a bite," Ed invited as usual.

"I don't mind."

Like a tree, Buck's girth took on a half-inch ring each year. Ed remembered only one time that Hal had refused an invitation to sit down for a meal— the time he had come for buckets and shovels as a forest fire blazed on his range. Even though Ed didn't mind if he sat down at the McLaren table often, sometimes Eleanor did. Today Buck was his usual autocratic, curiosity-ridden self.

"Mort don't want that kid Gaston for Congress. He's hinted to me to step on him. Mort always was sly like that; never does his own in-fighting."

"More pie?"

"Thanks. I don't know, though, about this business of steppin' on Gaston. A lot of folks feel he's done some studying before talking. Likely that makes a big hit with you for one."

"He comes from a smart outfit. He went to law school, too. Should be all right. To hell with Mort!"

Ed saw the resentment in Eleanor's face as she pointedly began clearing dishes.

Ed stood and pushed back his chair. "Got something to show you. Let's go to the living room."

He laid out all the papers, with a large manila envelope beside them.

"Here's the stuff we put together for the Forest Service investigation in '47. You mentioned it the other day."

"Yeah. Golly, you didn't really burn it—said you did."

"Sure felt like it at the time."

"Glad you didn't follow through. What's on your mind?"

"Ever drive to Conconully?"

"Once in a while. You mean you want to pass this material on to the candidate?"

"You might."

"Don't you want to take it yourself?"

"Naw, I don't want to get mixed up in the campaign. You don't even need to say where it came from—just from the Cattleman's Association. Besides, I'm gettin' ready to go east. Eleanor and I been figuring on visiting our other kids' families this summer."

"Sure, I'll take it up for you, if it's a favor. But what Mort wouldn't do to me if he found out! Notice how he jumped on that kid about tribal termination? Mort wants that land back in the public domain so's he can lease it."

As he handed the materials to Buck, Ed was dubious of the wisdom of his play. He was unsure of the reaction Carr Westmore's grandson would have to the gift. Did the new generation give any consideration to the long record? Would a political aspirant dare to base his platform on fact and be patient for the day of the triumph of the policy if not the personal political victory?

Eleanor, who had puttered in the kitchen until Hal left, looked through the doorway. "Thank goodness we're leaving town. You get so worked up over elections!"

"There's lots to take care of before we go. You're gonna have to go with me down to the courthouse at Okanogan. I've been roundin' up all the abstracts of title, blueprints, and warranty deeds. You have to sign everything over along with me. You also have to sign that contract to sell those trees to Biles-Coleman."

"Now don't you say anything more! I'm not going to sign away those timber rights. I think it's a decision for Bill to make now he's taking over."

On the previous day, the Biles-Coleman appraiser had come to the McLaren house with a contract to be signed. Ed had already shaken hands downtown on the deal. Eleanor had shown no compunction about causing Ed to go back on his word. "I never said I would sign anything!" she told the appraiser.

The lumber company representative went away red-faced and angry. To avoid an all-out hullabaloo, Ed had yielded to Eleanor's refusal for the moment. He told the appraiser in the yard, "We'll give Eleanor awhile to get used to the idea. We'll sell as soon as we come back from our trip to Iowa."

Ed and Bill rode in the pickup to the two hay meadows on the river—one the Johnston place, the other dubbed the England place after its original owner. The alfalfa mixed with sweet clover was virtually ready for cutting.

"Not as high as some years; it's been too dry," Ed observed.

"Still three hundred tons," Bill estimated.

"Think you can handle all three cuttings this summer? Hiring everybody? Susan has to feed 'em."

"We can do it. You had me dancing down the hay on the wagon when I was five years old. Remember?"

Ed inwardly conceded that he would have to trust to what he had already taught Bill. He changed the subject. "We have less rainfall every year."

"I've said before that you can irrigate from the river if you want to invest in a pump and a sprinkler system."

"We still get flooding every spring. No end to the rigs you can put your money into. You got that new baler I just got finished paying for, also the hayshed. Before you store, be sure the moisture is down. Let the grass lie long enough to get dry."

"You're tellin' me what I already know, Dad. What's really bad about the way we put up the hay crop is that we have to hire so much labor. What we need is a tractor and trailer. You can load hay with a conveyor belt powered by one portable Briggs and Stratton motor."

"You know what a rig like that would cost?"

"I was figuring on going to Spokane to find out while you were gone."

Ed held back a load of startled invective. "I'm lettin' you do things, I said. I see you're gonna do your damnedest."

Bill smiled broadly as he said, "You're dam tootin.'"

"It's gonna cost you sixty dollars to raise a cow that sells for sixty-five dollars."

"If you invest one time in a tractor, all the crew you'll need after that would be a swather and a baler."

"Those Clydesdales won't break down."

"Those Clydesdales are twenty years old, Dad. They deserve to go out to pasture."

"And I'm put out to pasture, too."

The elder and younger McLarens rode in separate cars to the attorney's office in the town of Okanogan, the county seat since 1914. Although it was no longer growing as fast as its nearby competitor, Omak, only four miles distant, Okanogan was still more impressive largely because of the three-story brick courthouse, complete with bell tower, on the hill above town. Okanogan could also boast of the First National Bank building, built in 1915, and the companion Cariboo Inn, built ten years later—adjoining two-story, light-colored brick structures on Main Street. Trees planted by the enterprise of the Commercial Club shaded the town's sidewalks.

Dwight Meeks, attorney, met them in his office on the second floor of the bank building. After a taciturn but polite greeting, he presented papers that he had prepared.

Without reading the documents, Eleanor signed at once. "If Bill is going to be manager, that's all I care about."

Susan, in her turn with the pen, studied the pages. "Two hundred thousand dollars in debt, Bill. The payments will add up to most of the cash off the top. What arrangements are there for buying capital?"

Ed was pleased that she asked. "There's enough capital in the Lazy Ear checking account for buying this fall. If you handle the selling right, you shouldn't have to borrow. But after this year, Bill is gonna have to get his loan someplace else if he needs it. I figure if I pull out, I should pull out with enough to keep your mother and me the rest of our lives."

"You got three hundred thousand in savings if you got a nickel, Dad."

"That's your mother's and my hay for winter. We're not putting any more into the business."

Eleanor came to attention. "You mean you won't finance the cattle buying for Bill!"

"That's what I said. After this year."

"Keep still, Ma," Bill said with a wink. "You want to queer the whole deal?"

"No."

Mr. Meeks interposed, "This is an excellent, generous arrangement, Mrs. McLaren. The way things should be done by families but seldom are."

Eleanor sat back in her chair. Soon she noticed Susan's lightened hair. She eyed it without comment.

The quartet ate lunch together in the Cariboo Inn.

"Why do they keep that mangy moose head up there on the wall?" Eleanor asked.

"That's not a moose," Bill explained. "That's a caribou. This town is on the old Okanogan-Cariboo trail."

"Everybody went up the Cariboo Trail to the gold fields in the early days," Ed added. "You oughta know that!"

"Let's have something to eat besides beef stew," Susan said as she read the lunch menu.

"How about caribou stew?" Bill joked.

They ordered chef's salads and angel food cake with strawberries to please the women.

After Ed paid the bill and they went to the street, Bill said, "Better be getting back to the range. Still some fence to repair before we start haying."

Eleanor began to follow Bill and Susan to the parking lot, but Ed surprised his wife by tapping her shoulder. "Wait a minute. Let 'em go."

"Why? What are we going to do but go home?"

"I thought I'd buy a pair of pants and a jacket. What you want?"

"Oh, I never wear anything but housedresses. I don't need anything."

"Get something to wear on the train, I mean."

"For goodness' sake! I haven't thought anything about it. I haven't bought any dress-up clothes for so long, I haven't the least idea what you do wear on a train trip."

Ed piloted her into Tremont's Boutique.

A slim, middle-aged woman in a black dress came to greet them. "May I help you?"

"Yep," Ed said. "My wife and I are going East."

"We have just what you want for your wife. Wrinkle-free linen suits are ideal for travel. What color do you like, ma' am?"

The clerk led them to a rack of "Better Ladies."

"Navy blue, I suppose," Eleanor said diffidently. "Something that won't show dirt."

"Nothin' doin'!" Ed vetoed. "One pink and one white suit. Blue dress, too."

Eleanor gasped. "Now, Ed! We have to start saving if you're retired!"

"That's next month," Ed declared. "Go on and try on some things."

To Bill's amusement, Dad McLaren made three final trips to the Johnston place to give counsel. Susan lost her irritation as she overheard her father-in-law say, "You're already a cosigner on the Lazy Ear account. Don't be afraid to spend for what comes up. Enough to cover most everything."

Yes, Bill was a cosigner on the account, but he had never yet written any personal checks—only such checks as payment for barbwire, tools, salt, or harness.

THAT EVENING, AFTER Ed and Eleanor had finally driven out of town in the Fairlane, Susan and Bill talked a while in bed before turning out the lights. "Your dad said we could use the check ing account. Let's give a party," Susan suggested. "I have my guest list all made out."

"Gonna play the Grand Lady of the Lazy Ear?"

"Any objections?"

"Nope. Only don't wear that Holstein dress."

"I made that dress myself. I've had more compliments on it than on any dress I ever wore. I copied it from *Vogue* magazine."

"You believe the Truway buyer took you down to the Peerless Room because you wore that dress? Makes you look sophisticated?"

"So you noticed!"

"So did everybody else from Oroville, Riverside, Tonasket, Omak, and Okanogan, not to mention Curlew and Twisp."

"You should recognize my technique by now—how I manage the football star with the high school sophomores. You aren't the only one who can attract an admirer."

"I have no idea what you're talking about," Bill mumbled sleepily. He squeezed his wife's breasts and fell to snoring.

Susan lay awake and planned the celebration. Because the house was so small, the event would have to be staged in the three-sided shed that ordinarily provided a roof for the car, the pickup, the mower, the baler, and miscellaneous junk. Dad, Sam, and Bill had made it with a hardwood floor to hold heavy equipment. If she sprinkled spangles on the floor, it would be slick enough for dancing. Larry McDonald, son of the famous three-fingered Larry McDonald, could bring the upright piano on the back of his pickup. He also enlisted musicians with other instruments—a fiddle, a guitar, and even a Jew's harp. The dancing would be preceded by a barbecue, of course. The shed was close enough to the house that it would be no great chore to carry out the food to improvised tables. She would have to persuade Bill to dig a barbecue pit. Thinking of all the details that must be worked out, Susan put herself to sleep.

Next morning she telephoned all their friends about town and sent notes to those in other towns. She invited the entire Fifty Couples Club membership. Feeling mischievous, she mailed a note to Judd Thacker, who had called at the ranch, although he had not come to the house. He had talked to Bill, who happened to be in the corral; he had given Bill a Truway business card with his name, address, and phone number. She sent a note to the architect with whom she had had a serious discussion lasting through two numbers at the most recent Fifty Couples gathering. He had assured her he could design a suburban ranch style home that would make her the envy of the Okanogan country. He had promised to do some preliminary sketching. On the note, she wrote a P.S.: "I have been waiting to see some plans for my dream house. Bring them along!"

Weston Sand, the architect, had only recently opened his offices and had joined the Fifty Couples as a way to meet prospective clients. At the dance, he had realized that Susan was a little oiled, as she rambled on about her dream home. On discreet inquiry, Sand learned that the McLarens in 1952 had bought three hundred head of yearlings at ten cents per pound at the Okanogan sales, wintered them through the fall and spring, ranged them during the summer, and sold them at twenty-six cents at the 1953 auction. He wrote in response to Susan's note that he would be happy to attend the party and to bring preliminary sketching and drafting.

He would not have been quite as elated at his invitation to the McLaren party if he were more aware of the constitutional aversion of cattlemen to splurging on the architecture of anything other than barns and toolsheds. Susan was aware of the aversion, but she was determined to have more of a share of the family income from now on. She imagined a spacious, split-level house on the hill above. The front, facing southeast, would be a solid glass wall through which she could look out over flower gardens to the hills, instead of the calving meadows.

Bill was not as excited about the party as Susan, but he was glad it was taking place. He had said nothing to his neighbors about the deed transfers, but the departure of the elder McLarens at the height of summer was a signal to the community of Bonaparte. Playing hosts alone at an open house would be what everyone expected of a new Old Man and his woman.

Susan coaxed Bill to write her a check, which she took to town and cashed. She shopped for and found a voluminous square-dance skirt and a ruffled blouse. For Glenna and Deanna, she bought flounced pinafores.

The day before the party, Susan drove the pickup into town to rifle the freezer locker for almost all of a two-year-old heifer, butchered into ten-pound packages. As the meat thawed, she removed it from the paper and swathed it in cheesecloth. Bill and their son Tom, just home the day before from his freshman year at Pullman, had spent the whole morning digging a barbecue pit. When they said they were ready, Susan handed down the hunks of beef. They shoveled gravel from the river directly on top of the meat, then laid wood planks over the pit for a lid. Bill sealed the pit with sand and started the fire. Everyone helped to heap on a mountain of apple wood that would burn all night.

Susan rose at dawn, to find the fire turned to a bed of glowing coals. The mouth-watering smell of roasting beef came through the sand.

The hostess put a butcher's apron over her Levi's and launched preparations for the rest of the menu. When Glenna and Deanna came yawning from their bedroom, she scarcely gave them time to finish breakfast.

Aided by her resigned daughters, she chopped cabbage to make coleslaw, enhanced the flavor of canned baked beans with onion and brown sugar, and sliced store-bought tomatoes and cucumbers. The vegetables were not yet ready in the garden, except perhaps the com. She and the girls picked what ears could be considered edible. The kernels were still small, but tender and full-flavored. Susan made apple pies while the girls manufactured a tubful of potato salad. If people wanted more desserts, they would have to bring them. Several good cooks would undoubtedly bring samples of their specialties— angel food cake, chocolate cake, or carrot pudding.

At two o'clock, Bill opened the pit and forked out a package of beef.

"Just right! Still a little pink!" Susan pronounced. "By the time people start coming, it will be ready!"

SUSAN DONNED HER skirt and blouse; the girls, their flounced pinafores. Bill and Tom went into the house, washed, and put on fresh shirts and Levi's.

Susan was concocting fruit punch of canned orange, pineapple, and grapefruit juice just as the beer and wine arrived by special truck. The beer was put out in a tub with a cake of ice from the ice house. A chunk of ice and a generous quantity of Concord wine were added to the punch. If Dad and

Mother McLaren had been in town, Susan and Bill would not have dared to serve liquor. Dad and Bill indulged in convivial drinks at public gatherings, but Ed upheld Eleanor when she refused to allow alcoholic beverages in her home.

In the kitchen, Susan put coffee and water into gallon enamel pots and began heating them on the electric range. There would always be teetotalers who preferred coffee to beer and wine. Everyone would need coffee to end the evening, at least.

Tables and workbenches had been set end-to-end in a long row at the far wall of the shed. White sheets draped over the sundry collection of furniture gave unity to the dining board, which was now lined with silverware, trays, and cups.

Bill stood at the driveway to greet each arrival and to direct traffic toward the shed. Susan came from the house with the first supply of punch in a stainless steel dishpan that now served as the punchbowl. Glenna and Deanna brought out the coffee and stood ready to serve it. Susan's friends and neighbors deposited their offerings directly on the table.

"If I didn't have a thing prepared myself, there's enough on this table for two hundred people right now!" Susan exclaimed.

To make room for the hot food, the punch bowl and the coffeepot were moved to a card table. Half a dozen women guests helped Susan and her girls bring out the serving dishes from the house. Bill enlisted two men to retrieve chunks of barbecued beef as needed. He allowed guests to serve themselves to the side dishes; then, as they reached him at the end of the table, he deposited a sliced serving of barbecue on each tray held out—a pound slice for a man, half a pound for a woman.

Judd Thacker made a late entrance; he was decked out in expensive gabardine pants, white shirt, black vest, and black string tie.

Susan shook his hand cordially. She had drunk several glasses of punch, and half-hoped to feel herself take fire at Judd's touch. But nothing happened with their handshake. Had the brushfire already gone through her? She would have to look elsewhere for kindling.

Larry McDonald and his troupe arrived in time for a hearty meal before performing. The musicians wore Levi's, cowboy shirts, Stetsons, boots, and red bandannas.

"Give yourself plenty of strength," Bill urged the orchestra, who were quick to comply.

The architect from Wenatchee strolled into the shed in the company of a young man. They approached the host. Bill held out his hand. "Where was it we met? I'm half-loaded."

"I don't believe I have had the pleasure of meeting you before, Mr.

McLaren. I am Weston Sand. It was your wife who extended an invitation. She said to bring a friend, so I have. This is my partner, Jamesey." He thrust forward the young man with a sulky face and a limp hand.

"Partner in what?" Bill asked, as he waved at Susan for help.

She came running.

"Oh, Bill! I forgot to tell you! Weston is an architect. At the last Fifty Couples dance, he promised to make me some house plans. Did you bring them, Weston?"

"Yes, indeed. I left them in the car. Run and get them, Jamesey."

Jamesey sighed as he left on the errand.

"What have you been up to?" Bill demanded of Susan, who batted her eyes and smiled.

"She has been dreaming," Weston Sand said. "I took the liberty of trying to make her dream tangible."

Jamesey returned with a roll of blueprints.

"I can't wait! I can't wait!" Susan squealed. She made room for the drawings on the loaded table. Sand arranged them in proper sequence.

"You spoke of your lovely view to the south. If you do decide to have a glass wall, I suggest a thermal pane that will keep your fuel bills down. In time, it would pay for itself."

"Dandy idea," Susan exclaimed. "Save, save, save! is what the McLarens do."

Bill grabbed Susan by the hand and pulled her across the yard and into their twelve-by-fifteen living room.

"What's got into you? You going off your rocker?"

Susan stood like a she-bear at bay. "Mother McLaren has spent her whole life in a shack. Do I have to do the same?"

"You're drunk, Buttercup," Bill said with unexpected tenderness. "I'll pretend to look at the plans."

While Susan and Bill had been absent for an obviously tense conference, friends had collected and rinsed dishes. The food on the table was covered when they came back to the party. Everyone sensed and understood the stress on the young McLarens in their new status.

The fiddler scraped his fiddle string; the Jew's harp player sounded a preliminary twang.

"Let's dance till morning," Larry McDonald yelled in a voice that echoed up and down the valley.

"I bet Old Hugo can hear that at the England place," Bill laughed. "Hey! Where's Hugo? Hugo's not here, the old sourpuss!"

Susan shook spangles on the floor.

While the orchestra played the set of fox trot, waltz, and drag, Susan and

Bill were left to dance almost alone, in honor of their new status as operators of the Lazy Ear.

Arthur Lund, the banker, Mr. and Mrs. Charley Blackwell of the mercantile company, and Frank Dallam, the newspaper editor, were behaving as though they were guests at an important occasion. For years, they had been heavily obliged to Old Ed, who had apparently relinquished the reins to Bill.

The only gloomy faces at the feast were Bill and Susan's children, who had been commanded to "stay home for once." With collegiate good manners, Tom danced with plump housewives and continued defiantly to drink cup after cup of punch, even though his father had already ordered him away from the dishpan. Glenna and Deanna danced half-heartedly with men old enough to be their fathers. Some of them actually were the fathers of Glenna's and Deanna's friends, who were all at a moonlight beach party at Osoyoos Lake.

At midnight, Tom said to Susan, "Mom, you're talking too loud. And look what you've spilled on your blouse!"

Susan glanced down to see a large smear of barbecue sauce. "Oh, damn!"

She wondered if it had been there at ten o'clock—when Judd Thacker sneaked out after her as she went to catch her breath behind the shed. She had good-naturedly accepted a kiss on the lips even though she thought, "Ugh!" She'd had enough of him! What if the barbecue sauce had been on his necktie and was applied to her like a scarlet letter!

"When is this party going to stop?" Glenna, worn out, shrilled at her parents.

"Go on to bed if you feel like it," her father told her.

"With this racket!" Glenna exclaimed. "I bet all the coyotes have been scared into Stevens County!"

"Coyotes are what you are!" Deanna accused. "A pack of coyotes howling at the moon!"

Her father, filled with beer and good will, began an imitation of a coyote howl. The crowd shouted approval. Half the men joined the serenade.

"How long did Larry tell you they would play?" Bill asked Susan.

Larry overheard and shouted, "I don't stop while anybody's on the floor. I can last till four if you can. We still haven't had a tag dance or a ladies' choice."

To loud applause, Larry began a tune he'd played fourteen times already. No one minded as long as he kept the beat.

Weston Sand approached Susan, "We have further to go home than most people. I do believe we must call it a night. Thank you for your hospitality."

"Thank you for coming!" Susan cried as she held out her hand happily. "Thanks for bringing the dream house. It's been on display all night. I guess we had better add on a ballroom. No more parties in the shed!"

The architect beamed. He crooked his finger at Jamesey.

Jamesey came forward to take Susan's hand. "If we leave the blueprints, we'll expect a token deposit, Mrs. McLaren," the junior partner delivered the blow.

Susan beamed to hide her shock and beckoned to Bill, who was urging other couples not to leave yet.

As he joined his wife, Bill said to the architectural partners, "You guys are softies. Nobody goes home till the sun comes up."

"The sun will be up when we reach Wenatchee," the architect responded. "As Jamesey just inquired, Bill, do you mind giving us a deposit on the house plans?"

Bill was equal to the occasion. "We'll have to go to the house. My checkbook's there. I'll write a check for however much you say."

Susan peeked through the window. The men were in the bedroom. The bed was littered with cups and paper plates. She saw Bill write a check even though the project of a new house was a total surprise to him. Her drunken heart warmed.

After the architects departed, she went to Bill. "How much did you give them?"

Bill looked eastward at the dawn. "Too damn much. Where are those plans?"

"Still on the table in the shed, I guess."

Bill walked over to get them, and Susan tagged along. "They made me pay a thousand dollars! What's Dad gonna say when he gets home?"

"I had no idea they'd charge just to give us some plans," she wailed.

Bill rolled up the sheets and carried them into the house. In fifteen minutes, everyone was gone, or on the way down the lane to the highway.

Susan flung her arms around Bill, who began to laugh. "Sue, let's go swimming and sober up."

"Are you out of your mind?"

"Nope. Just drunk. Come on."

He picked her up and carried her kicking and shrieking the three hundred yards to the river. He threw her into the cold water and jumped in after her.

"Not with our clothes on!" she screamed.

Sober from the bracing dip, they slogged back to the house and began to peel off their clothes in the bedroom.

"I got to get ready for the haying crew," Bill said. "So do you!"

Susan was already naked under the covers.

"Come to bed for a couple hours, anyway," Susan begged. "You need some sleep."

"You know what'll happen if I get in that bed. It won't be sleep. By the way…" He grabbed the blueprints off the dresser and unrolled them. Then he tore them in half.

Susan sprang from the bed and clawed frantically at Bill. "You bastard!"

He held her firmly. "It's morning, Buttercup. That dumb house didn't even have a loft for dancing in!"

She fell back on the bed. "The hell with you!" she said. She turned on her side and went to sleep.

When she awoke at noon, everyone was gone from the house, but the mess of the evening before remained.

She pulled on a bra, shirt, underpants and Levi's and began removing debris. Being head lady of the Lazy Ear did not seem a cause for joy. What would Dad McLaren say to a thousand dollar check on the account when there was a haying crew to pay? She and Bill had not had the courage to inquire how much was in the account. The statements still went to the elder McLarens.

She decided they would have to sell some steers. She'd heard Dad McLaren say the cattle shouldn't be kept on the lease land too long. Because of the underbrush, they'd grow thinner in stead of fatter.

Bill came in the back door and found her glumly clearing food off the kitchen linoleum.

"You still mad at me?" she asked in her kneeling position. "I think there's probably a thousand dollars in the checking account."

"Maybe so. Trouble is I wrote a check for a first payment on a tractor, too."

"Oh, God!"

"Tractor won't be delivered for a few days. We'll put off the haying until it comes. Better round up some steers and get them to the auction on Friday."

"That's what I was thinking," Susan agreed. "What if Dad McLaren wrote a check for some presents in Iowa and the check bounced."

"Old Lund wouldn't bounce Dad's check. He'd just see to it that I got bounced out of the cattle business before the ink is dry on the contracts."

SELLING HAD BEEN high on Dad McLaren's list of parting admonitions. Old Ed always shipped his cattle either to the Seattle stockyards or to the Old Union Stockyards in Spokane.

"Thought I might try the local sales rings for more business," Bill had said. "We got sixteen cents for those cows last month."

"If you're gonna sell locally," Old Ed was making a big concession, "your best bet is Willis Barker. He buys for Van Wegen in Wenatchee. He comes right to the place and makes a bid. He has a truck and trailer that can take twenty-eight head, same as a railroad carload."

"He buys by the head. I wanna try sellin' by weight."

"Willis is never more 'n ten pounds off weight, everybody knows."

"Ten pounds off in his own favor!"

Bill's father persisted. "Willis's checks are always good. One thing you got to watch. Some of these out-of-town buyers' checks are so rubber they stretch a mile. Somebody like their uncle in Toppenish has to make'em good. They get a temporary loan from a bank or a relative, but if the capital isn't behind it, you're in the soup. Find a buyer whose checks are good. Barker, for Van Wegen, musta written a million dollars worth of checks; never a one has been returned for insufficient funds."

"Truway buys by weight. Their checks are always good."

"They pay twelve cents for feeder steers on a thirty-day deal," Ed said. "That's a buyers' market if there ever was one."

The conversation, listened to avidly by Susan, had ended without any hard and fast order given by the Old Man.

"I'm gonna hold off for the best bid once in a while," Bill said.

"'Member when Willis makes a bid, he takes it with him," Ed gave a final caution. "You ask him again what he'll give, and it will be less than the first time."

"For God's sake, Dad! Where do you think I been all my life? Right at your elbow. I've seen you turn down some mighty good bids."

Now, facing the consequences of following their own impulses, Susan and Bill sobered quickly.

"I can't see why Dad didn't tell you how much was in the account," Susan complained.

"He said there was 'enough.' He meant enough to feed the hay crew and buy baling wire, likely."

"You were a real sneak ordering that tractor. Now I understand why no haying crew showed up this morning. You figure all the help you'll need will be a swather and a baler."

By Ed's agenda, he and Eleanor would ride in the Ford Fairlane as far as Walla Walla to visit Leila and her family first. From there, leaving the automobile, they would travel on the train to Sam's in Iowa.

Leila, a brunette beauty, had arrived as an infant in answer to her mother's prayer for a daughter. For her first two years, she had been like a doll decorated in hand-sewn dresses; but as soon as her personality emerged, she had eluded her mother's devotion and turned to her father for affection. She had a vague memory of an interval in which her father had not been with the family to give her a horsy trot on his foot or to swing her above his head while she squealed. She was left with a need to keep her father in her company and rebelled in early childhood at being a domestic assistant to her mother.

Leila's favorite creatures were the Clydesdale work horses. When she was eight years old, she and Mike, one of the neighboring Runnel boys, also eight, "drove derrick": they guided Clydesdales Kate and Jane as the team pulled slip loads of hay to the top of the stack. Underneath each load of hay, as it was transported on the slip, lay a chain net. This net, or sling, drew together to form a closed bundle as the load rose via the derrick pole, and was maneuvered to the proper spot for deposit. Leila was skillful at the use of the derrick arm to put the load at the spot her father designated.

When the load of hay, enclosed in the net, reached the top of the haystack, Ed yelled at Leila, "Trip 'er!"

Leila jerked the chain so that the sling, held together by detachable hooks, fell apart at the bottom.

Leila worked tensely and happily to please her father. Only when he snapped at her, "Don't let that sling drop so fast; you might bust some links!" did she take offense.

"I quit," she shouted at her father.

"Work inside or outside, makes no difference," he replied calmly.

She never went as far as the kitchen door before deciding to return to her job with the Runnel boy. She and Mike took turns, one walking behind the team and driving, the other leading with a hand on Kate's bridle. By comparison, the job of peeling potatoes all day ran a poor second choice.

Haying was the most incessant, yet most pleasant work for the family. The first process was the cutting, done by Ed with the big, steady Clydesdale team hitched to the mower. He trusted no one but himself with the sharp sickle bar that cut a swathe six feet wide. The mower was drawn in a geometrically exact square that became smaller with each turn about the field.

The fallen hay lay in the field for a day to dry, then the full crew went into action. Sam drove the team at a walk to rake the windrows. Three men on foot built the shocks, or mounds of hay, fluffed them up, and turned them over so that the bottom would dry.

Bill as the spike pitch stayed in the field. He kept three drivers and horse-drawn slips in rotation: one slip being loaded, one slip on the way to the stack, and one at the stack being unloaded. Each man who drove the flat bed, twelve feet long and the width of a team, put on his load with the help of the spike pitch. The flat beds were called slips because they slipped across the ground, any kind of ground. And because they were high-centered, they never stalled in the way that wagons did on rough terrain.

It required judgment to make an adequate load—it had to be not too light, not too heavy. The rhythm was disturbed by uneven size loads. When Leila, as a teenager, promoted herself to slip driving, she had to learn patience to collect a full load before heading for the haystack and the gallon jug of water wrapped in a wet gunnysack and stashed under the hay.

If Leila's load split, she knew enough to cower and remind her father and crew that, after all, she was "only a girl."

Eleanor and a hired girl cooked at the range in the Johnston house. Meals were served on a back porch that Ed had screened in to keep out flies. Several factors gave the Lazy Ear a good name as a place to work at haying time. In the hundred-degree heat, Eleanor served lemonade with chunks of ice. Unlike some of the other ranchers, Ed and his boys would take time during the winter to saw great blocks from the frozen river and store them in deep sawdust in the ice shed.

Eleanor was known for her "good grub." She cooked meat and potatoes for both noon and evening meals. She made five pies at once to choose from: lemon, chocolate, apple, berry, and cherry. At noon, pie or pudding were in order; cake or cookies were served with canned fruit at night. Coming from the field, the crew were often met by the inviting smell of hot bread, biscuits, or cinnamon rolls fresh from the oven.

Everyone got out of his bunk at five o'clock in the morning; the crew was in the field at seven. The usual lunch period was an hour, but on blazing hot days, the workers stopped at eleven, and returned to the field at four o'clock to work until dark The teams were not unharnessed at noon but were fed and watered.

Eleanor and Ed went back to their house in town on Saturday night. Eleanor left ground-up meat, potatoes, and onions for hash. She set the table and washed the dishes. What everyone did after Saturday night supper and until five on Monday morning was his own business.

The work detail moved from the Johnston place to the England place to the Carlson place. The Carlson field, higher on the hills and dustier than the other places, was least liked. Working in the coarse rye grass cut the hands and irritated the nostrils. Dad would not permit Leila to ride on the slip down the rough terrain because it made the load so heavy that it dug into the dirt.

Three crops of hay were harvested: in late June, early July, and mid-August. Because feed was so precious, Sam not only raked the field with the horses at a walk, but re-raked it at a trot.

At the end of summer, a great haystack loomed in each feedlot. Fences protected the stacks so that cattle could eat only at mealtimes, when sledge loads of fodder were strewn about the lot. The stacks must last all winter.

Every spirit was at its best during hay harvest. The men and animals working in harmony with the earth accepted the necessity to be productive. The crew vied good-naturedly for the favors of the hired girl—usually a Runnel girl—first Margaret, then Ellen, then Amy. Eleanor saw to it that her own family, including Ed, was served a fair share of every delicacy at the table.

Leila even helped with the dishes at night!

THROUGH HIGH SCHOOL, Leila retained her love of horses, and added an interest in boys, especially winners of bronc-busting contests.

She begged her father for a horse of her own, one that she could break and train herself.

Leila discovered what saddle horse she wanted and how it could be obtained. She came home excited after a visit with friends to Solar Hawk, son of Sun Beau. "You've got to get me one of his colts, Dad! He's the most beautiful thing I ever saw. He's so much taller than any of our stock He's steel gray, almost black, and his tail is black. He looks so powerful, but he's fine boned. He has a dish face. The Barnes's mare was bred to him, and the colt will be for sale."

"Missy, I'll thank you to get your mind off stock breeding, and on to setting the table," Leila's mother snapped. "You know your father can't afford a saddle horse for you!"

"But the government is making it so colts won't be so expensive," Leila persisted.

"I've heard how the Fanchers at Siwash Creek got to use him," Ed came to his daughter's defense. "The government has loaned him out on the condition that area mares are bred to him. They say they are giving us a chance to raise the level of quality of our stock horses. Solar Hawk is a remount stallion, a cavalry horse. He's a real thoroughbred. I guess that his blood mixed with the cayuse mares would make better animals."

THROUGH THE CHILL of the Great Depression, cattle ranchers had continued to use ordinary cayuses, catch colts, and cow ponies for herding. But with the United States' entry into the Second World War only a matter of time away, the government had begun to court the agricultural industry.

"When you get on him, it's just like getting on a powerful machine!" Leila rhapsodized.

ED BOUGHT THE Barnes's colt for seventy dollars when it was four years old. It was a combination birthday and high school graduation present, all twelve hundred pounds!

"It'll make a dependable horse for cow-cutting," Ed justified the expense to his wife, who sighed.

"Is that what my daughter is going to become, an expert at cutting cows?"

"She already is," Ed chuckled. "But I think you're right. She should go to college and learn something more."

"The boys have both gone to agricultural college. I wish one of my children could attend Whitman. Leila has no idea of how to behave like a lady."

"You had your way about a horse," Ed reasoned with Leila. "Try to please your mother for once."

Leila sent in her application for Whitman College, then turned her full attentions to training Smokey. At first, she was not able to mount him without assistance, but by the time she received her acceptance letter from Whitman a month later, she and Smokey knew how to cut a cow back and leave the calf.

She trained Smokey to stop on his hind feet and rear into the air. She had first experimented with a harsh bit, but found that Smokey responded better to a belt full of tacks running across his chest. While Smokey trotted, she would pull sharply on the belt. When Smokey felt the tacks, he rose on his hind feet.

Ed watched her in the corral, bringing Smokey up sharply with one hand and waving her hat with the other. "Why are you teaching him all those rodeo tricks?" he asked.

"Just for fun," she replied.

Leila was dreaming a dream that eventually came true.

When she arrived home for summer vacation after her first year at Whitman, she was informed by a suspicious mother that Claire Pentz, publicity chairman for the Omak Stampede, wanted Leila to telephone him.

Eleanor, listening in horror, heard Leila say, "I think so. I think so. Yeah, Dad will let me have the trailer to get down there."

With a look of pure bliss on her face, Leila hung up the phone. "They're going to continue the Stampede through the war! They want me to be queen!"

"What do you have to do?" Eleanor demanded. "I don't want my daughter running around with a bunch of rodeo clowns!"

"They said they want me because I'm a girl who's always had a good reputation, and besides, I'm the best girl rider in the country. There will be two princesses, but I'm going to be the queen!"

"What clothing will you need?"

"I wish I could have an English riding habit!" Leila ventured. Leila learned that she could wear any costume that she deemed appropriate, but that it would have to be provided at her own expense. "All I have are Levi's!" she complained to her new sister-in-law, Susan Buck McLaren.

Susan, married to Bill two days after college graduation, was living with her parents. Bill, who had been an R.O.T.C. officer in college, was at boot camp in Texas.

"If you can sneak me a pair of your dad's pants, some with a double seat, I can probably cut them down to fit you," Susan offered to Leila.

"Oh, you are so talented," Leila cried. "If you hadn't got married to Bill, I bet you would have been a princess."

"Not in my cards," Susan said philosophically. "Haven't you noticed how pregnant I am?"

Leila threw her arms around Susan's neck. "I'm so busy being important, I didn't notice a thing!"

Susan made over a pair of Ed McLaren's gabardine trousers and a rust-colored flannel shirt that fastened with snaps. Leila's Stetson and riding boots were new.

Ed was as proud as Leila of her being selected queen of the rodeo. He reconciled Eleanor to the news by saying, "If anything can give her the notion of being ladylike, this will."

Ed, in one of his terms as president of the Cattleman's Association, had joked about Leila in his opening remarks, "I always say for you fellows to study. Read everything you can get your mitts on. My daughter's quite a reader. Always got her nose in a silly book or a magazine, off in her room when there's dishes to be washed or clothes to be ironed. Won't even keep her room clean. My wife's got so she won't touch it; just keeps the door shut. The other day, she looked into Leila's room, and it was slick as a whistle.

"'What's come over you?' her mother asks.

"Leila says, 'I was reading the paper and saw a piece about Old Lady Haliday in Omak getting a year in jail for keeping a disorderly house.'

"So I say 'Read!'"

All the cattlemen roared.

THE GROOMING OF Leila and her two princesses was casual.

"When the left front foot comes up, your fanny comes up," Claire Pentz explained to the royalty.

When Claire Pentz asked the girls to provide advance publicity photographs, Susan took snapshots of the queen and princesses posed on horseback and on the Lazy Ear corral fence. The photos appeared in weekly newspapers across the Okanogan Valley.

Leila and her court reigned for three days of Stampede. Leila, whose father and brother had always told her, "Let your body go with the horse," posted down Main Street to the rodeo grounds like a British royal on parade. As they entered the gates, the girls were introduced over the loudspeaker; every tourist, cattleman, cowboy, cowgirl, businessman, and Indian clapped and whistled in homage. Laughing happily, with dark eyes flashing, Leila pulled up Smokey and waved her Stetson. As queen, she ruled over steer wrestling, bareback riding, calf roping, bull riding, and barrel racing. After the grand entry, she and her two friends stayed on horseback to help move animals through the chutes into the arena.

Climaxing each day, twenty cowboys and Indians on specially schooled horses lined up on the bluff across the river, rode their mounts down the steep bank into the water, across the river, and up the opposite bank to race hellbound for the middle of the Stampede arena. The event was aptly named the "Suicide Race." Ed gritted his teeth and endured the madness for Leila's sake.

"Nobody should treat horses like that!" he muttered in the company of other stockmen, who agreed. Numerous riders as well as horses suffered broken ribs and legs.

Nevertheless, these were Leila's days of glory!

In her second year at college, Leila, who had been somewhat distracted by public life, became even more distracted by the advent of love. "Nothing has ever happened like what has just happened to me," she wrote to her parents. "I am dropping out of school and coming home to get married."

Miss Leila McLaren became the bride of Harold Miller of Walla Walla at a large wedding in the Bonaparte Community Church. The Garden Club arranged flowers at the altar and in the reception parlor; members presided at punchbowls, invited guests to sign the guest book, and consoled the mother of the bride, who was braver than most mothers.

The men, including Ed in his best suit, and even the bridegroom in his best suit, stood by dumbly while the feminine rituals were carried out around them.

All of Hal Miller's family were present for the wedding and seemed highly satisfied to see it taking place. Ed guessed the father was willing for his son to marry young because he would be more easily exempted from the military with a wife. Ranchers' sons could be excused as necessary for the production of wartime crops. Sam, who had been working on a master's degree, and Bill, a senior, chose to take advantage of the status accorded them as college R.O.T.C. men.

Leila's parents arrived in Walla Walla to find her canning and cooking for a husband, six children, and six ranch hands. She was anticipating her seventh child, but she had not even bothered to inform her parents in letters to Bonaparte. Her brood was full of life and happy to see their grandparents, whom they had visited by turns in other summers. Hal, a wheat rancher, was the son of a wheat rancher.

Leila, it appeared, had known her own potential better than anyone else.

Now, a dozen years after her wedding, she was instantly agreeable when Ed brought up the matter of Bill's taking over the home place.

"Deliver me from ever being under Mother's thumb," she hissed in her father's ear.

Aloud, she said, "Hal's father can't possibly spare him here, can he, Hal?"

"Nope, I guess not," Hal said.

Leila signed her name with a chortle, "Hot darn! My nasty brother Billy has to pay me interest for thirty years!"

Eleanor, observing Leila's prodigious household burdens, needed persuasion to leave. "I better stay right here and take a hand."

Ed knew she nearly meant it. She continued to fret, but in the end, she went along as planned to Sam's family.

AS THE TRAIN rolled eastward, Ed felt each hour a heightening desire to renew the spirit of comradeship that had existed between him and his eldest son. Ed regarded Sam as having the most sense of his three children.

After coming home from the Second World War, Sam went through a hard adjustment period. He refused to discuss the armed conflict, except to say it was a bloody farce; that the only way the world could keep going was to develop people with enough guts to ignore orders.

"Somebody has to give orders in a large group," Ed had remonstrated. "You'd have nonsense otherwise."

"What I mean is that the people who make sense should be the ones giving the orders. The war was a headless horseman—at least where I was."

While waiting at home for final discharge papers, Sam daily slept late, then drifted downtown to drink beer in the tavern.

Ed, disturbed about his son's behavior, went to the tavern and found a place beside Sam on the stools. "Let's go to a booth."

"Sure, Dad. Have a beer on my severance pay."

"O.K. Sure."

Ed had never told his sons to stay out of the tavern. After they had come of age, he had even treated them to a cold beer himself at the close of the cattle sale. But as a whole, the McLarens had spent little time in the tavern because there was always something else to do. Now Sam seemed unable to find anything to do.

"I was reading Shirt Tail Bill's range book about grass last night," Ed said, making conversation. "Ever noticed it lying around the house? It isn't any textbook like you studied at Pullman, but it's got a lot of common sense in it. You'll have to read it. Make you forget about those atom bomb formulas. They're nothing compared to the formula of sunshine, soil, and seeds."

Sam smiled wryly. "Haven't cracked a book in four years. Funny. I forgot. I was going to be a college professor, wasn't I?"

Ed tried to remain casual. "Noticed in the paper this morning there's a short course on the results of some grass trials coming up at Pullman. Thought

I'd go down at the end of the week. Want to go along?"

"I guess so. Sure. Haven't seen the Pullman campus since I left school."

Ed thought that if anything would lift Sam's spirits, it would be taking a renewed interest in the science of agriculture. They took the trip to Pullman and came home with Canadian smooth brome seeds for trial. Sam planted the crop. It sprouted and started toward the sun. Sam would be safe from war now. All he needed was a chance to watch something grow. One thing you could depend on was that plants grew and provided for men and other animals. Somebody or Something caused the grass to grow and to heal the wounds of the Earth. Ed had shared his religion with his son.

Sam eventually went to Iowa State on the G.I. Bill to complete work on a master's degree in agronomy. He'd married and settled down in Ames, Iowa, after being invited to join the faculty.

SITTING IN THE railroad compartment as it moved with hypnotic smoothness toward Iowa, the state of his birth, Ed pondered whether he might be doing what he had noted as typical of others his age. People were like salmon returning to the head of the stream to complete the full cycle of their lives. Aging people journeyed to the places of their beginnings, ostensibly to visit relatives and former friends. Even the ones physically or financially unable to travel backward went backward in their thought. Despite the impassioned vow never to return that Ed had made to himself when he was coming westward on the iron horse, he was nevertheless retracing his way.

II.

Retracing the Way

6.

To the Gold Fields

Edward Everett Hale McLaren, age eighteen, six feet three inches tall, weighing a hundred fifty-five pounds, and wearing his dead father's trousers, bounded joyously from the station platform to a seat in the coach of the Northern Pacific Railway train the moment it pulled into Boone, Iowa, on the long trek west. It was a spring morning in the year 1897. There was no one but the stationmaster to see Ed off, but he did not care: in the vernacular of the pulp magazines he had read hungrily behind the haystack for years, Ed was "headed for parts unknown!"

As the train jerked to a start Ed had no regrets; the only person he thought twice about leaving was Meggie, a blonde girl who had been in his class at the academy. She had always giggled over his clowning with Arthur Meeker. If only she could see him in the drama of departure! No matter—girls could wait.

"Wild West, here I come!"

The conductor, as he punched Ed's ticket, smiled and whistled, "All the way to the end of the line!"

"Yep," Ed said firmly.

At the teller's cage at the Boone station, he had paid thirty-five dollars for a ticket to Washington Territory.

Ed's departure, although fairly impromptu, came only after what he considered careful planning. He would prospect for gold in the unsurveyed land of the Okanogan River valley. The *Des Moines Register*, subscribed to by all the families in Boone, touted strike after strike on what had been the Columbia Moses Indian Reservation in Washington Territory. The paper had information from the Northern Pacific that mining camps had sprung up at Ruby, Conconully, Oroville, and the latest, at Chesaw. The jumping-off point for the gold fields was the railhead at Sprague, described as county seat for a thriving wheat-and cattle-growing community and site of the Northern Pacific roundhouse.

Upon his arrival at the railhead, Ed planned to buy a saddle horse and make his way a short distance to the junction of the Columbia and Okanogan rivers. He would wait to buy his placer mining equipment until he reached Conconully, center of the mining region. In a small black notebook which he had found in his father's trousers, Ed had penciled a list, starting with "Miner's pick and pan."

As the endless fields of young com flashed by the train window, Ed congratulated himself. He was done with Ma's harangues, with being ordered about like a boy when he was a man grown. Reverend Thompson, minister of First Memorial Church, invited to Sunday dinner by Ma and waiting for the roast chicken to become tender, would never again hold Ed prisoner in the parlor for the purpose of casting out the Devil.

Neither would Ed translate any more of Virgil's *Aeneid* at Professor Elson's academy. He reviewed the swashbuckling glory of his last day as a student. He had been expelled! Meggie had nearly burst at his bastard Lord's Prayer at the close of chapel: "Our Father, which oughta be in heaven, came howling down the lane, with his shirttail full of hominy and never spilled a grain."

Ed's manly voice had boomed above the quavering tenors of other adolescents meekly muttering the correct version of the prayer.

As chapel adjourned, Professor Elson had beamed an angry eye at Ed. "I'll see you immediately in my office, McLaren."

As the professor sat at his official desk and his lanky pupil stood awkwardly before him, Ed's association with higher education terminated forever. "With considerable justification, Edward, I concur with your yearning to go west— where there may be room for such as you. Ordinarily I defer expulsion of a student until I have consulted the guardian, but your crude blasphemy this morning indicates that any more consultations with your excellent mother would be fruitless."

Ed rode home on the plow horse, which he watered and took to the barn before going into the house. It was noon.

Ma eyed him. She was as tall as most men and plain of visage. Early widowhood had left her humorless and severely righteous. Pa, originally a mining engineer, was trapped into farming when he married Ma—a young woman who had inherited a section of rich wheat land. After five years of matrimony, he went to explore Colorado. Pa wrote that he was building a mine there and would soon send funds for the family to join him. But before he could fulfill his promise, the mine claimed his life. His partner returned Pa's body to Iowa in a coffin and sent a brief note explaining that Mr. McLaren had tumbled down a mine shaft and died instantly. The partner enclosed the will that Pa had made before he died, as well as a check for half the mine.

As Ed, the outcast, entered the kitchen, Ma put down the ladle with which she was transferring strawberry jam to jars. She placed her hands on her hips.

'What are you doing here this time of day?"

"Prof finally kicked me out. I want train fare west. Even the Old Galoot said it would be a good idea for me to go."

Ma was prepared for the blow. "Professor Elson warned me that he was going to have to put you out, and I can't say I'm sorry. I'm tired of wasting money on the education of a walloper who doesn't want one. But Elson has no right to say you are free to leave home to become a useless hobo like your father was. There's plowing to be done here. The sows will be having litters."

"I'm leaving tomorrow," Ed said fiercely. "You'll still have Bob for farm chores. You've always let Bobby get out of work because I'm the oldest. He doesn't have enough gumption ever to leave home anyhow. And you'll still have Martha to bake your pies for the church socials. You'd never let anybody go of your own free will. You're still mad at Pa for getting killed on you. Maybe Bobby and Martha will put up with it, but I'm through being an unpaid hired hand!"

Ma gasped, "I shudder at the abomination that I have raised up in the sight of the Lord!"

Ed was unmoved. "Go to the bank and get me five hundred dollars. I'm leaving on the morning train."

"You'll do no such thing."

"Get me five hundred dollars, or I'll go down to the sheriff and tell him you're a thief. It's my money direct from Pa. You've always pretended you never got that will. Pa knew what you're like. That's why he made his will the way he did. He said his money was to be divided—half to you, and the rest equally among his children. You've never given us a cent! You won't even buy us clothes!"

Ed strode to the barn, harnessed the team to the buckboard, and drove the rig up to the door. In the parlor his mother sat with eyes closed as she mumbled prayers.

"The team's ready," he broke menacingly into her trance. "Do I have to take you to the bank, or will you go by yourself?"

She clapped on her bonnet and drove away.

Ed flung open the door of his mother's bedroom closet and pulled out the telescope bag that had belonged to his father. Pa had taken little luggage west; most of his clothes still hung there in the closet, including a dark suit that Ma had decided was too good to bury her husband in. Time and time again Ed had been denied permission to wear any of the clothing. Now he took it all, cramming it into the telescope bag without even removing the hangers. He laid out a pair of black trousers and a plaid checked shirt to wear on the train. The trousers he had been wearing to the academy were six inches too short; he would leave them for Bob.

Bob and Martha came home from elementary school to find him rummaging in forbidden territory. They sensed a major disaster.

"Where's Ma?" Martha asked fearfully.

"Gone to get me money for a train ticket west."

Bobby wailed.

Martha screamed, "What'll happen to us with you gone?"

"Ma's never treated you two the way she does me," Ed told them. "You can have the pants I've got on, Bob. They'll fit you in a couple years."

"I'm going to have knickers," Bob answered.

Ma drove the team and buckboard into the yard, and Ed went out to unharness.

Martha and Robert watched, silent and round-eyed, as Ma, her hand trembling, extended two hundred dollars in currency to Ed. "In the presence of your brother and sister, I say this is the last money you can ever expect from me."

"It's from Pa, and you know it. Besides, two hundred dollars isn't five hundred dollars. You're cheating me out of three hundred dollars."

"You are really not entitled to anything until you are twenty-one," Ma retorted.

"I'll take the two hundred. What do I care as long as there's enough for a ticket west!"

Ed stalked out of the house to do the evening milking for the last time. "You better come along with me and watch how it's done, Bobby," he said. "You're going to take care of the stock from now on."

"Do I have to, Ma?" Bobby sobbed.

"Go along," she ordered her spoiled favorite. "We must learn to manage on our own. I dare say we can. Martha, start paring the potatoes for supper."

Next morning Ma was up early and laid Ed's breakfast on the table. She had fried thick slices of bacon, three eggs, and a panful of potatoes.

Ed rose from the table when he had eaten the meal. "I gotta go, Ma," he said awkwardly. "I'll miss the train."

He hefted the telescope bag onto his shoulder and went out the back door. Ma stood on the porch, a stark, grim figure. Suddenly her body quivered. Was she about to cry? The lines of her face were deepening with gloom.

Ed stopped to look for the last time at the widow, whom he considered completely cold-hearted. He wondered what she had looked like before hard work and austerity had wrinkled and darkened her.

"Write to us, son. May the Lord keep you safe from filthy practices and bad companions."

"Thanks for breakfast," he said.

His usual breakfast had been cornmeal mush and skimmed milk.

On the train, Ed's stomach began growling promptly at noon despite being filled at dawn. He bought a pork tenderloin sandwich for thirty-five cents from the vendor passing through the cars; an hour later he needed a brains sandwich. His funds were reduced to one hundred sixty-four dollars and thirty cents.

When Ed left the train at the Omaha stopover, he found he could buy a complete meal for thirty-five cents. He vowed to pay no more exorbitant prices for sandwiches. Whenever possible he left the train to buy snacks in the railway station. Ed reckoned that he would need a hundred dollars to outfit himself for mining; that would still leave him a slight margin of capital.

Ed McLaren was not a "bad boy," but his adolescent brain had exploded. He could never be satisfied with rote perusal of the dull dogma that was forced upon him at the academy. He must see the whole of life, the whole of the real world, or he would suffocate! He had more reason to go west than simply to escape petty tyranny. He wished to test what he considered arbitrary "education" against the evidence of his own senses.

At a summer chautauqua in Des Moines, Ed had been entranced by a lecture on the theories of Louis Agassiz. According to Agassiz, many parts of the North American continent showed evidence of having been covered by gigantic ice masses in the days before history. The Swiss naturalist imported to Harvard University also advocated less teaching of Greek and Latin in academies and more study of facts as revealed by the face of nature.

When Ed reported the lecture with careful detail in his academy science class in the fall, Professor Elson had stated firmly that none of Agassiz's theories could be true. Scripture clearly taught that the Lord made the earth in six days; it had been in existence six thousand years at the most; and there was no time for extended periods under ice caps either in Europe or in North America.

Another dictum of Professor Elson was that the classical languages were the only subjects essential to a scholar: they were the original tongues of revealed Holy Word.

Ed devoutly hoped that his own senses, in the West, would confirm his prejudices in favor of anything that Professor Elson abhorred. The *Des Moines Register*, in its graphic reports on the gold strike country, said that the whole Columbia River plateau as well as the Okanogan Highlands showed claw marks of a glacier that had drifted down from the north in the Pleistocene period, over ten thousand years ago.

As the train clacked along toward the gold strike country, Ed had time to pore over a prized possession he had packed: a miners' and travelers' guide to Oregon, Washington, Idaho, Montana, Wyoming, and Colorado via the

Missouri and Columbia rivers. The manual was the work of Captain John Mullan, who had explored and constructed a military wagon road that diverged from the main Oregon trail at Walla Walla. Near the end of Ed's journey, the train route would be essentially along Mullan's road.

Captain Mullan, now a retired army man, advised a modicum of supplies: tin plates, kettles that fit one inside the other, knives, forks, brown sugar, coffee, bacon, flour, salt, beans, sardines, dried apples, a covered oven, a saddle with tapaderos, a gray saddle blanket, a snaffle bit, and a lash rope with canvas or leather bellybands. A horse's load should not exceed two hundred pounds, the Captain said. Ed worried that he really needed a covered wagon, but he did not have enough capital to purchase one.

What he must settle for was one horse to ride and another to carry supplies. The one hundred sixty dollars remaining in his wallet was far less than the amount he needed. He resolved to settle down immediately on a claim and pan for gold furiously.

All detailed planning was swept from his thoughts as the train pulled up at Sprague on a chilly May morning. Ed stepped out onto an unpainted platform made of new lumber. Instead of a depot befitting a county seat, Ed faced the burned-out shell of an isolated building. A burly, elderly stationmaster came from a nearby shack the size of an outhouse and swept an arm over the scene.

"Laid waste by fire!" he declared, as if in answer to Ed's look of shock.

Charred wood and ashes covered a flat square mile.

"Roller mills, the roundhouse—all gone up in smoke," the stationmaster mourned.

"When did this happen?" Ed stammered.

"Two whole years ago, 1895. They keep telling us they're gonna rebuild the roundhouse and everything else, but so far Northern Pacific hasn't done a lick."

"I was planning to take off for the gold strike from here," a bewildered Ed confided.

"Maybe you still can," the stationmaster reassured him. "Pack trains still go through here. Yonder's the Gehres and Hertrich store that the fire missed. You might go up there and ask if any pack train is coming through pretty soon. Garvey's livery stable is open again, too."

The stationmaster pointed toward what remained of a central business district, a quarter-mile away.

Ed thanked him, took another grip on his bag, and walked in the direction indicated. He passed the ruins of what must have been the roundhouse. One brick house and the Catholic church had been spared. He could make out a charred sign, "National Hotel."

Ed began to take heart as he approached the Gehres and Hertrich store, a two-story brick building with an awning over the entrance. Its business must be thriving, Ed figured, because many wagon tracks led up to the building along a street in which the mire was axle deep.

After scraping mud from his shoes at the mudguard beside the steps, he entered the store. He saw merchandise in long rows: sacks of sugar and flour, saddles, ox yokes, chairs, chums, coveralls, and mackinaws.

Ed moved diffidently down the center aisle to the counter, on which, he noted with awe, stood a gold scale.

A stout gentleman wearing a white butcher's apron asked, "Yes, young man! Is there something I can do for you?"

"Just got off the train. I'm intending to buy a grubstake later—for gold panning. But I don't have a horse yet. How does a person get out to the mining country?"

The man surveyed the prospective miner. Without answering him, he called out a rear door, "Hey Frank!"

A tall, sun- and wind-browned young man in overalls and mackinaw came from the back. "Yeah?"

"This beanpole dropped in. Came off the train. He wants to go on a gold rush. Maybe you can give him an idea of what's ahead."

Frank grinned and extended his hand. "Beeman's my name. Waitin' for my brother, Bill, who's overdue. He's bringin' in the horses from the waterhole."

"Frank's got the four-horse team and wagon out back right now," the storekeeper said. "They're on their way up to the mines with a string of horses carrying flour."

Towering Frank Beeman squinted closely at the eighteen-year-old as tall as himself. "I just told Jim half an hour ago we could use a hand. Know anything about horses?"

"Farm horses," Ed responded. "I've plowed a lot, and I always rode a horse to school."

"Straight off an Iowa farm," the storekeeper chuckled. "You oughta do for another hand. Might as well ride to the digging if you'll make yourself useful on the trail."

"I sure am lucky! Just let me know what's wanted."

"Mostly riding a mount, checking on the loads," Frank said.

"Long, hard trip. Sure you want to go prospecting? Not so easy anymore to make it with a pick and pan on Salmon Creek."

"You call it Salmon 'crick' The *Des Moines Register* called it a river."

"Make up your own mind when you see it. Looks more like a creek to me."

"I've come all this way to try my luck at panning. Reckon I won't change my plans just yet. I read there's been another strike—on Mary Ann Creek. I sure will appreciate it if I can tag along to mining country."

"Suit yourself," Frank said. "We found we make more buying flour for two dollars and fifty cents a barrel at Minnie Falls and selling it for five dollars a sack at the mines."

A string of thirty pack horses filed down the street and came to a halt alongside the store.

"Here comes Bill. Come on outside."

Ed's heart thumped as they walked to the front door. He saw his first pack train in the flesh-a seemingly endless line of muscular horses, whose dark hides gleamed in the morning sun.

Bill Beeman jumped down from a mount at the head of the column. "Let's go! We got a heavy date with them Injuns at the crossin'!"

Each pack animal's burden was a leather aparejo, or double pouch, loaded with two sacks of flour, one in each side pocket.

"Meet my brother, Bill," Frank told Ed. "Bill, this is Ed. He wants to go along with us to the diggings. I said he could."

Bill smiled a welcome and winked as he spoke. "Sure! Fine! Only you'll find out it's not a free trip."

"I'm not asking for one," Ed said as he took Bill's hard hand. He was also introduced to Jim Lovell, a man in his forties, who appeared to be a seasoned worker.

Ed felt a surge of triumphant homecoming. He was among people his own size and shape—no misfit, scrawny walloper, but a member of his real tribe! Ed guessed that, although they greatly surpassed him in experience, the Beeman brothers were not many years older than himself.

Within the hour, the string of packhorses, followed by the four-horse team and wagon, departed from Sprague. The saddle horse assigned to Ed accepted him graciously, in contrast to the characteristic resignation of the stolid Iowa plow horse. Frank, on his saddle horse, led the pack train; Bill brought the wagon. Ed was instructed to ride beside Jim Lovell for a while, midway down the line.

"Show the kid what he can do to make himself useful," Frank said to Jim.

At the first pause, three hours from town, Lovell said, "Let's ride down the back half of the line, see if everything is O.K."

After a moment of review, Jim pulled his horse to a stop. "Uh, oh, looka here! This horse's load has slipped. That's the kind of thing you're supposed to look for," Jim said as he yanked on the aparejo. "You gotta be sure the weight balances. Makes it easier for the horse."

The aparejos were cushioned on hay-filled gunnysacks. "Stick your hand in there and stir up the grass a bit," Jim told Ed.

Ed gamely untied the top of the gunnysack and stirred.

The pack train stopped for the first night on the flat plain—the only terrain they had had since the beginning of the trip. The ground cover consisted of sagebrush and clumps of wild sunflowers growing between large, black boulders. The camp was at the first running water, a sandy-bottomed, shallow creek that made no sound. Vegetation, even on the creek banks, was sparse.

Ed helped remove the aparejos from the horses' backs. Then each animal had to be watered, rubbed down, and staked out to graze on what natural forage there was. He would indeed not get a free trip to the mining country.

At the midday check of the aparejos, Bill Beeman had handed everyone a strip of beef jerky. It had taken Ed half an hour to chew his piece. His only other food for the day had been half a sandwich on the train at dawn. By the time they stopped for the evening, he was so hungry he was dizzy, but Ed was determined not to ask when mealtime was. Care of the horses came before anything else, he realized. He was greatly relieved when he saw Bill gathering sagebrush.

"We'll make a fire tonight," Bill said. "Sometimes if we're behind schedule, we travel too late."

"Need any help?" Ed asked.

"Naw," Bill replied. "We don't want a big fire. Just enough for coffee and biscuits."

Supper consisted of pan biscuits washed down with the strongest coffee Ed had ever tasted.

"We're not much for cookin' on the trail," Bill remarked.

Ed nodded, as if in agreement.

For dessert, he was glad to be given another hunk of jerky.

When the night deepened and the fire was only a bed of coals, Frank stood up from his seat on the ground and yawned. "Guess it's time to tum in."

Everyone agreed. Everyone but Ed reached for his bedroll. With all his planning, he had never once considered how he would spend the nights! He felt a twinge of humiliation.

"I reckon we have a spare blanket," Bill Beeman said.

From the wagon bed, he threw a wool army blanket over Ed's hunched shoulders. "Curl up tight, young pardner. Gets cold sleeping on the ground."

Long after the Beemans and Jim Lovell began to snore, Ed lay awake and stared at the infinite expanse above him. He had never seen a sky in which the stars were so close and bright. No houses, trees, or fences marked the line between the sky and the land, which lay endlessly black and empty.

He was a wild animal newly escaped from a cage.

In the distance he heard a coyote pack howling. In the creek, frogs croaked; above the fire, the nighthawks dived with a loud whirring of wings as they pounced on insects who betrayed themselves in the last gleam of light over the coals. Horses stamped their feet as they cropped grass. Ed felt the obstructions of civilization falling away from his spirit. He was seeing the universe whole! Professor Elson had been right about one thing. Here, in the vast emptiness, there was room for Ed McLaren.

Next morning the pack train continued northwest across benches still covered with sagebrush and some bunchgrass. As the train walked into a dry creek bed between high, layered walls of rock, Jim Lovell told Ed, "We're comin' to the Columbia."

Ed thought, "This is the coulee I read about—gouged out by the prehistoric river that was dammed by the glacier!"

He remarked to his companions on the layered walls of pale rock and clay lying east and west, a hundred feet high and thousands of unbroken feet in length. "I bet those are the banks of the river that ran off the glacier."

The Beemans and Jim laughed at him for proposing that this desert country had once been covered with a mountain of ice.

They crossed the granite floor of a three-mile coulee with cliffs three hundred fifty feet high. "It's almost more than a person can imagine how much water must have flowed through here," Ed marveled.

"I s' pose you figure that drop-off over there was a waterfall," Frank chuckled. "I admit it does look like it. How long ago do you say all this happened?"

"Maybe two million years ago it started. The melting lasted until eighteen thousand years ago."

Bill Beeman hooted, "Well, I dunno how you can prove it. Sure as hell nobody is alive as eyewitness."

Ed fell silent. His new friends were as hard to convince, in their own way, as Professor Elson.

As THE DAYS went by, Ed became familiar with the Beemans' past adventures. They had freighted supplies for several years to the Canadian border and considered themselves experts in their line. Their beginning capital had come through the sale of ten thousand pounds of bacon from hogs raised by their father at Genesee, Idaho.

"Couldn't give bacon away at Genesee," Frank explained, "so Pa made a horseback trip to British Columbia to find a market. We loaded up the bacon to pack it to the mines. Sold it for twenty-five cents a pound.

"Everything has to get across that durn Columbia. We found some cedar logs and made a raft; cinched the logs together with rope. First thing we had to get over was the wagon. We ran it onto the raft, then took off the wheels, to keep the center of the load down.

"Then after that we had to cross the Okanogan. It isn't near as big as the Columbia, so we tried to roll the wagon across, but just as the wheel horses got into the river, the leaders began to swim. The wagon started going this way and thataway over the boulders. I was standing in the wagon bed. I can't swim a lick, and the water came up to my neck. The bacon got all wet, and the water was runnin' out grease. The only thing that saved the load was that the Injuns finally took pity on us and went alongside and whooped to keep the horses going upstream.

"We finally learned to let the Injuns help us across."

Ed was perplexed by the distance between Sprague and the Okanogan mining country. He had envisioned a ride of a few hours in the saddle, but the trip was taking days!

"It's darn near two hundred miles from Sprague to the diggings," Bill told him.

They continued toward rendezvous with their Indian helpers at the junction of Foster Creek and the Columbia.

A DEEP, FIERCE torrent two hundred yards wide was the Columbia!

"You say you're at a crossing!" Ed expressed his doubts.

"This is low water right now," Jim Lovell told the greenhorn with amusement.

Waiting for the pack train were Ed's first wild Indians, a pair clad in buckskin, who talked with the Beemans in Chinook dialect. Their ferry consisted of canoes and logs lashed together. The ferrymen and the members of the pack train began at once to unload the flour and aparejos from the horses, and to place the freight in the canoes. Ed considered himself husky, but his legs trembled, and his head buzzed as he tried to keep pace with the other men. Everyone except him could easily throw a hundred and fifty pounds over a horse.

Repeated crossings were necessary. Three horses swam on the upriver side, and two on the downriver side of the raft, for each trip. The animals whinnied and protested at being driven into the water, but their Indian owners kept them swimming strongly in a direct course by whooping and hallooing and applying willow switches. The dismantled wagon was ferried across; then the men were given paddles to use as they made the final trip with the Indian team.

"Old Speelyi let us cross one more time," Frank said thankfully, as all hands put the wagon together on the far shore.

Although Ed had the advantage of the Beemans in being able to swim, he doubted whether he would have been able to keep himself from being swept away and drowned if he had fallen from the raft. The great, boisterous Columbia was the most menacing body of water that he had ever seen. Even the Indians had shown it respect.

The queue of flour-laden beasts followed the Columbia along canyon walls as the river neared its juncture with the Okanogan River. The two streams converged around a delta of sandbars and sodden willow thickets and came together in a flood three-quarters of a mile wide. On the brow, above the water, the Okanogan Highlands formed a guardian wall. On the west Okanogan River bank stood the abandoned ruin of Fort Okanogan, formerly a flourishing trading post of the Hudson's Bay Company.

Remaining on the east bank, the pack train proceeded due north up the Okanogan River trail for forty miles; then, again with the assistance of Indians and canoes, it forded to the west bank The going was a rough Indian trail winding among basalt boulders.

"Up there is McLaughlin's Canyon," Frank pointed out, "Chief Tonasket's territory. Folks say the Injuns holed up in the canyon in '58 and ambushed a pack train of one hundred fifty men and four hundred horses on the way to the Fraser River mines. Injuns still claimed this as their land. Six miners were supposed to have been killed in the attack and some others hurt. I guess the Injuns did kill some whites, but we've never seen any graves along there. Maybe the Injuns burnt the bodies up, or threw 'em on the rocks."

THE PARTY MADE camp at another creek bank This time they built a larger cooking fire than usual, for it was also needed to dispel enormous clouds of bloodthirsty mosquitoes.

Bill, who was attempting to make bannocks and coffee as usual, slapped insects from his face. "I say to hell with it. Let's move out of here to sleep. Who gives a durn about drinkin' a cupful of his own blood!"

An elderly Indian woman came smiling from the brush, and in Chinook, offered to prepare the meal. The mosquitoes seemed to drift away from her body. She chatted and joked with the Beemans.

"She says she sure is glad she has tough Injun hide and not thin paleface skin," Bill translated for Ed's benefit.

They gave the Indian woman the remains of a sack of flour as payment for her services.

"We're gettin' close to your Salmon 'River' mining claims," Frank told Ed, "but you better stick with us. You're a good hand with horses. Panning on some worked-over creek, you'll wind up with nothin' but a kink in your back. Storekeepers charge five prices for supplies and make all the profit in gold dust—if you ain't already been bamboozled out of it by the floozies and card sharks."

The first town they reached was Ruby.

"First and oldest camp on the Salmon," Frank said. "They say a curse is on the place. A miner who got rolled and robbed climbed a hill above town and yelled, 'May you be burned, drowned, and burned again!'

"That's just what happened, too. The '94 flood washed out Conconully and came on down to Ruby, where it did awful damage to the brewery. Towns ain't been the same since."

Ruby swarmed with male population—some sober and bustling, but most noisy, drunken, and idle-milling about the shanties, tents, saloons, and the hotel with a two-story false front.

AS THEY APPROACHED Conconully, five miles up the creek, Ed said, "I expect I better part company with you here."

So this was Conconully, described in the *Des Moines Register* as a prosperous mining center and Okanogan County seat in a sylvan setting! Now it was a town through which a flood had swept. Buildings lurched at crazy angles, with logs, planks, and debris heaped against them. The town, nevertheless, swarmed with people who seemed to be doing business in makeshift shanties and frame structures with canvas roofs. The hotel and the bank, probably the most substantial structures, still stood firm. The saloon was new.

"I never saw anything about a flood in the *Des Moines Register*," Ed mourned.

"Washout came after a cloudburst," Frank recalled. "Water fell a hundred feet to the mile for fifteen miles down the mountain. Above town, it was going thirty miles an hour. When it had to go through the narrow canyon on the end of town, all the logs and junk built up into a big plug. Didn't seem like the water could get around it, but it finally pushed through, carried half the town away.

"Neighbors at Loomis loaded up pack animals and brought in provisions and blankets. Three or four families lived in one house until the ones who'd lost everything could get some kind of roof patched over their heads. Mrs. Work, a rich lady with a big house, took up all her carpets and turned her house into an eatery. Lots of folks just cleared out of the country.

"Lucky the flood happened at nine o'clock in the morning when everybody was up and about. Bill Bowser's mother-in-law was the only person lost her life. She wouldn't leave the house. Bill came running home to sound the alarm. He and his wife grabbed the baby and beat a fast retreat. They say she couldn't seem to understand. When she saw the wreckage bearing down, she must have tried to run for it, but it was too late. They saw the water rise over her head. It took two or three days to find her body. It was lodged under ten feet of dirt at Harry Davis's place."

The pack train filed down the main street, the lead horse coming to a halt before the tent establishment of R. Hunter & Co., General Merchants.

Ed and Frank dismounted.

"This used to be the biggest store in the country," Frank said. "I'm asking you one last time. You want to stay here?"

"I planned on coming to this town when I was still in Iowa," Ed held firm.

Bill got down from the wagon, carrying the wool blanket in which Ed had slept on the trail, and also a Bowie knife in a sheath. "You'll need these. Watch out for that knife blade. Razor sharp."

Frank handed Ed a twenty-dollar gold piece.

"You don't need to give me anything," Ed protested. "Our deal was that you'd take me to the mining country if I made myself useful."

"Shut up," Frank said. "If you don't strike it rich before winter, you go to one of the cattle spreads toward Oro. There's squaw men in there, been there a long time, got families. They sell beef at the mines. Hire on with one of them, and you won't starve or freeze before next spring."

"Quit trying to talk me out of panning," Ed said. "I've heard 'tenderfoot' and 'greenhorn' too much!"

"Maybe you're right," Frank conceded.

"You guys sure were good to me," Ed told them. "Hope I see you again sometime."

"Oh, you will. We go through here twice a year."

A sizable group had stopped in the street to greet the pack train. A swarm even came from the saloon and yelled, "Come on in, you Beemans! We're settin' you up! Your whole gang!"

"I don't need a second invite," Jim Lovell said.

"I don't drink much," Ed said. "In fact, I've never even smelled liquor."

"You're in luck," Frank told him. "We're not introducin' you to Demon Rum this quick. Go on! Beat it while you can!"

Ed shook hands with the three men, who were washed away as by a tide.

The pack train waited in the street. R. Hunter would help the Beemans unload his order of flour in an hour or so.

7.

A Miner's Luck

Kneeling in the street and opening his telescope bag, Ed crammed the wool blanket and Bowie knife inside. Then he stood up, grasped the bag in his bony hand, and looked about him. He walked into a tent store in which a roly-poly owner with a roly-poly wife at his side assured Ed of his personal interest in newcomers. The pair brought out many items that a placer miner needed. Ed was forced to say, "My money sure would go fast if I bought all this stuff."

"Don't worry, son," the clerk hastened to assure the customer. "Your pan is money. You go down that trail leading south from town. There's a regular hive of gents strung along the stream bed. You build yourself a lean-to and stake out your claim. In a couple days you come back to town to register. We'll weigh your dust. Fairest scales in town."

Ed selected a miner's pick and pan, a shovel, and a nest of kettles. The wife stepped forward briskly to tote up the bill. She itemized the purchases with a pencil on a sales pad.

"You need a poke," the merchant suggested.

"I'll get that the next time. I expect what I really need now is a horse."

"Good place to buy is Lone Star Stable at the other end of town, across the creek."

"Thanks. I'll go along then," Ed said as he gathered his equipment. An aparejo would have been handy.

He walked the length of the street and crossed a footbridge. The livery stable proved to be a cluster of wooden stalls covered by a tent top. Several horses nibbled hay in the pen beside it. The proprietor came out briskly.

"The sorrel is only three years old," the owner said.

"Looks cranky," Ed observed. "His eyes are close together."

"Hunh! That critter is meek as a lamb."

Ed pointed to a pony whose hide resembled a crazy quilt of black and white patches. "How much for him?"

"Injun paint. Belonged to some breed kids. Gentle. Still a good general duty saddle horse. The kids traded him for a colt. Twenty dollars."

The pony walked toward Ed as he stood at the fence and sniffed inquisitively.

"Wants something to eat," the salesman explained unnecessarily to Ed. The horse, although not young, had evidently had good treatment.

"Twenty dollars is more than I figured to pay."

"All right. Seventeen. Then I throw in the saddle that came with him and a set of hobbles for three bucks."

The man went to fetch the accessories for Ed's inspection. He held out what appeared to be a leather pillow.

"What kind of a rig is that?"

"Good Injun saddle, made of buckskin, filled with hair."

After poking the object, Ed decided that it actually would make a resilient seat. He accepted the offer of twenty dollars total, the salesman concluding the deal with his anticipated profit achieved.

Hobbles had not occurred to Ed as a necessity, but he saw their value. He regretted that he lacked sufficient capital to invest in a saddle with tapaderos as recommended in John Mullan's guidebook.

The livery stable owner gave him two gunnysacks that lay in the straw in one of the stalls. "You gotta have somep'n to put your grub in," he pointed out.

"I was wondering how to organize the load," Ed admitted. "Have you got some twine? I can fasten these sacks together at the top and throw them across my horse, one hanging on each side, like an aparejo."

"You come in with that pack train?"

"Yes. They hired me on in Sprague."

The livery stable owner patiently supplied hemp twine and a needle for Ed to fashion his aparejo. "You'd do better to get rid of that stiff, store-bought bag altogether," he advised.

"Naw, it was my pa's, I'll keep it."

He decided it would be impractical to carry anything in his hands except his horse's reins. He was able to push the bag inside one of the gunnysacks as a counterbalance to the pick, pan, shovel, and kettles in the other sack.

He had yet to buy his provisions for the trail. For meat, he could catch fish in the creeks. The Iowa newspapers said the waters teemed with trout and salmon. At another stand manned by a husband-wife team, he chose fresh and dried apples, carrots, potatoes, lard, flour, sugar, salt, bacon and a dozen fresh eggs which the woman obligingly laid among wads of paper in a small cloth sack.

"See you're gonna have to carry your grub on horseback," the open-air grocer said. "Ma, can you spare him a fifty-pound sack?"

"For fifty cents," Ma replied.

With two gunnysacks and a bulging flour sack hanging behind his Indian saddle, Ed started on the trail to fortune. Despite his load, the horse picked his way easily along the path.

"I'll call you 'Stocky,' friend," Ed told his mount. "How do you like that— 'Stocky'?"

The saddle was comfortable, Ed decided. His spirits rose in response to the sunshine that found its way in spaces through the birch and poplar thickets along the creek bank.

AT AN OPEN spot where the creek widened, a giant, red-bearded man squatted. In his hands he rocked a shallow pan, eighteen inches in diameter, identical to the pan that Ed had bought. The basin was filled with wet gravel and dirt.

"You panning for gold, Mister?" Ed asked.

"Don't it look like it?"

"It looks like it all right. Only I've never seen it done before," Ed explained. "I'm a newcomer."

The man magically lost his grumpiness. He stood up, uncrooked his back, dumped his pan of tailings on the pile on the bank, and smiled widely. "New, hunh! Never 'a guessed it. Chew the fat a bit. Anything I can do to make you acquainted with the mining game?"

Ed marveled at the friendliness of everyone he met in the West. He dismounted from Stocky and held out his hand as his mother had taught him to do to the preacher. "Ed McLaren from Iowa. Pleased to meet you."

The giant pumped Ed's hand. "Never met a stranger in my life! Name's Clay Brown."

"I sure need help learning panning. People are neighborly out here!"

"Sun's goin' over the hill. I was about to knock off for supper. Got anything to eat in your pack? It's a long ways into town. My horse run off and left me. Can't catch a damn thing in the creek. Make you a deal. You share some of your vittles, and I'll teach you how to use a pan tomorrow morning."

"Got some fresh eggs and bacon. That do?"

"Jim dandy! Nothin' I like better, except maybe beefsteak. If you got the bacon and eggs, I got the pan."

Clay Brown dived into his makeshift tepee and reappeared flourishing a heavy, black cast-iron frying pan. Ed wondered how he had overlooked such a necessary item.

"I scrubbed it out real good with sand just this morning," Clay said. He kicked among the ashes of his campfire. "Bound to be a spark here."

Clay found the spark and nourished it with small twigs. When the blaze fanned up, Ed helped by pulling handfuls of weeds and grass. He scouted the creek bank until he found several pieces of dry driftwood; Clay Brown grandly threw them on the fire.

"There we got her goin," Clay said happily. "Now for the bacon and eggs. First the bacon, to make the grease."

Ed went to Stocky and relieved him of his load. He brought the bacon and eggs to Clay, then asked to be excused to take care of his horse. He led Stocky to the creek to drink, then fastened on his hobbles.

"Got any flour? I'll show you how to make biscuits in the pan."

"Yes, I have some," Ed was happy to say. "I've seen that done quite a bit already."

He rummaged in the gunnysack and came back with his ten-pound bag of flour.

Clay produced soda and salt from his tent, also a coffeepot and coffee.

"Take the pot to the creek and fill 'er up," he told Ed.

The meal was ready in short order, and they began eating at once.

"Come in with the pack train, hunh?" Clay said. "You were lucky. I wandered all over the country before I got my bearings. Didn't have a map even."

"I've been pretty lucky so far," Ed agreed. "Only thing that surprised me is how all the big towns I read about in the newspapers in Iowa have either burned down or been flooded out."

Clay nodded sagely. "It still ain't civilized around here. Nature can gobble up a mining camp in a minute."

As darkness fell in the creek bottom, the men stuffed themselves. Ed was enjoying his first full meal since leaving home. The railroad restaurants allowed only one spare plateful, and he had never encountered any people less concerned about when or what they ate than the slender, hard-driving Beemans.

"Tomorrow you can try your luck with my fishing pole," Clay said. "I cut a good willow switch and put on the store-bought hook and line, but I can't seem to catch anything myself. Never knew how to fish."

"I've caught lots of fish," Ed said. "I'll see what I can do for you, but I better get along soon to find a claim, after you show me how to pan."

"Stay right here, kid. Be my partner. People work with partners around here. My claim's already legal. You won't have to trouble yourself to file."

"Sure do appreciate your offer, but your—house," Ed hesitated as to how to describe the structure. "Isn't it small for two?"

Ed had made better wickiups himself as a ten-year-old, but supposed that Clay was concentrating on mining rather than on housing.

"I'll sleep in the tepee tonight, then tomorrow it's yours. Take turns. Or heck, tomorrow you could throw up a few more poles and cover them with willow boughs for your own place."

"I'd just as soon sleep under the stars the way I've been doing," Ed concluded. "I have a real warm blanket that the fellows on the pack train gave me."

They put the remainder of the bacon slab, the round of butter, and the six eggs that were left after supper into Clay's watercooler bucket in the creek.

When Ed started to wash out the frying pan and coffeepot, Clay protested, "I'll do that. You take my hatchet and lop down some willow boughs to lie on with your blanket."

"Yes, I guess willow boughs would be softer than the plain ground," Ed said. "I don't need to borrow your hatchet. I have a Bowie knife."

"A genuine Bowie knife! You are the lucky one!"

With his brand new tool, Ed quickly cut and heaped up a satisfactory bed spring.

Clay went into the tepee. Ed wrapped the blanket around himself and lay down on the boughs. He prepared his mind to review the many happenings of his first days in the West. Instead, he fell asleep immediately although he had consumed three cups of coffee.

He woke when he felt Clay Brown's boot prodding him; he blinked his eyes in bright sunlight.

"You're not gettin' rich lyin' there."

"Golly, no! Sure sorry to be so lazy."

Ed was up in a flash. He needed no time to dress, except to put on his shoes. He had slept in his clothes according to the custom of men in the West.

The pair devoured another meal: bacon and three eggs apiece. Then the master took the apprentice to the bar.

"First I'll just watch," Ed said.

Clay took the stance of a professor. "Some folks say all it takes is a strong back and a weak mind. 'Course panning is only half of it. See this pile I left last night when you showed up? Spent most of yesterday with my pick digging out from around the tree roots that go down to the water. You find gold where it can lodge someplace. I picked this spot because the creek levels off here after coming down those rocks."

Clay filled his basin with dirt from his stockpile and waded into the shallow stream. "What you do is wash off the extra dirt. Gold is heavy, sinks to the bottom when you rinse off the top."

He dipped the sand and gravel-filled pan into the water. "Just enough to cover the top, swirl a bit, then easy! Pour over the edge."

He dipped, shook, and poured artistically as Ed observed in a daze of concentration. Drip by drip the pan emptied. Clay scrutinized the bottom silt.

"Hot diggity! Pay dirt!" he exclaimed. He thrust the pan under Ed's nose. "See right there! See the trace of gold! I remember the first time I seen it. Ain't been the same man since."

"Holy mackinaw! I do see it!" Ed said reverently.

"Some of those little black lumps are gold, too," Clay added.

He outlined a method of procedure.

"We can work twice as fast if one digs and one pans. What say you use pick and shovel to clean out more dirt from the roots? I'll go ahead with washing."

"I'll get my own equipment," Ed said, proud that he had come to the gold fields prepared.

When he came back with his pick, shovel, and pan, Clay, with the palm of his hand, was carefully channeling the gold precipitate into the mouth of a flat whiskey flask.

"Where'd you get that bottle?" Ed asked.

"Always have one in my hip pocket, but not always empty."

He placed the flask with its precious contents upright on a stump. He left the cork off the bottle.

"Let 'er dry out, then into the poke."

All morning Ed dug with his pickax and scraped dirt from the rocky creek bank. After a lunch of coffee and bannocks that Clay made quickly with Ed's supplies, the master agreed that it was time for Ed to try his own pan.

Nearly at once Ed was as adept as his partner.

"By golly! Maybe we can still make a living here!" Clay marveled as he dumped the contents of the flask into his drawstring wallet in the late afternoon.

Ed had built up an impressive pile of sand and rocks. He estimated that he had added half the contents to the bottle. Even though he considered himself a novice, he had always prided himself that he could do as good a day's work as anybody.

Day succeeded day in the mining game. Panning for gold at the edge of a chattering creek was a release and a lark for a young fellow whose previous work days had meant twelve hours toil at plowing, haying, harvesting corn, piling silage, feeding livestock, or cleaning barns. Sunshine sparkled in the middle of the stream as Ed played with a washbasin of dirt with as much delight as a child making mudpies. He left his shoes beside his sleeping blanket and kept his feet in water all day. His companion wagged a garrulous tongue with countless stories of adventure and of hilarious high jinks.

"You been to Ruby?" Clay asked one morning.

"Yes, but the pack train didn't stop. Didn't seem like much of a town."

"Yeah, Conconully is taking over now. But there'll never be another camp like Ruby. When the *cheechakos* came in on the stage wearing their plug hats, the guys at the saloon stepped outside and took pot shots. The guy who shoots off a plug hat buys free drinks for the crowd.

"Miners hate swells. Old Man Bourne come in and started a silver mine with a quarter-million dollars. The guys got mad when he wouldn't raise their wages. When his son Jonathan checked in at the hotel, they gave him a serenade. Shootin' the windows out made lively music. They took a notion to dislike Jonathan as soon as he went into the bar wearing a bib and tucker. He bragged how his Pa sent him out here to gain experience. Got some experience fast."

Ed laughed. "Even if I'm a *cheechako*, nobody will take me for a swell. Maybe a scarecrow."

"I agree—you're some sight," Clay said. "Overalls six inches above your shoe tops!"

Clay's remark filled Ed with anger at Ma. He flushed and said, "One of the first things I'm gonna buy is some regular miners' clothes."

Clay Brown had been a butcher before coming West. He said that when the does' fawns grew older, it would be fun for Ed and him to go hunting. Clay bragged that he could skin a critter as well as any Injun.

Ed's unblemished good time was interrupted when he contracted a cold, accompanied by a painful sore throat. Sleeping in dampness prevented his recovery. He had enjoyed rising early and catching trout for breakfast; he could not understand why Clay had never been successful. But the soreness in his throat was beginning to interfere with swallowing even pan-fried trout.

Although it seemed that they were eating more trout than any other food, a pair of huge appetites had undone Ed's estimate that his supplies would last a month. Clay held the empty sack of flour.

"One of us will have to go into town and change our dust into something that mixes with soda and salt," he said.

Ed brightened. He would be the one to go. Clay had no horse; he had never made any attempt to catch the runaway. Ed saw himself stepping up to the gold scales in Hunter's store, determining his credit, and ordering supplies. His first purchase would be a drawstring poke of his own.

His presumptions were interrupted by Clay. "How about me borrowing your horse? Last time I hiked to town and couldn't carry much back—that's why I was in the fix you found me in."

"You sure you ever had a horse? I was planning on going to town myself. I think Stocky would rather I rode him."

"You got a bad cold, kid. You better stay here and rest up a day. You been swirling that pan pretty steady for someone new at it."

Clay's words drained Ed of self-confidence. Smart townfolks would probably gyp a greenhorn with a snuffy nose. He did feel feverish, and he ached all over his body. At home, his mother would have dosed him with quinine until his head swam. To lie on the ground in the sun all day would be in keeping with his true physical inclination.

"You take Stocky to town," he yielded. "He needs the exercise-hobbled all the time. I'll stay here and keep the mosquitoes from taking over the place."

Ed's words were scarcely exaggeration. It had become necessary to keep a continual smudge fire against the mosquitoes.

As ED LAY on his blanket, he wished he had asked Clay to bring some fresh milk. One of his kindest memories of his mother was that when he had quinsy, she heated milk that slid easily down the throat.

Ed drifted in and out of sleep throughout the day and into the evening. But by the time Clay returned, the night sky was already growing pale and the stars were gone. Ed pretended sleep, for Clay had obviously been detained at a saloon. He cussed and fumbled his way into the tepee.

By daylight, Ed noted a new horse grazing with Stocky. This time he was the one to wake his partner with the toe of a boot.

"You buy that horse?" Ed asked.

"Sure did. Three years old. Good buy."

Ed recognized the sorrel as the animal he had rejected in favor of Stocky. He went to the full gunnysacks dropped beside the firebed. "These the supplies? Hope you got some fresh fruit and milk."

"Heck, no. That stuff don't keep."

No milk, no bacon, no eggs! Ed took inventory. No additional drawstring poke. Only beans that must be soaked and boiled interminably before they became edible, flour for pancakes that fried black instead of golden, prunes tough as leather, dried apples, salt, oatmeal, coffee, lard, and tobacco.

"I brought you better-tasting supplies than you brought me," he said.

"I been around here longer than you," Clay answered firmly as he snapped his suspenders over his shoulders.

"Seems like you took enough dust to town to bring back at least one good thing!"

"Commonest mistake of new guys is to blow their poke on food and equipment," Clay undertook an advisory role. "You got to play it smart, spend less than you earn."

"How about that horse, then?"

"You're not really willin' to lend yours. I gotta have a mount. Even if we are partners, we can't ride double."

Ed felt furious. "You can't fool me into thinking all that poke of gold didn't buy more than beans and flour."

"Now listen, kid, I did things fair and square. Whose fault was it that you were sick and couldn't go to town?"

Ed hesitated to estrange the only person he could call a friend. "O.K. Guess I'm kind of cranky."

"You got a fever, kid."

NEXT DAY CLAY Brown confessed, "I was sort of disappointed myself with what I could bring back after two weeks work. This panning is small time stuff. I'd sure like to buy a rocker and make a real profit for us. You got any cash left, kid?"

Ed's stomach lurched with guilt as he evaded the question, but he would not part with his last silver dollar, two quarters, and a dime. Enough raw gold to buy a rocker had gone into the coffers of the town saloons.

"I'm as broke as you," he said.

ON THE CREEK, the reward of gold dust grew daily scarcer, the supply of trout also. Ed knew from experience in Iowa that creeks would be "fished out" at points used constantly.

A new kind of fish appeared: slow, fat creatures with heavy mouths, so sluggish that Ed feared they were sick. He caught and fried one of them, but the flesh was so full of bones and so tasteless that it was almost inedible.

It was clear to Ed now that Clay Brown was no more an expert than he was, on the wildlife or anything else of the area.

On the next trip to town, Ed went along. Both were disappointed as they found they had recovered enough dust for only a niggardly stock of beans, flour, coffee, and prunes.

"You fellows heading for Chesaw?" Mr. Hunter asked.

"Shut up!" Clay hissed at the merchant.

"What you mean 'shut up'? You told me yourself last time you were in here that your claim was about panned out and you were moving over to Chesaw."

"All right, big mouth," Clay Brown said with a show of patience. "I'll spell it out. My partner will think I been scheming to sneak out on him. I was just waitin' to tell him after he got over bein' sick. I been gonna ask you, Ed, shall we move up north across the river to the new strike?"

Ed was taken aback by the inadvertent revelation of Clay's plans. "Isn't that still Indian reservation across the river? I read in the *Des Moines Register* that the new strike was at Chesaw on Mary Ann Creek, but you couldn't file on Indian land."

"That don't bother nobody," the storekeeper said. "All we're after is the mineral rights, and they don't mean nothing to the Injuns. I'm going myself. This town's dead since the fire and flood. The bank's about to shut down."

"To cheer up my friend that you've got worried, how about staking us to credit for fresh eggs and bacon?"

"Nothing doing. Told you when you squared your account that I wasn't going to get in Dutch like that again."

So it was that Ed learned the truth: he had industriously helped Clay out of debts verging on bankruptcy; his partnership had been a partnership of equal liability. A silence of distrust having grown between them, they rode back toward camp.

"You think I'm a skunk, Ed, but I'm not," Clay pleaded. "I'm less of a gold miner. I'm a butcher at heart, and a darn hungry one. Hungry for a piece of steak."

When they half-heartedly resumed panning the next morning, they found no traces of color.

"We might as well quit," Clay said. "I've dug up and down this hundred feet at least twice. You can see we're the only people here. Last fall this place was alive with Chinks. They're all across the river now. Chesaw's named for one of 'em."

They went to the bank and put on their shoes. Clay had heavy logger's boots; Ed was still wearing his all-purpose ankle-top work shoes that came on his feet from Iowa. Clay had no stockings; Ed's were so full of holes, heel and toe, that his feet looked nearly naked. Ma, for all her meanness, had darned socks.

"Let's go back to the fire, and I'll stir up a batch of bannocks," Clay rallied.

"I'll fish a while," Ed offered, "but I'm not after any more of those suckers. Sure don't know why they call this Salmon Creek"

"You catch salmon at Kettle Falls," Clay said, "only Injuns are so thick over there, it's a good place for a white man to stay away from. During the salmon run, the west bank of the Columbia is covered with lodges and tepees. Some of the salmon weigh fifty pounds. Squaws catch 'em in baskets when they don't jump high enough to make it to the top of the falls."

"Maybe we could paint ourselves up like Indians. That's what the kids do in Iowa."

"Naw," Clay said. "But we're leavin' this place. Pick a few of those salmon berries from the bushes. I figured they was poison last week, but today I figure they ain't."

After a lunch of bannocks, trout minnows, and salmon berries, Clay stamped out the fire, knocked over his wigwam, and said, "Come on, I know what we're gonna do. Where'd you say that cattle layout was from here?"

"North. But you're not planning to ask for work as a cowhand?"

"Nope. Let's keep a lookout for deer tracks, though. You know—them split-hoof mule deer."

"Now, listen!" Ed laughed.

"Boy! Boy! Just wait and see what will look like a deer when you go without food altogether for a couple days."

"I'm not stealing anybody's cow!"

"In this country, people figure it ain't stealing if you kill one to eat. Ask anybody. They only send you to the pen for rustling cattle to sell. Besides, who said anything about stealing? We're going deer-hunting and then over to Chesaw. Ain't I spoken to you about going deer-hunting?"

Ed wondered how they would hunt deer. With bow and arrow? Neither of them had a gun.

"Let's load our mounts," Clay said.

As he rolled up his gear, Ed reflected, disheartened, on the difference in weight between the load he was carrying away and the load he had brought to Clay's camp the first time.

Clay, assembling his belongings, displayed for Ed's admiration a glistening collection of butcher knives.

"Might have to take a job using these in town some day," he said. "Thought I was done with blood and guts."

They retraced the road along Salmon Creek beyond Conconully, then took a trail northeast into the evergreen forest. When they came to a swift-running creek, Clay knew the geography. "This is the Sinlahekin; Conconully Lake is up at the end."

"You've been here before?"

"Sure. To look at me now, you wouldn't believe the lucky strike I made at Ruby and all the gold dust I spent on bar girls and whiskey. I should have my own cattle ranch by now.

"Came up this very trail one time with a couple of buddies. Heard there was a ranch for sale by a man named Wellington. When we were tanking up for a long ride, the bartender said he thought he'd heard the place had already been taken by some city slicker from the East—Guy Waring—but me and my partners decided to find out for sure if the deal was final.

"The barkeep said Waring had brought a wife with him from the East, a former widow with three children by her first marriage. None of us had even seen a white woman for a long time. The bartender warned us, 'If you guys are expecting a home-cooked meal, save yourselves the trip. This Waring guy is a skinny, educated type. They say he went to Harvard University and talks through his nose. His wife can do embroidery, but she can't mend overalls; can't cook either. All she knows how to do is set the table.'

"The bartender said the place came with a hundred fifty head of cattle, so we figured we could do our own cooking if we came within sight of a calf."

"I get your point," Ed said caustically.

"Never did get a meal, though. Waring was home. He was standing by the water trough when we drove up all tired and thirsty. He was a little squirt, all right, wore glasses. Didn't hap pen to be wearing a kitchen apron, though. He was wearing a Colt .45, heavy six-shooter.

"He asked us to state our business. We told him we were considerin' leaving our claim at Ruby and taking to raising cattle.

"'Beat you to the draw for this place,' he says.

"A pretty woman comes up from the garden patch with a load of ripe tomatoes in her apron. She was mighty pale, but she looked at her husband for what to do. He says to her, 'Put one of your tomatoes on the fence post and stand back.'

"She didn't say a word, but did exactly what he said.

"That city slicker raised his Colt to shoulder level, sights along the barrel, and gentle-like squeezes the trigger. After the smoke cleared, there was a wet spot on top of the fence post, but no tomato anywhere in sight.

"Three kids came out from under the porch. The boy was the oldest, or at least the biggest.

"'Put up another tomato, Harry,' Waring says.

"Harry took the tomato his mother handed him and stuck it on the post where the other one had been. That man fired his gun so fast all we could see was a blur. We heard the bang, though, and there was another tomato missing.

"The wife says, 'Will you please stop wasting my tomatoes!'

"Waring, with the sun glinting on his glasses, all of a sudden reminded us of a rattlesnake. So we lifted our hats to the lady and took off.

"Never saw Waring again. He was justice of the peace for a while, but he got disgusted because all the men he arrested for murdering people never got hung, and the drunk Siwashes were always overrunning his wife's vegetable garden. He went back East, but just heard he's come back to the Methow Valley and opened a classy saloon—Duck Brand, he calls it. Me and my buddies wouldn't want to go in there; say they throw you out first time you let out a whoop. What good is a drink if you can't whoop?"

Sinlahekin Creek, not fished out, yielded three ten-inch trout. Ed caught them, built the fire, and fried the fish.

"Nothing satisfies like beefsteak," Clay grumbled.

Next morning Ed found his partner's blanket empty. Had he become so disgusted with a fish diet that he had gone deer-hunting with a knife? His butchering tools lay open on the ground, some missing. He must be near, somewhere among the trees. Ed hiked up the gully as soon as he laced up his shoes.

Ed was right in assuming that Clay had not gone far. He was slitting the belly of a skinless animal that hung in professional butcher style from the limb of a tree.

Clay flashed Ed an impudent grin.

"Still got a dam good hand for dressing out a carcass, if I do say so myself. Told you I'd get us a deer. Tamest wild critter I ever saw. Didn't even walk away from me when I went up to it to slit its throat. Start a fire. We can roast kabobs on sticks. This morning air sure does give a guy an appetite."

Ed glanced at the hide on the ground, a messy pile of hair, skin, and blood. He could plainly see the brand mark AW. "I told you I wanted no part of livestock stealing!"

"Simmer down. To save your delicate conscience, I been calling this lovely, fat, young heifer a deer. I'm about fed up with your rube notions of what's honest. There's nothing as honest as hunger. Out here, boy, you're one more damn animal that's got to stay alive however he can. No town charity office. You make your choice; you either beg or you steal. Which is worse? Get the fire goin.'"

Ed shivered. He was dizzy from hunger, too. Was Clay's bitter logic unanswerable? Ed remembered his daydreams of becoming a daring Western outlaw. Now he had become one! Or would be one as soon as he started gathering firewood to roast a stolen cow. Rebellious as he was at his mother's righteousness, he thought of her now without wishing to do so. If she knew of this moment, she would snap in her sharp fashion, "See where worthless companions lead you!"

He was on the verge of fulfilling his mother's expectations. He wanted mightily to start gathering firewood, to fill his stomach with a square meal. At the same time, he knew he could not. His common sense presented him with a third choice. There was obviously a cattle ranch within a radius of a few miles. Opportunity to eat without stealing still existed. The Beemans had told him that he could find work as a cowhand. Besides, he still had an unconfessed dollar and sixty cents.

"You and I are splitting up," he said abruptly to Clay.

"Don't get sore. Suit yourself. Folks about to part should do it friendly," Clay chuckled in preoccupied fashion. "I can't be sore at anybody with good fresh meat under my nose. I'll build the fire myself when I get around to it."

Ed tramped back to the campsite. He rolled up his blanket, threw his saddle and gear on Stocky, and rode away. He chose his course due north along the creek through meadows of grass so thick and verdant that they resembled irrigated hayfields. Heavily forested mountains looked down on the Sinlahekin Creek valley, an ideal place for cattle.

8.

A Cowboy Eats Regularly

At midday Ed rode into another metropolis of the Okanogan country, a cluster of log cabins, unpainted shacks, and tents. The center of authority, apparently, was an elongated boxlike frame structure with a false two-story front. Large letters above the door proclaimed: Loomis Saloon, Ross Woodard, Prop.

Ed dismounted, tied Stocky to the hitching rail, and made his way through a bevy of Indians on the steps. He understood why the Indians remained outside when he saw the sign inside, on the mirror behind the bar: No Service to Minors or Indians.

Although the sign excluded him, too, he stood his ground. Because of his height, he knew he was often taken to be older than he was. His only intention was to ask directions, not to buy drink. No one appeared to notice his entrance. He approached the bar at which the barkeeper, in a starched white shirt under a black velvet vest, was polishing glassware and chatting with two resplendent creatures, certainly cowboys, arrayed in ten-gallon hats, red bandannas, woolly chaps, flannel shirts, and boots equipped with steel spurs.

The furniture in the saloon consisted of several circular, wire-legged tables, and wooden chairs. At one table, a man dressed in a black and tan checked drummer's suit was prying open a wooden crate with a hammer. "I'm gonna show my guns here, Ross," the man in the business suit said. "Bring you some trade."

"Can't stop you, I guess," the barman responded. "This is a public place. You won't do too well selling your merchandise. The settlers here don't carry firearms much."

The man shrugged and kept ripping boards and nails apart. "You're gettin' new people in the country. I bet some of them formed the habit of gun totin' before they got this far into Injun land.

"Springfield government breech loading rifles. Forty-five seventy. Thirty-three and five-eighths inch barrels. Used in all the wars against the Sioux and

Cheyennes."

The bartender, not answering, began to rub his counter with a cloth. To fill the silence, the salesman called to the cowboys, "Hey, you guys from the range, don't you need a gun?"

"Westmore doesn't let his help carry weapons, does he, Nathan?" the proprietor suggested.

"Just saddleguns," Nathan said. "I'd be scared to carry a thing like that. Might poke my eye out."

Ed could see what Cowboy Nathan meant. A four-inch spike bayonet was attached to the muzzle of each long barrel of the firearms for sale. Ed recalled that he had seen similar weapons on display on war veterans' gun racks in Iowa.

Rejected, the gun peddler snapped, "If you folks ain't interested, oughta be a way to get the damn Injuns out of the doorway so somebody else can come in."

"No law says they can't hang around outside," the barman said.

"At the hotel in Conconully these guns sold like hotcakes. People told me about an Injun scare."

"Nothing came of it," Ross Woodard said. "They were talking about the Cole murder in '91. Injun kid hung for killing a white man, but afterward they found out the kid didn't do it. The Injuns had a legitimate complaint. There won't be any more Injun scares, except maybe some yayhoo like you starts one."

The salesman's face broke into a grin. His eyes widened with an idea inside his head. "Damned if I won't start one!"

He selected one of the rifles lying on the table, inserted a cartridge, and closed the breech. He strode to the doorway, pulled back the rifle hammer, lifted the weapon to his shoulder, took aim, and squeezed the trigger. As he fired he yelled, "Got one!"

The Indians outside the door united in a wild cry. Woodard, the cowboys, and Ed ran outside. A young Indian, dying, lay in vomit. His chest was spurting blood. His companions dragged him from the saloon platform and laid him under a tree.

The peddler continued his ugly grinning as he watched from the doorway.

Woodard ran up the steps, collared the salesman, and shook him. "You bastard! You got some nerve! Committin' murder in cold blood!"

"Aw, don't get feisty," the peddler objected. "It wa'nt murder. Wa'nt nothin' but an Injun."

"He wasn't hurting you at all!" Ross continued in a rage. "You're in trouble. You'll get the whole country in trouble!"

"You tell me folks are gonna give a damn about one less Injun?"

"These cowhands saw you pull the trigger. They work for Westmore, who lives with an Indian woman. Fine people. They're my neighbors."

The salesman defied Ross with curled lips, "Knew there was somep'n funny about this neck of the woods! Forgot about them squaw men up here. Where I come from, they give you a free drink for killing an Injun!"

"Shut up! You're going with me to the marshal."

Ed, in shock, leaned against the platform. Wild West magazines had not hardened him enough. He retched at the sight and smell.

Still holding fast to the salesman, Ross Woodard addressed the Indians who were hovering and murmuring about the dead brother, "What you want done with the victim?"

"Find Black Robe *Suyapich*," one of the Indians called.

Woodard nodded.

"Annie, come out here!" he yelled.

From the hotel that adjoined the saloon, Annie, a girl in a mobcap, appeared; she observed the tragedy with startled eyes.

"Run get the Black Robe, Annie," Ross ordered. "He's upstairs in number four. I checked him in an hour ago. He was gonna try to get some sleep."

A slight, bearded young man who wore the black robes of the church of Saint Peter came back with her.

One Indian led the priest to the body and swept accusing eyes over all the white people present, "Bad *Suyapich* kill our brother!"

The priest knelt and felt for a pulse. After a brief examination, he stood and faced the company. "Who shot this man?"

"I ain't Irish. I don't owe no confession to the Pope!" the salesman snarled with all eyes upon him.

"God have mercy on you," the priest said. Then he turned to Ross Woodard, "Did this person do what the Inkamip says?"

"You bet he did!"

The owner of the saloon and the priest conferred in tones that not everyone could hear; then Woodard called, "Nathan! Will! Beat it as fast as you can. Tell Carr and Flower what hap pened so the People will know right away that nobody but this fool had any part in it."

"Right away, Ross!"

The cowboys jumped on their mounts at the hitching rail and galloped out of town.

The priest looked around in the crowd for help. He singled out Ed. "Lad! Do you think you can pull yourself together? Help carry this body to the marshal."

Ed braced himself. "All right, sir, I'll do it."

The priest waved the Indians aside. "Wailing helps nothing! We will seek justice."

Ross Woodard muttered to Ed, "It'll be a cold day in hell when they get justice."

The priest bent down and grasped the body by the armpits. "You, lad, take him by the feet."

Ed approached the corpse. A will that he had never known he possessed enabled him to girdle his hands around the ankles of the limp object that no longer contained a spirit. They proceeded along the street flanked by the now silent Indians. The townspeople, too, watched in silence. The only noise came from the gun salesman, who yelled with every yank Ross gave him.

Marshal Roy came from the small jail to meet the entourage; he was joined by a deputy.

"Get a move on, Bradford!" the marshal barked. "Grab the kid's end. He's about to pass out."

"I'm all right," Ed protested, but allowed the deputy to replace him.

The priest and the deputy deposited the corpse on a table inside the jail. Ross Woodard quickly recounted the tragedy.

"We gotta take you in, buster," the marshal told the sales man. "Into the lockup with you!"

The law officer shoved the peddler into the lone cell, slammed the door of iron slats, and snapped the padlock.

'What you think you're doin'!" the prisoner began to cower. "You can't lock me up! I ain't done a damn thing but plug an Injun!"

"Looks like we'll keep you a while," the marshal growled. "You pipe down right now!"

Marshal Roy inspected the remains on the plank table. "I don't know this Indian. Do you, Father?"

"He's Tommeo, I think. Member of the Inkamip family. He was too far south of home. It'll be tomorrow before his People find out. When they come to claim him, tell them to bring him to the mission for burial."

The priest made a sign of blessing over the departed soul. "I fear his burial won't be the end of the matter," he said. "It behooves us to be civil and sorry."

The marshal nodded agreement.

"Somebody can find out from his mother how much she will take to square things, can't they, Roy?" the deputy asked.

"Likely the best we can do," Ross said.

The marshal was exasperated. "Dammit! I hate folks gettin' by with murder; but more than one Indian family has taken payment for an 'accident.'"

"I plan to visit Carr Westmore today," said the priest. "His wife Opening Flower is the daughter of old White Stone Mountain, who died recently. The People listen to her. She's *skumalt*—wise and respected. I shall consult with her and her husband. They can probably arrange for a go-between with the Inkamip family."

"A good plan, Father," Ross Woodard said. "With things under control, I suppose I better get back to my business. Others will be wondering what the shooting was about by now. If there's a panic, we may get just what the peddler wanted—people buying his guns! But it won't happen on my place! I'll bring those guns for you to keep, Marshal."

"Better yet, I'll send Brad along to collect them," the marshal said.

Roy addressed the priest respectfully, "It sure was lucky that you were in town."

"You can thank Mr. Woodard that I was here," the priest smiled. "He gave me a room in his hotel for rest after riding all night."

"You never owe anybody a cent, Father," Ross Woodard stated. "You do the work of a dozen justices of the peace."

"You're excused, boy," the marshal told Ed. "First give me your name. You're a witness. You'll be around?"

Ed wrote his name on the marshal's pad. He tried not to sprawl his writing. He was relieved that the marshal did not request his address, for he had none.

As he stood in the street, his teeth chattered. The priest came from the jail and went to him.

"You did a hard job, lad. Thank you."

"It wasn't hard. I'll have to get tougher if I stay around here."

"I did not notice before how young you are," the priest said. "Maybe I asked too much of you—to carry a dead person."

"I'm all right."

"You alone, son? You're a long way from Iowa, aren't you?"

"Broke up with my mining partner this morning. How did you know I'm from Iowa?"

The priest smiled. "Many boys come from Iowa, Illinois, Indiana, how could one guess far wrong? Give me your name."

"Ed McLaren from Boone, Iowa."

"I am Etienne deRouge. One of my homes is at St. Mary's Mission, forty miles south on the Okanogan River."

Although Ed's upbringing had counseled him that horns grew on the papacy, he nevertheless felt drawn toward this friendly, brave human being. "I'm eighteen. I was trying to act twenty-one going into that saloon. Serves me right," he said.

Father deRouge laughed. "Your first experience in a Wild West saloon! A good one! Taught you to keep out! Are you sick to your stomach?"

"I haven't had a chance to eat breakfast. Do you know how much they charge for meals in the hotel?"

"I am a professional beggar. Mine are free. Come in with me and save a dollar. Mr. Woodard owns most of the public services in town. He knows what you've been through. I'm certain we can both be served breakfast."

"Still have some money," Ed asserted.

'It will go fast enough. Just say discreetly, 'Thank you,' when we get up to leave."

Ed's growling stomach impelled him to accompany the priest. As they entered the hotel dining room, Annie of the mobcap greeted them. "Will you and your friend have breakfast, Father? Mr. Woodard says you are always welcome as a guest. After what's happened already this morning, we all need food and cups of coffee."

As THEY FEASTED on eggs, sausage, and hotcakes, Ed admitted to the priest that his only home now was on Stocky's back, and that he hoped to find work on a ranch.

"*Mirabile dictu!*" the priest exclaimed. "I am on my way to a cattle ranch. I, too, hope to find employment there. I shall perform a wedding. We can travel together. I rode all yesterday and last night, but I must be on my way without further sleep to arrive at the time that I have promised."

Ed hesitated. "Maybe I better pick another day to ask for work if there's going to be a wedding."

"But no! If a choice of urgency is to be made, I suspect your business takes priority. Carr Westmore and his Indian woman have lived out of wedlock a dozen years. I have a continual quarrel with white men living with Indian wives.

"Incidents such as the one we've witnessed have convinced Mr. Westmore he must make his children legitimate. He will accept my offices willingly. It is Opening Flower who insists they are superfluous."

Annie came to their table and asked, "Did you have enough breakfast, Father?"

"Too much," the priest said. "Thank you."

"And your friend?"

"All I could eat! Thank you," Ed mumbled.

They went from the hotel into the street.

"Come, we shall go to the livery stable, where they are keeping my horse. I suppose your horse is tied at the saloon."

Ed quickly untied Stocky from the nearby hitching rail and led him across to the livery barn.

After three hours' travel over a rough but well-marked trail, Father deRouge said, "We take this side trail. See the large white house up there on the brow of the hill? It is the Westmore home."

"It looks like a mansion!" Ed exclaimed.

"Only from a distance. Finished with white stucco, it appears elegant from here, but the construction is relatively crude, the work done by natural ingenuity. For the framework, Westmore dragged cedar logs from the lake and nailed them together with wooden pegs. Opening Flower has given him so many children they were bursting out of the cedar cabin you see at the left. That is now the bunkhouse in which we hope you can stay. Better than your last accommodations, no doubt."

"My partner had a wickiup, but there wasn't room inside for both of us. I slept under the stars."

The priest laughed, "It didn't hurt you. I have slept under the sky myself."

After a few more minutes on the trail, they reached their destination. They tied the mounts by a water trough and went through a swinging gate into a fenced yard. A flock of Rhode Island hens cawed and clucked conversationally with one another; two milk cows cropped grass in the enclosure. Father deRouge led the way to the porch.

As soon as he rapped on the frame of the open door, a girl probably twelve years old came at once, her face alight with welcome. Her black hair hung in two long braids. Her copper skin and high cheekbones revealed her Native American Indian blood. She wore a pink, ankle-length dress that denoted the English part of her ancestry. In her pierced ears hung gold nuggets on chains.

She beamed as the priest took her outstretched hands and pressed them. "Father deRouge! At last you are here!"

"Analix! God bless you. How you have grown! How pretty you have become!"

"Thank you, Father! Papa sent to Vancouver for dresses for Mama and Bethany and me."

"I have brought a guest," Father deRouge introduced Ed. "This young man and I joined forces at Loomis. He wishes to ask your father for work."

"I could wait in the yard," Ed offered.

"Don't be silly!" she said brightly and smiled at Ed. "Come in, both of you."

She led them into a room in which the main piece of furniture was a table made from half a huge log, with benches to match. Woven tule mats covered the floor and three walls. A fireplace built of native stone filled the fourth wall. Before the fireplace stood an improvised prie-dieu hung with a beautifully decorated deerskin robe that was overlaid with chains of yellow and lavender wild flowers.

"See! Bethany and I have made everything ready, Father," the girl said proudly. "Bethany is a real artist. She painted the sunrise on the hide. We picked the yellow bells and shooting stars this morning. Everyone helped make the garlands."

"A lovely chapel for a wedding!" Father deRouge exclaimed. He took a Bible and another book from his cassock pocket and laid them on the prie-dieu.

Children sat at benches on either side of the log table. They were self-consciously bending their heads over primers as they snickered and darted black eyes sideways at one another.

'We saw you coming, Father," Analix said. "I made everyone sit at the table so you could see them studying. When we have the new school, none of us will be in the first grade."

She turned to Ed to explain. "I was old enough to attend St. Mary's before it burned. I read very well."

The children stood at her signal and recited in formal, parochial school voices, "Good day, Father."

"Good day, *mes enfants*. God bless you. I see you are being good and polite. Shall I go to the kitchen, Analix? Your father and mother are there?"

"Yes, go in, Father," Analix sighed. "They are still arguing. Papa wants Mama to wear her new dress, but she is slow getting ready."

After the priest went behind a portiere of woven grass, Analix addressed the young brood, "You behaved! Thank you!"

She turned to Ed with the pride of great responsibility. "I am 'the oldest,'" she said as though the title implied many duties. "I'll tell you our names. First is Bethany, my only sister, a year younger than me. She has a Christian name; next Leschi and Owhi, named for chiefs that Papa admired; then Tamma and Kahpat, Telah, and Antwine. There are two younger ones still napping. We are ten in all."

"My name is almost Christian, but with the 'lix' on the end. 'Lix' means in the Salish language that I am a girl. Sometimes Papa calls me just Ana."

"My name is Ed McLaren," he said with the most courteous tone he could muster. He had come to a warm home in which politeness and loving kindness ruled. He was inspired to behave accordingly.

As Analix talked, she revealed herself as a child needing reassurance almost as much as Ed. Her face became solemn with worry as she heard the exchange behind the portiere.

"Father deRouge is reminding Marna that she was baptized with all Chief White Stone Mountain's tribe when she was a child. It is important for my parents to be married by the white man's ceremony. So many settlers and miners have come to the valley, it is dangerous to be married only in the Okanogan way."

"Ssss! What you say, Analix!"

The portiere burst apart. Opening Flower stood in the door, a tall, exotic princess of regal bearing, wearing a floor length pink silk gown, high-waisted, with leg o' mutton sleeves. Father deRouge nudged her gently into the room.

"*Dans la mode Parisienne!*" he exclaimed.

But the Indian princess scorned the finery. She still spoke forcibly and at length in her own language. Carr Westmore joined everyone. He was shaking his head with a mixture of annoyance and amusement.

"The gown is the color of the flower for which she is named, but she will not accept it. She's talking so fast I cannot understand her. What is she saying, Analix?" he asked his daughter.

Analix rose to another important role—interpreter. "Mama says that her husband has forgotten that Chief White Stone Mountain's tribe assembled for a ceremony. The chief gave his daughter openly for a wife to Carr Westmore. Her marriage price was five cows, in a year in which few cows lived through the hard winter. At her wedding, the People feasted on deer stew and smoked fish. They jingled bells and danced all day. Her husband took her to a separate lodge and a separate fire; but now he has forgotten! He says this paleface dress is her wedding dress! Not the white doeskin beaded with the sunrise. She will not become a paleface!"

Carr Westmore's face grew sober. He spoke with an immaculate British accent, "Father, I am proud to hear Opening Flower express herself so well. There is some justification, don't you agree, for her attitude?"

"But yes! Tell her, Analix, that I do not wish to deny the first ceremony; I ask that she permit us to give it the blessing of *Mon Dieu*, who is not only God of the paleface, but God of the red People alike."

After Analix translated, Mama still spat. Analix retained her courage.

"Mama! You told us yourself what your father, the chief, ordered. He said that when *Suyapich* Black Robe, the Father came, you must stand before him with your husband. You did not have Father's blessing on your wedding day only because he was far south in Oregon then. You have waited many years to keep your promise to your father. And you are making a scene before company, Mama!"

With a swift hand motion, Analix called her mother's attention to Ed. The princess, instantly silent, studied the stranger in their midst. Her expression changed to one of dignity and decorum.

Subject to her gaze, Ed became conscious of his soiled pants, his ragged red and black mackinaw, and his worn-out shoes. He scarcely looked like "company."

Ed also felt the scrutiny of Mr. Westmore, who wore wedding garb himself: tan trousers and jacket and gleaming boots. A tall, broad-shouldered man in his thirties, he was a typical Englishman, with strong, regular features, sandy hair, and blue eyes; but he was also a man of the free outdoors, like his wildborn family.

"You are welcome here," he told Ed. "Father deRouge has told me about your circumstances. We'll talk later."

"Thank you, sir. Hope I'm not in the way."

"Not at all," the bridegroom replied, then turned to a son, "Antwine, go to the bunkhouse and tell Nathan and Will it's time to come."

The cowhands who had been in Loomis at the hour of the shooting nodded to Ed when they appeared with Antwine. Ed was humbly grateful for their recognition, which he had not expected.

"Is Flower still using one excuse after another, Boss?" Nathan asked.

"She has finally agreed. Come, Flower."

Mr. Westmore took his bride's hand and led her toward the prie-dieu.

Father deRouge drew a pair of silver candlesticks from the pocket of his cassock; next, two white tapers, which he placed in the candlesticks. He lit the candles with a sulfur match and placed them on the fireplace mantel.

"I shall not test your remembrance of the Latin you learned at Eton and Oxford," the priest said with a smile to Mr. Westmore. I have a surprise for Opening Flower."

The bride, restored to equanimity and kindliness as a response to ceremony, knelt with the bridegroom.

"*Nown empt an quelt utsen, ell egru gil tum asket an amyr, neur a quest…*"

The bride breathed joyfully to hear in her native Salish, "Our Father which art in heaven…"

As she made promises to love, honor, and obey, she laughed.

Father deRouge pronounced Carr and Opening Flower man and wife.

"But we are not yet finished with ritual," he stated firmly. "Your children must be made legitimate by baptism."

Analix said, "Weipah and Aeneas are still asleep." She pulled a rope that hung in a comer, and a pivoting ladder swung down. Analix climbed to the loft and handed down two baby boys.

"I shall bless the creek water," Father deRouge said. "I do not have enough holy water from Manresa for all of you. Outside we go!"

Yapping and tumbling over one another like rowdy puppies, the youngsters cheerfully accepted the sprinkles of water from the creek.

When Leschi fetched the record book from the prie-dieu inside, the priest produced another wonder, a fountain pen. "I write all names in the baptismal records of St. Mary's. Each of you must show me that you know how to spell your own name."

Analix quickly spelled first: "A-n-a-1-i-x."

"Now it's your turn, Bethany! Be careful! Isn't Bethany's blue dress pretty?"

Bethany, who was as quiet as Analix was sociable, smiled, and carefully as her sister bade, whispered, "B-e-t-h-a-n-y."

"Very good!" Father deRouge declared.

"My name is A-n-t-w-i-n-e," a boy said.

Father deRouge chuckled, "We shall write it that way, although I'll wager your father that it should be 'A-n-t-o-i-n-e' after a French voyageur who paddled down the Okanogan."

"That could be," Mr. Westmore agreed, "but most people here spell it 'A-n-t-w-i-n-e.' Also you will say that 'Aeneas' should be spelled 'I-g-n-a-c-e;' but I named him for Chief Aeneas."

As the name-spelling continued, the bride and her daughters went to the house.

"You will be surprised, Father," Carr Westmore said, "how quickly Opening Flower began to cook at her wood range. Analix is a great help to her because of what she learned at the mission."

The party returned to the dining room.

Analix and Bethany went back and forth from behind the portiere to the log table to set out an amazing feast: savory-smelling, steaming-hot slew in a large tightly woven cooking basket; slices of baked ham and roast beef; boiled potatoes with the jackets on; peeled, hard-boiled eggs; beef jerky; bread tom in chunks; cheese; butter; and raspberry and elderberry jam. Finally, Opening Flower with a flourish placed a heaping bowl of cooked roots in the center of the buffet.

The Indian princess felt herself again. She was no longer wearing the garb of an 1890s fashion plate, but a white, loose-waisted garment of doeskin sewn with glistening beads.

Mr. Westmore cheered, "Aha! You have changed to your real wedding dress!"

The bride nodded proudly. She handed Ed a tin plate from the stack at the end of the table as she addressed him in her own language. Her husband translated: "Opening Flower says she is always happy to have company. Take the bitterroot first. It is speetlum, my wife's name in the Sinkaietk tongue."

Ed was overwhelmed at the honor given him. Hoping not to be clumsy, he helped himself with a wooden-handled fork to a generous portion of boiled roots that resembled small parsnips or white radishes.

"Are these the roots of the pink flowers that grow low on the ground? I've noticed they open in the sunshine and close at night."

"You have guessed right," Westmore said. "They grow like a carpet."

As he tasted, Ed felt a mustard-like tang on his tongue.

"Try it with a slice of beef," Mr. Westmore said. "Come, Nathan and Will, join forces with this young man!"

Ed and the hands moved with common purpose down the long table. The boys started banging on their tin plates because they had been ordered to wait until after the guests were served.

Analix sent them a black look that stopped the racket.

"All right, boys," the priest said. "I'll hurry. I've been looking forward to eating as much as you. In France we call this a buffet."

"Mama says it is a potlatch," Analix countered.

"I stand corrected."

Opening Flower brought one more platter from the kitchen.

Nathan and Will prodded Ed to attention. "Smoked salmon! When you think you can't eat another bite, then you can eat smoked salmon the rest of the day!"

Ed experienced what Nathan and Will meant.

After everyone had finished eating, and Analix and Bethany had cleared the feast, Father deRouge said, "Now for the fun!"

He snuffed out the candles on the fireplace mantel and put the silver candlesticks back in his pocket. The flower chains and deerskin came from the prie-dieu, revealed as a pine slab nailed with wooden pegs to legs of lodgepole pine.

Seating himself at the stand, Father deRouge produced a tiny figure in a priest's robe. "See what my friend Maggie Bottomley has made with her clever hands? A puppet. He speaks.

"Good day, children. I am Frère Jacques. I congratulate you on your baptism today. I ask you always to say your prayers when you rise in the morning.

"It is easy for children to hop from bed and quickly say the rosary, but I am old and fat. I have been saying matins long years. My knees are sore; the floor is cold. The bell rings, and I must rise and say my prayers. I cannot! I cannot! The floor is too cold!"

The priest puppet flapped his arms and kicked his legs, but he could not lift himself from bed.

"Get up! Get up! Frère Jacques," the children called.

Groaning pitifully, Frère Jacques slid one foot over the edge of his cot and fell into a limp attitude of prayer. The children laughed merrily at the fat brother.

Father deRouge, in a light tenor, sang, "*Frère Jacques, Frère Jacques, dormez-vous, dormez-vous? Sonnez les matines, sonnez les matines. Ding Dang Don! Ding Dang Don!*"

"End of act," the priest announced. Loud applause followed. Father deRouge had further wonders—a doll pair, a boy and a girl, in bright clown costumes: "Pierrot and Pierrette, to dance a brawl!"

The hand puppets bounced in sprightly fashion to music supplied from

Father deRouge's chest. As they stopped, the boy and girl clown kissed with a loud smack. Nathan and Will whooped in delight, along with the children.

"That's as fancy a show as any on the vaudeville circuit at Ames, Iowa!" Ed ventured.

Nathan poked Will. "I dare you to ask Father who taught him to dance that brawling way in Paris."

Father deRouge smilingly stowed the puppets away. "I have left such sin in confession. I must go now if I hope to reach the mission tomorrow. There is much to do."

Opening Flower spoke to her daughters, who went out in a flurry to prepare a lunch for the priest to take with him.

As ED, NATHAN, and Will stood together, Will remarked in a troubled whisper, "I wonder what's going on across the room." The bridal couple and the priest, apart in a comer, were holding a low-voiced discussion.

"They're talkin' about that Inkamip who was shot … like family to Opening Flower. Indians and whites have always been friends around here, except when some fool tries to start something like this morning!" Nathan said.

"I never saw a murder before, and hope I never see one again," Ed said fervently.

"It'll be settled," Nathan assured him. "Indians take payment for a killing."

With the priest about to depart, Ed wondered what was to become of him. He did not wait long. Mr. Westmore came to speak to him.

"You accepted our family business with good grace, young man," the Englishman said. "They tell me you are a McLaren—good Scottish name. Do you know livestock, Edward?"

Ed flushed as everyone looked in his direction, but said straightforwardly, "I come from an Iowa farm. I know farm-horses and dairy cattle but never had anything to do with range cattle."

"Are you familiar with farm machinery?"

"I've put up a lot of hay using a mower and a rake."

"Good! Nathan and Will rebel at making haystacks with a scythe and pitchfork. In the barn we have a Buckeye mower and rake that my brother-in-law Red Curlew and I brought back from Fort Colville. The components are still in boxes. None of us has ever assembled such equipment. Could you?"

Ed had spent long winter nights oiling and repairing mower parts, and each June he had helped assemble the mower and rake for use with the workhorses.

"Likely it wouldn't be hard. Our mower was a Buckeye, too. Does it have fingers to catch the hay for the sickle?"

"I believe it does. We're in luck! Do you have your gear with you?"

"Still on my horse."

"Nathan and Will can show you where to put it in the bunkhouse. Twenty dollars a month and keep. Suit you?"

"Just fine! Thanks. I'll try to make myself useful."

He kept his qualms to himself about yet another summer jouncing on a steel seat mounted on a four-foot steel spring.

"About time you got us help, Boss," Nathan said. "You've had two hands and the biggest herd in the valley!"

"'Course the new help is only a greenhorn!" Will remarked. "We'll likely have to ride herd on him, too."

Everyone walked with Father deRouge to the gate. Ed's and the priest's horses were cropping grass along the fence with their reins dropped.

"I untied them," Leschi said. What's your pony's name, Ed?"

"I call him Stocky."

"Think how long he has had a bit in his mouth," Mr. Westmore said. "After Father leaves, Nathan, show Ed to the corral, and give him a bunk in the bunkhouse."

THE PRIEST GATHERED his cassock in one hand and swung lightly astride his mount.

"God bless you all, including you, young Edward McLaren from Iowa."

Carr Westmore laid his hand on Ed's shoulder.

"We'll look after him, Father," he said. "I suspect he's one newcomer who's had his fill of saloon life in short order."

As the priest went alone down the trail, Ed felt impelled to say, "That fellow reminds me of a prince in disguise that you read about in storybooks."

Mr. Westmore said, "That's nearly what he is. He is of French noble birth, son of a count. Without doubt he danced the brawl many a time in Paris. The romantic notion of seeking one's fortune in the New World takes varied forms. His dream is to build a school for the education of noble redmen. I intend to encourage his work here for the advantage of my own children, if nothing else. When I came to the Okanogan Valley, he had already baptized half the Indians, including Flower's tribe. He receives funds from his own family and from wealthy friends in the East, among them Mother Katherine Drexel."

Analix waved longer than anyone else to the departing priest. When he went out of sight, she bubbled, "All our family are of noble birth, too. Mother is a princess. Her father was Chief White Stone Mountain, and Papa—tell him who you are, Papa."

Papa laughed ruefully, "I am the descendant of one of those unfortunate second sons from Britain. However, I believe I am the happiest member of the Westmore family."

He hoisted a four-year-old to the sky.

STOCKY WAS USHERED into the corral that already contained half a dozen horses: four cow ponies and a pair of heavier animals that undoubtedly pulled the supply wagon.

Leschi and Owhi tagged along with Nathan, Will, and Ed to the bunkhouse.

"You know how to milk, Ed?" Leschi asked.

"Of course," Ed said at once.

Nathan emitted a sharp whistle.

"Skeedaddle, you Injun!" Will ordered.

"What's that about?" Ed asked.

"You greenhorn! He'll have you milking cows!"

"Shoulda thought faster!"

"You can have this place," Nathan told Ed as he held up the lantern in a dark room that contained a small stand and a narrow, home-carpentered bunk with a buckskin mattress.

Will brought a blanket from the next room. "See you got a cover in your roll, but I bet you haven't been sleeping too warm. This Hudson's Bay blanket will keep you warm at forty below."

"We'll let you have the lantern to get undressed," Nathan said. "We don't use it much. Guess you know how to put out a lantern?"

"Turn down the wick and blow it out," Ed assured him.

"You got it right."

Nathan set the lantern on the stand. "Sweet dreams!"

Ed enjoyed the luxury of disrobing by lantern light down to his union suit!

NATHAN POUNDED FROM the other side of the wall next morning. "If you want any breakfast, you better get out here. Quit decidin' what to wear!"

Deciding what to wear was exactly Ed's problem of the moment. When he and Clay had left their camp, he had put on the trousers he had worn on the train, but these were now grimy. The overalls that he had worn for grubbing in the creek were a repulsive wad. He had never yet had a chance to go systematically through his stolen wardrobe. He rummaged to the bottom of the bag and found a rolled pair of heavy black gabardine trousers and a blue cotton work shirt.

The three hands stopped at the pump to use a wash basin on a bench. Ed clutched the bar of Crystal White soap as though it were a strange artifact. With cold well water in the basin, he worked up a lather on his face and hands that caused Will to remark, "Careful, there, you might rub off your stubble!"

Ed felt his face. Yes, he did need a razor now. He resolved to buy one with his first wages.

AT THE HOUSE, Opening Flower and her daughters served a hearty breakfast of applesauce, hot cakes, syrup, sausage, eggs, and coffee.

"Aren't you glad you got your pants on in time!" Nathan joshed as Ed ate his sixth hot cake with syrup. "You musta been starvin' to death."

"I was," Ed said. "But I finally seem to have struck it rich!"

Carr Westmore stood up from the table first. "Today we're branding. Know anything about branding, Ed?"

"Only what I've read."

"Wild-eyed beasts with ears flattened against their heads, frothing at the mouth, dodging lariats while the cowhands whoop and holler?"

Ed caught the irony in his new employer's tone. "I always guessed magazine writers exaggerated."

"You can't be a tail-driver here," Leschi volunteered from the row. "Pop won't have a tail-driver on the place."

The boss, the hands, and the three oldest Westmore sons went to the corral to saddle mounts. Leschi laughed at Ed's saddle.

"You better ask Papa if he doesn't have something better for you. That's like a seat Mama sewed for me when I was little," he said.

"Suits me fine for now," Ed answered. "Genuine Indian saddle!"

THE PARTY RODE to a cache a mile from the house, a pocket between two hills. A sturdy gate made from lodgepole pine logs lay across the single, small entry to the naturally enclosed area.

As the party came through, the animals within the cache pushed forward with curiosity.

"What kind of cattle are these?" Ed asked.

"Mothers and calves," Will chortled.

Will's teasing was beginning to bother Ed.

"I can see that much! I'm wondering about the rust-colored bodies and white faces!"

"These are White-faced Herefords," Mr. Westmore said.

"All I know are Holsteins and Jerseys."

"Dairy animals. These are beef cattle. We at one time ran the usual mix of range stock—longhorns, shorthorns, scrubs—but with the help of my uncle in England, we are building a herd of purebreds. They adapt to this highland country. They're self-reliant, but don't go wild. They fatten well on the native grasses."

"I can see they are good stock," Ed said. "Are you the only person with Herefords?"

"No. Wellington French on Scotch Creek has brought out some registered Hereford bulls from Nebraska. Between us, we shall make the Okanogan Valley famous for its purebred stock."

The party halted beside a shed.

"Let's fall to," the Old Man said. "First we cut the calves from the mothers. Ed, stay behind and take it easy. You'll catch on. I can see already your horse knows how to work cattle. He's an aging but competent cowpony."

Ed could feel underneath him that Stocky was automatically assuming his duties. He needed no direction to hold his point as the cows were herded outside the enclosure.

The mothers waited in a bunch at the fence.

"You have little trouble with calves if they can smell their mothers not far away," Mr. Westmore told Ed. "Branding isn't a bad experience if you can jump up and run to Mama."

"How many calves you figure we got here, Boss?" Will asked.

"I judge seventy-five. Did you bring the tally pencil?"

Mr. Westmore brought six branding irons from the shed. He held one up for Ed's inspection. "This is our brand."

A tide of inner humiliation flooded through Ed as he recognized the brand that had been plain to see on the hide of the cow Clay had gutted.

"Let's start the fire," Mr. Westmore said.

The boys forayed into the lodgepole pine thicket nearby to gather brush and poles. Ed helped with his Bowie knife.

When the proper mix of dry grass and kindling lay in a heap, Nathan struck a match on the seat of his pants and lit the pile. It blazed quickly.

"We throw on some larger sticks now and wait for the bed of coals," Nathan told Ed.

To prepare for counting, Will leaned a board against the corral fence and placed a thick, black grease pencil atop the closest post. The calves clustered about the crew without fear.

Mr. Westmore arranged the brands on the coals that had dropped to the fire bed.

"Your job will be to keep the fire going," he told Ed. "Throw on only enough wood to keep it small and steady. We use six brands so that at least one will be red hot at all times. Pass me the hottest iron from the fire when I ask you to."

At a nod from his father, Leschi, holding a short piece of rope called a pigging string, approached an unsuspecting calf from behind. He deftly circled a hind foot and a front foot with the pigging string, gave a quick, gentle jerk, and the calf tripped to its side.

Leschi fell on the calf to hold it down with his weight. Swift as a magician, he whipped the pigging string around the other two legs. The surprised animal lay still. Mr. Westmore held out his hand toward Ed, "Give me a brand."

Ed promptly handed the boss a red-hot brand. The calf bawled once as the hot steam and stench rose from its hide, and bawled again when Nathan cut off its testicles.

As the morning passed, the air reeked with burned flesh.

"The new hand looks yellow around the mouth," Will observed.

Mr. Westmore asked Ed, "Think you can stick it out?"

"I can stand it."

"Sick at your stomach?" Nathan guessed. "Try smoking. Cuts the smell."

He offered his cigarette makings.

Ed shook his head. His attempts at smoking in Iowa had nauseated him; calf-branding was enough to endure. He stood his post until the last calf was shooed out the gate by Will.

"Go find Mama, feller," Will told the calf. "You'll feel all right when you suck a while."

"Put out the fire, boys," Mr. Westmore said.

When Leschi, Owhi, and Tamma brought rusty coffee cans full of water from the spring, Mr. Westmore poured them over the fire and stamped on the wet ashes.

"Less greenhorn in you than in most fellows who stop with us. You kept the heat of the brands even. Didn't have to remind you."

Ed felt a glow of pride. He had seldom been complimented in the course of his life.

"We'll go to the house for noon today," Mr. Westmore decided. "Red Curlew will be there by now."

"Who is Red Curlew?" Ed asked Tamma.

"He is my uncle, Mama's brother. He will have to go to Oroville to see what *N'Chi-lix-czin*, the People, will ask for the death of the Inkamip."

RED CURLEW, A tall, young brave who resembled his half-sister, was waiting at the watering trough, his mount cropping grass. He wore a deerskin shirt and trousers. Carr Westmore and the visitor greeted each other in Salish and spoke quietly for a moment.

The boss reverted to English to say, "We'll eat dinner first of all," and motioned everyone inside.

Ed sat between Tamma and Kahpat.

"You do eat as though you were hungry for a long time," Tamma observed.

"You' re right," Ed admitted. "All I had to eat for a week was fish from the creek. They tasted like wood, ten bones to every bite. They were fat and slow and ugly."

"Suckers!" Telah and Kahpat shouted gleefully.

Opening Flower spoke to Ed in her own tongue, and Analix interpreted, "Mama says the fish are fine to eat. You should have boiled them to make soup. The bones would have fallen to the bottom of the pot. Add roots, and you have a good, nourishing meal."

"We should have thought of boiling out the bones," Ed admitted.

"Mama says plenty of salmon berries are ripe, too."

"I saw all the berries but didn't eat many, afraid they would be poison."

"Mama says it is a good thing you have come to us. She will keep you alive," Analix relayed the message.

AFTER THE MEAL, Opening Flower, Red Curlew, and Carr Westmore withdrew to the yard to the shade of a tree.

When the girls had finished clearing the table and washing the dishes, their parents were still conferring.

Analix studied the trio talking in low voices. "It is serious trouble," she said.

Nathan told her, "Don't think everything depends on you."

She sighed, "We know what they are talking about. Red Curlew talked at Osoyoos with the Inkamip's family. The white person who took Tommeo's body to the mission was sitting on the coffin while he traveled! Red Curlew wants to know if the red men must forgive everything!"

Neither Mr. Westmore nor Opening Flower told the others what the settlement of the grievance was to be. At the evening meal, the branding finished, Red Curlew's visit was mentioned only in the context that he and three cousins would come to the AW ranch, named for Carr's father, Arthur Westmore, to help with the hay harvest.

"The tribe owns half the mower and rake," Analix explained to Ed. "Chief White Stone Mountain and Papa each gave five cows in trade for it at Fort Colville. Half the meadow hay will belong to Mama's People."

"Never heard of Injuns putting up hay," Nathan said. "Against their nature."

"You don't do it without a direct order, either, Nathan," Mr. Westmore observed. "But White Stone Mountain was a longhead. Red Curlew and the others are coming only because of direct orders he gave before he died."

ED WAS EXCUSED from riding for the next several days and remanded to the barn to grease, oil, and assemble the mower and rake. At last, gleaming in its cast-iron newness, the mower stood in the barnyard. Mr. Westmore inspected Ed's handiwork and found to his satisfaction that the fingerbar worked as the assembly instructions specified.

He told Nathan and Will, "Take Ed to the meadow at the far end of the lake to show him the grass we'll be cutting. He can decide if it is ready. Ed will be in charge of us greenhorns for the hay harvest."

Not to everyone's joy, Ed pronounced the grass tall and dry enough to cut at once.

The AW work horses had pulled a buckboard, but they did not take to pulling the mower and rake any more kindly than the impressed human crew took to the haying process.

When Ed hitched the two largest horses to the mower, the animals snorted uneasily. They reared when he slapped the reins along their backs to indicate that they were to pull the monstrosity behind them. Red Curlew came from the sidelines to hold the horses' head-stall straps and to talk in quieting language. It required a whole day of persuasion in the barnyard to train two teams, one for the mower and one for the rake. Lighter horses pulled the rake.

Ed, as he had glumly foreseen, operated the mower. The native meadow grass that looked like a deep, soft billow as it waved on the stalk was not an easy crop to harvest. Underneath was a bumpy terrain with no resemblance to the cultivated soil of an Iowa alfalfa hay field. Ed jiggled about on the high metal seat, knowing that he was expected to set an example of stoicism. Mr. Westmore drove the rake to gather the grass into rows. Nathan, Will, the tribal cousins, and the oldest Westmore boys forked the hay into shocks.

The grass was thick with rattlesnakes. As they tried to scuttle away, the ground crew pierced them with pitchforks until Mr. Westmore said, "Let us not kill the snakes indiscriminately. Because of the gophers they eat, they save grass roots."

Instead of slithering off at the approach of the rake and the team of horses, one large Western mountain rattler stood its ground and coiled into a circle. It raised its head, showed its fangs, and fiercely sounded its buzzer. The rake team rolled its eyes in fright, whinnied loudly, and tried to back up. Mr. Westmore jumped from the seat, grabbed Leschi's pitchfork, and with the handle, beat the rattler about the head until it lay dead.

"It would have struck in another second," Will voiced the general fear.

The sun was already hot and the dust thick in the nostrils of the crew.

"What time is it, dammit?" Nathan asked impatiently.

The Old Man drew his silver watch from the overall pocket on his chest.

"Only ten o'clock. Cuss all you want. You might as well resign yourselves to this work for several weeks. After we finish this bottomland, we still have the grass in the cache to cut. We'll make two haystacks for winter feeding."

When all the grass in the lake pasture stood in shocks, the crew expected time off. Red Curlew came to his brother-in-law to say that he and his friends would like to receive half their pay with half the job done. They had been working hard for four days. They wanted a holiday in town before starting the cache grass.

Mr. Westmore denied the request. "While the lake shocks dry, we shall cut in the other field. If I left you loose in town with ten dollars apiece, that would be the last we would see of you till you had drunk up half your wages."

Red Curlew insisted, "I told my friends that I could get them time off."

The boss was adamant. "We agreed you would stay until the work was finished."

The Indian men muttered in their own dialect. They drew aside.

"What are they saying?" Ed asked Nathan.

"They're mad at Red Curlew. He says they must do what the boss wants them to do."

Red Curlew's three Indian friends threw down their pitchforks in anger. They shouted words that shamed him.

"Now they're really talking foolishness," Nathan said. "They're tellin' Red Curlew he should act like a chief, not take orders from a white man. He is the son of dead Chief White Stone Mountain. Only trouble is old Chief White Stone Mountain never named anyone chief to follow him. The next chief is not always the son."

Mr. Westmore approached the argument. He ordered the Indian men to take up their pitchforks and carry them to the barn.

The Indians ceased their quarreling and grimly stalked the quarter mile to the bunkhouse. Red Curlew walked with the hands and the Westmores.

Ed and Mr. Westmore came last to the barn. As they unhitched the teams, Ed was acutely aware of the Old Man's worry.

"I hope I have not caused too much trouble in the tribe. On occasion, I am forced to remember that I am a white man among them."

Red Curlew came from the bunkhouse. "It is Saturday. Tomorrow is Sunday. My friends have gone camping in the hills for one day. They will be back on Monday."

"Thank you, Red Curlew," Carr Westmore said. "They will feel more friendly after a day hunting. I hope they did not have a bottle."

"No bottle," Red Curlew said morosely. His uncertain loyalty to his brother-in-law was apparent.

All four Indian men were on hand Monday morning.

"The Old Man won this time," Nathan said.

When Opening Flower served a plentiful noon dinner, the crew became a cohesive unit again. The Indians chatted jocularly with Opening Flower, who was, after all, a princess in their family. Besides, there was still the prospect of twenty dollars' wages.

The Indians followed behind the mower and rake to build shocks in the cache. Carr Westmore remained with the Indians and Will and Nathan and threw his clumps of hay into the wagonbeds, forkload for forkload. Ed agreed to direct the building of the two haystacks. To keep as much hay as possible off the ground, he made sure they were built to maximum height.

As the final chore, lodgepole pine fences were constructed to encircle the stacks, barring stock from access. For the present, the cattle fed over every hill and in every draw on the bunchgrass, which, although nourishing, could not be cut with efficiency.

On Friday, when the Old Man gave Red Curlew and his friends their twenty-dollar gold pieces, they hopped bareback on their mustangs and raced for Oroville.

Analix, standing next to Ed as her cousins disappeared through the trees, said soberly, "I wish they didn't sell liquor in Oroville. Mama doesn't like her brother to get drunk. As long as he drinks, she will not agree to his being chief."

"I'M EXPECTING YOU to stay on. Nathan and Will need you," Mr. Westmore told Ed. "The cows on Salmon meadows should be moved to the foothills. Then we'll dig postholes for the fence across the cache; after that, clean the waterholes and pack salt to the licks."

Nathan and Will listened with dark faces. The Old Man smiled at his hands, "I have one more chore that I didn't mention. I'm sending you to Loomis for supplies before we move the herd."

Three faces brightened to a degree that made the children laugh. After supplies were bought, there was a chance to hear community news at the saloon and to have the drink not allowed at the AW.

Next morning Nathan, Ed, and Will came expectantly from the bunkhouse. They had washed thoroughly at the pump. The Old Man, his plate pushed aside, was compiling a list; Opening Flower and the girls were offering suggestions.

"Thus far I have flour, salt, lard, coffee, baking powder, soda, prunes, dried apples, beans, and sugar," he read.

"And something good!" the boys added.

"You mean tea for Mama?" Papa teased.

"No! Jelly beans and licorice!"

"And peppermints!" Bethany said.

"That much candy will cost a great deal."

"Mama! Make Papa buy us some jelly beans and licorice!"

Mama smiled mischievously. "Beef jerky is good."

"Ugh! Oh!"

"If your pop is too stingy to allow a treat, I'll buy you two bits worth of junk myself," Nathan interposed.

Papa quit pretending. "Nathan carries the pouch. He can take some money for candy if he thinks you deserve it."

"Where are you going, Papa?" Analix asked. "You're dressed to go somewhere."

Mr. Westmore's face sobered. "I'd prefer to go to Loomis, but I must ride to St. Mary's to see Father deRouge."

"About Tommeo being killed?"

Her father nodded assent. "While you are in Loomis, Nathan, visit the marshal and tell him Tommeo's mother will take forty dollars as payment for her son's being killed. The drummer should pay; he has a good stake from all those guns he bought for sixty-five cents and sold at forty dollars."

No one remarked at the tears rolling down Mama's cheeks.

IN LOOMIS, THE wagon stopped first at the mercantile company. Shortly afterward in the saloon, the barkeeper slid three mugs of beer along the counter. Ed lifted the foaming stein to his mouth and tried to keep swallowing as long as Nathan and Will. At the end of their drafts, Nathan and Will emitted satisfied "Ah's." Ed decided that he could never become a drunk as his mother feared, at least not on locally brewed beer.

Ross Woodard listened gravely to the details of the settlement for the life of the Inkamip.

"Can't understand why drummers come to town and try to get the whites on the warpath. The Injuns don't want to fight anymore—not even old Joseph of the Nez Perce. He's minding his own business at Nespelem, or else he's dead. His People won't talk about him. Between the squaw men and the priest, we've never once had a real uprising in this country since Kamiakin.

"I reckon the marshal will be glad to have the gun salesman out of jail. He's been raising holy hell about his unlawful detention."

Nathan, Will, and Ed were back at the AW by nightfall. Mr. Westmore had already arrived.

"Everything calmed down at the mission?" Nathan asked.

The Old Man snapped, "An Indian mother settling for forty dollars for the death of her son! It is a judicial farce. I disapprove of many aspects of English life, but we could do with the importation of British jurisprudence. The next time a rascal expects to evade punishment because of lax local law enforcement, I intend to see that the judge and sheriff fulfill their duties to the letter of the law."

"Even for cattle theft, Boss?" Will asked.

"I've always tolerated the theory that no one should go to jail for killing a beef to eat when he's hungry, but the picture is changing. Organized bands of thieves are operating. I hear the butcher shops aren't particular where beef comes from as long as it 'dresses out pretty.'"

Ed felt his stomach tighten at the expression he had first heard from Clay Brown, his erstwhile mining partner.

"I stood in the brush last week," Mr. Westmore related, "while Cowboy Jimmie roped an AW calf, built a fire, and branded it over our brand with some iron I never saw before. Just as he let the calf up, I stepped into the open and asked him what he thought he was doing. He took to his heels. I brought the cow and calf home. They're in the corral. If you see Jimmie, tell him where our cow and his calf are shut up. If he thinks they are both his, he can come and claim them."

The Westmore household woke one morning to heavy winds and rain outside.

"It's too sopping wet for you children to be roaming the hills today," Mr. Westmore said.

"But what can we do inside?" Leschi exclaimed.

"All of you can review reading, writing, and arithmetic."

"I can be teacher!" Analix decreed.

"You know your multiplication tables best," Papa agreed.

"She is a mean teacher!" Tamma protested.

Mr. Westmore chuckled, "Get yourself a willow switch to crack over their backs if necessary, Analix!"

Analix scrambled to the sleeping loft and came down with a dozen pencils and ruled tablets, and an assortment of dog-eared primers.

"You should order us some more books from Vancouver, Papa," she said judiciously. "Everybody, take a place at the table. These texts will have to do for the present."

"She's a regular Madame Catechist!" Nathan exclaimed.

"Don't make fun of me!" she ordered. "You and Will and Ed should sit down at this table and write letters home. We have regular mail service now."

Although Ed had planned never to communicate with his family, he found himself at the table, pencil in hand, and a ruled sheet of tablet paper before him.

"How do you know I can write?" Ed quizzed his teacher.

"I know you can," Analix retorted. "Maybe Nathan and Will have an excuse to write poorly because there weren't schools when their families came West, but I can tell you've been to school. How many years?"

"Eleven long ones. I was hoping to be through forever."

"Eleven years!" the older children looked up from their tablets in astonishment.

"Analix went to the mission school three years before it burned down," Bethany said. "She learned everything. I only went two years."

"It takes more than three years to learn everything, Bethany," Analix reproved. "I'm sure even more than eleven years."

"Anyway, Ed's gone to school a lot longer than you," Tamma asserted. "He doesn't act so smart and bother everybody about it, either."

Analix faltered. Tamma had struck a vulnerable spot.

"Would you like to be the teacher, Ed?" Telah asked.

"Deliver me! Analix probably knows more than I do. Some people learn more in three years of school than others do in eleven."

Analix's face lost its shadow. "Then if you don't think you would like to, I may as well keep on. Kahpat, let me see how much of the alphabet you remember. Everyone else keep busy with your writing!"

"Isn't there something we should be doing, Boss?" Nathan appealed to Mr. Westmore, who was oiling his boots.

"If you'd prefer to go to the woodpile and split logs for the fireplace, you're welcome to do so."

"Ding blast it! Gimme a pencil!" Nathan sighed.

Ed wrote: "Dear Mother, Brother, and Sister:

"I have found a place to work. The country is full of mining claims, but a lot of people are leaving the diggings. I tried mining myself, but I found I can earn more in the cattle business; so I have taken a job on a ranch."

Up to that moment, Ed had regarded himself as a temporarily dislocated mining engineer, but now in his own words he had committed himself to a change of course.

"I expect to buy a few cattle whenever I get paid. When I have built up a small herd, I'll file on a homestead of my own. This country is now being opened for settlement by white people."

He concluded, "I am working for a man with an Indian wife. She is a good cook. Their ten children are smart as whips."

Mr. Westmore sent Leschi and Owhi to the post office in Conconully to mail the letters. Ed expected no reply.

Summer waned. A second hay harvest took place. The cowhands searched the hills for steers and herded them into the cache.

"We'll be heading for the railhead in a few days," Will told Ed. "You're in for a sad case of dust poison."

"Where do we drive the cattle?" Ed asked.

"Railhead's at Coulee City now. Takes a week to reach there."

"I got off the train at Sprague," Ed said. "I remember where Coulee City is.

First time I saw the Columbia."

"It's one long trip. The Westmores used to drive their herds up the Similkameen, but once you get the cattle to the railhead at Coulee City, they're carried all the way to the Seattle Union Stockyards. It's easier on the cowhands, but I doubt if it's any easier on the cattle. I've heard when cattle get to Seattle they look like they been run through a sawmill."

Ed's mental images of cattle drives came from the pulp magazines. Behind the haystack in Iowa, his eyes had bulged as he read of bellowing herds, pawing dust as they moved to market. His vision was of a thousand head of scrubby, longhorn Spanish stock pushed down the cowtrail to the din of whoops, cracking whips, and cussing that destroyed the immortal soul of every man on the drive. The cows' tongues were hanging out as they stampeded toward the lone waterhole reached at the end of the day.

His first real cattle drive was a complete letdown from the standpoint of drama. The cattlemen below Oroville—around Aeneas Mountain and the Salmon meadows—converged with their steers cut out for sale for a joint drive to Coulee City. Macaulay, Loudon, Griswold, Thorpe, and Westmore outfits were assembled in mid-September along Sinlahekin Creek, each herd cared for by two or three white cowboys and a handful of Indians. The biggest surprise for Ed came on the day before departure when he saw a familiar chuckwagon drawing across the meadow and Bill Beeman hailing him from his customary seat. Frank Beeman and another brother, Fred, whom Ed had never met before, were bringing a herd to join the drive.

"You guys quit the pack train business?" Ed asked.

"Heck, no. You'd be surprised how many businesses we need to earn a living! See you took our advice about finding a spread with a good cook. You must weigh twenty pounds more than when we saw you last!" Frank exclaimed.

"Come to think of it, I have been eating pretty steady."

"Somebody musta loaned you their razor, too," Frank observed. "See you lost that baby fuzz."

"Bought my own razor," Ed grinned back.

TOWARDS NIGHTFALL, NATHAN told Will and Ed, "The boss says we're pulling out early tomorrow morning. That means before first light, so we better hit the sack."

For the first time since he was six years old, Ed went to bed in broad daylight. At the end of the next day's drive, he was tired enough to go to bed before nightfall again. But by the third day, he had gained stamina—perhaps from the nourishing food from the chuckwagon and the purity of the air, but mostly because of pride. He was determined to be as husky as the others.

Westmore cattle were the tamest animals in the drive; some other four-year-old steers, whose only contact with men had been at calf-branding, were as dangerous as wild boars. But the crew skillfully cut out such steers from the main herd, and in a day or two had succeeded in punching and prodding the wild ones into acceptance that they were to move in one direction.

The combined herd of eight hundred steers moved at a steady walk from eighteen to twenty miles daily, were watered at carefully calculated distances, and then were allowed to graze or bed down for the night while five men kept watch.

The drive moved south on the west side of the Okanogan River to the fording place at the confluence with the Columbia. The Columbia crossing proceeded, dawn to dark, for two days, with the help of eight Indian cowboys whose ponies were even better trained than those of the white men. The cattle were driven into the water in V-shaped contingents, thirty at a time. Indians in bark canoes guided the animals. When a canoe overturned in the water, the guides swam calmly along with the cattle. Eventually the entire herd was transferred from one bank to the other. It was a time to celebrate.

The chuckwagons and cooks had made the crossing on rafts at three o'clock in the morning on the second day, in order to begin preparations for a huge meal. While the other men and horses began the struggle from bank to bank with the stock, the cooks slaughtered and dressed out a young steer. The carcass smoldered all day on a barbecue spit over a sagebrush fire. Beans simmered in tomato sauce in kettles; potatoes baked in the coals of the fire.

With everything safely over, the owners of the herds invited everyone, "Fall to!"

TWO DAYS LATER the journey ended at the stockyards at Coulee City. The Seattle Union Stockyards representative, who had been awaiting the arrival, signed a receipt after a count of the herd. The drive was officially terminated. The animals would be weighed upon their arrival by train in Seattle.

Each hand, with a twenty-dollar gold piece burning a hole in his pocket, made his way to downtown Coulee City. A banner across the main street proclaimed: "Roundup Dance at the Town Hall! Everybody Welcome!"

"Let's go!" Nathan exclaimed. "Come on, Ed!"

Ed hesitated. He smiled sheepishly, "Don't know how to dance."

"Neither does anybody else," Will said.

"I think I'd rather go sleep in a hotel."

"You coward!"

They grabbed him by either elbow and propelled him toward the loud music of B Flat Bill's Band. Four square dances were going full swing on a platform built in the middle of the street. Nearby, people were lined up before a row of beer kegs.

"Three beers are what you need!" Nathan and Will told Ed. They practically poured the beer down his throat, as well as his shirt front.

Ed began to see the fun and danced with the best of the frolickers. At four in the morning, a girl in a red dress asked him if he wanted to go home to sleep with her.

The next day he could not remember whether he had or not. He came to sensibility sitting alongside Nathan and Will on steps in the residential part of town.

Ed discovered that his twenty-dollar gold piece was missing, but he decided not to question Nathan or Will about his behavior of the night before. His companions themselves were in no condition to make a clear report. They hobbled into town to the livery stable, where a clear-eyed Carr Westmore had agreed to meet them. The three AW cowhands nursed headaches and refrained from conversation for the first day on the trail home.

When the men returned from the cattle drive, Analix flourished a letter under Ed's nose. "It's for you. It must be from your mother."

As she handed it to him, Ed recognized his mother's large, angular, upright script on the envelope. Wishing that he had resisted Analix's bullying, which had caused him to write to Iowa in the first place, Ed opened his mail and unfolded two sheets of lined stationery.

Resentment and anger overcame him as he read. As he had expected, his mother wrote bluntly: "We are glad you found work and are well, but can you stay free of lice working for a half-breed family? The pastor says that all people of mixed blood are shiftless, corrupt, drunken, and full of disease. I cannot imagine them 'smart as whips.'"

Ed stopped reading and shredded the letter to pieces. He dropped them into the kitchen stove fire.

"What a way to treat your mother's letter! You didn't even read it all!" Analix cried.

"There was nothing in it worth reading."

"The postage cost twenty-five cents!"

"I expect the expense hurt my mother, but I wish she'd saved her money!"

"I'd want a letter from my mother, but she can't write one."

"Even if my mother can write, she isn't as good a person as yours."

"Is she bad, like the white people who shoot Indians who stand outside saloons?"

"No, she wouldn't shoot Indians. She would only despise them and let them know it."

"I understand that, too. She is like Papa's mother in Victoria. She wants nothing to do with us because we are half-breeds. Did your mother say she despises half-breeds, too?"

"For some reason I thought your grandmother was dead."

"No, she is alive. Grandfather Westmore froze to death in the Hard Winter, but Grandmother was not here. She has always stayed in Victoria."

SIGNS APPEARED THAT the season was changing from fall to winter. A chill wind blew; squirrels stored pine nuts; tamarack trees shed their needles, leaving only a naked expanse of white trunks and branches. Mr. Westmore and his hands hitched four horses to the wagon for the trip to Blackwell's store and freighted home a supply of staples: barrels of flour and sugar, beans, rice, salt, soda, dry yeast, lentils, prunes, oatmeal, and cornmeal.

The porkers that had lazed in the pen below the barn all summer were slaughtered; their lard was rendered, hams and bacon were smoked. Opening Flower made corned beef by packing meat in barrels filled with a brine of water, salt, sugar, and saltpeter. She also cut beef into small strips and hung them to dry for jerky. Indian relatives brought her smoked salmon, deer meat, and dried roots. From a bee tree in the hills, she collected crocks of honey.

For winter fuel, the men felled pine trees and snaked them home with the team. The boys took turns at the sawhorse and axe to convert the logs into units suitable for the cook stove and fireplace. The mountain of wood covered the north end of the house.

Mr. Westmore laid an iron pipe from the spring to the water box, which he dug in the floor of the back shed. One no longer needed to lug in buckets of water from the frigid outdoors.

The children garnered the burden of Northern Spies and Spitzbergens, gift trees from Okanogan Smith years before.

Nathan and Will spaded up the Gold Coin potatoes and stored them in the cellar. To protect the chickens from weasels, the men plugged the holes in the coops with wire and tar paper. The household would have a supply of fresh eggs through the winter, and at a twist of the wrist, could enjoy stewed or fried chicken as a change from the salt and smoked meat diet.

WINTER, WHEN IT arrived, was hard; but the AW cattle were secure. The one- and two-year-old steers were fed from the haystack by the lake, the pregnant cows from the stack in the cache. Even Nathan and Will admitted they were glad for the grass mountains.

Once each day the hands drove a sledgeload of hay from the fenced-in stacks to the feedlot. When the cattle saw the laden sled, they plowed through the snow to meet it. They would follow behind in a long queue that gradually grew shorter as animals stopped by twos and threes at the carefully distributed hay mounds. Lowing and snorting, the herd wrapped their tongues about the feed. The steers drank from holes chopped in Conconully Lake, the cows from a trough at the spring that never froze.

The Westmore family and their hired hands spent the long winter evenings around the cedar table in the big house. By the light from the coal oil lamp, Analix helped the younger children read aloud. Nathan and Will tried to learn to play a guitar from the directions that came with it by mail order.

Bethany placed her hands over her ears at the dull twanging produced by Nathan and Will. She grabbed the guitar from them, and after a few sweeps of her hand on the strings, improvised a compelling dance rhythm. Mr. Westmore, working at his business ledger, looked up in surprise.

"Bethany," he said, "will play music for the winter dance at Osoyoos Lake."

Opening Flower smiled and nodded. Her daughter's talent did not surprise her.

Opening Flower, following the custom of Okanogan Indian women, kept her hands busy at crafts. All summer she had collected materials in her grass workbasket—porcupine quills, beads, feathers, grasses, furs, and bones. Now had come the hours of creation. She soaked porcupine quills to soften them and flattened each one with her teeth before she appliqued it to the grass baskets that she wove.

One evening she undertook a special project. She brought out a roll of deerskins, her awl, and sinews which she had cut into delicate slenderness for thread.

"I make Ed a jacket," she announced. "He shivers."

Ed was amazed to hear Opening Flower speak English.

"She can speak a good deal of English," her husband said, "but she will not speak it in front of outsiders. You are family now, Ed. She wants you as warm as the rest of us. Let her measure you."

With the change in weather, Mr. Westmore, Nathan, Will, and the boys donned jackets that Opening Flower had fashioned and decorated—soft, beautiful, trim-fitting, and fur-lined.

She propelled Ed to the center of the stage and measured him for the tailoring project.

Ed was nearly ashamed to show the eagerness with which he awaited completion of his new garment. The wind came through the holes in the elbows of the red and black mackinaw.

When the snow interfered with hunting, the Okanogan Indians came from the highlands and the Kettle River country to make winter camp on the shores of Osoyoos Lake. With the camp only a day ride away, Red Curlew now spent many evenings with the Westmores. He told stories for those gathered in the lamplight.

Red Curlew revealed that the Okanogan Mountains were people before the Earth turned over. "At the summit of the pass, where we go from the Kettle River country to this valley, a rock stands in the shape of a woman. Long ago she was a flesh-and-blood maiden, Amtoos. Some call her Namtuck; the palefaces call her the Hee Hee stone. Her People were the Kalispels, who live where camas grows."

In their summer wanderings, the Westmore children had visited the Hee Hee stone many times. It meant spring when their kinsmen, riding single file up the pass, stopped at the summit to lay a bit of horse's tail hair at the rock pile. For good luck, some travelers dropped ribbons or knives. Old men and women hit themselves with sticks in places that were sore. Amtoos would cure them of their pains, Red Curlew said.

"How did she get there in the first place?" Nathan asked the question that the Indian was waiting to hear.

Red Curlew lapsed into Sinkaietk. Analix translated.

"This maiden of the Kalispels came over here to get herself a husband. She had heard about Chopaka, who was a great brave and chief of all the mountains hereabouts. She wore a beaded doeskin dress and moccasins; she painted her face with red paint. In her hand she carried camas as treasure because no camas grew in the Okanogan country.

"She made camp for a while near Keller and sat down to rest from her trip. All the big mountains went to see what she looked like and decided she was the best-looking woman they had ever seen. There was no sense letting Chopaka have her. Moses and Little Moses jumped on Chopaka and started to beat him up. They treated him so roughly you can still see the wounds they gave him.

"But Chopaka was still the biggest and strongest. He saw the beautiful maiden and decided he would show her that he was the chief and the one she should marry. He knocked Moses' and Little Moses' heads together and threw them around the countryside. Nekotea tried to get into the fight and got smashed so flat that he was no mountain anymore. Moses had to go sit down above Omak. Joe Buck went up the Salmon River and sat down where he is now. That other fellow got put up at Camp McKinney. Bonaparte was split in half.

"The maiden went close to Chesaw, where she is now, and sat down and giggled, 'Hee, hee, hee!'

"They all watched her, but nobody got her.

"Chopaka said, 'See, now I am the highest of all around here.'

"But she said, 'I'm not going to marry any of you. I'm going to sit right here and make people pay me something each time they go past me, or I will give them bad luck.'

"Where she sat, she formed a rock, and nobody got her.

"And so I come back from before the Earth turned over," Red Curlew finished the tale. "*Ziken-kiken-splak!*"

"Why don't you go out to get yourselves husbands, Analix and Bethany?" Owhi joked.

"You tell us a story, Papa. Tell us how we came to be here," Tamma begged. "Tell us how you came here and found Mama."

Opening Flower lifted her head from her needlework and smiled permission.

As he and the other hands sat with the Westmores, Ed listened to the legend of how the settlers of the Okanogan learned to put up hay for winter.

III.

Hay for Winter

9.

Legend of the Hard Winter

Arthur Vestmore, Carr's father, was one of the horde who swarmed to America from the Old World during the Gold Rush period. On arriving in California, he was struck with a keen, unexpected sense of disappointment, for by the time he had rounded the Horn in a clipper ship, disembarked, and made ready to go to the mining fields, the first flush of the gold strike had passed.

Knowing nothing of minerals or where or how to find them, he had expected to scoop a fortune in nuggets hastily into leather pouches and rush back to England to rescue his beloved from the encroaching arms of his eldest brother, who had the advantage of being heir to the family estate. With no fortune to be found in the California desert, he rallied to the lure of tales of gold and silver newly discovered along the rivers in northern British territory. A wild stampede had started to New Caledonia, which later became part of British Columbia.

He paid sixty dollars to be crammed aboard the *Pacific Mail* coastal steamer, which was loaded to three times its capacity. The sea voyage ended at Fort Victoria on the Island of Vancouver at the mouth of Puget Sound, where Queen Victoria's subjects were busily constructing impressive buildings and doing their best to shunt away the unpleasant swarms of people pushing their way through the crown colony to the mainland. In the tent city of adventurers on the outskirts of Victoria, Westmore fell in with other Britishers, including a sailor, Billy Barker. Forming themselves into a party, they bought two Indian canoes at the Hudson's Bay Company for the trip to the interior along the Simon Fraser River as far as Fort Hope. They continued overland by horseback to Princeton; on to Keremeos, the 'meeting of the winds,' and into the Lake Okanogan valley.

Joyous participation in the Cariboo gold rush, named for the stately animals who roamed the forest, contributed a great deal of breadth to Westmore's previous education; and he, indeed, found fortune to equal that of his brother's in England. His party went first to Antler Creek, but there the

135

gold had already been exhausted. Hearing of a new strike at Williams Creek, the Britishers headed there, but found when they arrived that all the land worth pegging had been preempted. Although the creek bed above the canyon was rich in ore, the land below was without a gold trace. Billy Barker, who had assumed leadership of the party, persuaded his cohorts to stake claims in the supposedly worthless area. Barker guessed that the land below the canyon might not be the original channel of Williams Creek. If they dug down far enough, they would find gold. With a hundred feet allowed for each claim, they had a total of seven hundred feet which they would mine on shares.

Despite the amusement of other miners, Billy Barker coerced his group to dig a deep hole. As soon as their tents were set up, they began by felling timber to wall the sides of the shaft and to construct a roof over it. The preliminaries accomplished, the seven took turns laboring in their pit with a shovel. When they had burrowed to the depth of a man's reach, they rigged up a windlass to haul up loads in a bucket on the end of a rope. The first twenty feet were gravel; then the earth turned to slime. The Barkerites invested their last sixteen dollars in a pair of secondhand boots for the man down the hole. They went fifty feet; still no reward. Sailor Barker, who by now had the reputation of being crazy, delved on even by candlelight. His comrades were more than willing to give up, but he told them to lower him one last time. From fifty-two feet down he sent up a bucket with the usual load of slaty clay, but this time gold nuggets peppered the muck! Barker had struck a gold pay streak five feet thick—the old channel of Williams Creek!

As the news first traveled through the camp, it was considered as one more joke about the daft sailor, but when the truth became known, everyone who had been above the canyon pulled up his stakes and jammed them into the ground below, near the Barker claim. In days, a solid wall of tents belonging to claimants lined the ancient channel. On the eighteen-foot-wide business street, the establishments that accompany riches sprang up quickly. Most of the new wealth went the way of drunkenness, gambling, and whoring. Billy Barker treated the entire camp to drinks, then went on a spree to Victoria and came back with a wife, who soon showed her fickle nature and left him brokenhearted as well as broke.

Westmore, as convivial as the rest, soon saw that the difficult part of accumulating a fortune was in not squandering his earnings. All the while, he was still enamored of the memory of his English sweetheart. He must save sufficient gold to claim her hand, he thought. He began pouring his gold dust into canvas sacks obtained from the Hudson's Bay Company courier, and sending the tagged sacks to Victoria for deposit. He knew he could never ask Katherine Faversham to live as a miner's woman at the diggings. He must seek a way of life more acceptable to a daughter of an English aristocrat.

In 1863, with a reserve supply of gold in his leather pouch, he left the camp and traveled down the Similkameen River to the Okanogan River, which widened into Osoyoos Lake at the international boundary. He stopped to talk with Judge William Carmichael Haynes, the British customs officer, and to C. B. Bash, the United States official.

The native inhabitants of this region were the Sinkaietk, or Okanogan Indians, who gloried in their bands of ponies. They also owned cattle, acquired by trade and theft from white drovers; but their main meat animals were still the large mule deer that browsed on every forested hill.

At Osoyoos Lake, Westmore found trader Hiram "Okanogan" Smith comfortably established with his wife Mary, daughter of Chief Manuel. Smith grew all his own food—fruits, vegetables, and beef. He had planted apple trees, peach trees, and grapevines, which he had packed in by horses from Hope. Okanogan's twenty-foot-long dining table was often filled to its entire length with Americans who had come up the banks of the Columbia River and its tributary, the Okanogan River, on their way to the mines.

The trader assured Westmore that the land was free for the taking. The hay and grassland would provide abundant food in year-round pastures for all the livestock anyone could accumulate. If Westmore chose to raise cattle, he would find a ready market for beef with the hungry miners in the diggings. Jerome Harper, a prosperous cattle dealer above the line, had recently purchased an extra four hundred four-year-old steers from Dan Drumheller, who had driven them from the Walla Walla country. After feeding them on grass until December, Harper expected each to weigh nine hundred pounds. He would make fifty dollars a head on them. With so many cattle to oversee, he would likely be glad to sell the beginnings of a herd—not the steers, but a hundred head of his other cattle, cows with calf, and bulls.

"You could leave them here with my stock through the winter," Okanogan offered. "It's open grazing all year round."

Arthur chose land near Conconully Lake, a body of water smaller than Osoyoos, thirty miles below the boundary. On a hill overlooking the lake, he built a log cabin to establish squatter's rights. He returned across the line to dicker with Jerome Harper for a hundred head of cattle: cows with calf, and two bulls. Then Westmore drove them back to the range and left them with repeated assurances from Smith that they would grow and multiply during his absence until the following spring.

When the first snow threatened, Arthur Westmore retraced his way along the Cariboo trail to Victoria. Road crews were now building a government road, and stem-wheelers plied the Fraser River.

At Victoria, he went first to the Hudson's Bay Company to ascertain the state of his finances. His canvas bags of dust and nuggets, tagged with his name, stood on the open shelves at the rear of the store. The company's financial officer assured him that they contained the cash equivalent of fifty thousand pounds sterling.

He wrote to Katherine Faversham that he was coming in triumph to claim her hand at last, and landed in Britain with the same vessel that carried his letter. The dumbfounded young woman secretly and in haste canceled tentative plans for her wedding to the elder brother. In a flurry, she was whisked through a time-saving civil ceremony that made her the wife of a remote young man to whose tragic loss she had nearly been reconciled. She waved a fearful, unbelieving adieu to her parents as she and her husband boarded the *Great Eastern* for New York.

The new British ship, hailed as the largest ever built, stretched an endless six hundred ninety-three feet in length. It had a beam of eighty-two feet and a carrying capacity of four thousand passengers. The iron-hulled monster was equipped for traveling by both steam and sail, with five smokestacks and six masts each rigged for the square and fore and aft sails.

From New York to San Francisco, the bridal couple went by clipper ships, the Atlantic and Pacific sea voyages broken by an overland journey at the Isthmus of Panama. From California, they traveled on a wooden paddle wheeler to British Columbia.

On the long way Katherine was buoyed only by Arthur's reiterated dramatizations of herself as wife of a master of the New World, arrayed in finery in a faraway salon.

At Victoria, her husband gave her an opportunity to rest before they undertook the strenuous journey to the interior. When they attended services at the Church of England, the bride sensed at once that the female parishioners, who displayed every pretense of English ladies, regarded her as a creature on her way to doom. As she started the journey to the Okanogan country, the feeling grew heavy upon her that her sisters in the faith were right. Jostled by uncouth hordes of men, she and Arthur traveled on the stem-wheeler *Umatilla* along the Fraser as far as Hope.

Taking courage from the fact that she had packed her proper riding habit, she managed the horseback portion of the travel overland. But she went into a frenzy when her husband deposited her in a canoe manned by three savages. He coaxingly pointed out the beauties of the scenery and tried to divert her with Kamloops Indian tales. She heard nothing, feeling only the sting of the mosquitoes and the pinch of her shoes as she stumbled around the portages. Was she not awed by the magnificence of the cliffs at the coming-together of the valleys! She looked above to primeval wilderness and was overwhelmed. The whole forest moaned. She ran back along the trail in hysterical fear. She could not—would not—go another step! Arthur must return her to Victoria at once!

Nothing dissuaded her. Arthur Westmore escorted her back to the coast and negotiated, with much of the gold in his canvas bags, for the construction of a traditional English cottage resembling Ann Hathaway's. Katherine never swayed from her refusal to visit the faraway place of terror toward which she had been dragged like a captive. She would not even have been living on British soil! She occupied herself among the Episcopalians of Victoria, whose way of life approximated that of her girlhood.

Arthur visited her at intervals which she considered "furloughs," like those of British husbands home from India and other far reaches of the empire. She could well afford to remain in the New World, for her husband fulfilled at least part of her expectations: he arrived each fall after cattle sales with a seemingly limitless supply of wealth. His cattle ranged summer and winter on the lush bunchgrass of the Okanogan Valley.

BARKERVILLE, FOR A time the largest city west of Toronto and north of San Francisco, dwindled in population as the rich placer diggings were exhausted on Williams Creek. The hundred-foot claims fell into the hands of American companies that installed sluices and flumes, overshot wheels, pumps, and hoists.

The "pick and panners" emigrated down the Similkameen River to a site at which Okanogan Smith, the many-talented entrepreneur, declared he had discovered a mother lode. He had pegged the ground at the base of Mount Chopaka and bragged that he could pay the Civil War debt. When mining laws adopted by Congress in 1872 declared mineral deposits free to exploration and possession by the locator, Smith organized the Similkameen Mining District. Its membership included his neighbors who had settled on the Fifteen Mile Strip along the border. The majority had Indian wives and lived in friendly fashion with their wives' relatives.

ARTHUR WESTMORE, WHO continued to have a ready market for his beef, came to Victoria in the fall of 1873. Katherine, to celebrate his homecoming and possibly to protect herself from too abrupt intimacy with a bronze-faced, broad-shouldered foreigner, invited guests to a formal dinner party lit with candelabra. The two daughters of the household sat with guests, but son Carr, age seven, had long since been fed his supper. Hidden behind the portieres, out of the way of the servants who might order him to bed, the child listened to his father's talk.

Carr was not the only male in the dining room listening with rapt attention; for this reason, Mrs. Westmore allowed her husband's degenerated manners to go unrebuked, and his protracted anecdotes to dominate attention.

"Jack Splawn and I rode to Yakima this summer to bring back two hundred cows to add to my herd. Jack is a big, handsome American, with a head of bright yellow hair. He's been a cattle driver since he was eight years old. We bought our stock from Major John Thorp, who had them cut out and ready to start.

"We drove the animals slowly without incident until we came to the mouth of the Okanogan River, where it joins the Columbia. There were six Indians on the river bank who asked for the job of helping us to swim the animals across and to ferry our packs in their canoe. Jack and I would swim our own horses. The Indians yelled and waved brush to shoo the herd into the water, then took off right away in their canoe with our packs. The cows were swimming right along until the blinding sun got into their eyes. They were all bunched up in the middle of the river in the strong current. They started swimming around and around, getting closer together all the time. We called to the Indians in the canoe to come help us, but they kept paddling to the far shore. They dumped our packs on the bank and took off down the river. Jack and I were alone in the middle of the Columbia with two hundred crazy cows! Jack's cussing was the worst I've ever heard; I admit he wasn't doing all of it. While we swam our horses, we kept knocking the lead cows about the head until finally they strung out and finished swimming across. We didn't lose a cow, no thanks to the Indians!

"Those bucks had the nerve to come to our camp next morning. They said we owed them twenty dollars for helping us cross the river.

"'I'll pay you salmon eaters what you got coming!' Jack roars.

"He shoved and kicked them down to their canoe. I never saw Indians so obedient. They understood Jack!"

"You mention buying two hundred head of cattle," a guest spoke after the laughter died. "What cattle can you buy in the wilderness? Longhorns from Texas?"

"No," Westmore replied. "Shorthorns, Durhams. Cattle drovers have brought stock from California and Oregon for a long time. Jack Splawn plans to develop White-faced Hereford purebreds."

'What do you do for bulls?" another man asked. "Import them?"

Arthur Westmore shrugged. "We haven't yet sent to England. At present we follow what is not an ideal practice. When we separate the calves, we cut off most of the males' testicles, but spare every twentieth male for breeding."

Katherine stood abruptly. "Please! The ladies lack interest in the commonplaces of commerce!"

She invited the women to follow her to the parlor to see the new organ that had crossed the Atlantic in a clipper ship.

When the door had been closed a respectful length of time, Mr. Westmore resumed his description of life in the mining country: "A Campbellite preacher went into the saloon to haul his son from the gambling table; he began to watch what was going on. In chuck-a-luck, the dealer shakes a big dice marked 1, 2, 3, 4, 5, 6, in a leather box, then calls for guesses which number will come up on the roll. The preacher began to beg his son to save his immortal soul by leaving the premises.

"'Wait a minute,' the boy said. 'I have a bet going.'

"The father agreed to wait just a minute. After the announcement that Junior had correctly called the six spot, Papa laid down the whole family poke, maybe a hundred and fifty ounces, on the next roll. He lost it all, of course."

"Are the Indians friendly in the interior?" asked the Church of England priest.

"Moses, chief at Wenatchee, now behaves in a friendly manner to white persons," Westmore answered. "I suppose his manner does not reveal his true feelings, but he realizes that his People are outnumbered and that further resistance would result in their extermination.

"I met Moses once. He's an impressive, barrel-chested fellow. Jack, who has known him a long time, took me to see him at a big encampment at Crab Creek. While we walked toward the chief's tepee, we noticed that all the braves outside were tipsy and quarrelsome. They asked us what we wanted in their camp.

"Moses saved our skins by coming to the opening of his tepee and hailing us inside. He showed no effects of alcohol himself, but he must have been drinking. A ten-gallon keg of whiskey was standing in the middle of his tepee. He handed us one drink apiece with a tin cup, then said, 'I am your friend, but you should leave the camp. I cannot promise you safety for long.'

"He lifted up the skin of the tepee so that we could crawl out the back."

"It seems that he did not have any great authority as chief," the priest remarked.

"Perhaps it is because he is a chief named by white men," Westmore replied. "He was not a real Indian war chief like Kamiakin, who led the war against Governor Stevens. Kamiakin dressed in bright colors, wore a war bonnet, and rode a spotted horse with eagle feathers in its tail. The record is that Kamiakin fled to Canada in 1858, but Jack Splawn tells me of rumors that the chief is still hiding in the Palouse country. There were other warriors in the south central part of the territory: Owhi, Qualchan, Lokout.

"My Indian neighbors in the Okanogan River valley have remained peaceful for the most part: Chief Tonasket, Chief Susceptkain, Chief White Stone Mountain. They are trading for cattle."

"There seem to be a great many chiefs," a guest observed. "You are right," Mr. Westmore agreed. "Every family can have its own chief."

"I am curious as to how business is transacted in the interior without any currency," a Vancouver merchant remarked.

Mr. Westmore chuckled, "Happy you asked that question! It gives me the appropriate moment to display a souvenir."

With a flourish, Mr. Westmore produced a set of scales which he placed upon the bar. "Step right up, folks! A pinch of gold dust from your poke will buy you a drink. Sorry I don't have any tin cups!

"Every bartender in the mining camps has gold scales on his bar."

"How big is a pinch?" the merchant asked.

"These scales are only for appearance's sake. Drinks are 'on the house,'" the host assured everyone.

Amid cheers, he also produced a glass for each guest. The evening continued cheerfully with a round of chugalug and several more rounds of stories, both popular diversions in the Cariboo country.

NEXT MORNING THE seven-year-old boy in an Eton jacket sat at the breakfast table alone with his father, who had scarcely ever directed a word to him on the assumption that, raised by females, he would be a milksop. The boy cleared his throat, and gasping for breath, declared that although his mother and sisters could not bear mention of calf-breeding and Indians, he longed to see the frontier. Westmore for the first time felt a tug of affinity for his son. He broached the possibility to his wife that Carr should visit the Okanogan Valley for a summer.

Katherine shrieked, "Are you mad! He is no more than a baby!"

CARR WAS TEN years old before his mother could be persuaded to let him go to the cattle country. She always objected, "What will he do for suitable playmates? Associate as you do with savages and cowboys?"

The summer that Arthur responded, "Judge Haynes, the British customs official at the border, has a son," Katherine yielded. Perhaps a judge's son would be "genteel" enough for fellowship with a born aristocrat.

FATHER AND SON left on the stern-wheeler in April, 1877, and arrived at their destination on a bright morning when calves were being weaned on one side of Conconully Lake while their mothers were sequestered on the opposite side. Three hundred young animals demanding their mothers' milk made a deafening racket.

"You can stay with me as long as you like if you don't bawl like the calves for your mother," Carr's father said.

The boy laughed aloud and promised.

He adapted at once to the simple way of life followed by his father and the two young cowboys, Nathan and Will, who had remained with the Westmore cattle through the winter. He enthusiastically engaged in every activity from horseback riding to peeling potatoes for supper. After he had been at the camp three weeks, he asked his father, "When shall we visit Judge Haynes?"

Surprised at first, not remembering what he had said to Katherine about Judge Haynes having a son, Mr. Westmore took Carr with him to the British customs house.

The magistrate, who had come from County Cook, Ireland, in 1853, was not only collector of customs, but gold commissioner as well. His wife, Emily Josephine, daughter of a Crimean War veteran, had earned fame throughout the region by giving birth to the first white child.

Carr laughed to see a chubby one-year-old Valentine Carmichael Haynes wobbling on two feet from chair to chair in the Haynes residence.

"Is this my 'suitable' playmate?" he asked.

"Yes, but never tell your mother how old he is."

To CARR, THE Indians who had their summer lodge by Conconully Lake were by far the most attractive neighbors. He spied on them as he thought himself securely hidden in the cattails that grew at the edge of the lake. He had watched two women set up a lodge, a conical structure consisting of a frame of poles covered with deerskin. Smoke from the fire built in the interior rose above the tepee through open flaps at the top. Flaps on the side of the tepee could be opened and shut as a door.

One morning a pebble landed on the paleface's back and caused him to turn sharply. An Indian boy Carr's age dressed in a breechclout came forward. Carr moved sheepishly from the clump of cattails.

Despite the fact that they knew not a word of each other's language, communication was instantaneous between the two boys. They both were looking for a playmate. Red Curlew signaled to Carr that he should come along.

Red Curlew took Carr to the camp and presented him to his family. Carr was later able to translate their names: White Stone Mountain, a chief; Smiling Water, first wife; Cool Cloud, second wife; also Opening Flower, Red Curlew's half-sister. Red Curlew was the son of Smiling Water.

The two boys spent day after day together. They lassoed Indian ponies as the animals stood knee-deep, drinking from the lake. Each on a mount, Red Curlew and Carr rode over the hills until hunger called them to the tepee. The women welcomed them and fed them bowls of tasty fish and deer stews.

Every summer after 1877, Carr went with his father to the Okanogan and returned to school in Victoria in the fall. He seemed nearly a young Indian himself by the summer he reached fifteen. He and Red Curlew talked fluently in each other's language.

When the time neared for the drive to market and the trip back to the coast, Carr said he preferred not to return to Victoria for the winter but to stay with Red Curlew, to see for himself the excitement and spectacle of an Indian winter encampment, about which Red Curlew had told him a great deal. Chief White Stone Mountain's People lived in separate tepees scattered along the hills during the summer, but when winter came, they gathered at Osoyoos Lake.

Mr. Westmore said to Red Curlew, who had extended the invitation, "We shall call on your father, the chief, after your encampment is set up and we are ready to drive the cattle across the border."

Fall roundup took place. Carr assisted impatiently with the cattle drive as far as British customs. After Mr. Westmore had paid the two dollars per head, and other preparations were complete for the market trail, Mr. Westmore said to Carr, "Now we shall see if White Stone Mountain knows anything of his son's plans."

Carr had tied his bedroll to his saddle at dawn.

Chief White Stone Mountain and his People wintered close to the land on which Okanogan Smith squatted with Mary Manuel. The chief's camp on the east bank of the Okanogan River, just beyond the point at which the river came out the lower end of Osoyoos Lake, was an ideal gathering spot: a large tract of flat, open earth, circled by a mile-long race track. The pole frame of the chief's longhouse stood at Osoyoos the year round.

When Mr. Westmore and Carr rode into the Indian campground, the chief was established in his winter quarters. The women had thrown skin and mat coverings over the pole frame, and the chief's ensign, a white wolf skin, had been raised on the pole to indicate his presence.

White Stone Mountain stood at the door of his lodge greeting his tribesmen and accepting their tokens of respect in the form of food prepared for winter—dried berries, smoked salmon, and deer.

As the white visitors dismounted, the chief retired to the inside of his lodging. When Red Curlew ushered in Mr. Westmore and Carr, the chief was seated by the fire built in the floor. The interior of the dwelling was hollowed out two feet below ground level. The chief motioned for Mr. Westmore to be seated. From a fringed deerskin bag, White Stone Mountain took his pipe and filled it with kinnikinnick berries for smoking. He lighted the pipe with a burning twig and passed it to his guest, who took a generous puff.

Red Curlew, his face eager, acted as the chief's spokesman. "My father says you are welcome. Have you eaten?"

"Tell your father we have eaten. Thank him. We are glad to be here."

The chief nodded graciously, puffed on the pipe himself when Mr.

Westmore handed it back, and instructed Red Curlew what to say.

"My father, the chief, says he hopes you will let your son stay here for the winter. We have plenty to eat; our lodge is safe."

"My son may stay if he will obey the chief, and show proper thanks and respect as a guest."

"I will! I will!" Carr was quick to assert.

Chief White Stone Mountain smiled and spoke in a kind voice.

"My father will consider your son his son," Red Curlew translated.

The chief raised his hand to indicate the matter settled; then he spoke further.

"My father has something special he wants to say to you," Red Curlew explained.

"We shall listen carefully."

"It will soon be time for a hard winter when the snow covers all the food. My father is keeping count of open winters; luckily for cows and horses, many have gone by.

"White men who came here before Mr. Westmore owned as many cattle as are in buffalo herds across the Bitterroot Mountains. Those men expected grass always to stand above the snow. In a winter that the chief remembers, all the white men's cattle starved. In spring the valley was covered with rotting, dead bodies. White men who lost their herds left the country. Some drove the small numbers of animals that survived to the Bitterroot country."

"I have been told of those vast, untended herds," Mr. Westmore said. "Did the Indian livestock die as well?"

"No, they did not die. That is what I want to tell you. We have tamed ponies who have run wild. Ponies know how to paw below the snow for the grass. Cattle are not wise enough to do the same. Since Jack Splawn has come through with cattle to sell, I have bought many cows. When we see signs of the hard winter, we move our cattle to the headwaters of the San Poil, where we have a cache."

"Okanogan Smith never told me of such deep snow," Mr. Westmore said.

Chief White Stone Mountain was amused. "I have lived in this country longer than Okanogan Smith."

"You are shrewd and crafty," Mr. Westmore said. "I agree that leaving my cows with calf alone in the fields in the keeping of only two men is foolish. But I have a wife that I must visit."

"Perhaps you should take a second wife, one that will be here already. Then you will not have to leave your cattle in winter."

Mr. Westmore responded, "That would not do. If I took a second wife, my first wife would never let me come to her again."

Chief White Stone Mountain shrugged. "White men let their wives tell them what they can and cannot do?"

Mr. Westmore changed the subject. "I remember now that Jack Splawn told me that he was caught with a herd in the Okanogan for a winter so severe that supplies sent to him never reached him; he lived on nothing but cow meat for seventy days. The north wind blew constantly. The only shelter was to go behind brush and cover one's self with snow."

"I, too, remember Jack Splawn," White Stone Mountain replied. "We showed him where to take his cattle to a high stand of bunchgrass, and where to water his cattle at a swift creek that did not freeze. We also showed him white sage, a bitter bush fattening to cattle and deer."

"Perhaps I can be a lucky gambler this time," Mr. Westmore said. "The weather has changed and softened with the corning of the white men. I have been in this country now twenty years, and I have never seen a time like the one you remember."

Chief White Stone Mountain shook his head.

Red Curlew interpreted: "My father says he fears the weather does not change for any man, white or red. The Hard Winter comes and is kind to no one. If you are not taught the lesson, your son will be taught."

"I know the chief is a longhead," Westmore declared, "but I have given my promise to go to my wife. I charge my son to learn from you about winter."

CARR AND RED Curlew watched from a high boulder as Mr. Westmore, the three cowboys, and the winding line of steers disappeared along the trail northward. When the cattle drive went beyond sight and hearing, the boys clasped each other in friendly embrace and jigged about. "Yi! Yi!"

Then they hurried back to camp. Red Curlew had promised his paleface friend feasting, gambling, dances, storytelling, and mimicry. Women were still setting up tepees around the campground.

The chief's immediate family shared the lodge with several sons, their wives, and children. Each family had its private area and tended its own fire. Carr took his bedroll from behind his pony's saddle and placed it next to Red Curlew's mat.

Men had laid out the gambling table—an oval area market off with slats—for *iteh-le-cum*, the bone game. Two teams faced one another, each with its pile of twenty sticks as forfeits. A man chosen for his grace and skill as a juggler manipulated two small bones from hand to hand as he writhed and gyrated to the rhythm made by the players beating a clack-clack-clack with sticks on the slats. The plain bone was the "she," and the bone decorated with a black band was the "he." Players on the juggler's team chanted while the leader of the opposing side pointed to the hand that he guessed contained the black-banded "he." If the leader chose the correct hand, his team yelled triumphantly. Losers maintained stoical silence as they flung across a forfeit stick that represented some form of wealth such as hides, ponies, or food.

By firelight in the longhouse on the first night, the medicine men sat by the chief and shared a ceremonial pipe. Carr watched entranced as Opening Flower, now thirteen and a visitant to the menstrual hut, danced in the circle. She wore a feather in her braids, and a white doeskin robe decorated with a sunburst, the elegant garb of a chief's daughter. Her brown eyes gleamed with happiness and pride at being chosen to dance.

Every evening was a party. Sometimes storytellers repeated the legends of Speelyi, Coyote God; of the terrible Wish-poosh, the Big Beaver; of the Chinook winds, five brothers who lived on the Columbia River; and of Wa-Wa, Mosquito God.

In daytime, Carr and Red Curlew snared ducks among the tules at the lakeside or visited the steel traps they had set where the Okanogan River ran out of Osoyoos Lake. The traps were a gift to Carr from his father, and they proved to be invaluable for catching muskrats.

When Carr developed a cough and a runny nose, Cool Cloud sent him to the sweat house, a dome-shaped hut constructed from grasses, earth, and willow branches. Males taking the cure for colds, rheumatism, or other ailments baked naked inside the hut while women heated stones in the fire outside and passed them in. Carr dripped sweat and tried to overcome his embarassment at public nudity. His cold was cured.

Snow fell and remained on the ground in late November. Chief White Stone Mountain sent Red Curlew and Carr to round up the Indian cattle on the hills and bring them to the lake bottom so that if the snow fell too deep, the cattle could feed on the rushes at the lake. For a month the tribe kept to their tents except to gather firewood. The People danced long to summon the Chinook winds, who would melt the snow. The men dancers, their knees bent, remained in one spot and jerked their bodies up and down as the women wailed a sad, monotonous chorus. At length, the men began to move in a circle; they stepped for hours to the chant and rhythmic clapping of the women.

When the time came for the women to dance, Carr watched Opening Flower, whose face was somber now, as was appropriate for prayer to the winds that would release the tribe from the menace of hunger. Carr recalled what the chief had said to his father about winters in which livestock could not find grass, and he worried about his father's pregnant cows with only Nathan and Will to care for them

When Carr asked White Stone Mountain if he should go to Conconully Lake to see if all was well with the Westmore herd, the chief told him sternly to stay in camp. A strong north wind was blowing; the Sinkaietk did not wish to send out a rescue party for a paleface cowering underneath sagebrush.

Finally the Chinook came. The snow melted, and the Indian cattle wandered back to the foothills. More snow fell from time to time but did not stay long enough to cover the bunchgrass again.

In March, Carr went to the United States customs house. A letter was waiting from his father. Mr. Westmore would return to the Okanogan earlier than usual because he had learned of the severity of the winter. Carr was to bring his gear from the Indian camp and wait for his father at the customs house.

Carr went to the winter camp and packed his possessions, which had increased considerably from the time of his arrival. He thanked the chief for the many things he had learned as guest of the tribe. Red Curlew rode with him to the customs house.

WITHIN A FEW days Carr's father came across the border from British Columbia. On horseback, he proudly herded before him three heifers and two bulls, purebred stock, that his brother had shipped to him from the Westmore estate in Herefordshire, England. Mr. Westmore had freighted the white-faced, red-bodied animals by ferry up the Fraser River and carted them along the Cariboo road. He had decided that the livestock could walk from Osoyoos because he would have Carr's help with herding on the final lap.

When they reached the cedar cabin above Conconully Lake, the Westmores were glad to find that Nathan and Will had brought the cows and calves safely through the winter. The cowboys had a story to tell of snow and cold. They had lopped down willow boughs at the lake as survival food for the animals in the month of deep snow.

SOON AFTER THE Westmores arrived, Chief White Stone Mountain and his summer household settled into their tepee close to the water. Carr went happily to greet them.

He was expecting to stay with his father as usual until fall, but he learned with outrage that he was to be dispatched to Victoria at once for critical inspection by his mother. In spite of every argument he could muster, Carr was ordered on his way.

He went to tell his Indian friends that he was leaving the Okanogan for awhile. Inside the tepee, Opening Flower listened to what Red Curlew was saying as interpreter. Her face changed as the speetlurn folds inward in shadows.

"Come back," she said softly. She was learning English words to please Carr.

"I will come back and marry you."

Chief White Stone Mountain said gravely, "She will cost you some *wo-haws*, young paleface."

Carr responded with a man's tone of promise, "I will pay."

He had seen women who did not chatter constantly and nag their men; he wanted one of such a tribe for a wife. He would marry Opening Flower, who could talk with silence, or with a single word or two; who would follow over hills and rivers with pack horses; who would cook roots and meat over an open fire to sustain a man's strength; and who would never scream at her children, or slap or pinch them, but treat them with unvarying affection.

Wearing a dressed deerskin jacket that Smiling Water had sewn and appliquéd for him, he horrified his mother with his decline into savagery. Indian spirits had bewitched her son. Had his father been scheming to rear a cattle hand?

Carr refused to attend the tea dance that his sisters had arranged in his honor. Katherine responded by giving him an imperious command to learn civilized manners and dancing and be out of her sight until he did. Carr found himself sailing on a clipper to England with no opportunity to appeal to his father. He was sent to the custody of his Grandfather Faversham, who would arrange his admission to the proper institution of learning. If Carr remained in England and married an English girl of good family, his mother's prayers would be answered.

Carr had kept discreetly silent about Opening Flower, and he encountered no young lady in England who could alter his devotion to her. He was intelligent enough to apply himself to history, mathematics, and the other branches of knowledge that he could see were universally of value. He always needed fresh air. When the school bully attempted to put Carr in his place, Carr refused to engage in fisticuffs or wrestling but held the challenging oaf with his arms twisted to his back until he agreed to behave with respect toward the "New World Savage."

Rugby made Carr's life tolerable. His superior agility and stamina made him a legend of the public schools, but adulation did not tum his heart. At night, Carr dreamed of his father's pawing, bellowing herds, of riding an Indian pony, sleeping on the bare ground, and eating his food with his hands.

His father sent glowing letters that described the increasing prosperity resulting from breeding California stock with the White-faced Hereford bulls: "The country is so admirably suited to stock-raising that we can count on animals by the thousands. The bunchgrass remains abundant and the winters mild.

"Cattlemen hope that nothing will ever change in the Okanogan. Those of us who came here in the 1860s wish the number of white settlers to remain small, but I suspect that our hope is vain. Encroachments have begun on the open range.

"All of the Okanogan Valley, on both sides of the river, has been Indian reservation, except for the Mount Chopaka and Similkameen Mining District, which Okanogan Smith engineered as a cut-off. Now this strip is threatened because the part west of the river was proclaimed in 1879 as the Columbia Reservation, for Chief Moses.

"Our holdings are now technically on Indian reservation land. I doubt if we shall be forced to relocate. Chiefs Tonasket, Susceptkain, and White Stone Mountain are almost as concerned as the cattlemen and miners that all the land has been given to Moses, who does not even live in this area, but south in the Yakima country. Moses recently came to survey his expanded territory, and some of the cattlemen made leasing agreements with him.

"I am making my leasing agreement with Chief White Stone Mountain, who, I believe, is the one with true claim to the land. I give him ten animals each year.

"All the Indian tribes are bewildered by the procedure of selling their mother, the Earth."

MR. WESTMORE WROTE in a later communication that the Indians living on the Fifteen Mile Strip and on all the Columbia Reservation had been ordered to move across the Okanogan to the east side, which was now the Colville Indian Reservation. The entire Moses Reservation was restored to the public domain.

"White people are becoming insulting to the natives. The immigrants are overrunning all the land that has been the Indians'. Chief Moses and other chiefs were taken to Washington, D.C., where they were told that the United States government was purchasing the west side of the Okanogan from them. They could either move to the east side, or be allotted sixty or eighty acres in severalty.

"By the new ruling, any white settler can take 'four forties,' or a total of a hundred and sixty acres, in any shape he desires on unsurveyed land and maintain a squatter's right by living there, absenting himself for no longer than a six-month period. Families are traveling north from California in large covered wagons drawn by six horses, by way of Walla Walla.

"At the Columbia, at the mouth of the Okanogan, they pay Indians twenty dollars to take each wagon apart and float it across the river. They ferry loads in canoes and swim horses.

"One of these newcomers came to our place a few days ago and wished to hire out his services. He would take part of his pay in cattle. I shall probably reach some such agreement.

"To maintain our squatters' right to our place, I have declared my intention to become a United States citizen. I have already completed the qualifications of residency, of course.

"You will become a citizen of the United States when I do.

"General Miles of the U.S. Army has been quoted as saying there is danger of an Indian uprising. The Indians regard the order for evacuation as unfair, and I must say that I understand their feelings. They were hospitable hosts to early white invaders, and do not take easily to the role of varmints to be exterminated."

As he read his father's letter, Carr grew alarmed for the safety of Opening Flower. Where was she in the uproar and conflict?

MIDWAY THROUGH HIS first year at Oxford, Carr received a letter from his mother informing him that his father was dead. His body had lain in a snow-covered field a long time before anyone knew. Carr must come home at once. A surge of thanksgiving cut through his shock and grief. He was free of the straitjacket of civilization! With funds unhesitatingly provided by his uncle, now Earl of Westmore, Carr took the first steamship that crossed the Atlantic. He rode from Montreal to Vancouver on the Canadian Pacific Railway. A trip that had formerly required three months now could be made in three weeks.

He stopped two days in Victoria, where he visited his father's grave and heard the details of his death. His mother said that Arthur Westmore had come home early in November and remained through December, but when he received a letter from the men at the ranch reporting that six inches of snow had fallen and had not melted as usual, he took the train back to the Okanogan. He had promised to return as soon as he was sure of the safety of his cattle. Mrs. Westmore expected him after New Year's, but he did not return, nor did she receive any letters. Husbands of women in her circle of friends called her attention to newspaper reports that a blizzard was raging in the interior; train service and mail service were cut off. When asked how her husband was faring in the cattle country, she had nothing to tell.

The suspense ended when two inhabitants of the Okanogan country appeared at the Westmore front door with a grim parcel slung across the back of a horse. When told to go to the rear with deliveries, the strangers announced the contents of their package. Mrs. Westmore, frozen with terror, turned from the door and went to her bedroom.

The elder daughter Elizabeth stepped forward to invite the men into the house. They fetched the corpse from the horse and laid it on the parlor floor.

"Helen, go for Father Edmonds," Elizabeth cried to her sister. "I shall see to Mother."

The cook took charge of the crude guests and brought them to the kitchen, where she fed them. They said they had not slept for two days. Neither had they shaved for some time. From the Okanogan Valley to the Fraser, with the help of two horses, they had carried the body, lashed in canvas. One horse carried the frozen remains; the other horse carried the escorts, who alternated riding and breaking trail on foot. They had found shelter and bought meals at farmhouses along the way. At the Fraser River, they boarded the ferry, which made its way slowly through ice.

In the kitchen, the Anglican priest found the pallbearers and thanked them for their kindness. He assured them they would be reimbursed for their personal expenses during the trip.

The Okanogan men attended the memorial service and immediately afterward were handed their envelope. They adjourned to a Victoria tavern, where they promptly spent their wages on a display of drunken behavior that scandalized the town.

AFTER HIS BRIEF stay in Victoria, Carr set out towards the Okanogan country, promising to advise the family lawyer as soon as possible on the state of affairs as he found it. He boarded the *Otter* to New Westminster, then took a smaller boat that went up the Fraser to Hope. At the end of the water journey, he bought a horse and Indian saddle for twenty dollars. At Princeton, when he reached the Similkameen River, he traded the horse to two Indians in exchange for a trip in their canoe down to the Okanogan valley. He stopped at Okanogan Smith's trading post below the border.

Carr learned that many stockmen had lost their entire herds because of exposure and starvation. The four feet of snow that fell in January had made the bunchgrass inaccessible to the cattle that did not have the wits to paw down to food. The Chinook winds brought the thaw; but when the temperature plummeted sharply to zero, the melted water turned to a thick ice crust on the bunchgrass. The temperature fell further each day to forty degrees below zero in thirteen successive days of blizzard. No white man was prepared; all had come to the Okanogan with the prospect of open winters. Cows fell through the snow crust and were trapped belly-deep while they froze to death.

"The groaning and bellowing was hideous," Okanogan Smith related. "Some people cut down brush and willows for feed, but it was useless. Folks took their livestock into their houses and kept them alive on a mixture of potatoes and flour. Potatoes cost five cents a pound and flour five dollars a sack. Not many critters could be saved.

"Unburied, bloated, stinking cows lie all over the ground," Okanogan said. "If I were you, boy, I wouldn't even go for a look."

"I'll go certainly," Carr averred. "I may find some stock alive. Will there be anyone at my father's place?"

Okanogan shook his head. "No chance. If your hired hands are still in the country, they'll be at Conconully, the new town south of your place. A swarm of people have been coming on the land since the reservation was opened. Right now most of them are sitting in the saloons and talking. As soon as the ground thaws, they'll go panning on the creeks."

Carr borrowed a mount from Okanogan. After riding for a day, he came to the house of cedar logs that he had not seen for five years. At nightfall he pushed open the door and found a lantern where it had always hung on a hook. With matches that Okanogan Smith had given him, he lit the lantern and held it up. He saw that no one had lived in the cabin for weeks. Dirty cups and plates filling with mold lay on the table and sink counter. Rats had taken over the premises; their droppings were thick on every surface.

In the sleeping quarters he found a goat wool blanket still on his father's bunk. Carr was cold, hungry, and exhausted. Ignoring the holes gnawed by rats, he wrapped the robe about himself and lay down. In a moment, he fell asleep. Until daylight came through the window, he was beyond all discomfort.

In the morning, he found in the pantry one item of food that had not been destroyed by rats—a tin container of oatmeal. This he fed to the horse.

He cut over the hills toward Salmon Creek, where Smith had said the town would be. Late in the day he rode into Conconully, a duplicate of other mining centers he had seen. Outside the shacks waited a row of horses, reins dropped over their ears.

A dozen men huddled at the stove in the saloon.

"Anybody here a Westmore hand?" he called out.

Nathan and Will stood up uncertainly. Could this tall, authoritative aristocrat be the Westmore son and heir? The cowboys had changed from happy-go-lucky youths to confused, gaunt men.

"You can't be Carr," Nathan ventured.

"Yes, I can be," he retorted. "Can you explain what you are doing here?"

"Hangin' round," Will said. "Don't know what else to do. We left after the neighbors took your pa's body to the coast."

"So I saw. We're going back to find what's left on the range."

"We didn't just take off on our own," Nathan amended Will's statement. "Your Old Man fired us when we wouldn't cut willow boughs anymore. That's how he froze to death--out there loppin' off brush. Dead stuff. Cows couldn't eat it."

"You'll stay fired if you don't come with me."

GLAD IN A shamefaced fashion to have a boss again, they led him to the wagon behind the saloon. A meager pile of old bunchgrass lay in the wagon bed.

"These horses and buckboard belong to the ranch?" Carr asked.

The cowboys admitted that they did.

Carr noted that the animals were scarcely more than skin and bone, but at least they were alive.

"Give some of that grass to my horse; I've been riding her two days," he said.

The feed was divided in equal parts for the three animals.

"Harness up. We'll ride in the wagon and lead my mount."

At the end of the street stood a shack with a sign, "Eats," in the front window. Carr was ravenously hungry. He had a ten-dollar bill that he had exchanged at Smith's.

"I haven't eaten for two days. When did you fellows eat last?" Carr asked.

"About the last time you did," Nathan confessed.

Carr told Will, who held the reins, "Pull up!"

The three went into the shack manned by a smiling Chinese, who fed them mounds of pancakes, pork sausage, and scrambled eggs. When Carr took out the ten-dollar bill and said, "How much do we owe?" the Chinese, still smiling, said, "Ten dollars."

Without regret, Carr relinquished the last of his funds. When the trio returned to the wagon, they felt like new people. Nathan and Will were smiling like the Chinese.

"Boy, glad you're back!" Nathan said. "Will, look how he's grown!"

"Couldn't Father buy any hay at all?" Carr asked as they continued toward the ranch.

"He bought a little at forty dollars a ton," Nathan said. "Mostly there was none to buy. Nobody ever figured there was any need to put up hay."

WHEN THEY PULLED up at the cabin, Carr asserted his first prerogative as boss: delegating unpleasant chores. "I am not going inside that place till you fellows sweep out the rat droppings!"

Nathan good-naturedly hopped from the wagon and said, "Don't blame you. While you put away the horses, I'll take a hand with the broom."

The counters and floor were clear of most of the feces when Carr and Will entered. Nathan had also stacked the dirty dishes.

Nathan and Will found lard, flour, salt, sugar, coffee, dried prunes, and apples in crockery containers that Carr had failed to examine because of their outer appearance.

"There's potatoes out in the cellar, too," Will said.

The trio decided that they could live. For supper, they prepared what became the standard menu for weeks: fried potatoes and boiled coffee. They put prunes to soak overnight.

"We can have bannocks, too," Nathan volunteered.

In contrast with the general scarcities, the supply of cordwood was adequate.

After breakfast next morning, Will found a copper-bottomed washing boiler, filled it full of snow, and put it on the stove. When the snow melted into water, Nathan piled in the cups, saucers, and plates to soak.

"They'll likely be washable by night," Carr remarked.

"WHAT NEXT, BOSS?" Nathan asked.

"We're going riding. There's a mount for each of us. I hope Okanogan doesn't think I have stolen his horse. I'll ride it another day. Perhaps we'll find some cow ponies."

"We turned all the horses loose before we left," Will said. "We figured they could paw through the snow to feed."

Carr and the two hands rode till late afternoon through cold, snow-covered hills and meadows. Under a cliff in the cache, sheltered from the wind, they came upon sixty live head of cattle, a third of them newborn calves, fed from skeletal mothers. One of the cows was a White-faced Hereford, and her calf was a bull!

Two cow ponies were standing guard over the herd. Behaving instinctively and in keeping with the role they customarily played, the ponies had gathered the cow herd into the cache. They had even trampled a mat of bunchgrass out from the snow for the cattle to eat.

Gently, with the help of the cow ponies, the men on horseback urged the feeble livestock back to the corral at the cabin. When a cow or calf tottered and fell, the cowboys tugged the animal to its feet and coaxed it on. In the fading twilight, with the herd hungry in the corral, Carr, Nathan, and Will kicked and shoveled snow away from the meadow grass. They garnered gunnysacks full of grass and they threw it into the corral. The emaciated cows began to feed tentatively, as if they were no longer sure of the taste of grass. The men left the animals sniffing and went into the cabin for their own supper.

Will started the fire again and completed the dishwashing with a bar of Crystal White soap, also found in a closed container. Carr lit the lanterns, which were full of kerosene. Nathan made soda biscuits with the makings that had been protected by crockery. He spooned the dough in lumps two inches apart on a tin sheet and popped them into the hot oven. The trio marveled at the tastiness of their meal—hot bread and hot stewed prunes.

In the morning they continued feeding the cattle with armfuls of grass. They were able to disinfect and grease the open sores on legs cut by ice with materials found in a shed.

Day by day the snow pack sank into the ground. The cattle were turned out on the meadow where the new grass was starting.

"If they last another thirty days, they'll make it," Carr said.

The men tended the animals like babies. To encourage drinking, Carr took the sacks of salt from the pantry and spread them on the ground by the lake.

"It's time I returned Okanogan's pony," Carr told Nathan and Will. He left them in charge while he made the trip to the trading post, riding an AW pony and leading Smith's loaned mount.

Okanogan greeted him as one returned from the dead and listened sympathetically to Carr's tale of trouble.

"At least you're not in debt," Smith consoled Carr. "People who bought cattle with borrowed money will be paying on their losses for twenty years. Mr. Malott told me the other day that an acquaintance on the coast had financed him on a share basis."

"There is no money in the Westmore bank account in Victoria," Carr confided, "but my father had no great amount of outstanding debt, according to his lawyer."

"Your father must have had a thousand head of cattle," Okanogan surmised. "Dan Drumheller, who's been in the cattle business longer than almost anybody around, lost several hundred head. I've heard of losses of eight hundred head. There was just no food; no shelter. I heard that Gus Seigeman of Conconully had some hay that he sold for a hundred and five dollars a ton. He's the only man with money that I know.

"Mr. Sherman told me that he lost all his range cows; managed to save one milk cow and six calves. With sixty head, you're probably the richest cattleman in the valley," Okanogan concluded.

"We'll be prepared with winter feed from now on," Carr vowed. "Chief White Stone Mountain told my father that someday he would learn the lesson of the Hard Winter."

"Too bad that Death had to be the teacher," Smith said.

"Father let his herd expand without limit. I think we can be better off with a smaller herd that we can tend carefully and breed more carefully."

"You're a longhead, son. I'll give you what I don't always extend—credit for supplies until you can sell some critters in the fall. You must be close to starving out there. You could kill one of your cows for meat, but that would be foolish. One thing sure, cows will bring aplenty on the market this year."

A cheered and grateful Carr loaded as much as he could carry on his pony: dried apples and apricots as a change from prunes, salted pork and beef, dry beans, baking powder, and flour, plus two bars of Crystal White.

"Come back with a wagon," Okanogan urged hospitably.

"We'll get along with the bare necessities," Carr said. "I do appreciate the credit and won't abuse it."

"Yup! A real longhead," Okanogan said.

ON A MORNING at the end of April, the summer tepee of Chief White Stone Mountain appeared on the meadow by the lake. Because his father had written that the Indians were removed from the east side of the Okanogan, and because of remarks that Okanogan Smith had made, Carr had feared that his friends would not come to the old site a quarter-mile from the cabin.

He hopped on his pony and cantered down to the tepee.

As befitting his rank, Chief White Stone Mountain greeted the visitor first. He honored Carr with a handshake. Red Curlew joyfully thumped him on the back. The wives cried out and turned him about to see if it were really he.

Opening Flower said, in better English than she could speak five years ago, "Now my name is Flower. I have changed from Opening Flower."

"Your name is Opening Flower until you are married," her mother said sharply. "I don't know why you are not. A big girl like you should have been married long ago."

"I would not marry until you came again." Opening Flower looked at Carr with shining eyes. "Your father said you would come again from across the Great Waters, and you did come."

The chief frowned. "You talk first, as a woman should not do. Has he said he wants you for a wife? He has been across the ocean. He is not bound by words spoken as a boy."

Opening Flower's face clouded. Carr thought, "I want her. I have always planned it; but her father will expect payment."

"It is true your father said you would come again," the chief changed the subject. "Tell us, have you eaten?"

On the fire bubbled a pot of dried deer meat and speetlum.

"No, I have eaten nothing cooked by women for a long time. It smells like the stews I remember."

The chief motioned for Cool Cloud to fill a bowl for the guest. Carr, his hands shaking with eagerness, gulped the hot, savory stew. They filled the bowl for him a second time and let him finish.

"Your father is not here to greet you," Chief Stone Mountain said. "We are sad."

"You know that he is dead?"

"Yes. Susceptkain told me. I am sorry that I did not find your father. We always leave this place after the fall hunt. The Sinkaietk were ready for the Hard Winter. We took our animals to the grass in the San Poil until the snow melted. We knew that we must go because of the early fall of snow."

"I remember that you warned my father. From now on, I will have feed ready."

Red Curlew had waited a long time for a turn at conversation. He broke in, "You have come to help celebrate."

"What do we celebrate?" Carr asked.

"In ten days I marry Nanna of Chief Susceptkain's band," the Sinkaietk youth said proudly. "We feast and dance. You must be here. The wedding will be at this place."

"It will make me happy to be at your wedding," Carr said. "I shall find out what has happened to all the People."

Red Curlew hesitated, then spoke seriously: "You do not know much that has happened on the land since you have been gone. Many white people say that all of us Sinkaietk should move across the river. We have always had our summer camp here. The white commissioner has told us that we can no longer move about freely to fish and hunt, but must choose a home place in the white men's way. Rather than move across the river, we chose land in the hills above, where the graves of our People are. Your father agreed with us that we should always have the right to camp and fish by the lake. So we have come this summer."

"An injustice has been done to you," Carr said. "You will always be free to live on this land that was yours before we came."

"You and your father have been fair," Chief White Stone Mountain said. "We can share the Earth Mother with you in peace."

"In peace and friendship always," Carr agreed.

Ten days later he returned to the Indian camp for Red Curlew's wedding. The bridegroom, whose wealth was obtained from lassoing wild ponies and taming them, led two from his string to the father of the bride. All day the wedding guests, Susceptkain's and White Stone Mountain's tribes, feasted on deer stew and smoked fish, and danced about the fire to the jangle of sleigh bells.

People were eager to tell Carr of events that had taken place among them while he was away. A Black Robe, who would not wear a doeskin jacket when one was presented to him, had come to the Okanogan People with a story of a Great Spirit, Gitchee Manito—more powerful and kindly than Speelyi. This Great Spirit was known to the Mohawks, far to the east. Whenever the Black Robe came for a visit, he blessed marriages that had taken place in his absence. Red Curlew and Nanna would receive the blessing upon his return in midsummer. For now, the marriage ceremony simply consisted of its consummation. As the fête continued, Red Curlew and Nanna went into a separate lodge and a separate fire.

Carr concluded that the Black Robe was a Catholic missionary priest. The Black Robe's Manito put great bravery into a frail body. He had jumped into the roaring current of the Columbia River and pulled out a drowning baby when even the Indian men were sure it could not be done.

The Black Robe had stronger power than Tlekwilish, the medicine man. When smallpox invaded the tribe, Tlekwilish blew on people to keep the disease from them, but they died anyhow. Those who accepted the Black Robe's medicine stayed free of the disease. The man with the power of Gitchee Manito rubbed a person's arm until the skin bled. Then he made a scratch in the skin with a bone splinter. People with skin scratches did not catch the pox; they had only one sore place on their arms, and soon even that disappeared. One could believe the Black Robe's medicine.

Many, including Red Curlew and Opening Flower, had been baptized. The chief was still deciding about baptism because he must choose between his two wives. The Black Robe's medicine allowed only one wife, and this did not seem humane. Last summer the Okanogans had helped the dark-robed white man to build a lodge with a totem of crossed sticks on top. The *Suyapich* told the People to place this totem above the graves of any who died, and when he came to them again he would bless the graves.

Tlekwilish was not at Red Curlew's wedding, but was sulking at his hut over the hills.

"We are tired of Tlekwilish," a brave announced. "He is nothing but a fat coward when his mask is in his tepee; his advice does not make sense and does not work out. When the *Suyapich* gives advice, it is good."

White Stone Mountain approved of the priest in the main: "He agrees with me that everyone should lay stores by for winter and not gamble them all away. He tells people to keep clean tepees, to catch salmon and dig roots, and to cook food before eating it. He tells people to be brave and not lazy, all as I tell the People."

OPENING FLOWER, WEARING her white doeskin robe, did not look at or listen to her father. She gazed and beamed at Carr. She fed him by her looking. Time and space had done the courting for them. They each were the opposite of pretension. Carr's experience of English girls was that they let themselves be kissed, then ran to confess to their mothers in the powder room. Carr wanted no woman hiding from his passion by running to her mother.

NATHAN AND WILL had agreed to stay with Carr until the rescued cattle could be fattened and sold in the fall. Then they planned to go prospecting, and suggested that Carr might do the same. Many of the cattlemen who had lost their herds were already panning gold on the Tulameen or at Granite Creek. Carr and his hands, in the meantime, moved the sixty head from meadow to meadow. They kept salt at the lake and at all the waterholes. With tender care, the animals grew sleek and tame.

In September, Carr decided to keep part of his herd. With his two helpers, he separated the White-faced Hereford stock, including the bull calf, and fifteen other cows—the best of the shorthorn stock—from the rest of the herd and drove the selected animals to the cache in which they had survived the winter. The three cowboys drove the other thirty animals northwest of Conconully to Loomis, the town in which the mining population was now centered. They moved the stock at the side of the new wagon road, along which a constant stream of freight was moving—strings of pack horses, and overloaded vehicles on which tongues broke and wheels came off.

In Loomis at Woodard's saloon, a drunken freighter snapped a bullwhip that touched Carr's shoulder.

"You cowboys make room," the freighter ordered. "You're a bother on the road and in here besides."

At the second flick of the whip, Carr grabbed the stinging end. He reeled in the drunk along the lash of the whip. The man did not have the wits to let go of the handle. Carr grabbed the freighter by the scruff of his neck, marshaled him through the door, and shoved him off the porch of the saloon, all to the cheers of patrons who had endured bullying in their turn.

"I'll set you up," the bartender offered.

He shoved three mugs along the counter.

Carr inquired where he might sell thirty head of beef, and he was directed to the butcher at the end of the street.

"Twenty-five dollars a head—five dollars over the going rate," the buyer said.

Carr shook his head. "Cattle are so scarce, the price should be higher."

The buyer conceded, "You're right; it's a seller's market. Thirty dollars."

"Sold!"

Carr, who had observed his father bargaining, had known enough to be firm and calm, but his legs had shaken. He had conducted his first sale!

The buyer brought a leather pouch from the shed that served as his office and counted out twelve hundred dollars in twenty-dollar gold pieces with so quick a wrist that Carr suspected he could have asked for more.

In the street, Carr gave Nathan and Will a hundred forty dollars each for seven months of labor.

The sixty head had been bawling and milling in the center of town. Somewhat sadly Carr and his men herded the crop into the butcher's corral. The AW steers, even in the year of calamity, were the fattest of the animals on the buyer's premises.

Nathan and Will parted company with Carr at Woodard's saloon.

"I know you want to prospect," Carr said, "but as a favor to me, will you go back to the cache and stay with our cows until I can make a trip to Victoria and back?"

"We'll go back after we've visited every saloon in town," Nathan promised with a wink.

Whiskey was flowing at a dollar a quart in eight saloons. Carr knew his hands would soon return to the precious herd.

On his cow pony, Carr rode across the border. When he came to the Queen's highway, he made his way west along it to the Fraser River. After trading his cow pony for a trip in a canoe, he went home as a boat passenger. He dutifully took the remainder of the money from the cattle to his mother and sisters in Victoria.

Carr's mother accepted five hundred dollars with a disdain that angered him. She had sent him nothing in response to his letters, which had mentioned his lack of funds. He thought surely she had saved something from the lavish allowance given her for twenty years, but it became evident that she had saved nothing. Her only income now came from mining stock that her husband had purchased and placed with the lawyer for administration. When the lawyer asked Carr what value could be put on the real estate of the Okanogan, Carr explained that with all the cattle dead or sold, except for twenty cows and one bull calf, nothing of value remained in the Okanogan unless one counted a cedar log cabin and squatter's rights on two hundred acres of property. He said that his mother could have the income from the mining stock, and he would take the twenty yearlings as his inheritance.

He excused Nathan and Will to go placer mining when he returned to the Okanogan, boarded up the cedar house on the hill, and went to find the tribe of White Stone Mountain, who were in the highlands on the fall hunt. Before him, he drove the twenty yearlings, five of which he gave to the chief as the bride price for Opening Flower. Carr asked White Stone Mountain that his remaining fifteen head be allowed to graze on the Indian winter meadows while he and Opening Flower prospected. He promised that when the Black Robe *Suyapich* came from the south, he and Flower would receive the blessing of Gitchee Manito on their union.

With Flower riding proudly beside him, Carr went to the creek on which he had staked a mining claim during his summer months of cattle-tending. His claim was on a site where the   creek fell from a height into the Salmon River. The land leveled at the base of the cataract, which had gone dry earlier in the fall.

As his first task, he built a cabin. He dragged logs from the river with a rope, one end tied to the log and the other end knotted about the saddlehorn. As he had seen other prospectors build their shacks, he built his, from the ground up. Flower helped him pack the dirt hard for the floor. For the walls, he stacked logs, shaped by hatchet, one above the other. He plastered gaps with mud. He laid on the roof in one slanting plane of cedar poles covered with sod. In one wall of the cabin, he built a rock fireplace, at which Flower could cook Indian fashion. Carr and his bride were as happy as two fairy-tale lovers.

Before the ground froze, Carr sank a shaft a dozen feet to bedrock and water flow in the creek bed. He timbered the shaft and bailed it out. His reward came when he took his nuggets to town and found that he had averaged two and one-half dollars per pan. He was invited to step up to every bar in town to use the gold scales, but he spent little in bars. He hurried home to Flower in the snug cabin and hid his wealth in the chinks between the logs. He would spend his money when Dan Drumheller came through with cattle from California.

When he wrote to his mother of his marriage to Flower, her reply did not surprise him. "I can never accept a savage in my home," she wrote.

In the succeeding spring and summer, Carr panned gold while Chief White Stone Mountain's band tended the AW stock. Flower's mother, Cool Cloud, stayed with them for the birth of their first child, a daughter. Carr found two large gold nuggets on the day that Analix was born. He sent them to the coast to be made into a pair of earrings.

The yearlings became two-year-olds and were bred to the White-faced Hereford bull. When Carr sold the males of the calf crop, he sent his mother a small sum of money, receipt of which she acknowledged. She also sent news that both his sisters had married, and she herself was about to be wed to the Anglican minister of the parish, who, in common with her, had recently endured the loss of his spouse. Any income from the cattle would no longer matter. Carr saw that his family wished to forget him now that they had found better sources of maintenance.

NOT ALL WAS peace in the Okanogan country. Stephen, an Indian youth, lay buried in the mission cemetery at Omak, where the *Suyapich*, Father Etienne deRouge, had built a small house and chapel. In the Indian winter camps throughout the valley, the tribes danced a war dance. The white men cleaned their Springfields, Winchesters, and Enfields in preparation for an uprising that Father deRouge and Chief Smitkin of the Omaks were hard put to prevent. Stephen had been a pawn in the white man's justice. Accused of the murder of a white freighter, Stephen had surrendered to the law after being promised that he would be free on bail until his trial. Even while his chief was on his way to post bail, a vigilante committee rousted Stephen from the Conconully jail and hung him from a tree limb half a mile out of town. The committee cut his dead body down and placed it in a coffin to be delivered to the mission. Coming up the trail to claim their dead, the *tillacums*, the Indian's friends, met George Monk, seated on Stephen's coffin, on a bob sled. Old Smitkin was barely able to keep his people from overturning the bobsled and murdering the deputy. Monk agreed not to sit on the coffin during the rest of the journey to the mission.

In Smitkin's camp, the enraged dancing continued for two days before Father deRouge was able to persuade Loop Loop, leader of the dancers, to give up the body for burial.

MINERS AND PROSPECTORS were invading even the east side of the Okanogan River, the side to which the Indian population had been banished. A Chinese, Chee Saw, had married an Indian woman, Julia, and settled on the east side at the time of the Cariboo gold rush. Now prospectors on the east side at Myers Creek and Mary Ann Creek were insisting that a town of Chesaw be incorporated and withdrawn from the reservation. Circumnavigation of the laws protecting Indian rights changed the whole unsurveyed eastern slope of the Cascades from reservation to a white political entity—Okanogan County.

Chief Moses Reservation had been created by executive order of President Arthur in 1883, but the white men who had squatted on the Fifteen Mile Strip at the border soon straightened out the matter of infringement on improved holdings. The Indian Service in Washington, D.C., summoned Chief Moses, Chief Tonasket, Chief Susceptkain, and Chief Lot, heads of the principal tribes involved. The Indians agreed to cede the Fifteen Mile Strip but asked for compensatory unoccupied land. The government promised to give a saw and grist mill to Chief Tonasket; a boarding school to accommodate a hundred pupils would be set up as well, and a resident physician would be provided. Chief Tonasket would be paid a hundred dollars each year as a personal bonus, for which he relinquished all claim on the land on the west bank of the Okanogan River.

But Chief Susceptkain refused to move from his tribal lands on the west bank. Standing with him was Chief White Stone Mountain. The Indian Service, knowing when to yield, allowed these chiefs to take allotments on the west, where they had always lived. Lands of their choice were assigned to them in severalty. Susceptkain and White Stone Mountain each took four square miles of land, and each head of family or male adult was awarded one square mile of land.

Although the reservation was named for Moses, the chief and his own People lived considerably southwest at Moses Coulee and along the Columbia from the Rock Island rapids to Vantage, and also at Moses Lake. The Moses People objected to being uprooted from their ancestral haunts. Neither did the northerly tribes welcome them to what had always been their hunting and fishing grounds. But when the amended reservation plan was ratified in 1884, most of the Moses People began the exodus to the newly assigned lands, dubbed the Colville Reservation, on the Okanogan's east bank.

Paper agreement did not deter the Indians from inhabiting their traditional camps and hunting grounds. Indians scarcely understood the naming of any particular plot of ground as home. Home was where the fish jumped up the falls, in the hills where the deer grazed, and on the sandy meadows when the speetlum blossomed.

Those Indians who removed themselves to the east bank hoped to find freedom from harassment in their own territory, but white miners continued their invasion.

Having lost a million and a half acres from their reserved lands, the natives gravitated southward to Nespelem, where their tribal headquarters were eventually established. They were joined in exile even by famous Chief Joseph, vanquished general of the Nez Perce.

Ruby, a mining camp, was the first seat of Okanogan County. Liquor licenses were the main source of public revenue. The county treasurer kept the funds in baking powder cans buried in the dirt. For diversions, the population engaged in drinking, chewing dried venison, and singing ribald songs.

Stable citizens wrested control of the community from the miners in 1888, when Conconully became the new county seat. Stock ranchers began to pay property taxes. Duly elected county commissioners began a program of road building, and schools were established. Ranch women guided social activities toward parties with cake, sandwiches, coffee, and dancing. The white man's civilization had taken hold in the Okanogan.

"ZIKEN-KIKEN-SPLAK! AND THEN I came back!" Mr. Westmore said at the end of story hour.

SUCH WAS THE world that Ed McLaren entered.

Story hours ceased in February when calving began. The Old Man called four hours a night's sleep and expected his hands to do the same. He stood in the meadows in mid-storm and assisted at birth like a midwife. Most of the early Okanogan cattle had been born willy-nilly wherever the mother happened to be, with no help from man. But as new life struggled to its feet, to bow its head before the wind and driving snow, Westmore and his hands helped the weakened mother and calf to shelter, and the baby nursed in the shed in the cache.

The daily chore of feeding the entire herd continued. As he slaved for a seemingly tireless tyrant, Ed promised himself that he would try his luck again as a miner when spring arrived.

Bright sunny weather came soon after the Chinook. Doting cow mothers followed their rollicking calves and licked them with their tongues. Nathan, Will, and Ed joked with one another and played pranks in the sunshine.

Nathan and Will, a dozen years older than Ed, would be boys forever. Now, the Old Man seemed less of a cranky tyrant. Ed temporized with his vow to leave the AW.

He mentioned to the Old Man, "Now, with the ground softening, a person could go prospecting again."

Mr. Westmore shook his head. "Stay with us, Ed. My father struck it rich among the first at Barkerville across the border; even I dug out enough nuggets on Salmon Creek to begin my cattle herd; but I believe that agriculture is the future industry of this area. Mining is a sporadic game at best. The bottom has fallen out of the gold and silver markets. Most people are working in mining companies supported by Eastern capital. You would work underground. The creek beds have been worked out; the Chinese driven from the coast by labor troubles were patient and careful and got the last of the surface gold. Some high-grade ore has been found and moved by wagon to the Cariboo Mine stamp mill, but it's hard to say how much of this ore was treated.

"The people who will make money have the wherewithal to build the buildings and install the machinery to recover ore. They need steam and boilers. Prospectors lack a large area of knowledge. Rollers must be installed as primary grinders.

"I hear the Poland China Mine, being built with Eastern capital, has fifteen men at work; but the recovery has not proved high enough by amalgamation and gravity concentration. If and when the railroads come up the Okanogan Valley, there may be enough gold and silver to make mining profitable, but certainly not at present."

10.

The Rescue of Analix

The Old Man did not share entirely with his outfit in the open joy of the spring season. Silent and sober in his saddle, he watched the roaring, muddy creeks.

"What you thinkin' about, Boss?" Nathan asked.

"About the Conconully flood in '94. After the hard winter comes the run-off. A wall of water could flood the cache. It would have only one way in and no way out."

Mr. Westmore gave orders one morning to Nathan, Will, and Ed to ride into the hills to check the rise of water levels in the streams. Despite the mire in the road, he would have to take the wagon to Loomis because staples were used up after the long winter. When the children asked to accompany him, he said, "Not this time. I want to come home as soon as possible."

Ed, Nathan, and Will returned from the hills after their inspection just as Mr. Westmore drove into the yard with a full wagon.

"Wagons were stuck up to the axles along Sinlahekin Trail," the boss said. "How were the creeks?"

"If it rains much more, they'll start moving over the banks," Nathan reported.

"What I expected. Children, stay close to the house. No squirrel-shooting. No riding off by yourselves. Where are Analix, Leschi, Owhi, and Tamma?"

The four that Mr. Westmore inquired about were always first to run forward to examine the load and find treats, but today they were absent.

"Find Analix and her brothers," Papa said quickly to Bethany.

Bethany returned alone a quarter of an hour later. "They aren't in the barn, or the bunkhouse, or the house."

"Where are those rascals! This is no time to be wandering!"

He looked down the row of children standing before him. "If you know where they are, speak up at once!"

Kahpat, age nine, admitted, "I know where they are, but I promised not to tell."

"None of that nonsense! You obey your father, not your sister and brothers!"

Gulping for breath in his fear, Kahpat disclosed that Leschi and Owhi had teased Analix because girls were cowards and could never be chiefs. Analix had dared her brothers to name a deed she could perform to show she was the bravest in the family.

"What is this deed of valor?" Papa demanded.

"To ride a tree from Loomis all the way to Spectacle Lake. After dinner at noon," Kahpat went on, "they rode up the creek bed on their horses to Loomis. I rode along, but I came home when I remembered what you said about playing by the water. They pushed the biggest log they could find into the middle of the current with Analix on it. The boys were going to lead Analix's horse to Spectacle Lake.

"Don't tell them I told! They won't let me be one of the big boys if you do!"

Sniffling, he ran to his mother's arms. She knelt on the grass and clasped Kahpat to her bosom.

"Don't cry! Don't cry! You are a big boy."

Kahpat quieted.

Ed could not help comparing Opening Flower's behavior with that of a white mother under similar circumstances. He judged that any white mother would have been squawking like an old hen.

"Nathan! Will! Take the right bank Ed and I will take the left, back to Loomis!"

"Analix can swim like a trout, Papa," Bethany interposed. "What is the harm even if she falls into the water?"

"A fish knocked over the head with a stick can't swim. The water is running less than six inches under the tree limbs along the bank. I'll saddle a mount. You go on ahead, Ed!"

Mr. Westmore hurried to the barn.

Ed jogged on Stocky all the way to Loomis without finding Analix or her brothers, either on the trail or in the swollen stream. The current swirled with logs, bushes, and junk discarded by human beings.

The main street in Loomis had become a canal in which boys ducked one another and watched for thrills.

"Jones's outhouse is coming round the bend!" a youth chortled.

"Here comes your ma's chicken coop, too!" another yelled. "Look at those chickens on the roof! Wow, are they wet!"

Ed drew rein and called to the gang, "Have any of you seen Leschi and Owhi Westmore or their sister?"

"Sure," answered a lad who sloshed toward Ed in hip boots big enough to fit his father. "That smart-aleck Analix rode on a log, right through town! Her brothers were yellin' to her that they gave up; she could be chief. But she yelled back, 'I'm going to ride all the way to the river, through Spectacle Lake!'"

Ed turned Stocky's head with a tight rein, and galloped back the way he had come. He had traveled toward town while she was already past the AW downstream! She might even now be in the boiling flood of collected streams that became the Okanogan.

Maid of prowess though she was, Analix had not traveled successfully as far as the river. When Ed arrived at Spectacle Lake, ordinarily a shallow pond, he spied Owhi, Leschi, and Tamma jumping from log to log in a jam held together by debris. Their clothes were soaking wet. They screeched at Ed, "We can't get her out! We can't get her out!"

"Where is she?" Ed yelled.

"Over there! See her?"

Ed thought he saw a claw clutching at a log in the water. A hand!

"Is that her out there?" he called as he jumped from Stocky.

"Yes! Yes! The log went under a tree limb and she was knocked into the water. She can't get back on the log. It rolls away from her!"

In five minutes, or five seconds, a small animal could be dashed between logs or crushed by boulders on the shoreline. Ed leaped into the swell with logs clashing about him. He first saw her mat of long hair floating like willow roots tom up from the bottom of the lake. Reaching desperately, Ed grabbed her hair. She turned and saw his face. She stopped struggling and let Ed pull her to the shore by her hair. The boys lifted her together and laid her on the bank She began to scratch, spit, and scold like a cat. She panted and gulped for air.

"You're going to get a whipping like one you never had before!" Leschi shouted at her.

She sat up and pushed her hair out of her face.

"I know," she said and began to cry like a girl.

When she gained control of herself, she told Ed, "I'd never have made it out of there alone, but you shouldn't have yanked so hard."

"I'm sorry, "Ed said humbly, "but I had to get you out."

"She has her nerve! Complaining about her hair being pulled! She should be thankful to Ed she didn't lose her life! Analix is a fool instead of a chief!"

They staggered up the bank with their clothing sucked to their skins.

"Everybody's been out looking for you," Ed told the young people. "We'll have to get you home to Mama right away."

"It's not Mama to be afraid of," Tamma said dourly. "Papa is the one that licks us."

"Can't keep him from it, and doubt if I would if I could," Ed stated. "Where are your horses?"

"They've run away," Leschi said. "Horne by now, probably. We forgot to tie them when we jumped in for Analix. This high water spooks them."

The boys began the trudge home. Ed helped Analix up behind him on Stocky. Her dripping, shivering arms went round his waist.

"I wouldn't do this except that I'm tired. I know two riders wind a horse," she apologized.

"Oh, you're not fat enough to matter," Ed responded.

As the horse walked with them, Analix asked, "Do you think it was Speelyi or *Mon Dieu* who brought you to save my life, Ed? Out there in the water I was praying to both of them."

Ed started to say that he would thank Lady Luck that he arrived in time, but the flip answer would not come. The danger ended, he was overcome by a primitive fear unknown to him before in his life. He was overwhelmed by the natural force of the flood he had encountered, its death-dealing reality and power. God, or even someone the Northwest Indians called Speelyi, had shown Ed that he was a puny animal whose life was lost or spared according to the Deity's whim. In a flood, he had acquired more religion than he had in eleven years' instruction at a religious institution designed to form young Christians.

Halfway home they met Mr. Westmore. His face dark with anger and relief, he reined in his black and tan cayuse.

"Get down, Analix!" he ordered sharply. "You know better than to ride double on an old horse like Stocky."

Ed flushed with the realization that Analix's arms were tight about his middle.

"I wouldn't have let her ride, except she's had it hard. Half drowned. I had to fish her out of the lake."

Analix slid from behind Ed to the ground.

"Go find my pony, Ed," she begged.

"Nonsense! You children hike! I saw your mounts up the trail. I let them go home."

"Aren't you going to cut a willow switch, Papa?" Owhi asked.

His father made no answer to the question, but said, "Come with me, Ed," as he turned his cayuse. "We haven't time to herd rascals."

Ed dared not argue, but followed his boss at a quick trot.

Mr. Westmore and his hands were awake on horseback most of the night, watching for floodwaters that might threaten the meadow to which they had moved the cattle.

Ed was relieved to learn that he had not displeased the boss with his care of Analix. Mr. Westmore told Ed at breakfast, "You should have a new horse. Stocky is too old for a cow pony. Let the children have him with the saddle.

Red Curlew has just finished breaking an Appaloosa. I'm buying him for you. Also, next time we go to Loomis we'll get that Gaylin saddle Blackwell has in stock. Old Joe Gaylin, down in El Paso, Texas, makes a fine piece of leatherwork."

"How come you're playing favorites, Boss?" Will pretended jealousy.

"Ed was the one who dived into a mill after my daughter," the boss said quietly. "He deserves a reward."

A chorus of agreement went round the table.

Analix did not include her voice. After the cheers for Ed stopped, she sighed bitterly, "I am the Fair Maiden in Distress who was rescued."

The flood stage in the streams passed without further incident.

A LETTER WITH an Eastern postmark arrived. Father deRouge wrote that he would soon return to the Okanogan. He had been successful in obtaining an endowment from Mother Katherine Drexel.

"We shall have new buildings at Schall-kees," the priest wrote. "We can now build the church and school that a respectable mission requires. I have had my phonetic dictionary of the Salish language printed and shall teach children to write in their own language as well as in English. I do not wish any separation of the Indian children from their parents. Masses will be said in Latin for white members of the parish, but also in Salish for the Sinkaietk.

"To my regret, the boarding school will be only large enough to accommodate boys. The Westmore sons will be ready for Latin and algebra.

"In time, we shall have a day school for girls; and if Sisters can be found, we plan a boarding school for girls at a later date."

"'For girls later,'" Analix quoted in anguish and fled on her pony to the hills.

Opening Flower and Bethany cleared the table, doing work that Analix should have shared. Mama's face was dark with distress and bewilderment.

"It is hard for Analix to be a girl," Bethany said. "Don't worry about her, Mama."

SUMMER WAS ENDING in a blaze of red and yellow leaves when Father deRouge came at last to the AW. He arrived in time for the evening meal, which became a welcome banquet. Mr. Westmore made arrangements for the four oldest boys to stay as boarding pupils at the mission on the Okanogan River near Chief Smitkin's People. As partial payment of tuition, Mr. Westmore agreed to supply machinery needed for the mission farm.

"Also, I shall have the men drive down steers that can be butchered for beef as necessary through the winter," Mr. Westmore added.

"You should be proud of your husband, Opening Flower," Father deRouge said. "He is our most generous local benefactor."

"I also have the most prospective pupils."

"Eight lucky boys!" Analix interposed with an edge in her voice.

Father deRouge studied the tall, slim girl, who was English except for the copper color of her skin; he noticed the soberness in her eyes.

"I have not forgotten, Analix," he said. "You are the oldest and likely the brightest of the whole family. Have patience. I am determined that you shall have the education worthy of your ability."

The bitterness of being a girl showed painfully on Analix's face as she watched the loading of the wagon that would transport the four boys to the new mission school. At market time, Papa had sold his steers at the good price of twenty dollars a head. He had purchased school clothes, which filled a trunk.

Opening Flower was weeping at the separation of her family, but she had never objected to her husband's decisions.

Papa was driving the wagon instead of sending Nathan or Will as escort.

Analix stood cold with stoicism, particularly because Papa had insisted that she start to wear gingham dresses instead of buckskin shirts. She was dressed this morning in a red and black checked pattern that even Mama liked. It did not suit Analix's mood—until Papa, at the last minute, called out cheerily, "All right, daughter, climb on. We are taking you along for company on the way home, and to show your new attire to Father deRouge. Sit here beside me. The boys can ride in the wagon bed."

Analix gasped with delight, then shook her head. "I couldn't stand it on the way back."

A smiling Opening Flower led Analix to the wagon. "Go along, daughter. You need to see Father deRouge for confession. Besides, there may be a surprise for you."

"Go! Go on!" her younger brothers urged. "Make Papa buy candy."

"Candy!" Analix said contemptuously, as she climbed to the seat next to her father. "The surprise better be more than candy!"

After two days, Mr. Westmore and Analix returned with candy. Although Ed could discern no special gift that had been accorded Analix, she seemed happier than before the trip. She helped her mother and Bethany willingly with the household chores.

In the evening, by the lamplight, she responded to the small children's plea for a story.

"A family was once starving. The mother walked through the cold and snow for miles tracking a rabbit, to catch it and bring it home for stew. She at last cornered the scrawny animal when it tried to hide in a shallow hole. Clutching the rabbit to her chest, the worn-out woman staggered home at last with food for her children, who would be wailing with hunger.

"She came to the tepee, and sure enough, the children were whining about the dead fire. Mama told the children to cheer up. She built the fire and put the rabbit in a pot to stew. She kept the fire going for two hours. She put in roots that she had dug from under the snow with her bare hands. At last the stew was ready! Her children would survive the winter.

"'Come, my children! Eat! Eat! Your mother has provided for you!'

"The children looked at the stew. They sniffed it in their bowls. Guess what they said?"

"I guess they said 'Thank you,'" Telah, age seven, volunteered.

Antwine guessed, "It smells good."

Weipah guessed, "My brother got more than I did in his bowl."

Aeneas said, "I don't like rabbit!"

"That's the right answer!" Analix said. "For a while, I was like one of those children who didn't like rabbit stew! Now someone else must tell a story."

"Ed has never told a story," Will accused.

Ed was aghast. "I don't know any stories!"

"You do," Mr. Westmore contradicted. "I'll wager you know some Perrault or Grimm fairy tales. My children have never heard those stories from Europe."

Stammering at first, Ed found himself telling Little Red Riding Hood. He discovered that with no one belittling his efforts, he had quite a fund of tales to offer: Chicken Little, The Little Red Hen, The Three Little Pigs, and even Cinderella!

The story of Cinderella moved Opening Flower to say that children of first wives were sometimes mistreated by second wives, who wanted the best of everything for their own children. This was not true of the family of Chief White Stone Mountain.

As WINTER WAS about to set in in earnest, Mr. Westmore directed his hands to round up any strays and bring them to the cache feeding lot.

Riding through a pine thicket near the lake, Ed came upon Analix, who was sitting quietly on a boulder. She was studying a basalt wall painted with pictographs in red, black, yellow, and white. The primitive lines showed men, sunrises, sunsets, journeys, war parties, and hunting parties. Some of the human figures were drawn with heads of elk, deer, bear, beaver, or fish.

When she noticed Ed's approach, Analix smiled.

"I never saw these before," Ed marveled. "What do they mean?"

"I don't know exactly. Mama's People say even they do not know the full meaning. But before the Earth turned over, people were animals and animals were people. My Indian cousins think the pictures are magic. They do not want to talk about these pictures because they have something to do with their special spirit powers. If a person brags of his spirit power, he loses it."

"You don't believe that, do you?" Ed asked. "What would Father deRouge say if you told him about spirit powers?"

"I am not sure what he would say. But what he talked to me about at the mission when we took the boys to school has a great deal to do with why I am sitting here."

"Is it a secret?"

"I am bursting to tell you, Ed. It is a big plan that Father deRouge has made with Papa about Bethany and me—that we go far away, farther than to St. Mary's."

"Start from the beginning. I would hate it if you and Bethany went away. For how long? What would Nathan and Will and I do?"

"You'd get along fine. Besides, some day we would come back. I may as well tell you about it. You know I have been taught the Catholic religion, and I do believe in Father deRouge's *Mon Dieu*. The Indian Great Spirit is the same.

"In my mother's first religion, the boys and girls about to grow up go into the woods and seek their special power, and the wise men of the tribe go out to talk to their power before they go on a journey to a different place. They sit still and wait for the end of their thoughts. That is what I am doing here. Shall I leave this place where I belong, the same as trees and the rocks belong here?

"Father deRouge talked to me about the fact that I am half Indian, but also, I am half a white person of a great, educated family. I can hardly believe it, but Father deRouge says I have special power!"

"Father deRouge is right. You are a genie!"

"Remember that Papa said he would have a surprise for me the day we took the boys to St. Mary's?"

"Yes. You never said what it was."

"It is a really big one! Bethany and I have the chance to go away from here! All the way to Spokane, to a girls' academy!"

"Father deRouge and Papa told me about the power of a great church that extends all over the world and has many schools and universities. Father deRouge belongs to the Society of Jesus. With Father Jean Pierre deSmet as leader, the Society has established schools and missions west of the Missouri River ever since 1845. Gonzaga University and Preparatory School in Spokane is one of the places they have founded. They are all organized now in provinces. Gonzaga College is for men. The Sisters of the Holy Names of Jesus and Mary have opened an academy for girls not far from the college. Papa says that Bethany and I can get as good an education there as we could in Europe."

"I can see you are through worrying about whether your spirit power wants you to go. Let me warn you, there'll be days that you will want to run away home. From what I've heard of parochial schools, students have hard, long lessons; and what you will find hardest is having to keep quiet all the time."

"Don't joke, Ed. I am worrying. Will the white girls like us there? Will the sun and trees and rocks of this place know us when we return?"

"I think they will," Ed said. "The sun shines the same on everybody everywhere, but I agree that you belong here like the trees. We'll miss you at the AW. A lot."

"When Father deRouge said St. Mary's would take boys first and girls later, I was jealous. But Father explained to me that St. Mary's mission school, even when girls attend, will be mostly for beginners. I would be wasting time sitting in classes for other pupils learning the alphabet. Bethany and I already know most of what he will teach girls at St. Mary's. At the girls' school in Spokane there will be real nuns who will make you study such hard things that you will cry before you learn them."

"I suppose he meant geometry and Latin. They do get hard."

"I'll help in the girls' school at St. Mary's," Analix went on. "Father deRouge says he will need me because I know both Salish and English. Girls will not be afraid to stay at a school that has an Okanogan Indian catechist. Also, I can help the People in the hard times that lie ahead as the reservation grows smaller. I really want to learn everything there is to know."

"You're ambitious," Ed observed. "I never heard of anyone who knows everything. Some people think they do, I grant you."

"At least everything taught at the paleface academy," Analix amended.

A letter accepting Analix and Bethany as pupils at Holy Names Academy arrived from Spokane. Sister Mary Alodia wrote that girls in the academy wore dark serge dresses with white collars, and these would be provided by the academy in proper sizes. The girls should bring only underwear, two gingham dresses, and perhaps another good dress for Sundays.

"If I have to dress that way from now on, I will go to the academy wearing a deerskin shirt and trousers, with my belongings in a parfleche," Analix announced.

"I will, too," Bethany followed her sister's lead.

Opening Flower, who had been unhappy because of the decrease in the size of her family, raised her head and smiled.

"Yes, they will! I go, too, to the railway station. We ride our horses. You have not let me ride horseback for a long time, husband. Let us ride together."

Papa agreed. He and Mama could accompany the daughters as far as Colville, head of the new Corbin railway that went to Spokane. The girls would ride alone on the train. Sister Alodia wrote that she would meet the train personally to take the Westmore daughters in charge.

The day before the girls left, Ed found Analix again at the Indian paintings. He dismounted from his cow pony and climbed up beside her.

"Did you come to tell the spirits goodbye?" he asked.

She wore her buckskin shirt and trousers, and her hair hung in two black braids. "I am thinking this is my last day as a wild creature," she said. "I have been a deer. Perhaps I'll turn into a heifer."

"Don't let anything change you," Ed said gently.

Analix's face was somber. "I kiss you goodbye, Ed, as the Indians kiss."

She laid her fingertips on his eyelids. Ed reached up to take her hand, which rested warm and trusting for an instant in his. He smiled at her and stood up, still holding her hand. She looked directly at him, and he was filled with tenderness. But her eyes darkened; she grabbed her hand abruptly away, bounded to the turf below the rock, and was halfway out of the grove before Ed could clamber down. He was puzzled and surprised at her sudden flight.

"Your power will always be the deer," he called after her.

He thought, "She is a skittery, wild creature; half Indian witch doctor, half white lady. She'll never become a heifer. She is a doe, with its alert and fearful spirit."

THE STAY-AT-HOMES LINED up to see the travelers off at the water trough outside the fence. Opening Flower wore deerskin garments that matched her daughters'. Papa wore his beaded jacket, too. Nathan, Will, Ed, Telah, Antwine, Weipah, and Aeneas, a row of bachelors, were about to be on their own.

Nathan cheekily said, "Oh, Analix and Bethany, aren't you going to kiss us hands goodbye?"

As the AW's oldest hand, he was a privileged man. Mr. Westmore took no offense.

Bethany went cheerfully forward to give Nathan, Will, and Ed each a hearty buss in the style of Pierrette. Analix, however, hopped into the saddle and could not be coaxed to follow her sister's example. Ed glowed with his secret. He was the only one who had been kissed goodbye by Analix!

The quartet of riders kicked their horses' flanks and headed east on the trail to Colville.

When the party was out of sight, the four small boys at once lost their glum faces and even whooped with delight at being on their own. "Now we can ride with the men all day!"

"Oh, no you don't!" Nathan said. "You have to stay at the house and cook our meals for us because your mama isn't here."

Aeneas, age four, began to cry; Weipah, five, made a face of despair; Antwine, six, cried out, "That's not fair!"

Telah, age seven, grinned and said, "You're not getting away with any smart tricks like that!"

For a week, at nightfall, they all cooked supper together: bacon, fried eggs, fried potatoes, and steak. They chewed jerky for lunch. Nathan, responsible soul, cooked oatmeal for everybody's breakfast.

When Flower and Carr Westmore came home, they looked younger and happier than they had for many seasons. They had sold Analix's and Bethany's ponies at Colville and spent the money on store-bought goodies. Opening Flower's parfleche overflowed.

Shortly a letter came from Analix. She wrote that they had a safe trip on the train and were met at the depot by Sister Mary Alodia. "Her long, dark habit made her easy to recognize. She told us that we were easy to recognize, too."

Analix and Bethany were roommates in the dormitory. There were more than fifty resident pupils and at least another hundred and fifty day pupils whose families lived in Spokane.

"Holy Names Academy is a brand new brick building, two stories high," Analix described her new world. "It is in the middle of a prairie without trees. They call the road that leads to the door Boone Avenue.

"Willows and other trees grow along the banks of the Spokane River, which is close. Last Saturday, in free time, I went by myself to sit in the shade for an hour. The river is wider than the Okanogan. One of the Sisters told me that it also runs into the Columbia.

'When I went back to the dormitory after my visit to the Spokane River, I found I had done something wrong. I had left the grounds of the academy without permission. Sister Mary Alodia was cross with me at first, but after I explained why I went, to seem closer to home, she told me she would excuse me because she understood. She also came from a country of creeks, rivers, and hills. She agreed with me that the setting of the academy was dreary.

"She said I had given her an idea. Every year Holy Names Academy will observe an Arbor Day. Each class will donate a tree to beautify the grounds.

"All of you at home, start hunting for little maple trees and dig them up and plant them in buckets to grow until next fall.

"It is too far, we know, for us to come home for Christmas, but Bethany and I will have a good time because we'll have a party in the dormitory.

"Mama, you will go to the Christmas mass at the mission. Tell Father 'Joyeux Noel' for us, and say we are both studying hard, to show the Sisters how much we learned in the mission school that burned down.

"The Sisters come from faraway places, just like Father deRouge. Sister Othilia, who is German, makes handiwork that Mama would admire.

"There are twelve grades in the academy. The Sisters, at first, did not know where to place us. I settled that when I showed them I could solve algebra equations. I am in the eighth grade, and could even have been in the ninth grade if I had wanted to. My main teacher is Sister Mary Isadorita; Bethany's teacher is Sister Mary Alexina, for the sixth grade. Sister Cecelia Marie is teaching music to Bethany—piano and mandolin.

"Ed told me that I would have a hard time sitting still in school, and he was right. What is strange to us is that we are treated like babies almost. We do nothing but study. The Sisters do all the cooking and housekeeping; they even wash our clothes!

"Merry Christmas to you all! With love,

"Analix and Bethany

"P.S. Dear Papa: I gave the gold pieces to Sister Mary Alodia; she said it would be a long time before you need to send any more payment. You should have seen the look on Sister's face when I poured the money out of the parfleche onto her desk.

"The pupils must curtsy to the Sisters. Down, one, two, three. Rise, one, two, three."

11.

A Cowhand's Glory

Ed was the winner in a draw of straws with Nathan and Will for the privilege of driving to St. Mary's in the sleigh on Christmas Eve. Flower looked forward to attending Christmas Mass in the mission chapel and to visiting with her relatives, many of whom would be present for the spectacle that Father deRouge provided. He had learned well his parishioners' love of ceremony and music. After the festivities, the four boys in school would come home for a two-week Christmas vacation.

December 24 was a bitter cold day with deep snow on the ground, but Flower bundled Ed and herself in buffalo robes that Red Curlew had brought her from Montana. The bells on the harness of the team that pulled the sleigh jingled in the spirit of the season as Ed and Flower traveled the thirty miles.

Father deRouge greeted them at the door of the red brick building that served as the mission's headquarters: "Ed! How pleasant to see you again! And there sits Mama Westmore!"

The priest accompanied Ed to the sleigh to greet Mrs. Westmore.

"Such a cold Christmas Eve! We must take you in at once. We shall go to Pauline with you," Father deRouge said to Flower.

He escorted her to a side door at which he knocked. A smiling half-blood woman responded and in a soft voice said, "We are happy that you have come. You must not stand outside any longer. Oh, it is so cold!"

She drew in the guest quickly.

"The woman who is now in charge of Mama Westmore is Pauline," the priest said as he continued with Ed along the porch. "She and her husband take care of the dormitories and do much of the cooking, gardening, and interpreting. I could not maintain the mission without their help."

"Mama seemed to feel that she went off with a friend," Ed said. "Now where do I find the boys?"

"They'll be in the gang in the snowball fight out here," Father deRouge chuckled.

Twenty or thirty youths were sending out volleys of snowballs and ducking and dodging the return fire from around the corner of the building. The war stopped when Father deRouge stepped into the snowy yard and called, "Leschi! Owhi!"

The two came from behind the building warily. When they spied Ed, they hailed him happily, but in a subdued manner.

"Leschi and Owhi, take Ed to the dormitory to get warm. You can find a cot. Several boys have already left for the holiday. Bring him to supper. See that he gets a tin plate and cutlery when you go to the dining room."

"Yes, Father. Thank you, Father," the brothers said.

As the priest left them, Ed remarked, "You two seem mighty meek! This place taking the spunk out of you?"

The boys brought him to their corner of the dormitory. Ed gratefully soused his numb hands in hot water that Leschi fetched in a pitcher and poured into a basin.

"Father's a lot stricter here than he ever was at our ranch," Owhi said, aggrieved. "He says he's teaching us 'civilized' behavior and respect for authority."

Ed whistled, "Boy! That stuff's even come west! I know what you are putting up with. But your priest is really a nice guy."

"We know," the boys conceded resignedly.

The evening meal consisted of creamed salmon poured over homemade bread, boiled carrots, and cabbage, all parceled out family style on tin plates.

"This is good!" Ed exclaimed. He was famished.

"I guess it's good if you've driven in the wind for thirty miles," Leschi joked. "But we get a lot of creamed salmon. Papa will have to send down another cow."

"Then you'll say we get a lot of boiled beef!" Owhi predicted. At the close of the meal, a dishpan full of hot water and soapsuds was handed along the table so that each diner could wash his own plate, tin cup, and cutlery. The utensils were turned over to drain dry on the oilcloth-covered table.

After supper the students went outside to the mission grounds to watch the arrival of parishioners, both Indian and white, for the High Mass that would be solemnized in the chapel. A feast would follow, Leschi told Ed. "That's partly why we had a skimpy supper. Pauline was saving food for the company."

Deerskin tents and pine-bough huts popped up like a mushroom ring. Fires before each unit, with spits over the coals, roasted rabbit, quail, and deer.

"Everybody has brought something for the potlatch," Leschi said. "Nobody will go to bed hungry. You could still eat a horse right now, couldn't you, Ed?"

Ed grinned. "Darn near it!" he agreed.

"Wander around by yourself now as long as you want to," Leschi told Ed. "It's time for us to go into the chapel. We're singing in the choir for Mass. You can go in with everybody."

Ed, left alone, blew his breath on his hands and waited for the Catholic ceremony, which he had never seen before.

To signal midnight, which traditionally marked the birth of the Infant Savior, Father deRouge fired a pistol at the entrance of the chapel. Other guns answered. The congregation approached and began to file into the chapel, many carrying pine and fir limbs, and all chanting softly. Father deRouge's beautiful tenor voice rang in welcome, "*De Dieu on annonce la gloire.*"

Ed went in at the end of the line and stood near the door. Many others also stood for lack of room in the pews. Ed had never been in any church in which the people dipped their fingers in holy water and genuflected. Evergreen, stars, and ribbons adorned the altar. To Ed's Protestant eyes, the Corpus Christi, shipped from Europe, was garish. Father deRouge chanted first in Latin, then in Salish, to the rapture of his audience.

When the Mass ended, the flock knelt and crossed themselves upon leaving the pews. Laughter and conversation broke out as the congregation assembled in the churchyard. Mama Westmore, who had had an honored seat on the women's side of the chapel, joined Ed and her sons. The boys had quickly discarded their choir robes.

"Father deRouge said we are to go in with the guests served in the dining room," Leschi said. "It's because Mama is here."

The boys led Mama and Ed to the dining room, which had been enlarged by removing the partitions that had been in place for the boys' regular meal.

Campfire cooks brought in roast pheasant, squirrel, and quail to supplement the savory feast laid out by the lay brother and sister: roast beef, hot bread, butter, jams, jellies, cakes, pies, canned fruit, and vegetables. Giant enamelware pots breathed out the steam of boiling hot coffee.

"Where are Tamma and Kahpat all this time?" Ed asked the two oldest Westmore boys.

"They are having a separate Christmas party in the small boys' quarters," Leschi said. "They are considered too young to behave, and too young to stay up late."

As it had been suggested by Father deRouge, Leschi, Owhi, and Ed ate rapidly so that other guests could have their places in the dining room. After excusing themselves, they went to watch the feasting outdoors at long tables set up near bonfires.

"This must be the most people ever to come to the mission at one time," Owhi marveled.

The Westmore boys and their guest fell on cots in the dormitory at half past two.

Tamma and Kahpat were delivered to the rest of the Westmore contingent after breakfast. They told of a decorated Christmas tree, singing, and a visit from St. Nicholas, with oranges and candy.

After Mama and Ed thanked Father deRouge for the hospitality of the mission, the troop bundled itself into the sleigh and departed on the trek home. When they had come a mile up the winding road from the mission, all four boys stood up in the sleigh and yelled, "Yi! Yi! Yi! Yi!"

"You'll spook the horses," Ed cautioned, but he knew how the boys felt. School was out for two whole weeks!

The only chores during Christmas vacation were distributing wagonloads of hay to the herds and breaking water on the lake so that the cattle could drink.

Leschi, Owhi, and Ed accompanied Red Curlew to the Indian winter camp at Osoyoos Lake. Ed shook hands with Indian men; ate stew at the fire of Smiling Water, Red Curlew's mother; and watched the gambling. When invited to participate, Leschi and Owhi knelt with a team but soon lost the sticks that had been handed to them by Red Curlew. They stayed through an evening of dancing and storytelling.

WHEN THE BOYS returned to school, driven back this time by Nathan, the AW was left comparatively quiet and idle. The calves had not yet begun to arrive. Nathan and Will seemed not to mind lolling about the bunkhouse between ample meals that Flower prepared.

Ed mentioned to Mr. Westmore, "I ought to be thinking of a way of making my living."

Mr. Westmore nodded agreement.

"We're happy to have you stay as long as you like. Nathan and Will have been here for years, but I see you as a chap who wants to get ahead on his own."

Ed flushed as he said, "I haven't saved anything."

"Nathan and Will are to blame for that," Mr. Westmore accused as the stay-at-homes were gathered about the lamplight.

"Come on, Boss!" Nathan objected. "We made Ed buy himself two pairs of socks and some long underwear before we went to the saloon the last time we got paid. Besides, one shot of whiskey puts him under the table. We don't know what he does with his wages."

"Let me make you a proposition," Mr. Westmore offered. "You can work for board and room and one calf a month, instead of a twenty-dollar gold piece. Nathan and Will can do the same if they want to. I'll provide a little spending money whenever we go to town."

"No thanks!" Nathan and Will said in chorus, but Ed said, "I think I'll accept. I really like the cattle business. I hear some land is being set up for homestead entry."

"You can run your calves with the herd until you're ready," Mr. Westmore said. "Good for you!"

Nathan and Will laughed.

"The Old Man is awful tight with those gold pieces," they teased. "He's playing you for a sucker."

"I don't think so," Ed decided. He knew he could not be satisfied to work indefinitely for wages as Nathan and Will seemed content to do.

GOLD WAS STILL the bait the Great Northern Railway used to lure settlers. Reports were widely circulated of dividends totaling three thousand one hundred and twenty-five dollars paid by Okanogan Free Gold Mines, Ltd. On display at Rossland, British Columbia, were twenty-four-ounce gold bricks from the mine.

At Loomis, the Black Bear Mine was grinding away and producing enough ore to stay open. The Nighthawk Mine was being developed with Milwaukee capital. The Wannacut Lake Mining and Milling company had established a hundred-stamp mill to refine ore for the whole vicinity. The breakthrough to wealth was coming with the railroad!

Although the northern half of the Colville reservation was still legally closed to white people, Neil Hardy and Tom Stanton had been in the stagecoach business since 1896, when gold was found in Republic, fifty miles southeast of Osoyoos Lake.

Now, two years later, the land was being thrown open officially for mineral entry. Nathan, Will, and Ed rode over to the new boom town to see the show. The muddy streets, the saloons, the hotels, and stores milled with people who planned to take the stage to Rock Creek. In the dead of winter, with heavy snow on the ground, amateur prospectors in thin shoes and light wraps talked excitedly of their plans. Nathan and Will led Ed up to meet Neil Hardy, whose face was a gooey morass of handlebar mustache and dripping tobacco juice.

"How many loads you gonna make today?" Will asked.

"I'll drive till midnight," Neil said. "Gotta make my fortune, too."

Ed remarked, "I feel sorry for some of these women."

Neil shook his head in hopelessness. "I told a lot of' em they ought to get a coat on, and some other shoes, but they don't pay any attention. They jump off the stage into the snow thinkin' they're gonna find a gold mine!"

Ed was glad to ride home with Nathan and Will to the warmth of Flower's hearth. He would postpone finding a claim at least until the weather lightened.

Republic reached a population of six thousand, to become the fourth largest town in the state. Although the land officially belonged to the Indians, thousands of white people were squatting on tracts that they anticipated would be open in the near future for legal settlement. In fulfillment of expectation, the north half of the Colville reservation was opened for homesteading in 1900. The Great Northern Railway finished laying tracks to Republic and began regular runs to the town, simplifying travel for the region's newcomers.

Ed, who was sampling a beer in the tavern after loading the Westmore buckboard with groceries, barbwire, and harness, listened to white settlers justifying themselves. All adult Indian males had been given the privilege of moving to the south half of the reservation or accepting an allotment of surveyed land in the north.

"Give Injuns their choice of eighty or a hundred acres on the reservation. They take the eighty acres and get paid for the rest of their land in money. They build a house, but they put a tepee out in front and the cowhides in the house," a wiseacre chuckled to his cronies.

Ed could not resist an interjection: "Nobody can make a living on small allotments of Okanogan County land. Besides, the whites are slickering the Indians out of even their eighty acres as fast as they can."

"All Injuns care about is gambling and firewater," the man retorted.

"You're making a broad statement," Ed countered. "Indians here are more civilized than whites. Father deRouge at St. Mary's Mission has taught them how to behave. He's made friends of them."

"Yeah," a man called. "The Injun lover wears a long robe to cover holes in the seat of his pants."

"Maybe there are holes in the seat of his pants, but he keeps firewater from the Indians; he's made good people. Old Man Westmore has an Indian wife. I've lived with the family since I came west."

"I'm damned!" the wiseacre said as he emptied his glass and turned away. He called to the barkeeper for a refill.

Ed, who had thought to celebrate his twenty-first birthday by attempting, one more time, to enjoy beer, left his mug unfinished and walked from the saloon.

CARR WESTMORE DISCUSSED the inroads that the boisterous hordes were making on his livestock. "Val Haynes, who's foreman now for Tom Ellis, told me he'd seen an AW brand that had been altered. A gang is herding our cattle off, it appears. Val and I have agreed to get the goods on one of the big gangs and see it through the courts. Next time you see our brand or the Ellis brand in suspicious company ride like a bat out of Hades to let me know; but try not to attract attention. We're fed up with 'slick ears' and people who protect relatives by lying as to their whereabouts.

"Old Lady Haley's outfit is the worst. John and Lewis feel they are good boys minding Mama when she tells them to move a dozen head of cattle from place to place."

MR. WESTMORE RECEIVED an order from James Pearson, the butcher at Republic, for sixty steers. Although it was nearly Christmas time, the weather was still open. The Old Man felt that Red Curlew and Ed could deliver the beef without much trouble. Red Curlew, who had at length elected to take a hundred-acre surveyed allotment next to the AW, had leased his acreage to his brother-in-law and moved into the bunkhouse as a cattle hand.

To keep shrinkage on the way to market at a minimum, Ed and Red Curlew drove the herd only ten or fifteen miles each day and allowed them to graze on bunchgrass wherever it stood above the snow along the trail.

On the morning of the second day, Red Curlew told Ed, "I believe someone besides us is driving cattle along the creek. I see a horse dodging in and out of the willows. Let's find out who it is."

As they left the trail and rode nearer the stream, John Haley, the elder of Old Lady Haley's dutiful sons, rode from behind a willow clump. "Hello, you busters! Been trying to catch up to you. I'm driving this dozen critters up to Republic for Tom Ellis. Like to mosey along with you."

Ed and Red Curlew observed that the cattle had Ellis brands: ten animals marked HL on the left ribs, and two branded 69 on the right hip, both marks used by Ellis. But Red Curlew and Ed doubted that Tom Ellis, whose foreman was Val Haynes, would delegate any cattle buying or selling to a member of the local robbers' roost.

Red Curlew, quick with the knowledge of what to say, agreed to let John Haley's herd join the AW's. "Sure glad to meet up with you. Ed doesn't want to make the trip with me. He wants to stay at the AW so he can drive Westmore's wife to Mass at the mission. Ed can go back. With two of us, we can handle a combined herd."

"That's dandy!" John Haley said. "You and me, Red, can handle twice as many cattle as we got."

Taking his cue, Ed said he surely preferred to go back to the ranch. He walked his Appaloosa out of sight, then kicked him in the ribs and "rode like hell" as the Old Man had previously ordered.

"GET BACK THERE as fast as you can," Mr. Westmore ordered. "Say your Old Man told you there was no way you could be excused from a cattle drive to go to a Christmas party.

"Don't let John guess you know he is stealing the Ellis cattle. Stay with him. If we seize the cattle now, they become hostages of the law and must be moved at public expense. Let the thief do his own herding and driving into trouble. The dressed-out hides must be found in the butcher's corral in Republic. The sheriff has to see with his own eyes in the presence of witnesses. I'll drag him to the scene by the ear if necessary!"

Ed overtook Red Curlew and John Haley where they had stopped for the night at the Charles Pugh place. Mr. Pugh, who did blacksmithing as a sideline, caught Red Curlew's wink and unnecessarily reshod his pony. Mr. Pugh also offered the overnight use of his meadow for the herd. They were still eight or ten miles west of Republic.

In the morning they completed the drive to the slaughterhouse at which the beef were to be dressed for the butcher shop. Ed had not seen Clay Brown since the day they had parted company on Sinlahekin Creek, but was not surprised to find him in his former trade at Republic.

"Hi, young pardner!" Clay hailed him. "Glad to see you still alive and kicking. Worried about you.

"Let's put the critters in the corrals until morning. I'll go out with you with a lantern to open the gate."

'We need receipts," Ed said. "Red Curlew and I have sixty head."

"Sure, I'll give you a receipt," Clay agreed at once, "but we can't count in the dark. You find a bed for the night and come back in the morning for counting."

As the tired animals moved into the corrals, the sheriff of Ferry-Okanogan County, Sheriff Lowry, and two deputies rode up to tie lantern light.

"Whose cattle you got here, Brown?" the sheriff asked.

"After I slaughter 'em, they go to Pearson's butcher shop." "I mean, where'd they come from? Who sold 'em?"

"Mostly AW brand," Clay answered.

"Any Ellis cattle in this bunch?"

"No, not that I know of. If there is any, I don't know it."

"We'll leave 'em here tonight and come out in the morning to look at them. We got a report from over west some Ellis cattle are missing. Maybe they could have got mixed up with this herd."

"Where's Haley?" Ed whispered to Red Curlew.

"Long gone. Didn't you see Brown sign for him to beat it?"

Clay Brown told the officers, "I was just sending these fellows back to town for a good night's rest. Any objection?"

"Fine!" Lowry said. "Might as well ride back to town with us."

Ed noted that no deputy was left on guard at the corral.

IN THE MORNING, no Ellis cattle were found in the corral. The sheriff excused Ed and Red Curlew to return to the AW.

"If you come on any stray Ellis cattle, let us know," Sheriff Lowry told them.

As they rode off toward home, Ed asked Red Curlew, "Why didn't we say something?"

"Around most palefaces I cannot speak English," the Indian answered.

"Haley got away with the whole thing! He sure must have had a hard time cutting out those HL steers in the dark"

Red Curlew smiled. "He had plenty help."

"Where do you suppose they took them?"

"We just passed them. Didn't you see them in the field in the timber? They'll be back at the slaughterhouse by noon."

THAT AFTERNOON, VALENTINE Carmichael Haynes, Tom Ellis's foreman, was standing at the Robber's Roost Saloon bar in Republic when John Haley stepped up to buy a drink with a hundred-dollar bill.

Tom Ellis, virtually holding Sheriff Lowry by the collar, kicked through the fresh cowhides at Brown's slaughterhouse. He found two hides branded 69 on the right hip, and ten hides marked HL.

Carr Westmore, Val Haynes, and Tom Ellis accompanied Ed and Red Curlew to the courthouse to make a statement against John Haley.

It was the first time in four years that cattle theft charges had been filed in Okanogan County. Prosecution had been impossible because no one was willing to testify against a hungry person, but suddenly forty-seven witnesses were willing to appear for the state.

James Pearson protested that he had made a legitimate purchase from Clay Brown; he knew nothing of the source of the beef.

Trial of the cattle thieves was set for summer when people could travel readily to Conconully, the county seat. A two-story frame structure resembling an oversize saloon, except for the American flag flying over it, had been erected as the courthouse. Its chambers could accommodate a large audience. A dozen wooden steps led up to a railed-in porch across the front of the edifice; a railed-in balcony graced the second story front.

Hundreds were drawn to the courthouse.

Analix, home from Holy Names for the summer, played an official role as interpreter for her uncle, Red Curlew, and other Sinkaietk who had seen John Haley on the trail with the Ellis cattle.

Red Curlew, wearing buckskins, spoke through his niece, demure in the Holy Names uniform of dark dress with a white collar: "Ed McLaren and I spotted the Ellis cattle in the willows on Bonaparte Creek; then we met their driver, John Haley, who told us he was taking them to Republic for Tom Ellis. We got to Clay Brown's corrals about ten o'clock the second night. John Haley drove the beef he was herding in with the AW steers."

Ed noted the looks being cast at Analix and wanted to jump up and hustle her to safety.

At recess, Carr Westmore gave Ed two dollars. "Take her to the ice cream parlor for a strawberry sundae or whatever she wants."

As they sat in a booth, Ed looked across the table at the pretty young woman of mixed blood and wished that he could forestall the indignities that might be heaped upon her. He hoped that because Carr Westmore was her father, she would be protected.

Analix, whose cheeks were red with excitement, asked happily, "Do you think I did all right, Ed? Do you? Papa said I did just fine."

"You did a dandy job," Ed assured her.

Called next, Ed gave his version of the drive with Haley. He observed that persons in the crowd who had expected a tale of a pell-mell, hoof-hammering pursuit of a thief looked dissatisfied with his testimony.

Val Haynes presented more of a spectacle. Resplendent in a red and black shirt, twill pants, and riding boots, all topped with a black Stetson, he was the complete cowboy. He spoke with a trace of English accent that carried over from his childhood: "I am twenty-eight years old. I live at Osoyoos or Penticton, anywhere in between. I know the twelve head of cattle that the defendant is charged with stealing. I saw them last about December 7, 1901, on the United States side of the line, near Borax Lake in Okanogan County. I am foreman for Tom Ellis. I recognize the hides skinned from the beef—there they are on the table. At Torn Ellis's orders, I brought them to the sheriff's office from Clay Brown's cache behind his slaughterhouse. I don't know how they got out there after they had been called to the attention of the sheriff in the slaughterhouse."

Old Lady Haley had found a defense lawyer among the men who congregated at the Peerless Hotel bar in Oroville. Although he was a bona fide graduate of an Eastern law school, he had not opened an office after four years in the West, but saw what clients he had in his hotel room. Reputedly, a stipend from home covered the cost of his beverages at the Peerless bar.

After a desultory, mumbled cross-examination of the state's witness that changed nothing in the story, the defense attorney allowed Val Haynes to be excused. Old Lady Haley broke out in oaths, but quieted herself.

John Haley, on the witness stand the following day, told his story straight on the basis of a promise that James Pearson, the butcher, would also be charged.

"I am twenty-four years old. I have known James Pearson for the past six years. I was out at Davenport in the forepart of December, 1901. From there I came back to Republic, and after some conversations, I agreed to go and get these cattle. On about the eighteenth of December, I went up to Oroville and got ten head of the Torn Ellis cattle, and also two other cattle. One was a Coster steer; one was the steer owned by an Indian at Inkaneck."

"He's a weaseling little liar!" James Pearson bellowed.

The judge banged the gavel at the portly, outraged butcher. The defense attorney pulled Pearson back to his seat.

"At any further outbursts, I'll order you from the room," the judge stated.

John Haley continued his responses to the prosecutor: "It was after dark when we reached Republic with the cattle. Before we got to the corrals, Sheriff Lowry and two deputies came up there. Lowry was the Ferry County sheriff. He asks, 'Is there any HL cattle in this bunch?'

"Clay Brown says, 'None that I know of.'

"Lowry says, 'Well, it's too dark to see now. Put them cattle in the field, and I'll come out and examine them in the morning.'"

"What happened to the cattle during the night?"

"The cattle took a mope the next morning."

"How early?"

"It was quite a bit before daylight."

"Who took them?"

"James Pearson and myself took them out of there."

"Where did you take them?"

"Put them in Fuller's field, a big field up there in the timber."

"Where did you go then?"

"Went back to Republic."

"Did you get any money out of this cattle stealing?"

"Yes, I did."

"How much?"

"I got a hundred dollars."

"Who gave you this hundred dollars?"

"James Pearson."

Pearson yelled, "He's lying! Damn the walloper!"

The judge ordered a recess and instructed that Pearson be barred from the room until all references to his part in the cattle theft were completed.

Testimony continued for weeks and led to the verdict of guilty for both Haley and Pearson.

Protesting his innocence and reviling his co-defendant as a, back-stabber, Pearson escaped jail by a series of appeals. John Haley good-naturedly served his term in the penitentiary. It was part of his family tradition to "do time in the pen."

On the day of his sentencing, John nodded greetings to Red Curlew, Val Haynes, and Ed. He smiled at them broadly and called, "No hard feelings! You got me dead to rights!"

When Ed went to Loomis for supplies, he was pointed out on the street as the "guy who caught the cattle rustlers." In the bar to which Nathan and Will dragged him, owners of livestock doffed their ten-gallon hats in recognition.

Frank Beeman, now in the ranching business on Pine Creek, insisted on buying Ed a real drink. "None of that beer slop! Yeah, you're a comer, boy. You're gonna be a leading citizen. I done a good thing when I packed you in here along with the flour."

Ed shied away from the glory. "Old Man Westmore and Tom Ellis were the ones behind the trials. Red Curlew and I just followed orders. My boss comes from England. He said what the country needs is 'jurisprudence.' Guess they're great on law and order in England."

Frank Beeman swallowed as he considered Ed's explanation.

"I'm not in favor of too much 'jurisprudence,' but killing one to eat is a lot different from running a dozen of the neighbor's cows to the butcher."

EVER SINCE THE north half of the Colville reservation had been opened for mineral excavation, many white settlers had encroached on choice grassland by staking it out in mining claims. When the land was subsequently opened for homesteading in 1900, many of the mining claims had already been put to agricultural use. If Ed expected to find good grass meadow, he knew he should file a claim at once.

He selected a hundred and sixty acres lying between two creeks, Antwyne and Bonaparte, that ran into the Okanogan River from the east side, giving him water on three borders of his land. He filed a claim at the courthouse and received instructions about minimum improvement requirements. To "prove up, " he must live on the homestead part of each year for five years.

The Old Man agreed to Ed's absence at intervals from the AW. Ed continued to move Westmore cattle, build fence, and act as foreman at haytime. Sandwiched among the days as an AW hand, he went to his claim to construct a two-room shack with scrap lumber he bought from the new sawmill on Tunk Creek. After roofing and chinking the cabin, he cleared land. On the ground between the two creeks, he plotted his home place. His acreage was not big enough to grow sufficient wild grass for the cows he had purchased over a two-year period from the AW. He had sold six two-year-old steers and ten calves as part of the AW herd at the Seattle stockyards, and had placed his profits in the Moore, Ish & Finn banking house at Conconully. To feed thirty cows with calf, he would need to seed his ground with alfalfa and oats; also he would plant an acre of apple and cherry trees as a setting for his cabin.

To buy the seed, plow, and roller that he needed, he went to Pard

Cummings, whose landing place on the Okanogan River had become the terminus of the stern-wheelers that brought merchandise and passengers from the coast. Pard sold Ed the seed and equipment, and pointed out his need for a cookstove, a teakettle, a frying pan, a stewpan, and a folding cot for a bed.

He could buy seedling trees from Doc Pogue, who had begun an orchard on land that he irrigated. Doc had dug his own irrigation ditches three and a half miles from Salmon Creek.

"You have a natural site for an orchard," Doc told Ed. "Before you take the young trees, break your ground and dig your ditches; then we'll pick you out some likely young trees. I'll let you have them for next to nothing."

Ed replied, "That's how much I can afford, but maybe I can help you with some chores from time to time."

"Fair and square," the doctor said.

The doctor, who held a medical degree from Northwestern University, had become one of the most enthusiastic promoters of the development of the Okanogan country.

He offered, "I have a pair of Hamiltonian horses you can borrow if you do some plowing for me."

Ed gratefully agreed to the trade.

WORK WAS LIGHT at the AW just before the onset of winter. The Westmore boys were at St. Mary's, Analix and Bethany at Holy Names. Two high haystacks stood ready against the day the snow covered the bunchgrass. Cows awaiting the birth of calves were secure in the cache; the three-year-old steers had been driven to the railhead and sold.

"I could probably move to my own place now," Ed suggested to the Old Man.

"We'll let you go after spring branding," he said, "but here comes the snow now. You're lucky Flower is inside boiling up a pot of stew."

The snow was coming down in flurries in a strong, cold wind. Ed was glad to go into the house with the Old Man, Nathan, and Will. Flower had lighted the lamp.

"Ed tells me he is pulling out in the spring," Mr. Westmore said to the others as they ate.

"What you gonna do for Flower's stew and bread knots?" Nathan asked. "I'd think twice about leaving a good cook."

"A strong young man like Ed will have no trouble finding a cook," Flower said with a smile.

AS THEY FED cattle from the haystacks through the period of heavy snow, the

Old Man advised Ed, "You see how we can take care of our cows with feed and water handy. It's different from the way my father and others like Ben Snipes and Dan Drumheller left their herds on the range to fend for themselves on the bunchgrass and to have their calves with no help. There will never be such large, wild herds on open range again in this country. We've had to learn to keep no more cows than we can care for through the winter—hard or light. What the men with thousands of head had to learn is that cattle are essentially domestic animals and only flourish as such.

"Stock overran the range and broke the ground cover, too. Where the ground was churned up, brush took root and crowded out the native grasses. We shouldn't put our cattle on the bunchgrass until the roots have a chance to take hold in the spring, or there soon won't be much wild range. We have to divide our grazing areas. No use talking to some people like this, Ed, but I see you as a boy of some sense."

SNUG WITH THE others around the fireplace in the long evenings, Ed shivered at the thought of leaving such a comfortable home.

After the spring branding of new caves, Ed cut out his own cattle—he had devised his own Lazy Ear brand to mock the characteristic droop of his own left ear—and drove his herd to Mount Hull, to slopes that had never previously been grazed. He would let the alfalfa and oats he had planted in the fall on his river meadowland grow untouched for winter feed.

He rode to the AW to collect his gear. When he came to the corral that circled the bunkhouse, he dismounted from the Appaloosa he had ridden ever since rescuing Analix from the flood. He loosened the saddle and threw it over the corral fence.

The Old Man, who had been cleaning the water trough, said, "I'm giving you your horse. She probably wouldn't let anyone else ride her. Also, that's your saddle."

"I can buy my own horse," Ed protested. "You've given me a lot already."

"Not so much," the Old Man said. "You gave us something, too. If you hadn't come by to put the mower together, we'd still be using scythes to cut hay."

Nathan and Will, also in the corral, were hitching the workhorses to the buckboard. Ed supposed they were being sent to Loomis for supplies, but they drove the team to the front of the bunkhouse. Flower appeared.

"Nathan and Will will drive you to your cabin," Mr. Westmore said. He threw Ed's saddle into the wagon bed. Get your gear and they'll haul it. Tie your mount behind the wagon."

"I'll do it for him," Will said. "Get up on the seat."

Ed sputtered in protest but was too overwhelmed to do anything but obey.

Analix and Bethany had not yet returned from Spokane, but all the boys were home for the summer from St. Mary's. Tamma, Kahpat, Telah, and Antwine came from diverse directions and hopped into the bed of the buckboard with the surety that they would also be needed to help Ed get settled in his new home.

The Old Man, Flower, and their two oldest sons stood together. Leschi and Owhi, who in the past year had studied Caesar and algebra at the mission, were as tall as adults.

"I'm not needed for hay harvest this year," Ed thought with a twinge. "There are husky hands aplenty at the AW."

AFTER THE BUCKBOARD lurched into motion, Nathan told Ed, "Look behind you. Flower has put in a few presents."

Ed saw beef jerky, dried salmon, and jars of fruit. Telah called his attention to two rolls, which Ed recognized as blankets made of wild goat wool. Flower had garnered the wool in the previous summer from the bushes on which goats had scratched off their winter covering. She had carded the wool and woven it on a loom that had stood by the fireplace all winter. Ed had many times admired the work in progress, but had never imagined that such warm comfort was being manufactured for him. The only decoration on the blankets consisted of darker wool in bands at the tops and bottoms.

Ed marveled at the mystery and beauty of the tall woman, slender as her husband despite ten pregnancies. She had bid him a silent farewell with an Indian sign. People spoke of Indians as savages, but Ed had found them persons of dignity, courtesy, and loving kindness to strangers within their gates.

12.

Homesteader

Ed's first days as a homesteader left him lonesome for the spread in the hills. All that sustained him through the sweltering summer heat, as he carried buckets of water from the creek to his four-foot-high trees, was the prospect that one day he would be working in the coolness of an orchard. Sometimes he stopped to build smudge fires to abate the insects. In desperation he jumped on his horse and rode to the hills for an afternoon to escape the bloodsucking swarms.

Ed's only neighbors were Chief Ohotkolin and his large family of wives and children. Before the government had opened the land to white settlement, it had first allotted each Indian resident who so desired an eighty-acre tract. When the surveying crew had given Ohotkolin his choice of a part of the valley, the chief had gruffly and bluntly declared, "All mine!"

The Indians displayed no hostility toward Ed but ignored his presence.

Awakened by a racket one morning, Ed saw the chief's first wife chasing a young woman from the main tepee. The old woman brandished a stick as she ran after the fleeing girl, and from time to time succeeded in landing a whack about the young one's head and shoulders. The recipient of the beating managed to hop on one of the ponies that were grazing in the pasture; but the old wife snagged a mount of her own, gave chase, and overtook her rival. She grabbed the mane of the young girl's horse to hold the girl within reach of the stick Yelps of pain resounded across the hills and sent back echoes. Ohotkolin, who bragged about his ability to hear deer moving in the forest, stayed deaf in his shed. If he met the young woman again, it would have to be on the sly.

The valley was filling quickly with homesteaders. First dwellings, like Ed's, were one-room scrap lumber cabins with a lean-to on the backside. Charlie McGinty, who had tried mining with as much success as Ed, began an orchard, also with the help of Doc Pogue. Ben Ross came up the river by boat to the terminal at Brewster, bought a horse and saddle, and wandered around the north half looking for a location. He talked over with Ed the

193

Salmon Creek reservoir possibilities and shortly afterward settled on the river flat. Miss Georgia Warren filed in the Antwyne, too, and was snapped up by a suitor before the other bachelors could wangle an introduction.

Ed's first white neighbors were brothers, Morton and Buford Clements, who were husky but squatty in physique. When Ed called on them, he could tell they were intelligent enough, but they studied his attempt at friendliness with suspicious eyes. When they did not return his call, Ed supposed they wanted to mind their own business and left them alone. They carried water to their shack from the same rock on which Ed filled his buckets, but scarcely nodded their heads at meeting on the path.

Sven and Olaf Linstrom, immigrants from Norway, became Ed's best friends. They were sociable and full of practical jokes.

As soon as their cabin was finished, the Linstroms proceeded to break up a seedbed in preparation for growing a crop. Ed watched the brothers' attempts to use a primitive harrow which they had manufactured by attaching thornbushes to a log. They had chained the log to their two small horses, who were now trying to drag it behind them. When Ed saw the horses were finding it impossible to make any headway through the tough bunchgrass sod, he led his own horse across the field and offered to let the Linstroms use it. He stayed to see how things progressed with the extra horse and received the brothers' hearty thanks when the log drag began operating as it was designed to do. They invited him into their cabin for a mug of coffee from the pot on the back of their cookstove.

The Linstroms sowed their field with oats. By midsummer, their crop stood as high as Ed's. At Ed's suggestion, they jointly rented a mower from Pard Cummings and harvested their feed crops as a crew. The three bachelors surveyed their twenty-five ton haystacks and decided they had earned a vacation before starting fence-building and ditch-digging. Using the Linstrom wagon as conveyance, they went on a camping trip around the circuit of towns that were popping up like mushrooms. In the wagon bed they threw a jumble of bedding and cooking utensils, most valuable of which was a frying pan, used every time they came upon a creek and caught a mess of trout. In Chalkees, where one time a mission school had stood, they bought bacon, eggs, and a quantity of bottled beer. At each meal they filled up like boa constrictors.

When fat Sven was snoring heavily after one such meal, lying on his back with his paunch protruding into the air, Olaf and Ed dropped their empty beer bottles on him. Sven sat up with the snap of a jackknife. "You guys tried to kill me!" he yelled.

They scrubbed the frying pan in the creek sand and moved on.

Ed and the Linstroms, who also grazed their cattle on Mount Hull during the summer, undertook to build a road to the mount. They started with the cow trail because cows had naturally chosen an easy grade. In the heat and dust of August, the three young men plowed up the trail, widened it with a primitive road grader made of two boards nailed together at a V angle, and then used a King split-log drag, which they had ordered and paid for together.

People arrived daily in wagons loaded high with worldly possessions, built cabins, and tilled the soil. They settled in every draw that had a creek.

Poker and solo, long the ordinary diversions of the predominantly masculine population, now ceased to provide sufficient social activity because they excluded the increasing feminine element. Newcomers complained to other women, "What do you girls do to put in time evenings?"

Pioneer women hinted that pleasurable activity did take place in homes after nightfall, but prodded their husbands later: "Those uppity creatures with their clothes still fresh from the East! They don't have all the looks, anyhow! You should take us to a party once in a while!"

Shivarees for newly married couples brightened tattle at the store: "When that sissy, prissy Margaret from St. Louis heard the washtubs thumping and the whooping and hollering out side, she screamed, 'Injuns is a-comin!' We could hear her clear outdoors. When we shoved into the cabin, there she was down on her knees, eyes shut, pale as a ghost, prayin' for deliverance!"

Christmas provided another social highlight. Pard Cummings, proprietor of Glenwood Mercantile Company at Pard's Landing, began the custom of an annual open house in the unfinished upstairs of his large frame home on the river bank. Families jolted over hills in wagons without springs, children snug in straw in the back.

Three speedsters in a sleigh, Ed, Sven, and Olaf, zipped past the cumbersome wagons. At Pard's, a nook was arranged for coats and kids. All comers contributed to a potluck supper.

After the feast, the overstuffed children staggered to their corner and reluctantly fell asleep despite the inviting sounds of the musicians tuning up their instruments: B Flat Bill on harmonica, Charley Thorpe on fiddle, and Three-fingered Larry McDonald on piano.

In the attic full of dancers to "O, the moon shines tonight on pretty Redwing," Sven, Olaf, and Ed were as stylish as everyone else in their ten-gallon hats and shaggy, woolly chaps, black, blue, and orange, respectively. The rowels of their spurs jangled with every dance step and gouged the floor mercilessly.

At daylight, people thought of going home. Although Sven had consumed too many drinks even for him, he insisted on driving the sleigh. Not far into the journey, he rashly forced the horses to turn a comer too sharply; the sleigh overturned and plummeted the bachelors into an embankment. With snow up their sleeves and down their coat collars, they were cold, miserable, and sober the rest of the way to Bonaparte.

All three slept at Ed's place. At noon, when they sat down at Ed's table, Sven could still pile more and more hotcakes and more and more eggs and bacon on his plate, all the while waxing strong on the subject of how much he had eaten and drunk the night before.

"I don't see how you stood it to breakfast," Ed said testily as he emptied out the last of his flour sack.

He was reaching a surfeit of intimacy with the Linstroms.

DICK MIRVA AND his bride moved in nearby. Mrs. Mirva, Aggie, arrived at the homestead as a blonde with curls down her back; but after a few months in the cold, lugging wood to keep herself warm, griming her hands with the soot of the stove, she gradually came to look like other homesteaders' wives depressed by the woes of a harsh existence. Her hair began to hang like a witch's wig, uncurled.

When Ed dropped by, she grabbed the broom, swept out the cabin hastily, and apologized, "My hair is a sight!"

She retired to the bedroom and returned soon with her hair in a knot. She threw out old coffee grounds and started a fresh pot. As she served Ed and Dick with steaming mugs of coffee, she begged, "Why don't you fellows take me to a dance before I die of cabin fever!"

"I don't know of any more dances till the weather is better," Dick placated her. "We'll take you to the next one we hear about."

She continued to cry and rail. Ed decided to reduce the number of his visits if his coming threw her into a frenzy. He stopped going to the Mirvas' altogether when he overheard an exchange not meant for his ears. As he rode up to the cabin one afternoon on his horse, he heard shrill screams. Mirva was slapping his wife and cursing.

"Damn it, you're always whining! Shut your face before I shut it for you! You fuss over Ed like you're in love with him."

"Ed wouldn't treat a woman the way you do. Haulin' in my own wood and water! Nothin' to wear except this dress I made myself from flour sacks! Sure, I'm in love with him! He's lots better looking than you, too!"

Ed turned the Appaloosa away sharply. He lambasted himself for a jackass; he recognized trouble only when his face was pushed into it. What real defense had he before the embarrassing fancies of a silly woman? Some of his married friends had advised him that being married to one woman was the only shield from being an obvious target for the rest. For the first time, he gave a moment's thought to the advantages of the married state.

HE RESOLVED TO throw his excess energies into the job to which he had recently been elected—foreman of a crew to build a road from Bonaparte to Oroville.

The Clements brothers, who had struck him before as the stingy, self-centered sort, refused to assist the program even to the extent of letting the road cross their property. The Indian trail had always gone through the pasture, which was originally Chief Ohotkolin's. Gossipers said the Clements had bought forty acres from the chief in exchange for a pony and a jug of whiskey.

Ed had vowed never to set foot in the Clements' s cabin again after they refused him the right of way for the road, but his sentiment altered with the arrival of their sister, Eleanor. She had attended Marcus Whitman Academy in the settlement at Walla Walla. At age twenty-one she had come to prove up on a claim of her own adjoining her brothers' place. Her brothers built her a tiny sleeping shed on her acreage, but she spent most of her time keeping house and cooking at her brothers' cabin. All the unmarried men, including Ed, found business at the Clements's.

Eleanor brought back to Ed's memory what young ladies were like—those who attended church socials and academy classes in Iowa—tantalizingly fresh in smell and completely pure in body. She wore her abundant, curly black hair in a ladylike bun on top of her head, but short wisps escaped naughtily on the sides. Her skin was clear and smooth, with pink highlights on her cheekbones. She wore dark, ankle-length skirts and starched, ironed, white overblouses.

He sat in her brothers' shack while she served him coffee, homemade bread, and jelly. They first discussed the new dry goods store in the town that was forming at the junction of the river and Bonaparte Creek. Then she confided that a group of parents had asked her to teach grammar school next fall. Cooking for her brothers wasn't enough to keep her busy; and besides, she did have her "education going to waste."

All week Ed had avoided agreeing to go with the Linstroms to the Saturday night dance, which was being held to raise money for the proposed school. As he was about to end his call, he found courage to ask her to go to the dance with him. Ed was flattered when she accepted, for he knew that she had already refused half a dozen other invitations with the excuse that she planned to attend with her brothers.

She told Ed, "Mort and Buford have made up their minds that they don't want to go, so I'll be glad for you to take me. It isn't far out of your way. If it's to raise money for the school, I really should be present, don't you think?"

"Yeah, it would look peculiar if you weren't there," Ed quickly agreed.

He came for her Saturday night in his new buckboard, handed her up gallantly to the seat, swung himself up beside her, lifted the reins, and smacked them along the horses' backs to start them pulling.

As they bounced along the roadbed that Ed had helped build, they said scarcely anything to one another. Ed was preoccupied with displaying his latest acquisitions: a new buckboard and horses. He was astonished when he noticed that Eleanor squirmed and blushed every time the colt running alongside made an attempt to reach the teats of the mare that was part of the team. He had forgotten how priggish girls could be about the natural ways of animals.

At the dance, Eleanor was too popular to suit Ed, but she came back to his good graces on the way home when she invited him to eat Sunday dinner with her brothers and herself.

After the dinner, which was the best meal Ed had enjoyed since leaving the AW, Eleanor repeated her invitation for the next weekend. He drifted into the habit of eating Sunday dinners with the Clements. Eleanor assured Ed that her brothers liked him, a conclusion he never would have reached on his own.

Mort told Ed one Sunday, "We'd sure appreciate it if you keep the wagon road off our property. Feed him good, Sis."

Ed had enlisted and was heading the volunteer road crew, who called themselves the Good Roads Association. They plowed the natural trail along the river and widened the road with a V grader and log drag. Funds for equipment were raised by periodic dances. Ed had no intention of playing favorites with the Clements on the course of the road. He told Eleanor in the kitchen, "It's your brothers' tough luck that the grade goes naturally down the lower gulch. Everybody who's helped with the planning agrees. That's the way the cows go down to water. I learned that from working at the Westmores. They built all their roads along the cow trails because cows naturally choose an easy grade. Sven and Olaf and I made a good road all the way up the mountain."

When Eleanor told him he must be joking, he tried to explain to her that it would cost twice as much in time, labor, and materials to shunt the road in a devious circuit; there was no money to waste, no extra effort to spare. Roads were being built with donated manual labor. County road money was supposed to come from a four-mill levy, but so far there had been no increment. The county had little taxable property. Indians, who still held a good deal of the land, could not be taxed. Neither were homesteads taxable until the claim had been proved up. Exemptions also covered homesteaders' cattle, horses, and machinery—almost the total wealth of the area.

"We're going to put up barbwire if your gang starts to go through our land," the Clements told Ed by way of Eleanor.

"You'll be going against the statute," Ed asked her to explain to her brothers. "The legislature has already said that all roads and trails that have been used by the general public for seven years are declared lawful. You can't stop the road just by wanting it stopped."

"Mort and Buford have been to see a lawyer," Eleanor informed him.

"I wish 'em luck. They're going to need a lawyer."

He might not have gone back to the Clements the next Sunday had it not been for his degree of entanglement with Eleanor. In the kitchen, after the meal, Ed dried the dishes. He had never previously demeaned himself thus for any woman, but it permitted him a few minutes alone with coy Eleanor. When he first kissed her, she pulled away and insisted on getting the dishes done. But after the unpleasantness of the discussion about the right of way, she offered her lips for a prim goodbye and said, "We'll expect you next Sunday."

Ed, a full-grown, celibate male, was at the mercy of his natural urges. Her physical closeness turned his body into a piston wanting to drive. If she invited him back in defiance of her brothers' interests, she must like him for himself. He conjured up his memory of the blonde whom he had kissed in the coat room at the academy. He had intended to go back and woo her when he owned a gold mine in the Wild West, but she seemed silly and far away. Eleanor was sedate and uncompromisingly clean in the dusty Okanogan Valley. She would make a good wife if he could endure her hen spurs. He had been a bachelor long enough to appreciate the time and energy required to feed oneself and keep clothing presentable. He often bought new overalls rather than wash ones dirty enough to stand alone—not an economical operation, he realized.

Ed had kissed no one except Eleanor in the Okanogan, although some of the girls had indicated their willingness for him to do so. Then he thought of Analix, who had given him an Indian kiss with her fingertips. A yearning to see her wrenched him. She used to be very fond of Ed, but she would be growing up now. Father deRouge would marry her to an Indian Catholic youth—or keep her as an old maid catechist at the mission.

ELEANOR BEGAN TEACHING eleven pupils in a one-room shack that the menfolk, both married and single, had built. Inside the schoolroom were ten double homemade seats, with space for a younger and older child in each. The school raisers had built an outhouse and also donated a bucket and dipper to hold the drinking water that could be fetched from a nearby creek. The creek was handy, too, to supply disciplinary switches that could be cut from the willows along the bank

Until state funds could be secured, Miss Clements's salary was paid by subscription. New children enrolled daily. Soon all twenty seats were full, which was more than Eleanor had bargained for.

She became known as a successful disciplinarian, a role that she had promised the community to fulfill. One day near the creek, out of sight behind a willow clump, Ed overheard two boys who were fishing: "I bet Miss Clements don't act so bossy around that feller of hers. 'Go down to the creek and get me a switch,' she says, and dumb Billy, teacher's pet, does it! I wonder how long her feller would be sweet on her if he knew how she swats everybody with her old switch! Jeeminy crickets! We wanted a woman teacher because she wouldn't be as mean as a man! She's meaner 'n a badger by daylight!"

Ed was tickled. No doubt the future buckaroos deserved every whack they got! In his school days, he had earned his whacks, he realized now. He was beguiled, too, by the perception in the honest schoolboy minds that he was Miss Clements's "feller."

He came for her every night after school. When the children waited until he arrived and giggled to see Ed help her into the buckboard, she complained, "They're lively and unruly enough without you coming here to take away my authority!"

"What if I didn't come for you? Then you'd be mad, too."

"You just like to trap me!" she snapped.

He smiled victoriously. He could kiss her when they reached the willows, when she was sure no children could see. They were set on a road that led reliably to marriage, a sensible road for the prettiest girl in the country, and for a man with a big appetite and the need for sons to help with the cattle spread and orchard. From Eleanor's point of view, keeping house for surly, ungrateful brothers, and trying to beat the times tables and alphabet into the heads of oafish boys and tomboyish girls, was a less than promising way of life. Ed McLaren was easier to manage and kinder to her than anyone else in her rather harsh existence. Ed, she could see, would be the husband her mother had advised her to look for: a good provider. After the joint drive to Coulee City with steers, Ed had made the biggest deposit of any cattleman in Arthur Lund's new Okanogan State Bank She acknowledged that Ed was a natural leader of people, but with some misgiving. In her family, minding one's own affairs was a tenet.

She allowed their physical intimacies to develop more with fatalistic pragmatism than with personal ardor. When she said "yes" to Ed, she knew what she was in for, but decided never to flinch.

The Reverend C. V. Hall of Chesaw preached in the schoolhouse on one Sunday a month. Ed meekly escorted Eleanor to a service, at the close of which he asked the minister if he would officiate at a wedding. Eleanor had decided it should take place the first Sunday after school was out. The minister was "happy to oblige," and also remarked that he had available a suitable gold wedding band that an elderly widow had given him as a present on her deathbed. Ed agreed to a fee of fifteen dollars for both the minister's services and the ring, and the wedding plans were thus sealed.

On the day of Ed and Eleanor's marriage, the congregation trebled its normal size. Eleanor wore her usual white blouse and dark serge skirt, with the modest addition of a new wide brimmed leghorn hat, adorned with a billow of soft chiffon, lilies-of-the-valley, and a white satin ribbon falling behind. All the ladies had been admiring the hat for some time in the window of Mrs. Carpenter's Home Millinery.

The Methodist minister and the orthodox members of his congregation, far outnumbered, withdrew from the reception as soon as liquor was brought out and guests began dancing to the music of B Flat Bill's Trio.

In the weeks prior to the wedding, Ed had bought a load of lumber from the sawmill and constructed a bedroom on the south side of the cabin. He had also remodeled the back lean-to into a small kitchen and piped water from the creek He could hardly wait to surprise Eleanor with the fact that she would not have to carry water in buckets.

With the dancing at its height, Ed led his bride from the floor, amidst the cheers of the wedding guests. They rode away in his buckboard to Ed's cabin, where he gave her the grand tour of the residence in which she had never before set foot.

"Having water in the house certainly is nice," she said. She began to pick up Ed's overalls from the four corners of the main room, but Ed said, "None of that tonight!"

Ed's lovemaking was an awkward but enthusiastic onslaught. "There!" he exulted at the end. "I've got my brand on you."

She sat up in bed and slapped his face.

TWO NIGHTS LATER a horde of neighbors who felt themselves welcome by strength of custom swarmed in, shrieking and hallooing as they set up a barrel of whiskey and demanded something to go with it. Despite having attended twenty shivarees for other newlyweds, Ed was completely surprised. He was moved to boisterousness and expansive hospitality though he had given no thought to stocking provisions. Eleanor had been more foresighted. She was able to keep the table full in repeated trips to the pantry for cakes, pies, and fresh bread. Ed was awestruck with admiration for her capacities.

He went in a tender mood to the pantry to tell her, and found her wrestling with the lid of a fruit jar. She handed the jar to him with a cross look. "It's about time you came to help! I've been trying to get this lid off for five minutes. I'd get a jar easier to open, but it's the last jar!"

The lid was an intricate one—glass held on by a complicated wire clamp. The fruit undoubtedly came from Walla Walla. He loosened the lid for her.

"Something wrong?"

"No, of course not! Those Linstroms that you call your best friends!

They've eaten up a whole week's baking and three jars of peaches!"

Eleanor splashed the peaches into a serving bowl and handed them to Ed to carry to the table.

"Everybody help himself," he said for the tenth time, but now with a forced heartiness. He knew well that Sven Linstrom had a big appetite, but did Eleanor have a touch of her brothers' stingy streak? Seeming to know that they had worn out their welcome, the invaders left shortly.

Eleanor had kept her serenity before the guests, but as she stood alone in the center of the disarranged front room, Ed saw that she was white-faced and full of resentment. She had filled many stomachs and made polite responses to lewd suggestions concerning her newly married state. He would have to make allowances. He took her in his arms and carried her to the new bedroom.

"You've tired yourself out. You mustn't take Sven and Olaf so seriously."

"Ed, you're nice to me even when I don't deserve it," she softened a moment.

ELEANOR PLUNGED INTO housekeeping with such fervor that Ed realized that his living conditions as a bachelor had been far short of respectable. She exclaimed in disgust as she removed pair after pair of grimy overalls from the corners. Some of the garments had been lying about since calf-branding the spring before.

"I was gonna wash them sometime!" Ed said lamely.

His bride made a number of unexpected demands for household items. Happy Jones, who had tried cattle raising and failed, had secured the agency for the Maytag washing machine. While Ed was building fence, Happy paid a call to the McLaren cabin with a machine for Eleanor to inspect. At noon, when Eleanor announced to Ed what was on the back porch on trial, Ed snorted and said, "I don't trust any gadget that Happy sells."

Eleanor had ready a copper boiler full of hot water, a bar of Crystal White soap that she had cut into shavings, and a mound of overalls and underwear.

"The engine runs on kerosene. You have to start it for me."

Ed dumped the boilerful of hot water into the washing tub. Eleanor added the garments and soap. Ed pushed the lever, and the machine went "Swish-Swash!" with a clanking.

"Sounds like Happy didn't grease anything," Ed commented. He nosed about and used the grease gun that he brought from the shed. The machine was still inclined to hop about the back porch, but now it made less noise.

Eleanor called his attention to the roller wringer. "All you have to do is turn the handle and guide the clothes into the rinse tub. Men don't know how hard it is to wring towels, sheets, and overalls with your hands and arms. "

Ed grunted noncommittally and left Eleanor to finish the procedure. At the end of the day, she brought in from the line Ed's clothes, clean and dry, as he never hoped to see them again after the day they left the store. When Happy came for the verdict next morning, Ed was ready with his checkbook. He paid for the machine and even ordered a pair of zinc rinse tubs with a wringer roller.

Neighbor women, until now resigned to washboards, bustled over to see the bride's indulgence and mentioned the wonder to their menfolk.

Sven Linstrom hailed Ed, "Boy, oh boy! Happy sure is glad you bought that washin' machine. He was leavin' it all over the country. He had it last at Dirty Waters's, that old geezer's who keeps horses on Johnson Creek. Dirty told me that he didn't have any use for the machine and just let it sit by the creek. When Happy come to pick it up, a whole bunch of frogs jumped out. Couldn't have been nothing but tadpoles turned to frogs."

Ed decided not to recount the tale to Eleanor. Happy must have given the washer a good scrubbing with Lysol before he took it to Eleanor, or else the whole story was a lie. Jealous people would say anything.

THE CLEMENTS BROTHERS were summoned to court to show cause why the county road should not continue to go through Chief Ohotkolin' s pasture. Ed, as foreman of the road crew, was called as witness. Eleanor insisted on accompanying him to the court proceedings at Conconully. With his wife glaring at him as he occupied the stand, Ed implacably recounted that the Clements brothers, posted at their fence with shotguns, had threatened to shoot him if he cut the barbwire.

On the way home from the showdown, Eleanor burst out, "You really fixed things! It's your doing my brothers lost!"

"You ought to be glad I didn't repeat any of their cussing. What I testified was mighty cleaned up compared to what they said."

"You're president of the Good Roads Association, besides being foreman of the crew. Don't tell me you couldn't keep the road off!"

"Where'd you get the idea I was trying? I was bringing the suit. We're building the best road we can, and if it goes through Mort's and Buford's property—that they damn near stole anyhow—it's because it's the best way for it to go."

"You could have stretched a point."

"You must get your ideas of honesty from a bum source."

"Don't you dare insult my family! We're respected people where I come from!"

"Mort and Buford would have had more respect around here if they'd let the road go through of their own accord."

"Of all the disloyalty! I'll never forgive you!"

"For not letting you twist me around your finger for your brothers?"

"If I wasn't pregnant, I'd leave you!"

She stared fiercely at him. Her brutal words were true.

Ed shivered to consider what kind of woman would marry to protect her family's property. It was what Ma might have done.

During the remainder of the summer Ed lived in a tent, plotting the road. By lantern light, at the end of the day, he concentrated, making detailed notes.

"FROM THE CORNER *of sec. 11, 12, 13, and 14, I run North and retrace the line bet. secs, 11 and 12 over steep, broken N.W. slope.*

40.75 Falls lks W. of the 1/4 sec. cor. which is a quartzite stone 6x8x8 ins. above ground as described by the Surveyor General. The true course is therefore N 0°13' E. 40.75 chs. over ascending westerly slope.

55.76 Road bears N.W. & S.E. ascend steep slope.

65.90 Top of ascent on rock point, descend steep broken N.W. slope 14° to 32°.

81.00 Falls 28 lks. W. of the cor. of secs. 1, 2, 11 &12. A granite stone 6x8x6 ins. above ground mkd with 5 notches on S. and 1 on E. edges. Therefore the true course is N.0°11' E 40.25 chs. Land rough, broken and mountainous, soil sandy gravel and stony 3rd & 4th rate. Scattering fir and pine timber from 65.00 to 81.00 chs Sept 18, at this cor. at 4th, 50m, pm. l.m.5 by my watch, which is set for l.m.t. I set off 2°3' N. on arc and 48°49' on the lat. arc. and determine with the solar meridian and mask the line determined on the ground Maj. Var. 23°50E'."

He was instructing himself with the *Highway Engineers' Handbook* by Harger and Bonney.

Poring over his notes as he lay on his bedroll, he hypnotized himself to sleep.

WHEN THE ROAD construction was completed within the limits of available funds, Ed returned to his house. Eleanor, now at term, seemed relieved to see him.

"Oh, Ed, thank goodness you're here!"

He put his arms about her. "I guess we're tired of being sore at each other. I've had another taste of my own cooking on the road crew, too."

"If you only would pay some attention to what I say once in a while!"

MRS. BOTTOMLEY ASSISTED with the arrival of a boy they named Samuel, Eleanor's choice from the Bible.

"Now you have somebody you can boss for a while at least," Ed teased Eleanor. "He can't talk back for at least a year."

She was mellow in her happiness. "Oh, Ed. I'm sorry if I push you too much," she said. "I promise to be a good mother to our son."

"I'm satisfied with my bargain, Eleanor. You're a darn pretty woman and a darn good cook."

"I can hardly wait to get on my feet again," she said. "You need some hot meals. How is the hay crop? I hope Sven and Olaf are doing their part."

Ed and the Linstroms were harvesting a late crop of hay.

"Should have done it sooner," Ed said. "I don't know what we are gonna do about road building. It takes too much time from this place. The county ought to get state money to build roads—money from truces."

Eleanor had lost interest in the conversation. She took the baby from Maggie Bottomley' s arms.

"It's time for him to nurse," she said.

Ed waited for her to produce a breast, but she held the baby away from her.

"She's bashful about nursing in front of you, Ed," Maggie explained.

"O.K., I'll clear out," Ed said. He was nonplussed.

ELEANOR NURSED SAMMIE for nine months, but she seldom did so in front of her husband. Only at night did she let him bring the baby so that she could nurse him in bed.

She washed all the cotton flannel diapers by hand, and she prided herself that her baby was never wet. The house stayed spic and span. When Ed came in from chores, he could never hold Sammie until he had washed.

Maggie Bottomley, after a few weeks, told Ed, "It's all right for her to be so afraid of germs with a first baby, but if she has any more, she'll have to learn not to knock herself out."

When Ed reported what Maggie advised, Eleanor sniffed. "Living in filth the way some big families do is what would kill me."

AS A PRIMARY crossing point over the Okanogan River to the northern half of the county, Bonaparte was gradually developing a core of stable citizens within its population. Some settlers were acquiring considerable property by virtue of an amendment that allowed homesteaders to file on additional isolated tracts of land that adjoined the original homestead. Discouraged settlers sold a relinquishment for a few dollars; other claimants simply walked off their places.

Ed saw that the valley should be tied together by a highway built along the water grade of the river. At a meeting of the Good Roads Association, he insisted that sufficient roadway could not be financed by free-will donation. He and Wesley Brittain explored Remington and Ballinger's *Codes and Statutes of Washington*, chapter ten and following, relating to roads.

Under the stipulations of the permanent highway law of the state, roads, to qualify for state funds, must be built from a trade center and meet certain specifications. Every permanent highway must be graded to a width of not less than sixteen feet; must have proper bridges, drains, and culverts; and must be surfaced with macadam, stone, gravel, or other materials for not less than twelve feet. In no case should any highway be constructed with a grade greater than ten percent.

Wes and Ed were uncertain that Okanogan County, with its cul-de-sac nature and sparsity of trade centers, could qualify. Commissioner Wes suggested that Ed study some projected roads if he was willing to donate his time.

"I don't mind the time," Ed responded. "It's the writing everything out in longhand. When I took on road-building last year, writing out the survey with a pencil and tablet was a mighty time-consuming chore."

Commissioner Brittain agreed to the validity of Ed's complaint. He would try to find stenographic assistance. The next occasion of their meeting, the commissioner asked Ed, "Remember Analix Westmore? She interpreted at the cattle trial a few years back. You testified."

"Sure, I remember her. I worked at the Westmore place then."

"She's home for good from the academy in Spokane. Always was sharp as a tack. I saw her at the mission the other day when I took in Old Man Nelson—he was dying alone sick at his cabin on Antwyne Creek. They take in anybody down there—white or Injun—at their infirmary."

"You were starting to say something about Analix Westmore."

"Yeah, I'm coming to it. Analix was sitting in the Father's office typing big as you please on a shiny new typewriting machine with two sets of keys—capitals and small letters. She said she was mailing out letters for a fund for a new girls' school.

"She's taken on a sideline of writing letters—public stenographer for business people, also people who can't write, or ones with contested land claims and allotments. We could have your road surveys typed. Public records shouldn't go into the files in your handwriting."

Ed's heart warmed. He had an opportunity to see Analix once more. On the mission staff! She had reached her goal.

"I'll go down and talk to her," he said to Wes. "See how much she'll charge."

"Go ahead. We can afford to give Father deRouge a few extra dollars to keep the infirmary going. The county uses it a lot; we owe them some return favors."

ELEANOR HAD NEVER countenanced Ed's relationship with the Westmores. When they were first married, he had asked her to pay a visit with him to the home of the man who had taught him the cow business.

"I hear he's a squaw man. Is his wife a clean Indian or a dirty Indian?"

"Flower is a clean Indian," he had replied shortly, repulsed. He lost his desire to display his bride to the Westmore family. Her attitude was the common pioneer line.

ED RODE HORSEBACK to St. Mary's. The grounds sloping down to the mission buildings had been greatly improved. Orchard trees of fruit-bearing size grew along the main approach; vegetables flourished in the field beside the river. A baseball field and a skating rink had been laid out.

Only the church had not changed in appearance; it was still a typical pioneer Catholic church—a box built of lumber painted white, with a bell tower topped by a cross. The new brick building was undoubtedly the infirmary. Ed noted an excavation for what he supposed would be the new girls' school. He dismounted at the boys' dormitory, where Father deRouge's office was located.

Ed knocked on the door and heard a familiar voice say, "Come in." Analix smiled radiantly at the sight of him, and stood up from the desk where she had been typing.

"Ed! I was wondering if I would ever see you again!" she exclaimed.

"I was wondering if I would ever see *you* again!" he repeated happily. "I feel like doing an Injun jig around you!"

"Please, don't!" she said in good humor. "Father wouldn't approve."

Ed drank in what she looked like as a grown woman. Although she wore a starched white blouse and a dark skirt, appropriate garb for a lay catechist, she was still Analix, of the shining eyes. Her body had become tall and lean like that of her English father. Her high cheekbones and light brown skin showed her Indian blood. She now wore her black hair in braids coiled at the nape of her neck. The gold nugget earrings still hung in her earlobes.

"You deserted the AW altogether," she accused.

"I sure didn't mean to," Ed assured her. "You know how I got too busy to work for your Old Man after I filed on my place. Besides, I've been doing a lot of extra road-building. That's why I'm here. Wes Brittain told me to get in touch with you. The Good Roads Association needs some typing for projected roads. Could you do it if the county pays for it?"

"I know Father deRouge talked to someone. He's glad for a chance to help the valley. We won't charge much; every cent will go to the girls' school."

"I have some handwritten material that I can bring down right away. I pity you figuring out my handwriting."

"I remember your handwriting! I'll earn every cent we get."

"Is Father deRouge around?"

"No, I'm sorry, he isn't," Analix said. "He's out scrounging cement for the new foundation."

"Is he as tough and smart as ever?"

Analix's face became sober. "He is still tough and smart, but the life he leads is taking its toll. There must have been a great difference between his youth and his missionary life now."

"He was one of the first friends I made in the Okanogan."

"I know. Ed, you're becoming a leading citizen, aren't you? Remember how I made you write to your mother? She'd be proud of you now. I always knew you'd have your own place and get ahead. They tell me you are married, and your wife is pretty."

"Got a kid, too. Boy."

"Oh, Ed! How did we all grow up so fast!"

A shadow hung in the air. Ed felt the need to joke, to say, "I should have waited for you," but he knew it would not sound very funny.

Instead he asked, "How are things at the AW?"

She shook her head somberly. "Not as happy as they used to be. Red Curlew has gone to the San Poil. The family packed up all their belongings—rode and led horses over the pass. They won't be wintering at Osoyoos anymore.

"Mama went out to the trail to watch her People go. They all threw down ribbons, feathers, baskets, and blankets at the feet of Amtoos in spite of all that Father deRouge has said against sacrifices to heathen idols. Mother didn't cry, but when they were gone out of sight over the hill, she put down a buffalo robe for Amtoos, one that Red Curlew brought her from Montana."

"What's Red Curlew doing with his time?"

"He runs now with the men who hate the white homesteaders. He works on haying crews, then spends all his wages on whiskey."

"Never thought Red Curlew would act like that!"

"He is desperately unhappy. White Stone Mountain never named Red Curlew chief because of the company he kept. The old chiefs vow that there will be no more chiefs. Red Curlew has joined up with Pete, son of Chief Susceptkain."

"Sorry to hear all this."

"I am afraid Mama cannot endure what is happening. Everyone suffers because Papa and Red Curlew have been lifelong chums."

"Are your brothers and Bethany still living at home?"

"Yes, except for Weipah and Aeneas, the two youngest, who are still in school here. The Sisters at Holy Names discovered that Bethany has exceptional artistic talent and have urged her to preserve the native arts. It pleases Mama that Bethany wants to learn Sinkaietk handicraft and to write down the old songs."

"Bethany could play any music she heard once, I remember."

"Yes. Her watercolors are beautiful, too. Because she helps Mama with the housework, I am free to work here, to please Father deRouge. I'm doing my best to help the girls' school get started until Father can find an order of nuns."

"I hope you don't plan to be a nun!" Ed blurted.

"I considered it, but I know I love the outdoors too much. I'd hate the restricting clothing and life of seclusion. The Indian in me needs to be free to ride away to visit home and Conconully Lake."

WHEN ANALIX HELPED with his road projections, Ed found she had a better mastery of solid geometry than he. She could figure cubic feet of dirt to be filled and knew when it would be preferable to build a bridge across a gulch.

AT ED'S URGING, Analix and Bethany came with Leschi and Owhi to a Saturday night box social at the Riverside School. The event was being staged to raise money for road-building. Men paid admissions, and feminine guests brought basket suppers for auction at intermission.

Ed, who was on the arrangement committee with Wes Brittain, could not persuade Eleanor to leave the baby.

"We could take him along and lay him on the bed with the other kids," Ed suggested.

"And have him catch cold, not to mention fleas and mange!" Eleanor snapped. "Besides, I'm certainly in no shape for waltzing around a roomful of people."

She was pregnant again, and by contemporary mores justifiably excused.

The gathering was a mix of cattle hands, mostly single young men, and young homesteaders with wives. Proceeds of the event would go to finance a lawyer to represent the Good Roads Association at the next session of the state legislature.

A committee had engaged the services of Gerald Gaston, who had opened an office in Conconully. He had earned a law degree from Princeton University, which deeply impressed the selection committee.

"I've seen him in court fightin' roads," Ed had pointed out.

"He told me he's merely presented cases for all clients who sought his services. He's likewise available to people who want a solicitor for roads. He's familiar with the issues," Wes Brittain said.

"I give up," Ed had said. "I guess lawyers have enough sides to their mouths to argue for anybody who can pay the fee."

Gaston was a smooth-tongued, personable fellow who made Ed uneasy. He was more good-looking than strong, Ed judged. He appeared at the box social in a plug hat, a dark sack suit, and a white shirt with a high, starched collar.

Brittain remarked to Ed, "He's eating Sunday dinners at the Westmores."

Ed knew what that state of affairs presaged. Unquestionably, Gaston had discovered the valuable services of the public stenographer at St. Mary's.

"I hope Analix can see through him," he muttered. When he saw Gaston claim Analix for a dance, Ed scowled.

The Westmore sisters behaved with charm and dignity. Analix wore a yellow silk dress with a ruffle at the bottom, Bethany, a blue dimity, both garments no doubt designed and sewn by Bethany.

On the sidelines, dancing with no one, Ed overheard, "Who let the Injuns in? What are they looking for? A drink of whiskey or a toss in the hay?"

When he turned to look at the speaker, Ed recognized Eph Perkins, accompanied by a young wife who had snickered at her husband's slur. The homesteader was wearing a pistol in a holster although the rule was that all firearms should be checked at the door. Ed pointed the man out to Wes.

"Yeah, I noticed him myself. Has a flannel mouth. Been drinkin' too much. He's about to bust his buttons over his fancy new imported 1902 Eagle Luger, nine millimeter. It'll never replace the Colt. I'll go take it away from him."

Ed saw Wes going outside with Perkins, presumably to settle a disagreement over possession of the pistol. Such a drunk could disrupt the festivities if not handled with tact in private. Ed saw Analix standing a moment alone on the edge of the floor, like a wild deer sniffing danger on the wind. Ed went to her and asked with a smile, "Want to take a turn around the room with an old married man when the music starts again?"

She responded gratefully, "Of course, Ed. I don't know what's happened to Leschi or Owhi."

As the band began "The Missouri Waltz," they moved to the floor. Analix had learned to dance exquisitely in Spokane. She had no trouble following Ed, who had learned to dance by plunging into the fray after cattle drives. He did, however, have a natural sense of rhythm.

"Come to think of it, where are Leschi and Owhi?" Ed wondered. "Before we dance anymore, I better take a look outside."

As he approached the main entry, he heard the German Luger firing outside. Everyone in the hall yelled, "What's that?"

"Everybody stay inside!" Ed ordered as he swung the door open and went through. At the foot of the steps, the Westmore brothers were fighting with several homesteaders. Wes Brittain and Perkins were rolling on the ground, struggling over the pistol. Wes was on the bottom, but he had the firearm, and his arms were long enough that Perkins could not yank it from his hand.

Ed elbowed his way through the melee, grabbed Perkins by his gun belt and shirt collar, and dumped him like a length of cordwood into the horse trough.

Wes, still clutching the seized pistol, stood back to back with Ed.

"Anybody want the same treatment?" Ed challenged.

All the other combatants decided it would be more fun to spend the remainder of the evening dancing than shivering like Perkins, who had climbed out of the water.

"I'm going home. Gimme my Luger," he whined.

"You can come to the courthouse for it in the morning when you're sober," Wes told him. "I'll fetch your wife for you. Everybody apologize to Leschi and Owhi, go back inside, and act like nothing has happened."

"No harm done," everyone agreed. "Pistol just went off in the air accidentally."

They shook hands all around, except for Perkins, and went inside.

Mrs. Perkins scurried from the dance hall under escort. The musicians began to play, and the mood changed in a moment. They were accustomed to such conflicts and knew well the value of a fast schottische to restore the spirit of conviviality.

Ed claimed Analix for the remainder of his dance. They pretended that it had never been interrupted.

"Which basket is yours?" he asked her as they passed the large center table, on which the supper boxes were displayed.

"Since you can't bid, being married, I guess there's no harm telling you mine is the one with the silk rosebuds on the handle. Bethany made them."

Ed tried to grin.

Analix danced the last dance before supper with Gaston, who had won the lively bidding for her box.

"Wish I hadn't come tonight," Ed said grimly to Wes.

"Couldn't make my wife come either," Wes commiserated.

"Damn good thing you were here from my standpoint, though. The situation was going to hell in a handbasket before you busted out the door."

"Hope we haven't got a bunch of folks spoiling things for the Westmore girls," Ed worried.

"They were still the belles of the ball," Wes concluded. "Whole trouble is they're too damn pretty to suit the white wives."

"Maybe so," Ed agreed. "Everybody's stuffing his face, and we got nothing to eat because our wives didn't fix us anything. I feel like leaving."

"Go ahead," Wes urged him. "I'll lock up."

At home, Ed climbed in wearily beside Eleanor. She woke when he pulled at the covers.

"Have a good time?" she asked with an edge in her voice.

"Nope," he said. He knew better than to amplify his answer.

HOPES ROSE HIGH in the Okanogan County Good Roads Association when a new bill was introduced in the state legislature. Its passage would provide a half-mill levy on each dollar's worth of property in the state to build roads in the underdeveloped areas, which surely included the trail from Wenatchee to Tonasket, Chesaw, and Bonaparte, and the road from Republic to Loomis and down the San Poil River.

Ed had done the preliminary scouting and formulated a typewritten draft with Analix's help. It would be Gerald Gaston's function to lobby for the new bill in Olympia, then to secure a direct appropriation of twenty thousand dollars for Okanogan County. The construction program would mean more local wages. All the road construction, improvements, or repairs of two thousand five hundred dollars or more would be let to contract by the county commissioners. Plans and specifications were to be prepared by the county engineer.

"Since we don't have an elected county engineer, I guess you're it by appointment," Wes told Ed.

Ed hoped that Gerald Gaston had an iron grip on what was needed. The rumor was everywhere that the Eastern fop was filled with romantic notions regarding Analix, a genuine Indian princess.

Sven and Olaf told Ed that the Westmore girls were to have a double wedding, but it turned out differently. Bethany was married at St. Mary's Mission to George Naches, an Indian youth who had distinguished himself as an athlete. He had been pitcher of the St. Mary's baseball team that won the championship of Okanogan County several years in a row against the public schools. Bethany's husband had run cattle with the Westmores even before the marriage.

Ed, without Eleanor, went to their wedding. Analix stood beside her sister for the brief ceremony in the white church. A celebration and picnic followed outdoors.

Analix came to Ed. "Mama says to tell you she's glad you are here."

"Thanks. Is it true that you are going to marry that lawyer who's been squiring you to the Good Roads meetings for you to take notes?"

"Yes, it is."

"Some people said you were going to be married along with Bethany."

"Gerald does not want a religious wedding," Analix stated frankly. "He is not Catholic."

"How does Father deRouge feel about that?" Ed could not resist asking.

"He doesn't like it, of course," Analix admitted while a shadow of regret clouded her eyes. "It's the first time I have defied him. He said he thought I never would."

"I thought you wanted to be a teacher at the mission."

"I wanted the mission to have a girls' school. It will. A group of Lady Catechist Missionaries are being sent from the East, with money given by Mother Katherine Drexel."

"Far as I can see, that Gaston is an educated fool who'll say anything you'll pay him to."

"You sound just like Papa!" Analix said. "You're both jealous males. You married the prettiest girl in the country! Why can't I marry the best-looking man?"

"I better shut up," Ed yielded ground.

He went to greet the parents of the bride and the bridal pair, then Nathan and Will, who hailed him as "that greenhorn!"

Feeling out of place, he left for home before he would have to shake hands with another guest at the wedding—Gerald Gaston.

BILLY WAS BORN when Sammie was eighteen months old.

"Now you have a pair of cattle hands," Eleanor observed.

"I won't put 'em to work until they are at least six years old," Ed promised.

Analix and Gerald were married in a civil ceremony at the Conconully courthouse. Wes Brittain was chief witness.

Wes asked Ed to help him arrange one more dance to raise money for the attorney's trip to Olympia. The Good Roads Association could congratulate the bride and bridegroom, on whose shoulders lay a considerable community responsibility.

Ed insisted that Eleanor attend the reception with him. She wore a new dress that Ed had persuaded her to order from the mail order catalogue: a pink shirtwaist that showed her figure was still good after the birth of two babies. Ed complimented her on her appearance before they left the house.

"I never eat between meals," she said, turning aside his praise.

At the dance, Wes, in his capacity as chairman of the board of county commissioners, greeted them. To please Eleanor, Ed said, "Eleanor, have you ever met Mr. Wesley Brittain?"

"Good evening, Ma'am," Wes said. "Your husband is a prince of a fellow; don't know what the county would do without him."

Eleanor restrained a sniff, but later in the evening, she accepted Wes's invitation to dance with good grace.

When the commissioner brought Eleanor back to Ed, he asked, "Could you come to town in the morning? I have something I want to talk over."

"Sure. I'll make it a point to be there," Ed answered, assuming the discussion would be about road-building.

But the morning conference was on a different subject. "I'm leaving Conconully," the commissioner told Ed. "Your neighbors have decided that you ought to run for commissioner in my place. You know the mechanics of the road-building process. You'd still be main road-builder."

"Holy mackinaw! I'm not the kind that gets elected to office," he protested. He considered himself a strong-muscled ignoramus. "I'm a pick-and-shovel type."

"You're as much the type as I am," Wes said. "This is a new place. The people need roads, and you seem to be the only man around with the gumption to see jobs to the finish. We need a pick-and-shovel commissioner."

"Who put my name up in the first place? Not my brothers-in-law, I hope."

"No, a bunch at Pard Cummings's store."

"O.K. I know about who all it would be. I guess I can run for road-builder."

When he revealed to Eleanor that he had been asked to run for commissioner, she sighed resignedly. "I knew that Brittain wanted something the other night at the dance."

Under sponsorship of the incumbent, Ed was elected county commissioner in November.

The newspapers from the coast, which reached the Okanogan a few days after publication, reported that the bill for roads in mountainous regions had passed in the state legislature.

Okanogan County commissioners soon began to receive petitions from owners of the required two-thirds of the lineal feet fronting upon the proposed public highways. The commissioners passed the proper resolutions and transmitted them to the state Highway Commission.

The Good Roads Association waited for word from Gerald Gaston that money was being transferred from the public highway fund for their projects, but the wait lengthened. The board of commissioners, convened in emergency session, delegated Ed to go to the legislature to unearth what was holding up due process.

"Looks like I'm on the spot," he told Eleanor. "I've practically begun advertising for bids. Men are counting on jobs on the road to earn money to buy cattle in the fall market. Why should I have to go over there? Gaston is getting paid to heckle the legislature."

The only evidence of Gaston's activity on behalf of the Okanogan Valley had been publication in the *Seattle Times* of a photo of the Good Roads attorney of Okanogan County with his bride, an Indian princess to whom he gave the pet name "Pocahontas."

Ed exploded into profanity.

The caption under the picture said that Gaston's chief purpose was to secure road support for outlying districts of the state. Okanogan Valley residents wondered whether publicizing one's self was a valid method of putting pressure on the legislature. So far, it had not sufficed.

"You're tickled pink at a chance to visit the legislature," Eleanor told Ed. "Don't make a fool of yourself."

After an all-night train ride, Ed arrived, tired and rumpled, in the state capital. He went to the hotel at which Gaston was reportedly staying and asked at the desk for his room number.

"I'll phone," the clerk said. "Who shall I say is calling?"

"Ed McLaren."

The clerk spoke his name into the phone and listened. "Mr. Gaston inquires if you have an appointment."

"Let me have the phone," Ed said.

The man handed it across the counter.

The Good Roads attorney, the fuzz of alcohol on his tongue, finally was made to understand who Ed was. Instead of inviting him to come upstairs, Gaston said he would meet Ed in the office of the chairman of the highway committee at ten o'clock.

It was now eight o'clock.

Ed bought his breakfast in the hotel dining room and washed his face in the restroom. He hoped not to waste much time in Olympia and wanted to be sure he was staying overnight before he tried to find a hotel room. At a quarter to ten he went to the highway committee office and sat until nearly noon. The place was empty, without even a receptionist to take his name. Finally, weak around the eyes, Gaston came into the suite.

"I'm sorry to be so late, but days don't begin until noon here. We hold most conferences until midnight or later."

"Sorry I'm on the wrong schedule," Ed answered shortly. He took abrupt initiative. "Came to see what's holding up the road money for the Okanogan."

"Just for your own interest?"

"Nope. I'm county commissioner now. My job's the roads."

Gerald put more civility into his manner. "Glad you came. Need all the support we can muster. Let's go to Room X for a conference."

"Isn't this place good enough?"

Gerald said fraternally, "Just wait till you find out what Room X is."

As Ed expected, Room X was the committee room maintained by the liquor lobby for all visitors to the legislature. Samples were free. They had their choice of a place to sit, with no one else but the bartender in the room. The attendant brought two glasses and a bottle to the table and left them alone.

"I know the money should have been given to the Okanogan before this, according to the passage of the highway bill, Ed, but after sitting here a few weeks, the knowledge has been forced upon me that the liquor and fish industries control the legislature. Their business comes first."

Ed snorted, "I bet you mean 'sitting here'—right here!"

Gaston chuckled as though Ed had made a funny remark.

"What I mean is that certain factions have the power to hold up appropriations till they get our promise to support some of their legislation. I'm doing my damnedest—in fact, I was out with the liquor lobby last night. You have to work that way."

Ed did not touch his drink. As Gaston took his time with his, the attorney rambled about life as a lobbyist at the legislature as though Ed were a schoolboy come to learn about the mechanics of state government.

"Did you get those plans and specifications we sent you?" Ed attempted to bring the conversation back to the issue.

"Oh. You mean for the Okanogan highways? All those plans are in the highway commissioner's office."

"I went to a lot of work sending plans and specifications direct both to you and to the state highway commissioner. I hope you haven't misplaced your mail."

"My secretary files correspondence," Gerald said impatiently.

"What secretary? Where'd you get money for a secretary? Thought Analix would be your secretary."

"My secretary is a volunteer, not Analix. The young woman isn't efficient at clerical details, but I need her more for social responsibilities. There's lots to attend to, Ed. Just meeting the public is a chore. Everybody in the home county sneaks over here and wants something done. 'Keep the road here!' 'Put it there!' You'd think I was Santa Claus."

Ed felt an inner urge to rise and bellow like his bull, but he said instead tersely, "Okanogan County sent you over here to do one special job, and you'd damn well better remember it! You never even gave those specifications to the highway commission. That's why we haven't been given our money!"

Gerald pondered a moment. "I suppose Maybelle could have failed to call your correspondence to my attention."

"Where's Analix? If your 'secretary' is no good, Analix could copy the highway commissioner's copy—if he hasn't lost his."

"Poor Analix! It might be good for her to have something to do. She isn't having as good a time as it seemed she would at first."

"Why not? I saw her picture in all the papers. Seemed like she was the most popular wife in town."

"It was a mistake letting people know about her Indian blood. She can pass for a white person. As it is, I can't take her places where liquor is served, and that leaves her alone more than she should be."

They found Analix in the hotel lobby. She was reading *Les Miserables*.

"It's thick enough to last me until we go home," she said. Her eyes were alight. She stood to greet Ed.

"We have a job for you," Gerald announced brusquely. "I didn't think of it. Ed did. We need a detailed copy of the plan for the road from Loomis to Republic. You can type from the commissioner's copy if he'll lend it. Something seems to have happened to the copy Ed sent me."

She looked suddenly relieved. She squared her shoulders.

"I told you, Gerald! But never mind. After all the work I did on those specifications, I can make another copy in a jiffy."

"We might borrow one of the committee typewriters, I suppose," Gerald said. "Ed, could you come back and bring it to Analix? I do have some appointments waiting."

"Why don't I type at the office?" Analix asked.

"You know I can't have you there," Gerald said bluntly.

Ed was horrified. Analix's eyes went black with hurt. She said nothing in reply. Ed saw that she had already lost in previous discussions. Her face closed, assuming a cast of stoical acceptance that she was in a trap, a half-breed Indian woman married to a white man.

"I'll go up to the room and wait for you to bring the materials, Ed. I'm sure Gerald can arrange it. I hope the typewriter won't be too heavy to carry a quarter-mile."

"I've carried heavier things than typewriters."

AT THE HIGHWAY committee office, Gerald, instead of making requests himself, told Ed, "It will probably be best if I leave you to your own resources. They'll be more inclined to cooperate with a county commissioner than a lobbyist."

Ed wondered if the man was a moral coward or merely lazy. In any case, he was a weak, disillusioned woolgatherer.

A receptionist was now sitting at a desk in the outer office that Ed had inhabited all morning. He established himself as a commissioner of Okanogan County who wished to use the copy of plans for Highways No. 4 and 10, previously submitted by mail; also he wished to borrow a typewriter to be taken from the building. Ed was never introduced to the committee chairman, but after the receptionist went back and forth from outer to inner office for fifteen minutes, Ed was given custody of a twenty-pound Underwood and the rolled sheets of the highway projects.

As Analix typed in the hotel room, Ed sat beside her. Whenever sketches were required, he filled them in freehand.

Gerald came through the door four hours later as the drafts were completed. He announced importantly that he had learned that the highway appropriations committee would meet at two o'clock the next day.

"I'll take the specifications to the meeting. And don't think I have been wasting my time this afternoon. I got the promises of six men to expedite our appropriation."

"Made in Committee Room X?" Ed asked.

Gerald shrugged, "Where else? Lawyers for poor special interest groups don't have private offices."

"Hope that your six men are able to remember their promises tomorrow," Ed replied. Then he saw the pain in Analix's face and was ashamed of his sarcasm.

He decided not to wait to attend the appropriations committee session. It was Gerald's job to be there, not his. Analix said they would write as soon as the Okanogan County roadbuilding program was included in approved expenditures.

Ed carried the typewriter back to its stand in the highway commission office. The door was open, but there was no one to thank for the loan. Apparently everyone in Olympia quit work at five o'clock instead of at dark. He went to the depot cafeteria for a late meal, then caught the night train across the Cascades.

NOTIFICATION THAT FUNDS had been transferred for construction of Highway No. 4 came to the Okanogan County commissioners a week after Ed's visit. Presumably Highway No. 10, from Wenatchee northward, would be provided for in a later session of the legislature.

When Gerald came back to his law office in Conconully after the session, he was a hero. The townspeople listened raptly to his description of the ramifications of high finance in securing the road money. Gerald hailed Ed on the street.

"There, you see, all your fears were groundless. You didn't have to come over and check up on me at all! Let's go have a drink. I forgive you for your well-meaning attempt to jack me up! I had the interest of my clients at heart all the time, now didn't I?"

Thinking what he did not utter aloud, Ed said, "Fine. Let's have a drink."

He wanted to avoid a state of open hostility between himself and Analix's husband. Let the fellow have the credit for obtaining the appropriation. The Good Roads Association would have to send him back to Olympia for more money for roads. In the next biennium, funds must be secured for completion of Highway No. 10.

IN THE NEXT year and a half, Ed labored as he had never done before. He cared for the cattle on his range and meadows, fulfilled his duties as county commissioner, and did most of the on-site supervision of the road-building.

The members of the Good Roads Association, who at last had noticed how much time Gerald Gaston spent in the tavern compared to time on legal duties, sent the attorney to the January session of the legislature with some misgiving. Ed, trying to work with the state highway department, was impatient with the finagling necessary to get appropriations. He hoped for the best; maybe Analix could keep her husband on target. He heard that she did most of the work that came from Gaston's office.

Halfway through the session, Analix wrote to Ed: "Gerald is in trouble. I don't know if he can get the funds needed. He drinks all day every day. He says he is unhappy because he has lost the friendship of the right people, and blames me for my Indian blood."

Ed, appalled, showed the letter to Eleanor.

"I don't see that you have any obligation to her," Eleanor snapped. "Why didn't she write to her parents?"

"She won't want them to know how she's being treated. Besides, I'm responsible for roads."

"Maybe her main reason for writing to you is that the Old Man's hired hand always had to wait on the children, too."

Ed shut his jaws on words better left unsaid. He ached with helplessness.

Three weeks later Ed received a message at the courthouse that Father deRouge would like him to come to St. Mary's mission. Could he provide transportation for a pregnant woman to her parents' home near Conconully?

Ed had bought a horse and buggy mainly for Eleanor's use, but occasionally in his capacity as commissioner, he transported indigents from the tavern or lonely cabins to shelter at the mission. Explaining the nature of the trip, Ed asked Eleanor for loan of the buggy.

"Seems you spend half your time running around on some do-good, no-pay errand. Take the buggy. I never use it."

"Thank you for coming, Ed." The priest, who was becoming frail and graybearded, rose from his desk, shook hands, and said, "I need your help."

"Anything I can do. Be glad to!"

"You will never guess who is waiting to see you in the reception parlor."

"No, I can't, unless it's..." his voice trailed off in sudden clairvoyance.

"Yes, it is," the priest said. "Analix needs to be taken home. She rode the train this far from Olympia and stopped to see me. I am sending her to her family."

Ed's knees buckled with alarm. "Is she all right?"

"She is not all right, but will be. Let us go to her."

Father deRouge led the way to the tiny parlor at the end of the hall. "See whom I have brought, little sister?"

Analix's face flooded with shame and relief. "I ran away!" she confessed, with agony in her voice.

Her body was full with pregnancy, her face sharp and drawn.

"Father deRouge says you need a ride home," Ed took charge grimly. He had always known that Gerald was *cultus*—an Indian way of saying he was a no-account.

"Analix has suitcases," Father deRouge said. "Shall we fetch them? They are in the room in which she stayed as a catechist."

He led the way to the second floor over the dining room and kitchen.

THE PRIEST BENT to kiss Analix's hand as they said goodbye. Ed helped her into the buggy.

As they went up the winding road to the highway, Analix remained silent. Ed finally asked, "What did Father deRouge say about you hightailing it off from your husband?"

"He said 'I told you so,' though not in so many words. I must not let myself suffer too much; I must keep hope alive for the child that is coming."

"I suppose he thinks you must make up with Gerald."

"Perhaps. I don't know what Gerald will do now that I have come home without him."

"Did you leave because he threatened you, or beat up on you?"

"No, although he has done both of those things. He has been angry a long time because I refused to practice birth control anymore and became pregnant. But I really came home because I cannot endure life as the half-breed wife of a white man! I have to go out and sit on the boulders on the hill over the lake. The wind in the pine trees will wash away some of the hate and hurt that is in me now. When I have my baby, I believe I'll feel that I belong with the earth again."

At Pard Cummings's store, Ed went in to buy cheese and crackers for a lunch. One of the men on the porch called as Ed was returning to Analix, who had remained in the buggy, "Hey, Ed, you left your wife and taken up with a purty squaw? Got her in the family way?"

Ed made no reply in his anger. He would never understand dirty minds.

Analix at length poured out her unhappy experiences. Gerald's companions in Room X had plied him with liquor one evening until he was senseless. They had led him to a bed in a downtown hotel and left him there with the door open—a standard trick. A blowsy lady of the night had charged ten dollars to crawl into bed with Gaston. As a lobbyist for Good Roads, he had become worse than useless.

"How long is it to the end of the session?" Ed asked.

"Two weeks."

They went the rest of the way to the AW without talking. Analix seemed to be asleep. She roused once and opened her eyes with a start, then relaxed.

"I haven't had much sleep for days," she said.

"Just rest," Ed told her.

AT NIGHTFALL, THEY reached the AW. Opening Flower, coming out the front door, clasped her oldest child, her pride, in her arms.

"Come in," Carr Westmore invited Ed. "Thank you for bringing her home."

"Papa, Ed needs a fresh horse," Analix said through her weariness. "He's been driving the one at the buggy all day."

"Yes, of course. Leschi, take care of it. Charley would be a good one, broken to harness."

"I'll ride your horse down to you after it gets a rest," Leschi told Ed.

AT HOME, AFTER midnight, Ed met a chilly Eleanor.

"The whole valley knows that you drove that Analix person from the mission to Conconully. Kicked out by her husband. Don't blame him for not wanting children with Injun blood."

"I expect such talk from ignorant newcomers, not from you, Eleanor," he said in the coldest voice he had ever used with her.

"You've humiliated me more than I can stand!" she shrilled. "What kind of hold does that half-breed have over you?"

"Now see here! I've had enough goddamn trouble without you lighting into me after I've traveled eighteen hours straight."

"A long time getting here, you were!"

"You knew all the time what I've been doing."

She broke into sobs.

Ed put his arms about her and tried to be gentle. "I had no idea of disgracing you. We'll fix it up in the morning. Let's go to bed."

"Not till you eat the supper I cooked."

"Well, all right."

He ate a great deal because he had not had a square meal since he had left home at dawn.

Eleanor cried herself to sleep. Tired as he was, Ed lay awake burning with chagrin. For the sake of peace with Eleanor, he must stay away from the Westmores, although it made him angry to think that he should.

A month later he heard that Analix had a baby girl. Gerald Gaston returned shortly to Conconully and was occasionally seen in his office. Not long after the birth of her child, Analix resumed residence with her husband.

Ed understood that Analix would live with Gerald because a child needed a father, no matter how weak.

She settled into her husband's office as a public stenographer to help settlers and purchasers of allotments with correspondence to the land office. Her baby, in the back room, slept in a hammock and crawled on the floor.

THE VULNERABILITY OF his claim to his grazing land struck Ed one morning when he went to Mount Hull to clean and to check on the adequacy of the water supply at a spring he had improved as a waterhole for his cattle. In the open grass beside the spring stood a sheepherder's wagon; and sheep, never before on the range, were cropping grass. A man holding a pan in which bacon and eggs were frying squatted before a bonfire. He had set himself a table on a box with a tin plate, cup, and coffeepot. Ed moved his horse into the clearing and dismounted.

"Morning," Ed said civilly. "Haven't seen you around here before. What you doing?"

The Latin, with a dark, heavy beard, shrugged at Ed's question. "Cooking breakfast."

"You figuring on running sheep in this country? You can't run 'em on this creek. I hold the water rights."

"No rain in Nevada; no grass. I think you have the rights for the waterhole, but not the range."

"Ever hear of riparian rights?"

"I'll move on. Mind my sheep taking a drink?"

"Looks like they've had it."

"Gonna let me drink my coffee?"

"Oh, sure."

Ed left the sheepherder to have his meal in peace, but he was disturbed by the invasion. If nomadic sheep bands from the Southwest began to wander about, the waving fields of bunchgrass would soon be destroyed. Sheep ate grass to root level. He went to the post office at mail time for a conference and learned that Al Thorpe, John Beal, and the Beemans had had experiences similar to his.

"Drought must be fierce in the Southwest, but we can't be kindhearted enough to let all these sheep destroy the Okanogan range," Thorpe said.

"I read the other day that the federal government is organizing a forest service," Ed remarked. "There's talk of a grazing permit system."

"You mean the Great White Father's worried about you and me on Mount Hull?" Frank Beeman chuckled unbelievingly.

"It wouldn't hurt for one of us to write in and find out about it."

"To Washington, D.C.? Hell, you do it if you want to, Ed."

IN PRINCE'S STORE, he bought a package of envelopes and an ink tablet. He returned to the post office to use the pen. In the clearest language he could muster, he explained practices in regard to rangeland in Okanogan county.

"Carr Westmore's AW is below Oroville; Al Thorpe runs his cattle on Mount Chopaka; John Beal is above Conconully; Guy Waring, on the northeast; Tom Ellis, near the lake; Sven and Olaf Linstrom and Ed McLaren, on Mount Aeneas and Mount Hull, also some on Mount Bonaparte.

"Is there anything the original settlers can do to protect their ranges from wandering bands of sheep owned by people who don't have homesteads and who don't pay taxes?"

Ed saw his handwriting as an angry, illegible scrawl; but he had written the straight facts, he told himself. He folded the sheets of tablet paper and placed them in a stamped envelope that he obtained at the post office window. He addressed his message to Department of Agriculture, Washington, D. C.

In reply he received a printed bulletin: "Extracts from the Public Lands Commission … Appointed by the President … 1903 … To Study the Most Effective Use of the Resources of the Public Lands."

ED'S NAME WAS placed on a number of mailing lists as a result of his first letter to Washington, D. C. He received a circular from the U.S. Department of Agriculture asking for suggestions from stockmen as to what they thought should be done about the public range. Did stockmen feel that some form of government control was necessary? A commission was studying grazing systems in various sections of the country and was preparing a map of the general locations of summer, winter, and year-long ranges. The department requested that a representative of each grazing community call a meeting to obtain a consensus of opinion.

Ed induced twenty men to come to Pard Cummings's store in the evening. When all were present, chewing tobacco and spitting politely at the stove instead of on the floor, Ed called the meeting to order.

"I got this circular to fill out from the government and want to hear you fellows' opinions.

"Grass is going down fast because everybody has been pushing out on the range in the spring before the new stuff has time to take root. With so many people in the business now, shouldn't grazing areas be divided and a few rules made about the season?"

"I sure as hell want my stock to start eating as soon as yours," Sven Linstrom responded.

"We're getting no place fast if we turn personal. If you guys don't want to help fill out this circular, you don't have to. But it was sent to me. No law against me sticking my own neck out, is there? Under my own name, I'll send it back with what I think."

"Don't get your feathers ruffled," Olaf soothed. "You go on and fill out the circular—use my name if you want to. Anything you say I said, I said it."

"Sure, Ed. They sent you the thing. You fill it out to suit yourself. Say we helped you."

Olaf handed him a cup of coffee from the pot on the heater. Ed tasted brandy. The fellows thought the meeting had been called under the guise of a range meeting as a good pretext to duck the women. Decks of cards were thrown on the table.

"Not so fast!" Ed objected. "I mean it about grazing districts."

"Sure you do. Let's keep outsiders off the grass. You're fighting nobody but yourself here, Ed. Cut!"

ED FOLLOWED THE news of meetings about the public domain throughout the West. Theodore Roosevelt and Gifford Pinchot proclaimed that government supervision of natural resources must be implemented. A Department of Agriculture commission recommended that the department be given authority to set aside the grazing districts or reserves by proclamation. The Secretary of Agriculture proposed to classify and appraise grazing value of public lands and appoint officers to care for the districts and make regulations.

OKANOGAN CATTLEMEN FELT the direct result of the president's executive order with the establishment on March 1, 1907, of the Colville National Forest. The area consisted of 747,875 acres of government land that the community used as a basic source of income.

The *Oroville Register* carried the announcement that Carl Reed, representing the United States Forest Service, would meet with interested parties at the Riverside School to explain new forest regulations.

Assuming that the government representative would arrive on the afternoon train on the scheduled date, Ed drove to Oroville with his buckboard and easily spotted the stranger in the hotel lobby. Ed approached him with his hand outstretched, "You must be the government man. I'm one of the fellows going to the meeting tonight. I'll be glad to take you to Riverside—probably farther than you counted on."

"Thank you for your courtesy," the man responded with alacrity as he accepted Ed's hand. "I'm Mr. Reed."

Ed choked over calling himself "Mister" McLaren, and said instead, "I'm Ed McLaren."

When they reached the schoolhouse, they found the yard full of horses tied to the rack. Men in overalls, mackinaws, chaps, and spurs filled the schoolroom. The young visitor, who wore a Sunday suit, with a starched white collar up to his rosy chin, announced, "I am a graduate of the Yale School of Forestry. I'll soon have a Forest Service uniform to wear."

None of the men saw him in a starched white collar again.

He said that a Forest Service office was to be opened at Republic and that the residents of the countryside could go there for permits and other business. Grazing season for cattle and horses would be from May 1 to November 30 for the district including Republic, Malott, Curlew, Orient, Boyds, Tonasket, Bonaparte, and Oroville. He read to them from what he called "The Use Book," and outlined regulations.

"You will be asked to obtain permits for which you will pay a nominal fee based on animal units. Fees collected will be used to give you roads through the forest, to clean out waterholes, and otherwise maintain the property as a government benefit."

"Now," said Mr. Reed, "are there any questions or comments?"

Frank Beeman, who had been leaning against the wall, pushed himself to a standing position and began rolling a cigarette.

"Yeah, I got one," Frank said with a grin, "A government guy like you reminds me of a Bible story. The Devil took Jeez up on a high mountain, showed him a lot of land, and said, 'This is all yours if you will come in with me.'

"But Jeez said, 'Old Billy, you don't own a foot of it yourself.'"

As the laughter burst out, the young foreigner standing at the head of the room blushed to his hairline, but said cheerfully, "Good story, friend. I imagine it's one I can use for the rest of my talks on regulations around here. I admit that I, personally, don't own a foot of government land."

The men decided that maybe they could like the kid, after all.

They came forward to talk to him cautiously.

"Reed, did you say your name was?"

"That's it. Call me Carl."

"Carl, what's this 'commensurate' business?" Ed asked.

"In order to qualify for a permit, you have to be commensurate. This means that you have to own enough property to care for the stock in the winter months when they aren't on the range."

The men communicated to one another with glances. This regulation would keep out itinerant sheep bands.

"I don't mind parts of the regulations," Bill Beeman admitted. "As long as nobody is out on the range ahead of you for the grass, you can afford to stay off until May."

After the forester pulled his collar loose, Frank Beeman explained. "We kid everybody who sticks his neck out in front of a meeting. Let Ed McLaren tell you how we heckle him."

As HE RODE in the buckboard back to Oroville, Carl Reed confided to Ed that he had nearly bolted from the room like a jackrabbit when Frank Beeman told his joke.

"But I knew if I did, I'd be known as a fool around here for the next twenty years. I'm the person assigned to open the Forest Service office and remain here."

"The men want their range legally," Ed reassured him. "Don't let 'em bother you. They just like to try for the upper hand."

MR. REED'S WIFE and baby arrived from the East, and the family rented a house in Republic. In due course, when the Forest Service office opened, men in the cow business began to visit Carl Reed to formalize the use of their grazing land. Everyone wished to be considered "commensurate."

Ed applied for and received a permit for the same lands he had been using on Mount Hull and Mount Bonaparte, choice grazing range. Each two acres would feed a cow for a month. The new leaseholders expressed their satisfaction to one another. Because of the population growth, the time had come for legalizing possession of land.

ED BEGAN INSTALLATION of barbwire fence to keep off other men's strays as well as the sheep bands that were still in the country due to the continued drought in the Southwest. He took the boys with him to keep them out from underfoot of Eleanor, who was cross and nervous in her efforts to be as meticulous a housekeeper as always despite her state of early pregnancy.

"I pray for a girl this time," she said. "I need someone to help with the work that men cause."

On the mountain, Sam and Bill carried the fence posts from the stack on the wagon bed, brought Ed drinks of water from the spring, and joyfully fetched the lunchbucket when the sun said high noon. Ed dug holes with shovel and pickaxe, then pounded in the posts with a sledgehammer. The boys vied for their turns to hold the post upright for Ed's blows. Sundown after sundown, their faces black with dirt, they came home so tired they staggered.

"Shed your overalls outside!" Eleanor snapped as she stood guard at the kitchen door.

She dispensed bars of soap and sent them to bathe in the river. Clad in their long cotton underwear, they stumbled through the orchard. When they came back clean, Eleanor gave them cotton robes with tie belts. The overalls for dirty work never reached the inside of the house. Eleanor shook the worst of the dust from the fence-building clothes and hung them on nails outside the back door, to be put on again at dawn.

The redeeming feature of the summer evening was a delicious hot meal of oven-roasted beef, browned potatoes, carrots, peas, canned grape juice, sometimes two pies, and a chocolate or apricot upside-down cake.

As soon as they stuffed themselves full of supper, the boys fell into their bed in the back room. Ed was tempted to do the same, but he sat in the front room in the chair that Eleanor had insisted he buy for himself at Prince's store. By gaslight, he read doggedly in the journals that described how livestock men in California selected their breeding stock. Now, he picked his bulls from the herd, but buying a registered White-faced Hereford bull was his dream.

Eleanor sat at the dining table and quilted a laundry basket in pink for the baby girl, to be born in February.

Ed pored over the livestock pictures and pedigrees until he fell asleep sitting up. At midnight, Eleanor came from bed and shook him. "There's a full day's work tomorrow, isn't there?"

"You're right. Guess I better hit the sack."

SOME INDIAN DEERHUNTERS that Ed encountered while rounding up his cattle from the hills in the fall pointed out signs of a hard winter, the same signs that Old Man Westmore had counseled Ed to observe. When the snow, as predicted by the Indians, came early and stayed on the ground, Ed braced himself and fed his hay with scrupulous portions. A prolonged winter could exhaust his haystack. By December there had already been a long pinch of freezing weather and deep snow.

The spirits of the homesteaders rallied somewhat when the children brought home notes from school that a Christmas program would be given—with treats afterward! An old bachelor, dying in a shack on his claim, told the men who had stayed with him in his last hour, "Divide my poke among the kids at Christmas."

The money had been delivered to the schoolteacher, who said she would spend it for candy and nuts to be passed out at the end of the evening. She was coaching the children in a pageant of the nativity.

Sam and Billy looked forward with eagerness to the celebration. Eleanor remarked, "Believe me, when I was teaching, we didn't waste school time on practicing for a Christmas pageant!"

The program was to be held on the evening of the day school let out for Christmas vacation. Eleanor made sure that her husband and sons were bundled up warmly in the sleigh before they set off into a bone-chilling night. The boys were wildly excited as the sleigh runners cut through the ice-encrusted snow, which covered the ground a foot deep. Ed's responsibilities weighed on him. He could feel little Yule spirit with the prospect of three months more of feeding from the haystacks.

At the schoolhouse he joined in the fellowship of everyone trying to rid himself of the devils of gloom. A large star, made of cardboard and covered with tinfoil, hung over the audience. Red and green paper chains extended from the star to the corners of the room.

The boys left Ed in the audience and found their places in the chorus that was to sing Christmas carols. The program went as rehearsed with minor variations. The littlest angel could remember only the first line of his solo; he sang again and again, "The stars shine bright on Christmas night."

Finally the first-grader burst into tears and rushed from the stage to the comfort of his mother's bosom. Santa threaded his way through the folding chairs to give a candy bag early to the angel, who stopped wailing. The program resumed on the stage.

Ed noticed that Sam and Billy were singing unrestrainedly. He leaned over to whisper to Sven, "My kids can't carry a tune with a wheelbarrow, but I guess they have as much right to make racket as the rest."

"You bet!" Bachelor Linstrom chuckled. "They sure are whooping it up, aren't they?"

ON THE WAY home the boys gobbled their nuts and candy but saved their oranges to eat on Christmas day. As they put the horse in the barn, Ed's mood was somewhat brighter. "Dibs on being first to put my feet into the oven!" he shouted and raced the boys to the house.

They burst through the kitchen door to find Eleanor waiting up for them.

"I finished these while you were gone," she said, and held up heavy knitted woolen socks.

"Do we have to wait till Christmas to wear them?" Billy asked. "My feet freeze solid when I get in wood in the morning."

"I suppose you might as well wear them now," Eleanor said. Billy, more than anyone else, seemed to get his way with Eleanor. Ed opened the oven door, pulled up a chair, and stuck his feet into the hot cavern that baked bread.

"I never let the boys do that!"

Ed grinned defiantly. "I don't let 'em either till I've had my turn!"

"I give up. You might as well drink this cocoa. Made it half an hour ago. Probably has scum on top, but it won't hurt you to drink it."

Sam and Billy accepted their steaming cups and carefully licked the scum off the edges.

"Scum is my favorite part," Billy said.

"Go on up and kiss your mother for making you the socks and cocoa," Ed suggested to his sons.

Gingerly, they approached their mother.

"Ugh! Your runny noses!" she said, but bent down for their pecks on her cheek.

Ed went out to the porch to blow his nose, which was also runny. He shut off one nostril with his finger while he blew out the other nostril. Suddenly, through his cleared passages, he smelled the Chinook—warm wind rising from the west! The treetops spoke along the river. The thaw was on its way! The cattle could forage enough to ease the feeding from the haystacks. Maybe there was a Santa Claus besides Arthur Lund in a long red union suit.

When he returned to the kitchen, he saw that Eleanor had shooed the boys to bed. He put his arms gently about her swollen body.

"Sure hope you get your little girl."

"We'll just have to wait and see. I have other presents that I've made for the boys," she confided. "That's why I let them have the sock' tonight."

"I'm going to Pard's to pick up the sleds in the morning after we finish feeding. The boys have used those things I made with wooden runners for three years. Kids should have a Christmas!"

"Yes, they should!" Eleanor said briskly. "That's why I've made you a whole dozen handkerchiefs out of salt sacks so you won't have to blow your nose with your fingers! I heard you out back. Where did you get that filthy habit?"

Ed had never paid any attention as to how he blew his nose. He was astounded to find one more flaw in his manners.

"Done it all my life. Does it bother you?"

WHEN HE CAME in from the calving meadows after dark on a February night, he found Maggie Bottomley presiding over the kitchen. She was taking a brick from the oven to wrap in a towel as a bedwarmer.

"Shh!" the midwife whispered. "It's all over. I'm putting this brick to her feet."

Ed flung aside the curtain that separated his and Eleanor's bedroom from the kitchen. Eleanor's eyes had been closed, but she opened them at once. Maggie brought the lamp, and Eleanor triumphantly held a pink-clad bundle in the cradle of her arm.

"Her name is Leila," she said.

"Where'd you get that name?" Ed blurted.

"I don't care if you don't like it. I got it from a story."

"Suits me," Ed was quick to say.

Eleanor suffered his kiss.

"Where are the boys?" Ed asked.

"Over at my place," Maggie said. "Eleanor arranged that when she thought the baby was coming, the boys could run over and get me. Then they'd stay there."

"Sure. Fine. Sorry I was out so late," he begged pardon. "The kids could have come for me, too."

"It doesn't matter," Eleanor said. "It's better the boys weren't here. They're getting too big to be around childbirth."

The boys had seen birth in the pasture all season, Ed thought. Why should they be banished from witnessing the coming of a human animal? He had always been puzzled by Eleanor's wish to remain apart.

ED WAS ELECTED first president of the Okanogan County Livestock Association. The charter members were impressed with themselves when Spokane bankers and representatives from the Seattle and Spokane stockyards asked to attend the first annual meeting at Omak.

Everyone was interested in knowing that calves could be bred with smaller heads to prevent calving trouble, and which cattle withstood hot weather better, rustled well for grass, and achieved the most growth for the amount of feed consumed.

13.

A Flower Closes

In every gulch in which homesteaders built a cluster of cabins, a need ensued for a schoolhouse in which growing children, more bounteous a crop than any other, could learn reading, writing, spelling, geography, history, and arithmetic. By higgledy-piggledy finance, numerous boxlike structures sprang up, often on hillsides, with the front parts propped on stilts to make the floor level.

School each day opened with a salute to the flag, a prayer, or a rendition of "When the Roll is Called Up Yonder," with no one concerned about the separation of church and state. Grades one through eight took turns trooping to the bench in front to recite. First-graders chewed on their pencils while they listened to the upper grades, with the consequence that bright pupils could do considerable skipping.

Outdoors, at noon and recess, the school yard rang with the noises of such favorite games as "Pom Pom Pullaway! If you don't come away, I'll pull ya away!"

Dare base, steal sticks, ante-I-over, baseball, and quick fistfights were spring and summer games. In winter, great snowball battles took place, with teams dodging from behind forts. Pupils lucky enough to own sleds, either homemade with wooden runners, or steel-runnered "boughten" sleds from Glenwood Mercantile, zipped down the coasting hill, sitting up and steering with their feet, or lying flat on their bellies, head first, then trudged to the top for one more ride before the bell rang.

Lunches were hard-boiled eggs and sandwiches of homemade bread with jam and peanut butter filling. On hot spring days just before school closed, the children ate in the shade, under the front part of the propped-up schoolhouse.

When Sam reached school age and Billy was approaching it, Ed, despite his aggrieved memories of his own formal education, found himself on the school board. He felt a duty to look into information that state funds were becoming available to finance new school districts. The legislature was beginning to sell the newly surveyed sections 16 and 36, which, as a stipulation of the state constitution, had been set aside to finance education, both construction of schools and payment of teachers.

Eleanor said she wished the state had paid teachers' salaries when she was a teacher. She envied the current schoolteacher, who had come from Maine. On her way from the East, she had visited the Exposition in Portland.

"She's filed on a homestead east of town. I saw her yesterday at the store. She was wearing a white linen suit. She'll soon change those clothes in the Okanogan," Eleanor predicted.

Ed—who sometimes found Eleanor's brown ginghams too bleak even though she said they disguised dirt—told her that if she wished, she could send for another dress from the mail-order house. "We'll have some money this fall if the cattle prices hold up."

"If! If! I don't build my life on 'if.' Have you heard me complain about working hard and doing without?"

"No, I haven't."

He could say for Eleanor that she was willing to economize, sometimes even more than he.

"If we ever have any money, we won't waste it," she said firmly. "My brothers are buying up all kinds of Indian lands, and we've never added an acre. I'd rather you spent money on property than on clothes for me. Who is there to see me but you?"

Community conversation focused on what parcels of land had been considered for purchase. School sections, which could not be sold for less than ten dollars an acre, often seemed high-priced.

The survey showed that the meadow next to his homestead that Ed had appropriated for extra hayland belonged in a school section; he would have to purchase the property if he wished to retain possession. His savings account held five hundred dollars, not enough to finance a cash deal.

"I better write to Olympia," he said to Eleanor. "I hear you can buy state lands under a ten-year contract, ten percent down."

Ed went to visit Analix; he had not seen her in more than two years. She had become known to the public as an expert with land correspondence. Analix worked in a glass-fronted office located in a real estate building on the main street of Conconully—an office Gerald had largely deserted. It was sparsely furnished with a desk and a typewriter behind a wooden railing. A wooden settee outside the railing accommodated customers waiting their turn.

As Analix stood up to express her pleasure at seeing Ed, another man came banging through the outer door and flung a sheaf of papers on her desk.

"What's the idea of you putting the Injuns up to this junk?" the man demanded.

"Sales of Indian allotments are a matter of concern to me, Mr. Adams," she said quietly. "I wrote those letters for my friends in the hope that you will turn them over to the deputy auditor for consideration."

"The Injuns have agreed to the terms of the sales. What's it to you?"

"The proposed sales are theft on the face of them. The land commissioner should study them."

Adams spluttered, "I'm not showing them to the commissioner. I'm dumping your meddling back on your own doorstep."

"I'll send the correspondence to the commissioner myself."

"I'll have nothing to do with it."

As Adams turned to go, he noticed Ed. "Sorry if I barged in ahead of you. Sort of mad!"

When he had gone out, Ed asked, "Who was that?"

"The Indian agent from Nespelem. That's how he protects the interests of his charges."

Ed handed Analix a penciled version describing the hayland on which he wished to bid.

"I have forms we can fill out," she said. "First we make application for appraisement that precedes all sales."

A PROMPT REPLY from the land department informed Ed that a state inspector had appraised the property in question at ten dollars an acre. If Ed wished to purchase the land, he was to advise the department so that notices of sale could be posted for a period of five weeks in the office of the Okanogan County auditor and advertised for a similar period in a newspaper of general circulation in the county.

He showed the letter to Eleanor.

"Hurry and send in your bid!" she exclaimed excitedly.

AFTER A TRIP to the general store, Eleanor announced, "I put Mrs. Dorman in her place! She said to me at Blackwell's that she noticed in the *Register* that the meadowland next to the McLarens' was being advertised and wondered if you were buying it."

"That's what she'd naturally wonder, isn't it?"

"I told her that I didn't know anything about it if you were."

"What did you do that for? I haven't kept it a secret."

Eleanor looked at him as though he had never said anything more stupid. "Don't you know that if you shoot off your mouth about plans to buy land, somebody will run up the bid on you!"

He knew from her idiom that she was quoting her brothers.

DESPITE ELEANOR'S FEARS, no one but Ed bid for the land. He was advised that he could pay one hundred sixty dollars down and sign a note to pay for the balance in equal annual installments with interest at six percent per annum on the deferred payments. The transaction could be completed through the office of the Okanogan County auditor.

At the auditor's office in Conconully, the clerk took the down payment, which Ed had withdrawn in bills from Arthur Lund's bank, and gave him a receipt.

"As soon as the payment is received in Olympia, you'll be sent an acknowledgment."

ED DECIDED TO stop at into Analix's office to tell her of the successful conclusion of his business.

"People tell me I'm a fool to pay ten dollars an acre," he told her. "They say I'm not smart signing a note for fifteen hundred dollars."

"I imagine. Mort and Buford Clements are getting Old Alec's family allotments for three horses and a hundred dollars, with a jug of whiskey to seal the bargain. At least you're a square shooter."

"Forgot to ask about your family the last time I was in. How's your mother?"

"Not well, Ed. She has been pining for her People. Gerald and I may move back to the AW. I can help out with the cooking for twelve men. The last time Gerald and I were at the ranch, we heard a loud blast and a pile of smoke rose up in the pass. Father and I rode over there. Someone had dynamited the stone maiden—Amtoos, remember—and all the gifts left over many years were nothing but smoldering ashes. Mother has been sick ever since. Father has built her a sweat house. She steams in it for a while. After she comes out and bathes in the creek, she says she feels better to please us; but I can tell she doesn't really."

"I hate the way white folks are treating your mother's People."

"I know you do, Ed."

Ed was angry with himself that he had permitted Eleanor's contempt for squaw men's families to separate him from the AW. If she would not go with him for a visit, he would go alone. He was concerned as to how the Old Man was faring.

WHEN ED WENT up to the AW, Old Man Westmore himself answered the knock on the door. He came out to the porch instead of asking Ed inside.

"I've been home all morning. Flower isn't well."

"Analix told me. She is ailing because of her People."

"We white people, we're all trespassers in a way," Carr Westmore said soberly. "I didn't do Flower any favor by marrying her."

"She worships the ground you walk on, and you know it!"

"Maybe. But Red Curlew hates me now. He's gone off on all this Dreamer stuff."

"I haven't heard too much; but I guess Indians have it in their religion now about the white settlers," Ed said.

"Indians say people can't own the land; they just live on it by the kindness of Mother Earth, same as the ground squirrels. The Prophet Schwapsch had a vision of the white man coming to the land. Schwapsch prophesied about the wars, the tribes broken, and the People sick because somebody wants to own the land."

The Old Man was unburdening; Ed listened.

"The United States thought they bought the land from the Indian chiefs at the Walla Walla Council in 1855. All the chiefs met there at Walla Walla," the Old Man began a story. But before continuing, he suggested, "Let's go sit on the corral fence. I'd ask you in, but Flower wouldn't want you to see her as she is now, thin as paper. She'll blow away soon."

Ed followed him to a familiar perch on the lodgepoles.

"'Lawyer,' he called himself," the Old Man went back to his story. "He and Sticcas of the Cayuses, and Garry of the Spokanes, worked the deal with Governor Stevens. Most of the chiefs didn't want to sell—didn't think they had a moral right. My two oldest boys are named for chiefs. Flower says her father told her about Owhi of the Yakimas and Leschi from the Coast—they asked if man could steal the land from the Great Spirit and sell it? Could man give away the body of which he was a part?

"Not all the chiefs went along with what Lawyer did. That's why they got together and fought the Joseph war in 1877. That's when the Nez Perces came in here to the Okanogan. They put Joseph, who surrendered, on the reservation at Nespelem. He wasn't well-accepted for what he had done. I think he died a year or two ago. He used to be Hin-Male-Too: Thunder Rolling in the Mountains. He was no better than a poverty-stricken prisoner in the end.

"I believe that there is a great deal to what the Indians say about the Great Spirit owning the land—same as the Bible. I'm no scholar, but doesn't it say somewhere in the Bible that the earth is the Lord's?"

Ed recalled the nasal drone of his pastor back in Iowa: "The earth is the Lord's in the fullness thereof."

The words had held no significance for him then, but now as he sat on the corral rail in view of the lake, the meadow, and the hill range, Ed's imagination expanded. The support of man was the ground. The wealth of man was the ground. The hay that grew in the sunshine was man's by the grace of the Great

Spirit. Maybe Flower, who said the least, knew the most.

The sound of a pony coming down the path interrupted his reverie. Ed thought the rider vaguely resembled Gerald Gaston. As the pair drew nearer, he was astonished to see that it *was* Gaston, despite the Levi's and broad-brimmed hat. Stopping his mount before the two men, Gaston nodded to Ed, and Ed, nonplussed, nodded back. Gaston addressed the Old Man.

"Nathan wants to know if you want those yearlings in the cache or in the meadow."

"In the meadow."

Gaston kicked the pony in the ribs and rode back up the trail on which he had come.

Carr Westmore smiled. "Surprised at my new cowhand?"

"Sure. I'd have thought you'd run him off the place if he came around. Instead you have him working for you. You were plenty sore the day I brought Analix home."

"I knew Gaston didn't have much staying power," the Old Man said. "When he came back from the coast and came out here to see his baby, he looked forlorn. He was a hungry man.

"Analix said half the reason she'd left Gaston was because he didn't want a child with Indian blood. He told Analix he was sorry he'd said that. I thought to myself maybe we ought to give him another chance. He offered to go back east because he couldn't practice law anymore.

"But Analix said she would go down to Conconully and work with him. He had scarcely any legal business. Analix mostly kept them going. Now they're coming back here to stay. Father deRouge tells Analix that any husband is better than none. She'd never have felt right with herself if she'd sent him packing."

"Seems like you and Father deRouge are asking a lot."

"Work with muscles is helping Gaston. He has only known how to get by on his looks and his tongue. He's no worse than half the city men who came west."

"He'll have to dig a lot of postholes before I have any use for him," Ed muttered.

"You don't have the motherly tendencies of women," the Old Man said.

They got down from the rail together.

"Tell Analix I said 'hello.' Flower, too."

"I'll do that. Maybe you and I should write our ideas about use of the earth to Washington, D.C. Seems like everybody else does."

GRATEFUL FOR BALMY weather, Ed studied the grass roots of his new meadowland. As he felt the rise of the west wind that came at ten o'clock every morning, he caught the whinny of a horse. Nathan, his former cohort at the AW, came into view. Nathan rode an Appaloosa and was decked out in formal attire—bearskin chaps, beaded buckskin jacket, and a ten-gallon hat. Ed expected to hear a yell of salute, but Nathan approached him in silence. With decorum, the aging cowboy dismounted before he spoke.

"The Old Man sent me to tell you Flower has passed on."

A gust of wind—or an inner stab of loss—took Ed's breath.

He stammered, "She was always good to me."

"There is a gift for you. She divided up her treasures the way Injuns do. She never forgot you. She always talked about scrawny Ed, who ate half the vittles cooked for her second wedding feast.

"Father deRouge will say Mass at the AW on Saturday. Afterward, we'll have a meal. The priest won't let it be called a potlatch. He wants Flower buried in St. Mary's cemetery, but the Old Man is gonna bury her where she wanted to lie—in the graveyard on the hill, where the old chief and her mother are already buried. Analix and Bethany are sewing her into a caul."

"Saturday, you say?"

"Bring your wife, the Old Man said."

"Yes, we'll be there. Tell the Old Man and the others I'm sorry Flower is gone."

NATHAN RODE ON to spread the word to Flower's tribesmen at Nespelem.

As ED WENT to the house, he dreaded what Eleanor would say. When he delivered the Old Man's personal invitation to her to attend the funeral, she rejoined, "You can't drag me to any heathen burial."

"It won't be a heathen burial. Father deRouge from the mission is going to conduct the service."

"Popish! What's the difference?"

"Better come. Lots of old-timers will—for the potlatch at least. You'll see the tribes dressed in their best clothes."

Eleanor's curiosity impelled her to yield to Ed's wish. Still disdainful, on Friday night she asked him to bring in extra firewood for the stove. "I'll have to heat the flatirons if I'm going to wear my meeting clothing like everybody else."

She would honor the occasion by making ready the garments she wore to the Protestant church services held intermittently in the school.

"I have only this one good blouse left," she said as she guided the iron over the intricacies of its starched ruffles. "Never have seen the sense of your being such close friends with a squaw man and his family."

"Don't say that again! Westmore is the wealthiest cattleman in the

Okanogan. Doesn't that impress you?"

Eleanor sniffed.

THEY LEFT THE children with the Bottomley family and rode to the Westmore ranch in the hack.

The Westmores' enclosed yard was filled with people, white as well as Indian. Some of the natives were clad in blankets, as Eleanor had foreseen; others wore beaded deerskin garments or white peoples' clothing. The county sheriff, the superior court judge, and county officials from Conconully were all in attendance.

Chief Ohotkolin, displaying a mixture of cultures in his garb, nodded in greeting to his neighbors from the lower end of the valley. He remarked to Ed politely, "Opening Flower became Flower. Now she is Closed Flower, like speetlum at night."

He spoke in labored English for Eleanor's benefit.

Val Haynes, son of Judge W. C. Haynes, the first British customs officer, attended with his wife, Elizabeth, a niece to Chief Nespelem George. Chief George had in his company a Nez Perce, an exile who spoke a strange language. The sons of Chief Tonasket shook hands respectfully with the Nez Perce, who had fought beside Joseph, the great war chief, in the last stand in Montana.

Mary Manuel and her sons were there from their nearby homes at Osoyoos. Mary had moved ten years ago to her own corner of Okanogan Smith's orchards and fields. Okanogan, who in his later years became intrigued with politics and had been elected to the state legislature, had abandoned his common-law wife to marry a young white woman in Seattle shortly before his death. When the second wife had come to Osoyoos expecting to take over the aged entrepreneur's wealth, Old Mary and her sons had run the interloper off the place. Okanogan's lands had reverted to the original royalty that possessed them, descendants of Chief Manuel.

Aunt Smiling Water represented the family of the deceased White Stone Mountain. When Father deRouge long ago had decreed that the chief must give up either his first or his second wife before he could be baptized, White Stone Mountain had consulted his two mates. Smiling Water, who had already borne six children, cheerfully agreed to become the chief's older sister. When White Stone Mountain found that absolution could be obtained for occasional lapses into adultery, he had permitted himself and his women to be baptized.

Flower had been the chief's last child. She would rest in the square mile of land that White Stone Mountain had set aside, his allotment in severalty, as his scattered People's final gathering ground.

Father deRouge, accompanied by two Indian youths who were pupils at the mission, arrived in a hack. Mrs. Bottomley, who served as both seamstress and midwife to the settlers, had turned the priest's robes inside out so that today they appeared renewed. St. Mary's Mission was growing large, but the balance between mouths to fill and the mission's income was never enough to allow him a new cassock.

The Westmore family were waiting inside the house, seated around Flower, who lay in a handhewn, oiled coffin, inside a deerskin caul. The priest carried his holy water and the *Booklet of Prayer*, in Latin and Salish, which had been printed in France.

As the signal for the start of the Mass was sounded, those who were not members of the family found places on log benches in the yard. The house door remained open. All could witness the ceremonies and prayers.

Father deRouge was interrupted in his hymn of consecration. Old Man Westmore came out of the house alone and went down the front steps to the gate, where Red Curlew stood, clinging to the pickets. Flower's brother was swaying with grief, illness, or drunkenness, or a combination of the three. He wore blue denim overalls and a plaid gingham shirt which was tattered but clean from recent washing.

Carr Westmore unlatched the gate, put his arm about Red Curlew's shoulders, and led him through the midst of *N'Chilix-czin* to the house. Both men were weeping.

Flower's six oldest sons carried her casket on their shoulders up the hillside to the burial ground. Red Curlew and Carr Westmore followed closest behind, then the two youngest sons and Analix and Bethany, with their husbands and children. Men who had previously conjectured at Pard Cummings's store that Analix kept her husband sleeping in the bunkhouse could see today that their guesses were incorrect. Analix was pregnant.

When the procession of mourners had surrounded the grave, Leschi and Owhi filled shovels with dirt. The Old Man came forward, took a handful of soil, and threw it gently on the closed coffin that had been lowered into the ground. Each mourner took a clod; even Eleanor threw down a handful of earth.

Old Man Westmore's tears were over. He led the way back to the yard. Analix and Bethany, with other Indian women to help them, brought food from the house to the long table that had been moved to the yard. Each person was given a tin plate.

Eleanor chose foods with which she was familiar: roast beef, baked potato, glazed carrots, and canned prunes with white cake. Ed, singled out for attention by Leschi and Owhi, took the same food as the brothers: boiled venison, smoked fish, pemmican, speetlum, and a bannock.

The Old Man ate nothing. He was setting up another long table with the help of Nathan and Will. They brought boxes from the house and spread out the contents.

After all had laid aside their plates, the guests went forward for their gifts as their names were called by Mr. Westmore. They received porcupine quill baskets, soft leather mittens, mats, jackets, and skirts.

Mr. Westmore handed Eleanor a piece of Flower's handwork. "This will be suitable for a sewing basket or fruit," he told her with grave politeness.

Eleanor perforce uttered a hushed, courteous thanks.

For Ed, the Old Man held out a deerskin shirt decorated in brown and gold.

"Flower asked that this be given to you, and no one else, Ed."

"Thanks. I'll never part with it. Still have the jacket she made me the first winter I arrived in the Okanogan."

Analix stood with Father deRouge at the bonfire that had been lighted to turn aside the chill of the coming sundown.

Ed went to speak to her. "Flower lived a good life," he said.

"Yes, she gave Papa many children, and she always spoke to us with love and softness."

Father deRouge laid his hand on Analix's shoulder. "Your mother was fulfilled, and for her there need not be too much regret. Isn't that true, Ed?"

"Yes, sir," Ed answered, but he was thinking that carrying another child emphasized Analix's sorrow and fatigue.

"I hear you have moved back to the place," he said.

"Yes. Bethany's family is growing, too. We can all live here more comfortably together. Gerald is no longer interested in practicing law."

Ed glanced at Gerald Gaston standing alone. He had lost his suave, aggressive manner, and appeared at peace. Ed had heard that Gerald had stopped the use of alcohol entirely, but he noted a puffiness to his hands and features. He seemed bent for a young man.

The assemblage had begun to disperse. Ed rejoined Eleanor, who had been standing with two other white women.

"We've been away from the children long enough," she said.

Ed could agree with her for once. In the rig, they started down the trail.

"I noticed you talking with that Analix. In the family way again. She doesn't look too cheerful about having her husband back, does she?"

"Her sadness likely comes from the death of her mother."

"Those women I was talking to said that her mother died of pneumonia from taking sweat baths."

"Maybe so, but I reckon what really killed her was grief for her old way of life.

"Being with those people wasn't as bad as you expected, was it? Isn't Mr. Westmore enough of a gentleman?"

"Oh, I suppose so. They say squaws were about all the women there were in this country when he was young. He had to take an Indian if he had anybody. And you might as well admit it—if it weren't for me, you'd have taken up with a halfbreed yourself. That Analix stared at me as though I'd stolen something from her."

Ed had noticed Eleanor staring, too, but he refrained from saying so. The period of his life with the Westmore family was closed. He need not make it a bone of contention with Eleanor. He would turn his energies to being a citizen of Bonaparte. The community was about to be incorporated as a town. Ed was one of the six members of the Bonaparte Townsite Company, which also included the Linstrom brothers and the town banker, Arthur Lund.

CREATING A TOWN sensation, Billy Domino, sired by a grand champion, trod royally along the Bonaparte main street with Sammie and Billy McLaren yelping and scurrying on either side. The bull, Ed's first purebred Hereford, had been shipped in the railroad livestock car from the Old Union Stockyards in Spokane. From the station, Ed led the tame eighteen-hundred pound, red and white animal on a chain half a mile to his place. Sammie and Billy ran into the house to announce the arrival to their mother.

Eleanor came out to watch while Ed turned the bull into the pen at the barn. "No stopping you!" she sniffed when Ed came into the house for lunch.

His masculine conceit collapsed. All the way from town he had fancied himself a personage to those watching the parade. Had he really imagined that Eleanor would be as proud as he to own a purebred bull?

AS A RECRUITER for the Cattleman's Association, Ed called on John Bennett, a former Montanan, who had recently bought the O'Neill spread.

"How do you like the Okanogan?" Ed asked his new neighbor.

"Grazing is as good or better than in Montana," Bennett replied. "One thing we had in Montana you don't have here worries me."

"What's that?"

"Statewide branding law. Here I am using the ON brand now, registered in Okanogan County, but the son of the man I bought from—over in Lincoln County, fifty miles away—is using the ON, too. In Montana, only one person in the state can use a particular brand."

"You have a point," Ed agreed. "You come to the cattle meetings, and we'll bring it up."

AT THE NEXT session, the cattlemen discussed the problem.

John Bennett observed, "In Montana, we had a cattleman run for the legislature and fix it up for us."

A call came from the back of the room, "I make a motion that our president, Ed McLaren, run for the legislature to put through a uniform brand bill."

"What walloper said that?" Ed snarled.

The idea took hold as a joke on Ed, then became a serious request.

"Sure! Ed for the legislature! Why not for governor! President!"

"THEY SURE ARE hard up for suckers," Ed told Eleanor when he came home from the meeting. "They want me to run for the state legislature."

"I was hoping that when you got done with that commissioner business, you'd had enough of politics."

"I got no interest in politics as such," Ed answered.

"Hunh! I see you took it seriously when they asked you. All you do is involve yourself in other people's schemes and get nothing from it. If you'd kept the road off Mort and Buford's land when you were Good Roads president, I might have felt that you accomplished something."

"Quit bringin' that up!" Ed flared.

"All right, I'll just mention instead the time you've spent on the townsite company. All that free planning for grading the streets and putting in a pipeline water system."

"It's just good business for the town," Ed said for the fiftieth time. "If we want Bonaparte to be the trading center, we have to move fast. Requirements for homesteading have been reduced from five to three years."

"If you worked for local option for liquor, I could go along with that; but you wouldn't do that in a million years."

"No, I wouldn't. The country around Oroville wants to separate from the south half so they can keep their bars; but the south half would be stuck without revenue for roads and schools. The Oroville bars bring in almost all the tax money."

"I'm all for letting Oroville go. People off the train for the overnight stop in Oroville have nothing to do but pass the time getting drunk! Let them be ignored and the bartenders can be separate from decent people! I'll have you know the Christian people have a petition going."

"All that does is bring the issue up in the legislature. I signed the petition myself. Let's vote it out."

ELEANOR HAD JOINED a group to establish a new community church. She took an active part in the Ladies' Aid and the Prayer Meeting Band. When Ed occasionally came home from the tavern after a drink with the Linstroms, Eleanor greeted him with scripture about winebibbers. She demanded that Ed escort her to church services. When he declared, "I got enough of that in

Iowa," she announced her position:

"If you want to be a heathen, that's the act of your free will. But I'm not going to endanger the souls of my children. They will go to church and Sunday School."

"Sure, make 'em go," Ed responded. "I had to suffer. My kids shouldn't have it any better!"

Eleanor sniffed. "Lately I am finding it necessary to go a different path and bear many crosses. I hope you understand that clearly."

"Sure, I understand."

His wife now reminded him of his mother in Iowa. Eleanor had even sought acquaintance with Ma. She wrote a letter and received a reply. All women, it seemed to Ed, matured into the same pattern of fanatical respectability. He supposed it was due to their early training: little girls were warned from the start to protect their virtue.

Ed campaigned against the division of Okanogan County and gloated when his faction defeated the teetotalers.

14.

Campaign Issues

Eleanor became pregnant a fourth time, but she suffered a miscarriage. Maggie Bottomley advised her to stay in bed until she stopped bleeding, but she was unable to follow such a suggestion. She fumed while she lay helpless. The house was filling up with dust! She dressed herself and dragged over the house, brooding, dustcloth in hand. Members of the Ladies' Aid came to call in sympathy.

After one of the visits, her face working with desperate feeling, Eleanor told Ed: "They say they are going to build an irrigation dam on the other fork of Bonaparte Creek. I hear you can file on that land for a hundred and sixty acres. Residence requirements are reduced to three years, or you can live there fourteen months and pay a dollar and a quarter an acre.

"It would be like my folks' place in the Walla Walla country—garden truck and wheat. You wouldn't have to travel miles on horseback to work with those filthy, stinking cattle. When you're branding, your smell makes me sick to my stomach. It won't come off you or the boys even after you bathe in the river with laundry soap!"

She burst into tears and begged, "Please, let's stop this dirty cattle business and find some nicer way of earning a living! Frogs do come out of my washing machine, just like people said!"

Ed had worked long that day, but he would be patient. He saw her drawn, white face; he felt guilty that he had not paid more attention to her.

"Sorry if you think cow smell is stink. But I already have my homestead, remember. What would it look like if I sold my spread now? I've promised the cattlemen to run for the legislature to get a branding law. We need it to operate."

"I won't go to Olympia with you, even if you win the election. I couldn't stand the drinking parties and all the cheap politics I hear about. I had to give up my own homestead claim when I married you. I could file for another. Letting me stay here on a homestead while you're away would be reasonable. If you could build a cabin for me before you go, I could add two months to the residence requirements."

Her mouth jerked. Ed saw that she was far from him in her thoughts. She was not well, he knew.

"She drives herself crazy over cleaning," he thought. "Maybe I better not cross her."

Even if Eleanor would have no respect for a political victory, she would not object to his absence for two or three months. She had made herself clear. He would have to hire a man to see the herd through the calving season in midwinter. Eleanor could have a whole bed in which to rest without a stinking man to disturb her.

The cattlemen advised Ed that to cinch the nomination, he should go to one meeting of the Waterusers' Association, the organization promoting the dam in which Eleanor had so much faith. Ed accepted the counsel of his political advisers; they obtained. a few moments on the program for him. He learned that Judge Pendergriff was to be the main speaker.

Judge Pendergriff, with a reputation as a gifted orator, brought the newcomers to the Waterusers' camp up to date: "Five thousand acres in Aeneas and Bonaparte valleys, and the benches, can all be watered from Lost, Bonaparte, and Aeneas creeks, streams now wasting their waters in the Columbia.

"Our land is fine range country, we know already. To become the nation's leaders of the livestock industry, all we need here is a sufficient water supply to produce hay and corn for fattening purposes.

"Figures show that Loop Loop Creek now waters fifteen hundred acres of fields and orchards, the largest unit being the six hundred acres of the Boston-Okanogan Apple Company. We can anticipate this sort of development everywhere in the valley—in the places that have soil good enough for dirt farming!"

"That last line is all that makes sense—'places that have soil good enough for dirt farming,'" Ed thought.

When his turn came to speak, he stayed where he was in the front row and did not go up to the platform. He said, "I am not exactly swept away with this business, the way some others are. Maybe places in the valley have good enough soil for dirt farming, but not every place by a darn sight. The original squatters have tried out the land long enough to know what it is good for by now.

"If you are all bound to have an irrigation project, it at least should be one big project instead of a number of small dirt-fill projects as proposed. Any project should include Indian lands, too."

Ed's companion from the cattle faction whispered to Ed as he sat down,

"You didn't speak up the way they expected."

Ed shrugged. "The whole thing is too flimsy."

Eleanor, who had come along to a political meeting for the first time, kept her face straight ahead.

C. W. WILDROOT, imported as an expert from Spokane, stated that one foot-second would water a hundred acres. The annual irrigation cost would be eight dollars per acre; annual return, fifty dollars per acre.

"Now you take an average farm of twenty acres, or a home for five families, or twenty-five people. You have a hundred acres of irrigation land worth six thousand dollars."

Ed listened all the way through.

"Can you follow those figures?" he muttered to Tom Eder. "Just a bunch of presuming."

One fact crystallized: for the irrigation setup to be put in, a forty-mill levy would be required. That would be two hundred forty dollars in taxes on a twenty-acre farm.

After doing the mental arithmetic, Ed stood up again. "The community ought to go easy on heavy increases in taxation like this. We're not fixed for them yet."

Some hearty hurrahs came from nearby chairs, but the spellbinding from the rostrum continued to dominate the gathering.

"We have made great progress this evening," the chairman summed up the occasion. "Our next meeting will be the first Monday of next month. See you there!"

"THAT WAS ONE bunch of people you couldn't swing," Eleanor said smugly on the way home. "They ignored you properly."

"I'm not sure I'm for a dam at all," Ed told her bluntly. "I saw in the Spokane paper that some government construction engineers are coming to Washington next month. If they go to Seattle from Spokane, maybe I can route them up this way to get an opinion on how far it is to bedrock. That Wildroot says you can build a dam for a hundred and ninety thousand. I suspect it can't be done."

Addressing his letter in care of the Spokane postmaster, Ed wrote to the government construction engineers whose names had been listed in the paper. He described Okanogan County plans under the Newlands Act. Was there any chance of obtaining the opinion of federal experts before he, a candidate for the state legislature, committed himself to vote for an Okanogan dam?

Next Saturday morning a Reo automobile drove up to the front of the house, and four men in tourist dusters got out. Ed went at once to the yard to greet them and invite them in. He had stayed at home in the eventuality of any such visit. When he introduced them to Eleanor, she was her most gracious self.

"Have you had breakfast?" she asked the men.

When they confided that they had had nothing but coffee and doughnuts, she went to the kitchen.

"I'll have hotcakes and eggs in a minute; you can talk your business with my husband."

The engineers said that on receipt of his letter, they had decided that it was feasible to inspect the proposed irrigation site on Bonaparte Creek. They had already been instructed to view the Pogue River project on Bureau of Reclamation land around Cummings's landing at Riverside; the trip to Bonaparte wasn't much out of the way.

Eleanor's stack of hotcakes vanished. She invited the men to come into the house again after they saw the dam site. When the experts returned with Ed at noon, a chocolate cake was placed hospitably on the dining table with forks and plates. Ed recognized the cake. Eleanor had told the boys before they left for school that she could not give them pieces for their lunches; she was saving the cake for the church Sunday night supper. Yet now she cut generous slices for the engineers.

She listened in silence while the men told Ed, in all honesty, they doubted that a hundred and ninety thousand dollars' worth of digging would reach bedrock in the sandy soil at the proposed site—or even seven hundred fifty thousand dollars' worth of digging. The federal government already had been disappointed on several similarly proposed projects for which it had loaned money to states.

Eleanor tightened her lips. She wiped her hands on her apron and retired to the kitchen until Ed came for her. The men, about to leave, wanted another chance to thank her for the delicious refreshments. She returned to the dining room, but she responded to their compliments with a blank face. At a signal from Ed, she accompanied him to the yard. When the engineers donned visors and gauntlets, got the spark set, and finally made the engine turn over with the crank, they bade a last cordial farewell, but it was returned only by Ed.

"If I had known what they were going to say, I wouldn't have put myself out so much," she said as the clouds of their departure billowed along the dusty road.

"Experts can't change facts for a piece of cake," Ed told her.

"Experts! Fiddle diddle! What do they know? They're here four hours and give an opinion."

EVERYWHERE HE ELECTIONEERED, Ed reported the words of the engineers when he was questioned about the proposed dam, and he added his own observations: "Bonaparte Creek dries up some summers. We've had several wet years in a row, I know. The spring runoff has cut a big gully down my place. But you'll get a dry bed there some years."

At the next Waterusers' meeting, Ed said to the group, which had become a permanent organization with a paid secretary and a lawyer: "I'll look into the matter of state aid for the dam if you send me to Olympia, but you all know what the federal engineers told me. This dam may sound like a good thing, but I've heard that the Waterusers at Quincy, in a project supplied by the Columbia, are having a hard time. The cost of construction is raising the cost of the land way above the estimate of twelve to fifteen dollars per acre. Some say it will go as high as thirty-one dollars before it's done. I don't want to seem like a wet blanket, but your community, if it wants irrigation, can't afford to waste that much money on a dam that won't do what it's supposed to do."

On the way home, Eleanor stayed withdrawn in anger, but Ed did not apologize for what he had said. People could vote for him for what he believed, or not at all. He must speak his mind.

As required by a new direct primary law, he had filed as a candidate for the primary election. He would have to be formally nominated by his party, although he seemed to be the only candidate.

"Unless a dark horse comes forward in some new party, you won't have to do any campaigning after the first election," Tom Eder said.

Not wanting to appear unprepared at the state capital, he sat down in the evenings with government manuals, session laws of the state for the past legislatures, and the recently published state code book.

Fatigue distracted him sometimes. He preferred to play with a tot who twisted his heart with a smile of worship. When his boots sloshed with river muck inside, Leila patted them as though they were making music. Eleanor rushed between Ed and Leila. The infant took after her father! Filth must not be victorious!

Eleanor's agitation soon reached a peak. A glitter in her eyes, she met him at the door one evening. "You can't keep me from getting ahead!"

"Now what?"

"There was no sense waiting to look for a homestead after all the land is taken. Mort drove me to Waterville to the General Land Office today. I've been allotted a hundred and sixty acres."

"You filed on some land by yourself?"

"It's perfectly legal. Lots of wives are doing it. You can live with me. This place is all proved up. I filed for my other homestead land and had to give it up on account of marrying you."

"Your brothers aren't letting any consideration stop them from adding one more parcel of land to the family, are they?"

"I'm like my brothers," she spoke with fever on her cheeks. "I believe in seeing opportunities the way they do. People call them longheads. I'm going to be one, too."

"What if I haven't time to run a dirt farm for you? I don't want to be a truck gardener and live out there on the flat. I've spent ten years getting a herd going, gouging myself for twenty dollars for every heifer. And you know it! I hated dirt farming in Iowa even when it was the right kind of dirt!"

"You've spoken your piece a dozen times. But I can at least homestead the land and sell it for a profit when the irrigation comes in."

"Is that what your brothers told you?"

"Yes, they did! I can always depend on you for some slur on them. You can't stand it because I admire their gumption. But let me tell you—if you won't build me a cabin and live out there with me, I'll live out there by myself! My brothers said they would help build me a cabin if I needed them to."

She stared at him, defiant, pale, and almost without feminine attraction. He could indeed see in Eleanor a shadow of the greed that showed so plainly in her brothers' faces. She did resemble them!

"Eleanor, don't be like this," Ed pleaded for the first time in his life. "We'll let you homestead if you want to so much. I'll build your cabin."

"All right! For once, this family will do what I want to do!"

THE BONAPARTE COMMUNITY took on the aspect of a religious sect in the fervency of its faith and hope in the dam. Ed ceased his public doubting, in view of Eleanor's filing for a claim.

As he was planning to start fall roundup, Eleanor demanded, "When are you going to start building my cabin?"

"You said your brothers would help. When can they start?"

"They're busy with land sales. They told me to let you go ahead. They'll lend a hand when they're able."

Ed had expected such an evasion. "I don't want 'em around anyhow," he muttered.

He hired two men idle in town. In a week, they and Ed constructed a cabin partly of chinked logs and partly of lumber from the government sawmill. They nailed shakes on the roof and built a makeshift porch with a rail.

The site was a few rods from the course of a creek that emptied into Bonaparte. From the stream, Ed troughed water to the side of the cabin and directed it into a short pipe with a faucet rigged on the end. The spring itself was high in the hills on someone else's land.

"There's your cabin," Ed announced to Eleanor when the work was complete. "If we must sit out here in the plain, we're better off than most. I can't understand why you want to live out here on bare land instead of in the orchard."

"We've never really had a good house yet. You threw it together a room at a time. This cabin will do for the present. What I want in the end is a two-story house with a garden like other people are planning. It can be built here on the flat."

Her brothers at last appeared on the property.

"Sis said for us to O.K. the job," Mort joked. "Shack's good enough to live in awhile—especially if you earn a hundred and sixty acres by doing it, Sis."

"It's not much now, but I'll have something when irrigation comes in. I can manage till then!"

"You can live here just as long as somebody farther up the creek doesn't use all the water before it reaches you," Ed corrected.

"There'll be plenty of water," Eleanor retorted. "You won't admit it because the dam was somebody else's idea. You can't stand anyone but yourself saying how things should be run."

In the heat of late August, while dust clouds rose on the new lanes among the cabins, the McLarens piled some of their belongings into the wagon. Ed protested to Eleanor that she was taking more than necessary to a temporary dwelling. She sent the boys to catch the poultry.

"If you take your hens out there to run loose around everybody's cabin, they'll be popped into the closest stew pot," Ed warned. "I don't have time to build a coop right now. Leave the hens here. I'll feed 'em night and morning when I bring the horses to and from the barn."

Eleanor was reluctant to leave the hens, but the boys quit chasing them.

As Ed turned the soil of forty acres with a disk, he knew that the homestead land would grow neither wheat nor vegetables abundantly. In her haste and covertness, Eleanor had selected a poor acreage. It was suitable grassland for spring and early summer grazing. Some people were planting their ground with Jones' Fife wheat seed freighted in by steamboat to Riverside. Ed did likewise; even though the wheat might not mature, it would make hay next summer.

Tom Eder, current president of the Cattleman's Association, rode on horseback through the acreages of the proposed irrigation project one evening to Ed and Eleanor's cabin. Eleanor had gone to a meeting to organize a church mission society, which would be still another activity for the women who already belonged to the Ladies' Aid. Eleanor had taken the children, who could play with the other youngsters that would be at the meeting. Sam had driven the buckboard.

Ed was freeing his horse from the plow after turning up a promised garden patch near the house. Tom burst into laughter at the sight of a cowboy doing the work of a farmer.

"Caught a nester!" he teased.

"Not funny!" Ed said. "Can't believe I'm doing it! But come into the house. There's nobody but me home."

The coffeepot was on the back of the stove. Ed poured them each a cup, and they sat down at the round table that nearly filled the main room.

"Got something on your mind?"

"Yep. I hear a lawyer from Okanogan has been asked to file against you for the legislature. The new primary law gives them a chance to form another party. Did you know it?"

"No, I didn't. I haven't done any campaigning. Let 'em pick a lawyer. Is he the Waterusers' lawyer?"

"You guessed right. You didn't come out strong enough for a dam."

"I can't change facts to suit the get-rich-quick schemes of Mort and Buford Clements. I don't care whether I win or not."

"The cattlemen have got to have a brand law, remember. Get ornery. Stir around and talk to ranchers. If there's going to be a double election, you'll need the next six weeks. The new people aren't backward about using politics to get what they want."

Ed muttered, "I can't understand why everybody goes for this hogwash about a boom dam—a hole that won't hold water, dug in dirt! All the people who've filed here are going to be crying."

"If you don't count on a dam yourself, Ed, why did you move out here in the sagebrush?"

"Eleanor gave me fits till we did."

Torn ceased his line of questioning, but Ed read the thought behind his look: "You've become a henpecked husband."

WHEN ELEANOR AND the children came home at ten o'clock, Ed said abruptly, "Let's get off this flat! I'm not one of the caboodle counting on a crackpot idea. What have we to gain from one hundred and sixty acres of dusthole? The Waterusers have picked a candidate of their own. Let him fight their war."

Eleanor's eyes narrowed, and she braced her shoulders.

"I knew they were going to nominate Mr. Travis weeks ago. If the fight for the dam was left to you in the legislature, it really would fall through. Mort and Buford told me not to let you know about the new candidate. People are going to have their dam whether you like it or not. I'm not leaving this place!"

Sam, Billy, and Leila looked exhausted from being up too late. Their faces showed their dread of another confrontation. Eleanor did not notice them retreating like a huddle of forlorn calves to the straw ticks in the back room. She continued relentlessly, "If you don't want to stay here, I can't make you. Anyhow, as far as I can see, you and I don't get along anymore. I've been coming to a decision for a long time that we should go our separate ways. I can't stand your godlessness and roughness."

His knees turned to water. He had felt her affection receding, but he had kept pretending to himself. He had built the foolish cabin merely to please her, to win a kind word. Now he was left with no excuse to pretend; he went wild in the head. "I guess you were always too proper and clean for me. It was a mistake you made—marrying a cowhand."

She did not respond.

Ed went to the bed comer and hauled out the valise that was serving as his dresser drawer. He took his saddle from the porch rail. "I'll go to my own house and bunk."

"You're slow to catch on about some things, Ed," she said almost mockingly. "A smart man might have suspected that I wanted to split up when I insisted on this cabin being built before you went to the legislature. You didn't even worry when I said I wouldn't go to Olympia."

Ed could only think that now he knew how three-year-old steers felt when the butcher struck them the stunning blow on the head and slit their throats to bleed them to death. He understood the bafflement that clouded the eyes of animals as they died at hands they had trusted.

"I didn't know what you were scheming," he said. "I was too busy working."

One conciliatory word would have kept him, but she did not say it. He walked into the night and found his saddle horse drowsing by the creek. Bewildered by being used in rest time, the horse stumbled away with Ed on his back. The horse's gait suited his owner's state of mind.

WHEN ED REACHED his barn, he dismounted and took off his horse's saddle before leading him into a stall. Rather than go to the trouble of breaking into the house in the dark, he lay down and slept on the hay.

Ed woke in creeping daylight to the realization that he had slept on a pile of straw, and that his wife had ordered him away in the same fashion that a dog was ordered out of the house for the night. Only he was ordered out for keeps.

He climbed to the hayloft, where he had nailed some tools, and selected a hammer. Climbing down, he went to the house and yanked off the board that he had nailed across the kitchen door.

For food, there was not so much as a handful of flour or cornmeal.

Eleanor's canny preparedness turned him cold with rage. First he had been hurt; now he was belligerent. Married to her twelve years, he deserved better treatment! Wait till she sent one of the boys to collect the eggs! In the chicken house he found eggs in several nests.

He scooped a tinful of wheat from the chicken feed sack. He'd batched too long to let himself starve. He put split wood into the kitchen stove, splashed on kerosene from a can on the back porch, struck a match and produced an instant roaring fire. He boiled the grain and the eggs in the only utensil available—the tin can from the chicken feed sack.

Even though the day was Sunday, he rounded up calves in the hills. By nightfall, somewhat recovered from the dizziness of shock, he bathed in the river and put on clothes that Eleanor had not considered essential to transfer to the new home. For his evening meal, he ate leftover boiled eggs and grain.

The first thing he would have to do would be to recover his work team and wagon that were still at the new homestead. When he had left in the dark on Saturday night, he had fled instinctively on his mount.

Monday morning he rode to the flat. He went before dawn to avoid rousing anyone in the cabin. The team and wagon stood as Sam had left them after returning from the Saturday evening meeting.

He had done the best he could, Ed thought; Sam had unharnessed the horses, tied them to the porch rail, and thrown down some straw. The doubletree, tongue, and harness were in the wagon bed. Eleanor had evidently forbidden Sam to bring the wagon back to the barn where it belonged. How did she plan to care for horses without even a pen? Ed hitched the team to the wagon and drove away, his lately overworked saddle horse tied at the rear of the wagon.

If she had the temerity, she could ask for the use of the buggy, still in the barn, and one of the light horses. Eleanor had never taken any joy in her buggy. Let her walk! He needed the wagon for hauling salt and hay.

Ed was the first customer at the general store. He bought flour, lard, salt, sugar, pepper, coffee, beans, and baking powder. For immediate consumption with more eggs, he bought tinned corned beef and a ham to cut into slices as needed. There were still corn, string beans, and tomatoes in the garden. Eleanor should have thought twice before abandoning her vegetables.

Charlie Blackwell himself was waiting on Ed. "I thought you folks bought a load last week. How come you have to bring the wagon to town so soon again?"

"I'm staying at the main house sometimes," Ed said. "Things to do around the place at night after I get back from riding. That other load of groceries was for Eleanor's claim on the flat. Got to live there three months."

Charlie stopped questioning.

Again at his own place, Ed unloaded the supplies, drove the wagon to the barnyard, and unhitched the team. He led the horses into their stalls and forked them hay from the loft. They began to eat hungrily.

Sam appeared at the barn door.

Ed's first thought was that Eleanor had sent him to say that she had been silly, that he should come home; but Sam brought no such message. "When I got up and saw the team gone, I thought at first it had been stolen, so I came to check if you had taken it," Sam said.

"Yes, I took it! Isn't it mine?"

Sam, age eleven, began to cry. "Dad! Mother says you walked out on us! You didn't, did you?"

Ed's profanity ripped out like a fire over brush. "Your mother's gone crazy. That's all I can figure. She let me have it with both barrels—she was tired of cleaning up after me. I stink. I have to make my headquarters somewhere else."

"Billy and I knew you wouldn't just plain walk out on us."

"You're darn tootin' I wouldn't. Maybe your mother will get a bellyful of that homestead. She's not all to blame. It's her smart brothers put her head full of big ideas. You stay there, Sam. She'll need you. Maybe she can grow a crop of wheat."

"She'll have to keep charging groceries at Blackwell's. She can't do anything else. She doesn't know how much it costs to live. She's not going to build herself a mansion as fast as she expects."

"She told me to bring back some rags."

"Rags! What for?"

"She's going to braid rugs for the floor in the cabin. She said the rags are in the two bottom drawers of the dresser in the bedroom."

Ed swallowed. He had nearly arrived at a state of sympathy for female aberration; but if she was calm enough to put her mind to braiding rugs, he, too, would be able to keep cool possession of his faculties.

"Wonder to me she even left rags," he said. "She took every other blame thing."

Sam took a gunnysack from the barn for carrying rags. They found odds and ends of cloth in the dresser drawers as Eleanor had said.

"Criminy, Dad!" Sam quavered, "I don't want to go back there! Can't I come and live with you?"

"No. Kids need someone to cook regular meals for them. You go on back."

He gave Sam two dollars, one for himself and one for Billy. "For school books and paper. If it's any more, come and tell me. School starts next week, doesn't it?"

"I don't want to go to school."

"That's got nothing to do with it."

WHEN ED WENT to vote in the new and novel primary election that came before the general election, he saw his name on the ballot as his party's candidate for state representative. Also, he saw the opposition party's candidate on the ballot and felt an impulse to vote for him.

"Maybe it would be better if a city slicker won," he thought.

His nomination formalized, Ed lengthened his days to make up for lost time on his cattle spread. Most outfits had long since sold their one- and two-year-olds and branded all the strays.

Members of the Cattleman's Association appeared one evening as Ed was taking his tired horse from the water trough to the barn.

"What's the matter with you, Ed? Aren't you coming to the meeting?" Tom Eder scolded.

"Is it tonight? I forgot, I guess."

"All us guys come to town, and our candidate doesn't show up to the meeting!" Sven added his reproof.

"You shoulda been at the ballgame Sunday," Olaf said. "That Travis was there umpiring and handshaking for all he was worth."

"If people want him for representative, they can have him. I'm not pushing any dam."

"You jackass, none of us cattlemen are dying to see a dam go in. Get garden patches, there'll be no grazing," Tom Eder pointed out.

"Why don't you fellows use someone with less on his mind? You know why I've lost interest. My wife's given me my walking papers. She's gone goofy over that dam."

"What this bird needs is a jolt from the drug department at the store," Tom Eder decided. "They got in a new barrel. Let's take him downtown and have Georgie siphon off a quart. Then let's go! We have to plan a strategy!"

"You said it," Sven spoke for everyone. "Between local option and dams, the cattlemen are losing ground fast!"

They took him protesting to his water trough and washed the dust of the day's riding from his face. They herded him downtown into the beanery and forced him to eat a meal. Eder stepped over to the "drug department" for "medicine." They dosed him well while and after he ate, then led him to the meeting, which had been postponed until he could be rounded up.

At the meeting, it was decided all around that Ed would appear at the rodeo next Sunday. Georgie had informed Eder that the Yakimas were bringing some cayuses to town. No one could ride their animals, they boasted. What they won, they would spend for firewater medicine.

Aversion to fighting had almost overwhelmed Ed when he had been alone to brood on the range. In the company of sympathetic friends, his heart thawed and his courage returned in a measure. These men had been counting on him all along. He owed them something.

On Sunday, a goodly number of people gathered at the bucking contest, which took place in the corral behind the store. The element who attended were scorned as sinners by the churchgoing, Sabbath-keeping faction.

Before he went downtown, Ed pulled on his boots and chaps. He seldom wore chaps anymore, but had a pair of shaggy black bearskin that he had not worn because he married Eleanor shortly after he bought them. She had turned up her nose at them and called them hideous.

Ed, at the rodeo, did his best to follow the suggestions of his political advisers. Perched on the corral rail, he talked to anybody who would talk to him, although he felt in no mood for aggressive campaigning.

The onlookers included some new settlers who had borrowed money from the Eastern Loan and Trust Company of Spokane; they had come mainly from the Walla Walla country and had already begun to dig ditches in anticipation of irrigation.

Okanogan and Columbia Moses Indians were present in force to root for a sorrel brought by the Yakimas to challenge all comers. From up and down the valley, the cowhands had traveled to town arrayed in chaps and spurs, ready for whatever danced out of the chute. Plump ranch wives had come along to the rodeo for a day away from cooking at home.

Georgie was keeping the bets.

Two strangers, a middle-aged man and a young woman companion, reminded Ed of the people who drifted from mining camp to mining camp in the days of the fever—the dude card players or the sharp investors who took the wad of the gullible and temporarily flush. The pair promenaded the length of the crowd. As they passed Ed, he smelled the man's cigar smoke, and the odor of brandy as distinct from moonshine. The young woman, despite her expensive clothes, showed that eagerness for life displayed by good-looking Indian maids when they first considered more glittering possibilities than those shown to them at St. Mary's Mission.

Slim Figlinski poked Ed in the ribs. "Let's not talk politics. You got my vote already. Let's get on something interesting. How about that girl?"

"Who is she?" Ed asked with perfunctory interest.

"That man who brought her—he's her father—is president of the Eastern Loan and Trust Company. He lives in Spokane, but he can vote at the Waterusers' meetings because he holds title to a lot of land that is going to be irrigated."

"They look like a couple of sharpers."

The rodeo had drawn a professional concession. A barker stood at the counter of a shooting gallery crying, "Step right up! Shoot the duck and win a beautiful kewpie doll. Fill the water pistol and squirt! Win a gorgeous cutie for your best girl!"

The president of Eastern Loan and Trust beckoned to a boy whose yearning to shoot the duck was obvious.

"Here's a quarter. See if you can win a kewpie doll for my Nancy."

The boy darted forward at once, and at the first squirt knocked over the duck on the traveling belt. The concessionkeeper awarded him one of the tiny figures done up in pink silk and feathers from the row on the shelf. The sharpshooter gave it triumphantly to the bank president, who in turn handed it to his elegant daughter.

But it took more than an exotic woman to hold the center of the stage. B Flat Bill started on his fiddle and men on the fence began to sing, more heartily each time the bottle of medicine went along the line. Ed could think of no reason for refusing his turn. Eleanor had almost stopped his drinking, but he was no longer responsible to her!

AT LAST THE ringmaster strode into the center of the corral and sang out, "Well, folks! It's quite a party! Now let's get the bronc busting underway!"

Ponies were jumping and snorting in the chutes.

The show opened with the youngest Brinkly boy, Zeb, taking his first-ever rodeo ride. He was pulling leather when he burst from behind the gate. Lasting two seconds on the back of the bucking pony, he landed flat on the ground with a force that must have hurt from the sound it made; but, laughing, he stood up immediately and dusted himself off while the cayuse continued to kick his heels high.

"I'm surprised I got him through the gate," he told the crowd cheerfully.

HORSES AND RIDERS tumbled out in successive fights for mastery that lasted only a minute or two. The cowpokes, whooping as they flew into the dust, had scant concern for the spectacles they made of themselves. They scrambled up and scooted for the fence, where the railsitters helped them from the reach of hooves that meant to kill.

Joe White Cloud, the Yakima Indian visitor, held his sorrel by the rein and waited for the champions to emerge. The well-oiled men who had lasted their time on other ponies surveyed the main challenge.

"Nothin' here we can't tame. Tame already," they told one another.

The horse stood quiescent beside his owner; but as soon as Joe White Cloud let go the reins, the animal was transformed to a devil, bucking, rearing, and biting. He frothed at the mouth and kicked himself in a fury of hate for strangers who dared mount him.

Dressed in gentlemen's clothes, Lawyer Travis, candidate for the legislature, made his entrance. He overlooked no one in his greetings. He demanded introductions and put his hand in all directions. He went to greet the president of Eastern Loan and Trust, and came to an urbane stance beside Nancy.

"Bet that fellow paid twenty-five dollars for that suit in Seattle," Tom Eder remarked to Ed.

Ed was glad he had worn his bearskin chaps. He was a cowpoke himself and proud to wear the clothes.

None of Ed's cow ponies bucked. If they had shown tendencies to do so, he had sold them. He had not ridden a bucking horse for years. But now it became imperative to show what a "ride 'em cowboy," real he-man he was—not a city slicker come to put something over on the country folks.

"Joe," he addressed the Indian in a voice that he forced to be loud enough for all to hear, "I'm the one fellow who hasn't tried to ride your pony, and I'm the one who can do it. If I win, you don't owe me anything. If I can't, I give you two dollars fare for the ride."

Family men laughed. Ed McLaren was cutting loose! "Don't break too many bones. You gotta get to the legislature," his gang yelled.

"Do your damnedest, sorrel," thirty-six-year-old Ed muttered.

In the role of wild, bumptious lad, he hopped from the fence and approached the sorrel while the Indians among the crowd eyed one another solemnly.

"Ed, you stay off that horse!" Narcisse Nicholson, a halfblood friend, advised.

"Try and stop me!"

Narcisse dropped from the fence and walked to Ed. "Think you might be liquored up. How many swigs did you take from the bottle?"

"Four, but it doesn't affect me at all."

Narcisse threw up his hands and returned to the fence.

Nancy had let go of her father's arm and was coming his way.

"Just look who is watching!" Ed congratulated himself. "I know the tricks to steal the women! Her Old Man and the lawyer can fry an egg. She left 'em for me!"

Ed spat into the dust and flipped himself on the outlaw.

The sorrel quivered, doubled, and rolled, but Ed knew how to hold his head. Bounces jolted Ed's teeth, but he had yet to disgrace himself. Cowmen weren't ready to allow clodhoppers to come here and see the fancy chaps boys on the decline!

His next thoughts had to be assembled from the dust in which he lay. His mouth was full of dirt; blood was running from his nose.

"What happened?" he asked a grinning Tom Eder, whose face came into focus.

"Figure it out for yourself. Nobody can tell you anything."

Tom helped him up from the ground.

As Ed eased himself back on the rail, Joe White Cloud came to collect his two dollars. Ed winced at Nancy's amused smile as the Yakima folded the dollar bills into two small sticks and stuffed them into his money belt.

Nancy strolled away, again on her father's arm.

"I'll be darned if I do any more campaigning," Ed told Tom as he rubbed his sore shoulder. "I proved how much sense I have. Nobody'll vote for me."

"Nobody cares if you're thrown by a wild cayuse," Tom comforted him. "Even the nesters know the same thing would happen to them—especially if they're lit like you." The cattlemen's committee took Ed home in his sorry state.

"Beat it! Leave me alone!" Ed snarled through his dizziness.

"We're not leavin' you alone till you promise to keep stirring your stumps and calling on people," Tom said.

"All right, I promise, to get rid of you guys!"

"Nobody seems to give a damn about how hard I got hurt," he sympathized with himself as he blundered into bed.

NEXT MORNING, AFTER greasing his boots, Ed recalled what he had promised the night before and groaned.

"How many days is it till election? Thirty? All right. I'll ride for votes instead of strays that long."

He'd even visit Old Man Caliente whom he had a fight with every spring about moving on the range too early. Enmity between Ed and his neighbor on rangeland went back twenty years. Caliente had taken his wife, Geraldine, from a job working in the tavern before local option. When she had worked there, Ed had joshed her a bit. She'd changed as Mrs. Caliente. The last time Ed had seen her, years ago, he had gone to the place to solicit Caliente's membership in the Cattleman's Association. Corning to the door with a battered face, holding a baby, she had directed Ed wordlessly to her husband in the corral. Ed mentioned to Caliente that he had been acquainted with Geraldine when she worked in the tavern. Caliente had grunted contemptuously. Ed realized at the time that he would make no progress by using the ordinary political formula, "Be nice to women and children."

Now, as a candidate for the legislature, he dived into his current objective: "Wonder if you'd be interested in supporting a brand law. We're getting all the cattlemen behind a bill to take to the legislature. Know you don't belong to the Association; could if you wanted to pay dues; but you might want to support the branding bill by voting for me as a representative."

Caliente drew his mouth sideways. "That's a laugh."

"How come?"

"You're askin' me to support a brandin' bill when I stole my first hundred head!" he chuckled viciously.

As Ed rode on to the next place, he thought seriously, "That man will never lose his hard core. Some toughs are straightening up—county is becoming civilized; but men like Caliente will stay all for Number One, ignorant, cruel to their livestock and their women."

AT THE COMMUNITY meeting in the new schoolhouse, Ed was invited to sit on the platform with the other candidates for office. Finally the chairman announced, "Now it's Ed McLaren's turn to stand up and shine!"

Ed related how he "went into agriculture" when panic hit the miners.

"Turned cowpoke!" Sven Linstrom corrected from the rear.

Ed reviewed how homesteaders had come into their own: "We've had our lands surveyed and entered under the homestead laws. We've practiced economy. We've established our forest rights. We are well on our way with a program of school and road building, fencing our land, building better houses and barns, putting more land into hay, and increasing our herds."

He outlined what he proposed to do in the legislature.

"If I make it to Olympia, I'd work up a brand law with the help of other cattlemen in the legislature and submit it to the House."

People could always call on him in case of emergency. He promised to support schools, churches, and law enforcement.

Lawyer Travis said much the same, and added that if he were elected, he would bring the irrigation dam to the Okanogan.

People stomped and whistled when Travis sat down. Ed was sure he had lost the contest to the Waterusers, but the stomping and whistling after Travis's speech had indicated only relief that the speeches were over.

Ed, with a record of friendliness and an obliging nature, won over his opponent by a large majority. He brightened for an instant when Tom brought him the news, but late in the night, without a family to care whether he won or lost, he felt the victory go dead.

IN PREPARATION FOR being absent from his place for two months during the upcoming legislative session, Ed finished marketing his steers and brought the cows with calf to the haymeadow. He cleaned the watering places on the river. He let it be known that he was on the lookout for a man to feed for him through January and February. The only applicant with livestock experience was a Portuguese named Joe, who told a hard-luck story of being run out of

Nevada as a sheepherder. Ed hired him although he would have preferred a cattleman.

During Christmas vacation, Sam and Billy came to visit their father. He loaded them with candy and oranges and sent trinkets to Leila. He had made a profit on his steers. He told himself that Eleanor might not have booted him out so quickly if she could have foreseen how much money was in his bank account at the end of the year.

Leila cried for him every night at bedtime, the boys said.

"Why won't you come to the cabin, just once, Dad, to show Leila that you're still alive and all right?"

Ed's heart thumped, but he decided that he would go near Eleanor only when she sent him an engraved invitation.

15.

School Lands

The state legislature would convene on the second Monday in January. Ed planned to go to Olympia a day or two early to get his bearings. In preparation, he examined the telescope bag crammed with the garments he had taken by force from the closet in Iowa. Eleanor had sent the bag back to Ed from her claim, by way of Sam and Bill. Pa's Sunday suit had been too large for Ed in the year he left home, but he likely would fit into it now, he thought. The crumpled trousers, vest, and coat would have to be pressed before they could be worn in public. He washed some of the white shirts in the horse trough, but the results caused him to buy two new shirts from the dry goods store. He would have to locate a laundry in Olympia.

Wearing his best saddle clothes, he boarded the train for the coast. Tom Eder came to see him off early in the morning. Sam and Bill were shadows on the sidelines until Ed called them over to him on the platform and shook each small right hand.

The excitement of traveling to the capital as an elected official was tempered by thoughts of his family troubles. Through his haze of gloom as he registered at the Olympic Hotel, he discovered that he was a Big It! When he wrote on the blank line to specify business, "Legislature, Okanogan County Rptv.," the desk clerk looked from the register to Ed, then whistled peremptorily to a bellhop, "Show the Honorable Mr. McLaren from Okanogan County to his room! Three forty-two, on the comer, windows over two streets!"

"Yes, sirrr!" The bellhop snapped to attention, received the key from the desk clerk with a bow, hefted Ed's bag, and grandly led the way to the elevator. After admitting Ed to Room 342, he bowed out, quarter in hand.

"For service, push the buzzer on the bedstand."

"O.K. But I don't need anything."

As he shut the door after the bellhop, Ed was reeling—from the elaborate nature of his reception, as well as from the speed of the elevator. But before he could undo the top button of his shirt in the privacy of his own room, a knock sounded on the door. In response to Ed's doubtful, "Come in," a young man wearing a starched collar and clothes in keeping, strode into the room on a wave of effusion.

"Mr. Ed McLaren? Okanogan County? Welcome, distinguished freshman! Maybe you don't recognize me—I've grown a foot since we left Bonaparte, but I certainly know you! Understand you won the contest in your district hands down."

"Only sucker they could find to leave home at calving time," Ed replied, disclaiming any glory. "Can't say I remember you. How come you spotted me so fast?"

"I'll give you a couple guesses. I was in the bunch milling around in the lobby waiting for you to arrive. My father suggested you might like to have someone assist you with the onetwo-three of procedure for legislators new to the city."

"Who is this guy?" Ed asked himself. "Must be the kid of nogood Bill Brewster, who was too lazy to work a ranch; he finagled some soft job here."

Never before had Ed been the object of such tender concern.

"You a Brewster?" he asked aloud. "What you got up your sleeve?"

"All kinds of things! First, my front name is Edgar, same as yours. Can you imagine anything more coincidental? Call me Ed, of course. Or else Eddie— really Eddie. I want to welcome you to the capital, take you out to lunch, show you the sights of the town."

"I'd like to have the capitol buildings pointed out, but I'd better get my breath first. Just made it from the train."

"Sunday morning?"

"Tomorrow's Saturday, isn't it?"

"Yes, but you'll be getting ready for the governor's ball. The whingding on Saturday night is the real opening of the legislature, not the first sessions on Monday. Command performance for you."

"Wow!" Ed had given a ball no consideration whatever. He hesitated. "I suppose everybody wears a suit."

"Not just a suit! Tie and tails."

"Whaddya mean? Some formal thing like a magician?"

"Exactly. But don't worry. This is where I come in handy!"

"I got a suit in my valise," Ed said as he removed it from the bag. "I'll have to get it pressed. You know some shop where they can do it fast?"

"You'll pardon my saying so, Ed, but your suit isn't the right kind for the ball."

"What's the matter with it? Hasn't hardly ever been worn."

"Take my word. You'll need a rental. I happen to have a card right here."

He presented a printed card: "Van Kamp and Hibberd's. Cor. Capitol Way and Vine. Retail Clothing. Men's. Sale or Rent."

Mr. Brewster's son finally went his way with a promise to return Sunday for the sightseeing tour.

Ed had noticed that everybody in the lobby was wearing a suit. What he had brought was for general daytime wear for a legislator. Charcoal gray and with a hard finish, it seemed to Ed like all the Sunday suits he had seen in the course of a lifetime.

He pushed the button on the bedstand; the bellhop arrived in one minute. "Know where I can get this suit pressed?"

"Yes, sir! One trousers, vest, and coat. Back here at four o'clock sharp."

"Fine."

"Now, about your shoes. If you wish to have them shined, put them in the hallway."

"Is that safe?"

"Nobody steals anybody else's shoes unless they want bunions, now do they?" The bellhop was relaxing as he became aware of the country origins of Honorable Mr. McLaren.

"Guess you're right. I'll put them out when I get ready for bed. Never thought of bringing shoe polish along."

WITH HIS SUITCASE unpacked, Ed noticed that he was hungry. He rode down the elevator to the lobby, where he was hailed by Paul Nelson, a man he knew from Stevens County, who was also a new representative. They went together for a meal in the hotel dining room. As they looked over the menu, they agreed that the food cost three times what it should.

"We can scout around for a cheaper place when we get the lay of the land," Paul said.

"What's this business about a governor's ball? Some walloper told me we need 'formal' wear," Ed ventured.

"There's places where you can rent it," Paul said as he produced a card identical to the one that Brewster had dispensed to Ed.

"Must be Eager Beavers all over the place," Ed concluded. "Where'd you get your card?"

"From Senator Handy. He's the old-timer from my county. He says you better be there first thing in the morning if you want a suit to fit."

They made an appointment to scout for the rental store in the morning.

ED HAD PLANNED to save money from the five dollars a day that he understood was allowed for representatives' expenses, but he gave up the idea at Kamp and Hibberd's Retail Clothing. Rental of a suit for one evening was five dollars. He and Paul were tactfully informed that they needed, in addition, dress shirts and black ties. By the time they were in the street again, Ed was wondering if he could live to the first payday with the funds he had in his wallet. He would have to go to a bank, establish credit, and write a check. The Honorable Paul Nelson expressed similar worries. They bought ham sandwiches and coffee away from the hotel.

They agreed to attend the ball together as stags but not to dance. Paul asked Ed if he minded if Senator Handy went with them. He was a widower who also wanted only a place on the sidelines.

At nine o'clock that evening, they identified themselves at the door of the armory in which the gala was to be held. The only other persons inside were onlookers in the balcony, preempting the front-row seats. Shortly thereafter a number of freshman legislators arrived, scrubbed and groomed, and mutually aware that they had met earlier at the rental store. The exception was Senator Handy, a veteran legislator with graywhite hair. He was dressed in a tuxedo of greenish cast, which he undoubtedly owned himself—and had for a good many years.

Senator Handy explained that most of the balls began late because many legislators attended private dinners prior to the large event. Handy said that he didn't care for dinner parties now that his wife was dead—tired of them before that, to be truthful.

The dance orchestra, in formal garb, assembled at the front end of the room. They settled themselves in their chairs; removed their instruments from carrying cases; leaned toward the concertmaster, listening to the A from the fiddle; and began the scraping and squealing that Ed was accustomed to prior to the start of the music in the Okanogan.

At half past ten, Governor Lister, who had been reelected a few weeks before, came in with a chattering party including a group of women in bright, swishing gowns. Lister's popularity with women was evident; they swarmed about him like a harem.

"How come he does so well with the ladies?" Ed asked Senator Handy.

Handy chuckled. "Oh, he's a real favorite with the clamorous, emerging female in the state of Washington. He saw to the passage of a widows' pension law, also statewide prohibition."

"I didn't vote for him," Ed said. "Glad I didn't."

As the orchestra struck up the Grand March, the governor, wife on his arm, opened his second inaugural ball. Couples began a John Paul Jones.

ALTHOUGH HE REMEMBERED that he was in a pact against dancing, Ed saw within the radius of the room one female with whom he might have danced: the young woman Nancy, from Spokane, daughter of the president of the Eastern Loan and Trust. He wondered in what capacity she qualified as a guest. He pointed her out to Paul Nelson; she was easy to see with male eyes.

Even Senator Handy saw her.

"Her pa is the new right-hand man to the new director of conservation and development," Handy informed Ed and Paul. "Robinson."

"Things sure happen fast," Ed said.

"Yep," Senator Handy agreed. "If I were faster on my feet, I'd beat you over there."

"All I meant was that when I saw her and her father a couple months ago, he didn't have the job he has now."

Handy yawned. "I'm going home. I'm in a different age group from you two."

"Dare me to ask her to dance?" Ed asked Nelson as the senator ambled away.

"Dare me?" Nelson returned. "But after you."

THE FEMALE MAGNET remembered Ed. She hailed his approach.

"I'll be darned, the he-man from the cow county! So you made the grade."

"Yep. In spite of being thrown off that sorrel. Care to dance?"

She went into his arms at once. "You're a good dancer! Do they have dancing teachers up there at the end of the railroad?"

"They hold dances. You learn rhythm keeping the beat for B Flat Bill."

"I've heard of those dances. I'm told boys bring their horses inside for company. Is it true?"

"A guy did that once at Pard Cummings's. Up to the second floor of the house. Went through the ceiling."

Nancy giggled. "I think I could live there and like it. Tell me, are you in favor of the dam?"

Ed and Paul had braved themselves for the occasion with two snorts apiece from a bottle Paul had brought in his valise from Stevens County. Alcohol always had the effect on Ed of making him lugubriously honest. He would be perfectly honest with this young woman. He told her that the United States engineers and Okanogan County old-timers thought there was too little water in the small streams that were to be used to fill the dam, a dirt-fill dam, at that.

"You, from Okanogan County? You aren't pushing the darn? You're the elected representative!"

"Some of my neighbors who elected me aren't too sharp about putting two and two together. The Waterusers bunch had somebody lined up to introduce their bill. I knocked him out of the election, but the Waterusers will get around that, likely. If anybody asks me, I'll tell the reclamation committee straight facts as given to me by experts."

"My father is in the Reclamation Service now. Can't you take his word as an expert?"

"What I heard before is that your father is an expert in making loans."

"There're uses for investment officers in the reclamation business. I do hope you will give both sides a fair study."

"I have."

"Maybe you would come to Daddy's and my apartment sometime to tell what you would say at a committee hearing."

Ed considered the possibilities. What if he told her father that he didn't agree with all of Okanogan County that the dam is a good thing?

"I might give your Old Man an honest opinion," he warned.

"He would respect it."

The music ended. A man, nearer to middle age than Ed, found Nancy with signs of annoyance on his face. His suit did not come from Kamp and Hibberd's.

"Nancy, you were supposed to be dancing with Jim Brewster. Didn't you look at your program?"

"Sorry, darling," she said.

She introduced the man to Ed without giving his name, "This is my fiancé. He's an engineer."

After she danced away with her betrothed, Ed realized he had never told her his own name. "So her fiancé is an engineer," he thought. "On account of him, she favors the dam. Sorry I can't be more obliging to her and provide her boyfriend with a job."

As the evening went on, he took note of her whereabouts from time to time. It was useless to ask her to dance again. She kept the men hovering three deep, among them Paul Nelson, who was waiting a long time to fulfill his part of the dare to dance with her. If she had a program card at the start of the evening, she had lost it.

Ed was pulling the pillow over his ears to keep out early morning stirrings in the hotel when a rap sounded on his door. Grumbling to himself that he might as well be home on the ranch at calving time for all the sleep he was getting, he hoisted his legs over the side of the bed, and in his long johns, went to answer the door.

Eager Beaver stood splendid in a Sunday suit.

"You forgotten our plans to see the town this morning?"

"Darn! Just woke up! Come in. I'll dress." Ed found his own Sunday suit hanging in the closet. It had been brought back neatly pressed Friday at four o'clock as promised.

After half an hour in the fresh air with the ebullient guide, Ed's natural interest in the world about him returned, and he hiked about the capital longer than Eager Beaver enjoyed.

Ed's appetite for food, which transferred with him from the Okanogan, brought them into accord when they were passing a Chinese restaurant. Eager Beaver said, "I promised to buy you lunch, remember?"

"None o' that! We'll go dutch. Then I can eat all I want with a clear conscience."

He still wondered why the young man wanted to be such good friends. It was five o'clock before Eddie Brewster left Ed to his own devices.

NEOPHYTE LEGISLATORS SEEMED to have the propensity to appear first at every congregation. Ed McLaren and Paul Nelson were among the early ones to present themselves at the entry of the House chambers on Monday morning. They satisfied the bailiff that they belonged on the floor and found the desks assigned to them side by side.

Other elected representatives of the people of the state of Washington wandered intermittently into the chambers. By their assured deportment, Ed could tell the holdovers from previous sessions. They greeted one another as long acquaintances. Nobody bothered with inconsequential freshmen from the cow counties. They were worthy of one quick glance.

The Speaker of the House entered and took his chair on the podium.

When the chaplain moved to the lectern, the legislative body stood to hear a prayer for the blessings of God upon the deliberations. The House sang "The Star Spangled Banner" and saluted the flag. Ed's throat choked. He was in deeper emotional water than he expected.

"What the devil is a cowpoke like me doing in this high and mighty patriotic outfit?" he asked himself.

He resolved that no one should know how inferior he felt in his company. The clerk called the roll.

"Mr. McLaren?"

"Present," came his booming voice, startling himself.

The Speaker read a message of greeting from the state senators convening simultaneously in other chambers.

A guest United States senator was escorted with honor to the platform by the sergeant-at-arms as the House stood again. The senator reminded those present that the sessions in Washington, D. C., were conducted by just such men as they, some Republicans, some Democrats. All must keep in mind that they were Americans first, party members second.

The senator said further that the Washington State House of Representatives had a high calling in its responsibility for the tax structure which maintained the schools and highways.

Ed was hypnotized into a glow of exaltation that made him forget the dull place at the bottom of his heart where he felt the lack of home and family.

He came again from the realm of the ideal when Eager Beaver clutched at him as he emerged from the floor at noon adjournment. "Ready to visit the land office?"

"Land office? What for?"

"No time like the present for getting acquainted, is there?"

"I guess not."

Eddie piloted him through the press of members and firstday visitors to the state building across the lawn.

Inside and down a corridor, Brewster brought Ed to an office. "Chief Clerk Endicott, this is the Honorable Mr. McLaren from Okanogan County to see you."

The clerical gentleman, whose rounded hips and sloping shoulders told of long hours in a chair bent over books, was more outwardly wary of strangers than Eddie; he held forth his hand as though it might be bitten.

Ed pumped the limp hand and did his best socially, "Just got over here the other day. Pleased to meet you."

"The same," the clerk responded, and waited to learn the reason for this intrusion upon his valuable time.

"He's a brother-in-law of Morton Clements," Eddie interposed as if the detail would explain everything.

"Oh," said the chief clerk. "He was here himself the other day. I did just like they told me."

"Did *what* like they told you?" Ed wondered to himself. He realized that, identified as a brother-in-law of Mort, he might be expected to hold identical interests.

"The land will go up for public auction at the Okanogan County courthouse in about two weeks," the clerk volunteered.

"That's what I wanted to know," Ed decided to play out the game. He had expected any skullduggery of Mort's to be along the lines of dam promotion, but the present references were apparently to still another matter.

The clerk seemed relieved of doubt. He launched on a compulsive summary of his years in the land office: what party work he had done, names of people he had pleased, most of which was lost on Ed but not on Edgar Brewster, the Eager Beaver.

"Father says Bill Endicott is the real main cog in the land office machine," Brewster rattled on.

"I'm new to politics," Ed said, surmising it would do no harm to state the self-evident. "I'll have to get acquainted with the 'main cogs.'"

Endicott glowed. Here was no special interest force before whom he must cower, but one with whom he could play a benignly condescending role.

"A freshman legislator! Welcome! Welcome!"

"THAT WAS CORDIAL treatment you got in there," Eager Eddie said when they were on the sidewalk again. "Did I do all right by you, Ed, old boy?"

"Oh, just fine!" Ed answered, though he failed to understand what Eddie had done for him. "Thanks a million. I better get along to my room, I reckon. Studying ahead like a kid in the first grade. Have to."

Eager Beaver continued to trail him all the way back to the legislative chambers. Ed resolved to keep free of sudden friends who seemed to know more about his business than he did himself.

AS THE SESSION continued, Ed acquainted himself with men who, as livestock owners from Stevens and Yakima counties, would be interested in a branding law. Beginners together in writing bills to be introduced, they mapped a brand law that could be administered by a self-supporting system. Every cattleman in the state would pay a fee to register his brand, thus creating a fund for administration. They chose Ed to file the bill with the chief clerk.

"You can put it on paper best," they insisted.

The title of Ed's composition was read on the floor of the House. Paul Nelson moved that it be referred to the standing committee on agriculture.

Ed loitered in the agriculture committee room in daily expectation of his bill being brought up for discussion. After he had been patient ten days, the committee chairman introduced the branding proposal. The group kept a dead silence.

"We've never thought it necessary in the state of Washington," a west side farmer said at length. "Registered livestock brands are what they need on the big cattle spreads in the Southwest, where you don't see your cows from one season to the next."

Another committee member waved his hand vaguely as if to brush away a gnat from the day's business.

"You could stir up a lot of trouble with a bill like that—what if people in different counties happen to be using the same brand?"

A motion followed to lay the bill on the table.

Ed, on the edge of his chair in the visitors' ring, stood to ask if he might be heard by the committee.

"Please limit your remarks to three minutes," the chairman said. "I see this is your bill. But we have to get ahead with some tough snags today in the poultry statistical division. We have big business breathing down our necks."

Ed held the floor long enough to name some of the livestock owners of the state who would like to keep their cattle from being stolen by unscrupulous predators who took advantage of the lack of a statewide brand law by the very means a committee member had mentioned—by use of the same brand as another cattle owner in an adjoining county. Ed had begun with names of the legislators who had helped prepare the draft when the west side farmer-legislator interrupted, "I'm afraid that little, if any, statewide support for such a bill can be found at this time. I move that we take up the next item of business."

"Do I hear a second?"

Ed had been clipped down by a hay mower. He walked from the committee room. He might just as well walk away from the rest of the legislative session. He could take the train home, feed his own cattle, and monitor the birth of his calves. His one objective had been lost.

In a study of self-disgust, he collided with Nancy Robinson, the young lady conservationist. She gave him the smile that in Bonaparte had first seemed friendly, then later, mocking, as though he amused her vastly.

He suppressed his gawky, cowpoke uneasiness when she asked, "How are you coming with your pet bill? I've looked for you, to invite you to supper. You and Father must discuss the dam project."

"Nothing I say would count one way or another. I had my bill on the branding law thrown into the wastebasket by the agriculture committee."

Her eyes widening, she smiled. "You expect to see your bill through the first time it's read in committee? You have to feel around and line other factions behind you. You trade support for support; don't you know the first thing?"

Where had he heard such a program outlined before? From none other than Gerald Gaston, in his period as a lobbyist for the Good Roads Association.

"I don't know the ins and outs. Never figured politicking amounted to a hill of beans. All us cattlemen want is a common sense brand law that protects our property and won't cost the taxpayers anything."

"Darling, I can see you don't know the ins and outs. Somebody will have to teach you."

Ed felt his color rise.

"What do I have to learn? How to make shady deals?"

"Oh, no—just to talk about your particular interest; then let somebody else talk about his—in a pleasant, social way. You come to an understanding. Look around you at these men, all simply money changing, inviting one another to dinner to consider a point or two better."

"I don't get invited to cozy, quiet dinners."

"But I've just invited you to one, Mr. McLaren, darling! May I call you 'Ed' to keep from calling you 'darling'?"

"I'm no 'darling,' but everybody calls me 'Ed.'"

He was about to explode with social embarrassment. He'd been told there were stylish, smart people who carried on bright conversation, calling one another 'darling.' She had also known his name all along, or had been interested enough to find out his name, anyway.

He looked along the hall where people were clustered in small groups. "By golly! You're right. You do it like the gypsy fortune-teller at the rodeo. Stand in the door of your tent and look as though you have something priceless to offer."

"Now you're catching on!" she exclaimed and laughed as she strolled away.

In his mail pigeonhole at the hotel, he found a note from her. It read: "Come Tues. evening before the conservation committee meeting at our apartment. The Okanogan dam will come up for discussion."

The address was printed on her notepaper. Her writing was a bold backhand.

On Tuesday, Ed put on his suit, pressed a second time. He had left his shoes in the hall to be shined. He put on his second new shirt. What more could he do?

He could comb his hair, he decided, as he gave himself an inspection in the mirror. He winced as he considered his weather-beaten cheeks and shiny nose, and he settled on the sour conclusion that he had no reason ever to look into a mirror. He could always recognize himself by the flap of his left ear that fell comically out from the side of his head. His "Lazy Ear" brand fitted him to a T.

He rang the bell of the Robinson apartment. Nancy herself met him at the door and opened her eyes wide in her practiced way.

"Come in, Handsome Ed!"

Was it possible that he didn't look like a monster to her? Nancy was a stunner in a red and gray dinner dress sewn with blue beads and edged with shiny fringe, one of the garments pictured on girls in the barber shop magazines.

When they reached the parlor, they were joined at once by Mr. Robinson, who held out a big paw and repeated the joyful welcome words, "Happy-to-make-your-personal-acquaintance-after-hearing-so-much-about-you-from-Nancy," ending with the offer of a whiskey highball.

Ed wondered if he should blurt out, "Look here, did you catch my name right? I'm only the freshman representative from Okanogan County—one of those sparsely settled areas of the state."

He took a nip of the whiskey drink instead. It nipped him, too, he noticed.

A fire was burning in the fireplace. It seemed to him that it made the room too hot. Half an hour passed before any other guest arrived. Ed had again displayed the country cloddishness of being on time, as if in the middle of a January night promptly reaching the barn when a calf started to come from a bellowing mother.

Nancy excused herself "to complete some preparations."

Mr. Robinson came to and from the room. Each time he entered he asked brisk, jovial questions and answered them himself.

Finally Nancy returned to the sofa and seemed prepared to settle. She moved close to Ed and squeezed his arm as she said, "Now I want you to tell Father, when he asks you after dinner, exactly how you feel about the dam in the Okanogan Valley. He wants to know how far it is to bedrock and all those things the government engineers told you. Promise that you will give him the benefit of your information."

Ed flexed the muscles that Nancy grasped. He wished he had a corner in which to assemble a few items on the back of an envelope.

The doorbell signaled the arrival of more guests.

"I'll answer," Mr. Robinson called from another room.

Mr. Robinson brought in six men. Ed rose and wished that he had deferred taking a drink until now. Mr. Robinson insisted on refilling his crystal glass for the continuing introductions and conversation. Eventually dinner was served, not by Nancy, but by a male waiter in black and white.

Salmon was the dinner entree.

"Fresh off the boat from Alaska," Mr. Robinson boasted.

Ed ate more than he needed. But everybody else was behaving like an animal, he thought, as he watched the tableful of mouths open and shut.

As the party rose from the dinner table, Lamonte Robinson came to Ed and took him by the elbow. "Instead of going to the parlor, you and a few others of us will go into the study for brandy. We have a special interest in what you have to say about the proposed Okanogan dam."

"Glad to tell you all I know, but maybe you won't like it."

"We'll respect your candid opinion. Show Mr. McLaren to the study, will you, Nancy? I'll collect the rest."

She obediently led the way.

She seated herself in a chair opposite his, crossed her knees and clasped her hands across so that Ed could not fail to see the mammoth sparkling ring she wore on her engagement finger.

"Now I have you all to myself for a minute," she said. Ed had been thinking the situation was intimate, but he wouldn't have mentioned it himself.

"I see your diamond. Where's your lucky man tonight?"

"He's in your home town."

"Didn't catch his name the other night. Are you planning to be married soon?"

Nancy smiled demurely. She twisted the ring on her finger.

"I haven't set the date. My thinking is a little blurry. It's true that I'm engaged to Bob Thornton, but it's only engaged."

"So his name is Thornton," Ed echoed, unable to think of anything else to say.

Maybe all unmarried girls talked in this style nowadays. Nancy gave him her long glance and sly smile. He fidgeted and wished the other men would appear. When they did, Nancy excused herself.

Ed had been introduced earlier to all the guests, but now the spotlight focused on him. Mr. Robinson made him the man of the hour. The host made sure that everyone had a drink in hand and was comfortable; then he said, "Mr. McLaren is the authority we're consulting at this time. Shoot, young man!"

"I'm the representative from Okanogan County," Ed said, and cleared his throat. "Everybody thinks that anybody who lives up there would naturally be for a dam. We've got several small irrigation projects going from the river and are growing some good fruit. But I'll tell you men something: some of that land is all right for orchards and gardens, but that's mostly the low land, along the river, and places like that. Other places are bare hills made by the glacier. The soil is thin. It's all right for grass, but it never will be good enough for general fanning and wheat-growing. You need a thousand acres of land to graze a small band of cattle.

"I know people are talking up the dam and counting on the water supply in the creeks; but some federal engineers went in there a while back, and they looked over the site in question, Whitestone. They said it wouldn't be an economic operation, that it was too far to bedrock under the gravel. Concrete pilings are too expensive.

"The people who own property up there, the ones who know these things I'm telling you, aren't talking them up because they are counting on getting large payments for their water rights along the streams. They can get all these newcomers to buy up or homestead small-acre tracts, then buy them back for nothing when the dam falls through. That's the way their minds work."

His thoughts expanded and came freely from his mouth.

"For instance, I got a couple brothers-in-law. They don't care what they do to get what they want. They are working on their first million right now, just buying up land. They'll sell it to cattlemen someday at twenty dollars an acre after getting it for a dollar an acre."

The talk was interrupted momentarily by the reentrance of Nancy.

"Don't get up, gentlemen. What is being said?"

"Mr. McLaren was just telling us, Nancy, that they are getting the millionaire bug in the Okanogan, too."

"Well, that's commendable."

"I'm not the one with that bug," Ed refused the compliment. "In fact, I'm worried that you people think I'm pegged to introduce the bill for the dam in the house. But my brothers-in-law are too smart to ask me to do it. I guess anybody can make a million on land these days if he doesn't care how he does it. All you men must have heard the same talk we hear."

Sympathetic smiles and nods agreed with him.

"What did you say your brothers' names were?" Nancy asked.

"Brothers-in-law," Ed amended. "Buford and Morton Clements. But the fact is, I got no use for them. I'm sort of separated from my wife—their sister—right now, but I had no use for them long before that."

"We all have family troubles at one time or another," one of the men commiserated.

"Of course that's neither here nor there on the merits of the dam," Ed tried to return to honest consideration of the topic. "My opinion is that a dam on Aeneas and Bonaparte creeks won't hold water, and if it does, there won't be enough of it. One large dam, with adequate financial backing from the federal government, might be another story; but nobody wants to wait and do it right. They're railroading this other deal through, knowing it won't work."

"We thank you, certainly, for expressing your honest opinion," Mr. Robinson summed up the discussion. "Everything you have said will be of considerable interest to Commissioner Ross."

"You're prepared to give this information to the committee in the morning?" a portly guest asked. It was the first time the man had spoken, to the best of Ed's recollection.

"I'm planning to attend the hearing and speak my piece for what it's worth. I think every fact should be presented before the state invests seven hundred and fifty thousand dollars. They started with talk at a hundred ninety."

Nancy squealed, "You can't be against it! What about my Bobby? He needs money before we can get married!"

"There should be better jobs for an engineer," Ed said.

The others laughed indulgently at Nancy's concern.

"I'd be obliged if you'd regard what I said as confidential until after the hearing," Ed was at last reaching a point of caution. "Don't want to tip my hand to those brothers-in-law I mentioned. You can bet they have some shyster lawyer with big mule ears up to hear all he can."

"Most assuredly."

"Shall we join the other guests?" Mr. Robinson asked. "Our thanks to Mr. McLaren. Nancy, see that he gets another drink."

"Yes, Father."

The men left the study.

Ed, who had not yet managed to rise, saw Nancy standing in front of him with a highball in her hand. He was having difficulty seeing clearly. Food, drink, and cigar smoke were overwhelming his senses.

"Here is your drink, as Father bade."

"You are a dutiful daughter," he said, trying to be gallant as he took the glass.

He came to his feet, but the warmth of the room seemed so oppressive that he knew at once he would have been wiser to remain seated. He could scarcely keep his eyes open, and he needed fresh air. He was shocked to see his hand drop the whiskey glass. He knew he was unable to pick up the mess.

"I better take myself home," he said. "If you'll show me where my coat is."

She helped him gently across the room, sympathetic with his inebriation.

In the hall closet, he found his coat after lengthy deliberation. "If you don't mind, I won't say good night to anybody but you."

"I'll excuse you to Father. He'll understand. If you are saying only one good night, let's make it pay."

She languidly put her arms around his neck and pressed the length of her body against him. "Tell me what you think of me," she whispered.

He was seeing her double. He disengaged himself. He was drunk enough to be completely truthful. "I think you are a mighty fast girl."

"You dumb country hick! You rube!" She slapped him hard on the cheek.

The world was receding from him. He must breathe fresh air or pass out like a greenhorn on his first drunk with the busters. Stumbling down the apartment house steps, he came finally to the street level. He recognized his hotel but walked past it, too ashamed to ask at the desk for his key. He could not remember his own room number. A great weight was on his shoulders; the night was as dark as pitch. Soon all the streetlights would go out, and he would be in total darkness. Realizing this, he concentrated on self-control and entered the hotel.

At the desk, the clerk gave him his room key without asking for his number. 342! Of course! It was tooled in large numerals on the hard leather chip attached to the key by a chain.

Rather than call attention to himself by taking the elevator with other waiting guests, he headed for the staircase in a far comer of the lobby. He walked up the steps and round the turns of seemingly endless flights. At the third floor emergency exit, he recognized two spittoons with Chinese decorations, and the location of his room came to him. His limbs were almost too heavy to lift. His eyes fastened on a beam of light. At the end of the beam, Analix came toward him. The blackness gave way in her path. "Ed, finally! I was thinking perhaps you were in your room gone to bed for the night and sound asleep, but you were out."

"Yeah, I'm out. I'm in now, but I'm still out."

"You're drunk." She took the key from his bumbling hands and unlocked his door.

When they were inside, he put his arms about her and began to cry.

"You're so pie-eyed, you're revolting. You're worse than a drunk Indian," she said disgustedly.

THE SCENE FADED out, and he knew nothing further until broad daylight of the following morning.

Analix, still real, and Leschi, also, stood in judgment over him in his bed.

"We got you to sleep, and now we can't wake you," Analix said.

"What time is it?" he croaked as he tried to spring from bed.

"Afternoon, but you are staying where you are."

Ed was easier to restrain than he believed possible. He groaned and sank back on the bed.

"The hearing must be over."

"You can't help it," Leschi said. "Whatever hearing it was."

A knock sounded on the door. Analix answered and admitted Senator Handy.

"Huh! Still undressed at two o'clock."

"Just didn't wake up."

"Let me guess. You went to the Department of Conservation dinner party at Lamonte Robinson's last night, and the beauteous daughter plied you with drinks."

"How do you know all that?"

"Few freshmen representatives wake up early after their first political dinner party."

"That outfit sure fixed me."

"I'm surprised at your coming through in your right mind this soon. Conservation is a new department, but the special interests gang is still the same old bears' jaws. They play rough with anybody standing in the road of any of their legitimate interests."

Analix put her hand to Ed's forehead. She felt as cool, smooth, and tough as willow bark.

"You're still clammy," she was grudgingly sympathetic.

"No use getting up today," Senator Handy said. "Better stay out of sight for twenty-four hours at least."

"That's a cock-and-bull notion! I'm not hiding from those bastards."

"You are the scandal of the day. You've committed the unforgivable sin for a man in public office."

"Getting liquored up?"

"Not that. You have failed to avoid the calamity of compromising yourself with a woman. Nancy Robinson has told everyone in the House lobby that she had to slap you last night."

"She slapped me all right; did she say what for? I'll slap her back!"

Senator Handy's eyes twinkled. "You better get out of the game if you strike the ladies, no matter what the provocation!"

Ed's fury turned to gloom. "I'm a jackass! Those guys at home were counting on me to put through a brand law, but I couldn't even bring it into committee discussion. Have people heard about that, Analix?"

"Yes. Your county knows you tried."

"First mention ever made of a brand bill will be something to be proud of in time," Senator Handy soothed. "Six sessions from now, the bill will go through. You have a lot to learn about political victory. It's always Pyrrhic."

"The Indians aren't the danger in the West," Analix said. "It's the treacherous palefaces."

Senator Handy studied her sharply. He clucked his tongue.

"I remember you now, dear!" he exclaimed.

"I don't doubt it," she returned. "The Indian princess who came as a bride to the capital—and the misfortune that befell her bridegroom."

"Now, now! You mustn't let it make you cynical. This warrior here isn't your husband?"

"No, I'm her brother," Leschi said. "This visit the Indians are going to do better among the palefaces."

"Leschi and I are representing our family," Analix said.

The world was coming into immediacy for Ed at last. "Has something happened at the AW?" he asked.

Analix turned to him and said, "We came to you in trouble and find you in your own!"

Ed decided that he could sit up; he swung his feet over the edge of the bed. "All right! Explain."

Leschi took the lead, "Your brothers-in-law, the Clements's, have applied to the state land office to buy our cache under the mountain. The Old Man has used it for feeding always. The trouble comes from its being partly in one of the school sections that the state is selling."

"Gimme my pants!" Ed commanded.

Senator Handy obliged.

"Nobody will stand for them picking on you people. The whole valley knows you've been in possession of your land longer than the first white man in there!"

"Analix made Mort sore one time," Leschi said. "She pushed him off when he came to see her when she was still working in Conconully."

"Hush, Leschi!" Analix said sharply.

Nausea overcame Ed again. He had always half-believed the tavern gossip about the Clements men's lechery.

"He was full of liquor," Analix said shortly. "Anybody in a public business has drunk customers."

Senator Handy laughed, "I can see he was a poor show against an Indian princess."

"He found out he had to do more to get Westmore land than offer refreshments from the saloon to me," Analix said. "I was always worried when Papa failed to look into the added land regulations after the new survey was made. Papa depends absolutely on the right of prior possession. He says he was given the cache by Grandfather White Stone Mountain, who had a better right than anyone on the face of the earth to its use. The first surveyors left it off the maps as land not open to settlement because it was held by us. It is on a section 16 now. State courts have ruled several times that the state can't take section 16 and 36 land from Indians, but Father is not an Indian."

"He holds it under squatter sovereignty, if nothing else," Senator Handy deliberated. "Is your father a citizen?"

"Yes. He remembers a letter written to him by his father Arthur Westmore saying that he had applied for citizenship status. One reason we are here is to locate Grandfather Westmore's papers. They may be with his wife, who never left the coast. Father was born in Victoria, but Grandfather was always a settler on the States side, and children of citizens become citizens."

Ed raged, "People know your grandfather arrived in the valley in the 1800s and opened up the country alongside Okanogan Smith. He ought to take a shotgun to anybody trying to move in."

"That wouldn't settle the matter," Leschi said. "Father is enough of an Englishman to need his title settled by law.

"The parties who are trying to obtain possession have advertised in the *Methow Valley News* that the property is to be sold at auction. Father doesn't subscribe to the *Methow Valley News*. He lives at Conconully."

"The Old Man is smart," Senator Handy concluded. "Smart, too, to stay home to patrol his land. Do you have any idea how to proceed with the land office?"

"That's why we came to our representative," Analix said.

"Right procedure!" Senator Handy said. "I've had a few runins over there. If you want any help for these constituents of yours, Ed, count me in for knowledge of the record. I have a few private bones to pick with the land sharks—men who have no intention of living on the land, but who want to buy the public domain and divide it into lots to be sold like dozens of eggs at the grocery store."

"Why doesn't somebody ask for an investigation of the land office?" Ed challenged.

"Try that and you have a can of worms. It has been considered," Senator Handy said.

"Somebody like you should do it!" Ed exclaimed.

The senator smiled, but shook his head, "I've served in the legislature five terms and plan on two more before I retire. Public investigations are the province of young men like you who won't give a hoot in hell for their personal welfare."

"The more I think how I was hornswoggled last night, the madder I get," Ed muttered. "I've been a strawberry roan rider before. I might be one again."

Senator Handy's face grew increasingly cheerful. "A young buckaroo like you jams into the legislative cogs on a fluke once in a while. He starts rearing up, and for a while this place is interesting. But you must accept it that the young buckaroo is among the missing faces at the next session."

"You couldn't hog-tie me to run again for the legislature."

"It would be fun for the newspapers and for us timid solons to watch—the birth of the inevitable state land investigations," Handy opined.

"I'm just doggone crazy mad enough to blow my top. I don't mind speaking out," Ed declared.

Analix was dubious. "You better think about what you are saying. Leschi and I were simply going to the land office to protest and ask for a hearing. You need more bed rest. There's been too much disturbing conversation."

"Have you any appetite?" Leschi asked. "You haven't eaten anything yet today."

"Can't stand the thought of food."

"Your system expelled everything more than twelve hours ago," Analix said. "You need water, too."

"Sorry I'm causing everybody so much trouble. All I remember is that you helped me into my room, Analix; and the next thing it's today."

"The night didn't pass that quickly for us," Leschi joked. "Notice all those wet towels hanging on your chair backs? Analix rinsed them out in the bathtub down the hall. You ought to award her a medal."

"I only dropped by to see if you were among the living," Senator Handy said. "I wasn't sure you would be. I'll excuse myself, and you can take your friends out for a bite to eat."

"You must be ready for a meal after nursing me through the night watch," Ed told Analix and Leschi. "Let me take you to the dining room downstairs. I feel well now."

Analix hesitated; her face darkened. "Let's not eat here in the hotel dining room."

"Why not? I'm flush. Expense account per diem and all that."

"Leschi and I might be refused service. I know local rules."

"I'll urge the waiter by the collar if he refuses you service!" Ed snapped.

"Exactly. That's why we won't eat here. You're not ready for fights tonight at least. Besides, a walk in the fresh air will be good for you."

"Do you have some place in mind?"

"A restaurant off Capitol Way. It caters to plain trade, but it has comfortable booths. I ate there sometimes when Gerald wasn't with me evenings."

Leschi helped Ed on with his shoes.

They walked at a pace suited to an invalid.

At the restaurant to which Analix guided them, Ed's appetite, though poor for him, was good enough to satisfy his nurses.

Analix and Leschi had established themselves before coming to find Ed at the hotel. They were staying in a huge old house, obviously no longer in the possession of the original owner, with a sign in the window: "Bed and Breakfast. Reasonable Rates."

They stopped at the Westmore quarters for a short rest for Ed's wobbly legs before they took him home to his hotel room.

ED WAS RECOVERED enough next morning, Thursday, to go to his desk on the floor of the House. Analix and Leschi had sought an appointment at the land office.

After the first recess from the floor, Ed stood, feeling angry and queasy, in the hallway. He absorbed the amused looks cast in his direction as his due. Paul Nelson came to stand beside him, clapped him on the back, and refrained from remarks. Senator Handy approached through the press of bodies.

"Thought any more about speaking on behalf of your friends?" he asked. "They're not going to have any luck at the land office until pressure is brought to bear."

"If you'd help me with facts, I might have the nerve."

"I have facts in volume. The land office is glutted with people with petitions and problems."

"Would you come to my room tonight?" Ed asked. "Analix and Leschi are coming to let us know how they made out."

"Surely, I'll come. Also include Paul."

"Want me, Ed?" Paul asked. "They're your constituents with a legitimate grievance; the outcome affects Stevens County just as much as the Okanogan. We're the outlying districts that are being looted."

"I'll take all the help I can get."

Paul Nelson and Ed joined Analix and Leschi for the evening meal again at the restaurant on the unfashionable, tolerant street, where the price of a meal was within reason. Senator Handy arrived soon after the other four at

Ed's hotel room.

"Yes, brother and sister are impressive Indian royalty," Senator Handy commented.

Leschi smiled ruefully. "It's never done us much good to be Indian royalty. *Suyapichs* don't recognize it. One of the main cogs at the land office told us that we couldn't obtain a hearing for at least two weeks."

"That soon? Perhaps it's best for you, too. We need time for research and other preparation. Let me suggest a plan for Ed."

"Any plan based on me making speeches needs preparation," Ed observed.

"Speeches are only final touches. Leschi is mistaken when he pooh-poohs the value of the blood of Indian chiefs. 'The Noble Redman' isn't a worn-out phrase to those palefaces who are privileged to stand in his presence and feel his nobility, given from Mother Earth, to the strongest bodies and keenest minds of the People. Analix has rare beauty; and Leschi is the handsomest man in Olympia today."

He turned to Leschi and chuckled, "I shudder to think what I could do to defend myself if you took a notion to spring on me and strangle me."

"It is my understanding we 'scalped' everybody," Leschi retorted.

Senator Handy continued his speculations. "Ed tells me there are seven more young men like you at home."

"That's right. I'm the oldest male, and I lick the lot."

"Big Grandson of Chief, you write home quick as morning comes and tell those brothers to come to the hearing."

"All of us? Why so many?"

"For the effect it will have on the floor of the House as they sit in a row in the visitors' balcony awaiting land office attention."

"Their father is royal, too," Ed said. "Mr. Westmore was from British titled parentage."

"I surmised as much. I noticed their perfect British diction. Ed, you should have Analix coach you on grammar for your blistering attack on the land sharks."

"I've drifted into the speech that I've heard around me for the past dozen years," Ed conceded.

"Don't try to be eloquent, but leave out the 'hornswaggled' and 'doggone.'"

"Will all this work to our interest—making such a public noise?" Leschi hesitated. "We intended to argue only with the land office."

Senator Handy shook his head. "That won't work."

"We'll do as he says, Leschi," Analix decided. "Simple justice isn't enough of a defense except to Father deRouge."

The senator continued, "You say you are planning to establish your father's citizenship by calling on the lawyer who settled your British grandfather's estate?"

Leschi produced a folded note. "Father says this was the lawyer's office twenty years ago."

Senator Handy studied the name and address. "William Blythe Scarborough. Hmm. A man with a name like that hasn't moved in twenty years. You people go to Vancouver as soon as the first business of the hearing is fixed. By all means take Ed with you. He needs more time to recover socially from his drunken spree."

ON THE WEEKEND, Analix, Leschi, and Ed set out for British Columbia. The first day they rode by train to Seattle and stayed overnight in a hotel on Second Avenue. They took the ferry across Puget Sound into the Straits of Vancouver.

As Senator Handy guessed, Mr. Scarborough was still a living resident of Vancouver at the twenty-year-old address.

"Oh, yes, *mirabile dictu*, I'm still here. We won't go into how long it has been. But I have long since let my secretary go. I no longer practice," he said.

He was alert and quick to remember the Westmores, their prosperity, and their disaster. His immediate response was that Mr. Westmore had become a United States citizen.

"He left with me at one time papers showing declaration of intention. He certainly fulfilled the simple residence requirement."

Analix leaned forward. "Do you possibly have that paper in your files now?" she asked anxiously.

His trembling hands, covered with brown spots, wandered in a gesture of unhappy admission.

"Perhaps the papers are in my files; but I unfortunately have cataracts over my eyes and cannot wade through the morass. For anyone else, I am afraid the task is impossible.

"Papers that would establish his residence could well be in possession of his daughters and widow in Victoria. His wife married again, but I understand she still resides in the house Westmore built. It's a big showplace among those antique cottages that tourists come to see as facsimiles of dwellings in the mother country."

"I think we should go there," Ed agreed at once.

"Not so fast," Analix decided. "I'm married to a lawyer who has stopped practice. For quite a long time, I kept his files in order; and besides, I've been a public stenographer. I expect that if any papers are in your files, I could find them."

"Yes she could, sir!" Leschi chimed in. "My sister knew the alphabet when she was two years old."

"You're certainly free to poke in my files," Mr. Scarborough said. "Gracious,

I thought their usefulness was long past.

"I might have you for company two or three hours. You good people deserve tea."

He rang a bell; an elderly woman wearing a white cap came immediately to the office door.

"Yes, sir."

"This is my housekeeper of an indefinite number of years like mine," the lawyer said. "Alice, do you think you could rummage tea for guests?"

Alice smiled. "I'm sure, sir. Bring them to the kitchen in ten minutes. There's scones and petits fours going to waste. You should have sandwiches, too."

Analix laughed, "You men go ahead. I can work better without conversation."

Ed and Leschi learned the history of the Fraser River and Cariboo gold rushes from the New Caledonia aspect as they devoured countless hearty beef sandwiches, cakes, and sweet biscuits, with pot after pot of tea.

Analix found her way to the kitchen by the sound of the lively jabber. She flourished a rectangle of paper.

"Grandfather's certificate of citizenship! Right where it belonged, almost. I straightened the W file for you."

Mr. Scarborough took the paper and brought it close to his nose.

"Yes, yes! How lucky that I have been so lazy all these years and never discarded a paper!"

"Sir, we're grateful to you," Leschi said. "You will give us permission to take this with us?"

"Surely. It's your property. Let me know if it assists your case," he obliged.

"And you, Analix," Mr. Scarborough continued, "how I wish I could see your face clearly. Your Grandmother Westmore was ravishingly beautiful in face and form. Unfortunately it made her vain. She kept her husband in hell. You are a different strain of life."

"We've always wondered about our fine lady grandmother," Analix said. "Because of our mixed blood, she has never been like a grandmother to us. She and Papa do not write to one another."

Mr. Scarborough sighed, "Katherine is still the same woman living in an English world in a house with an English garden. Her daughter brings in a spot of tea to her and her guests, and she can be pleasant. But she is like many others, handicapped with too much pride in their origin.

"Visit the island. Enjoy the sight of the Parliament buildings. Know something of the heritage she has kept from you."

Leschi growled, "That grandmother has never seen me or wanted to see me. I won't go."

"I am a woman and haven't so much pride when I am fighting for my father," Analix said. "Ed, will you go with me to Victoria? It can't be more than an hour boat trip."

"You bet."

Leschi agreed to meet them at the hotel in Seattle rather than to wait for them to return to Mr. Scarborough's. They would take direct boats, Leschi from Vancouver, and Analix and Ed from Victoria.

THEY PULLED UP in a rented buggy before a great half-timbered residence on a garden-like way of the capital city of British Columbia. Ed felt Analix's hand quiver as he helped her from the buggy to the sidewalk. He had seen Analix endure flood and heartbreak with courage, but now she trembled.

"Perhaps they will ask us to go round to the back entrance as they did the men who brought Grandfather's body from the Okanogan."

"We'll do like they did. We won't go."

Ed punched the bell.

A faded yet beautiful middle-aged woman answered the chimes.

"I am Analix Gaston, born Analix Westmore. The attorney William Scarborough sent us."

The face sharpened to astonishment. "One of Carr's children! Not really!"

She hesitated, then decided, "You must be invited in. Please come in. I am your Aunt Elizabeth, already a widow and back with Mother. Mother will be surprised!"

She led them along a broad hall while she repeatedly took quick glances of avid interest. "We saw your picture in a Seattle paper one time, Analix—when you came with your husband to the state legislature as a bride. Is this your husband, the attorney?"

"This is Ed McLaren, not my husband. My husband isn't well right now. He couldn't come with me. Ed is an old friend who once worked at the AW."

Aunt Elizabeth stopped her eager glide down the hallway. "Oh. Is he your carriage driver? He can go for tea to the cook."

"Oh, no," Analix hastened to reprieve Ed. "Mr. McLaren drove the buggy, but he's not my carriage driver. He's a member of the Washington State Legislature. We've appealed to him for help with a problem of property ownership."

Elizabeth's brow cleared. She started again toward the parlor. "I might have known better. Mother is here in the music parlor. Never mind if she doesn't receive you properly. Some days she doesn't receive me properly; but I'll bring a spot of tea, and she'll pull herself together."

KATHERINE HAVERSHAM WESTMORE Brighton, a fragile piece of elegance like an antique bone china cup, was seated on a sofa with a footstool in front to support her feet. She wore a blue silk dress with a gray wool shawl over her shoulders, and a pink and yellow afghan spread across her lap.

"You will scarcely believe this, Mama, but Carr's daughter is here to see you."

The old lady peered up crossly. "What did you say?"

"This is your son Carr's daughter, Analix. You must greet her."

Ed was dumbfounded to see Analix step forward and make a curtsy that she had been taught at Holy Names Academy—the ancient bob—down, one, two, three; rise, one, two, three.

"Good morning, Grandmother," she said.

"You say this is my son's daughter!" the old lady shrilled. "My only son married an Indian! Is this woman half-breed? I can't see."

"She is a refined woman, very genteel, Mama."

"Do tell."

The old lady straightened herself. Her voice wavered with age, but nonetheless conveyed arrogance. "Drat, I wish I could see. How old are you?"

"I am old enough to be the mother of three children," Analix said.

"I'll be blessed! And who is this other person, Elizabeth?"

It was more than Elizabeth could do to make the elderly woman comprehend the identity of Ed McLaren.

"I'll bring tea, Mama."

"Yes, do."

Aunt Elizabeth whisked herself away.

Grandmother fidgeted. "I can't see why Carr had to marry a squaw after all the advantages his father and I gave him. Great sakes, girl! You're my own flesh and blood—part of you, and you're genteel, Elizabeth says. Do you realize she is your Aunt Elizabeth? But there it is, you're half savage; and there's nothing you or I can do to overcome it."

Analix kept her equanimity. "We shan't bother you long, Madame. You don't need to give us tea. We came to inquire if you have any of Arthur Westmore's papers in your attic—business papers. We need proof of his residence in the States."

"Eh? I'm sure I can't say. Elizabeth ought to know. We give everything to charity sales."

"The papers we need would have no value as charity."

ELIZABETH RETURNED WITH a silver tea service and china cups.

Analix was on her feet. "Thank you for bringing the tea, but we can't stay. You shouldn't have gone to the trouble."

"Now sit right down," Elizabeth contradicted. "I know Mama has said some mean thing or other. We just ignore you, don't we, Mama?"

"Yes, ignore me. I'm a crotchety relic with a death chill in my bones. Too old for learning manners with Indians."

Elizabeth adamantly poured the tea. It occurred to Ed that the widow resembled her brother Carr in some respects. She was not subservient to Old World pretension, but as much as a daughter could be, a defiant New World child.

Ed had remained seated; Analix reluctantly sat down again.

"Am I tail-driving, Ed?" she asked.

"Maybe a little. You should give your aunt a chance."

"Yes, dear, do," Elizabeth said. "I know you have a serious purpose in coming."

"You are right," Analix responded, with less defiance in her manner. "We came in the hope that you people would have some of Grandfather's personal records about. We are desperately searching for his business records."

Elizabeth smiled and handed Analix a cup and saucer.

"You see I have to treat you as I treat Mama, with a little patience. You're welcome company to me at least. Our usual callers are as old as the lawyer who sent you here. How is Mr. Scarborough?"

"Quite well," Analix said. "He let us search through his files. We may already have found enough to establish the Westmore claim."

"Let us hope so. I'm afraid Mama and I shall be little help. I knew this day would come, Mama! What have you to say now for your actions?"

"Oh, pshaw! I shan't apologize. I ordered all my first husband's effects burned. It wasn't that I failed to care for poor, rough Arthur. It was just that it gave me hysterics to be reminded of how his cold corpse was dumped in the middle of the parlor."

"Do forgive her," Elizabeth begged.

"Of course," Analix said.

"It is a shame that Mother was so in haste to burn Father's personal things after the funeral! She waited until Carr returned to the interior; she knew he would have prevented her destroying everything related to my father. Papa made us comfortable and happy while he lived."

"There was no income from the Okanogan after Arthur died," the old lady recited a litany. "Carr knew nothing of management—and taking an Indian wife! I couldn't abide that! I had to hide the disgrace."

Elizabeth steered her mother's attention, "Here is your tea, Mama."

She filled cups for the two guests and herself.

"The Westmore claim to property in the Okanogan is valid if first settlement counts for anything," she said as she offered cakes.

As Ed drank carefully, he observed that tea agreed better with his stomach than anything he had ingested since the Robinson party.

"Was it clear in the strait when you came across on the ferry?" Elizabeth asked.

"Yes, the sun was shining," Ed undertook small talk. "You must have an earlier spring than farther down the coast. We noticed beautiful flowers in bloom on the way here."

"Flowers bloom all winter long," Elizabeth said. "You must come back sometime to visit the Butchart Gardens with the great fountain. The Japanese current gives us the mild climate.

"Also, have you seen the Parliament buildings and the Empress Hotel?"

"Yes, we hired the buggy in the square in front of them. Like buildings in England, are they?" Ed asked.

"Quite like, we are told. We girls have never been to England and probably never will go there, for lack of funds."

Analix stood again, this time calmly.

"To be back in Seattle by nightfall, we had better go," she said. "Thank you for your kindness, Aunt Elizabeth."

"Goodbye, dear," Elizabeth said, and leaned forward to give Analix a timid peck on the cheek. "It warms my heart to see you. Even if we haven't communicated with Carr, we love him. Give him greetings from his family. Tell him, in some ways, he's the luckiest one—able to live as a free agent."

"We'll tell Papa," Analix assented.

Analix curtsied to Grandmother Katherine. "Thank you for tea, madame."

The old lady came to agitated life. "Elizabeth, did you see what she did? She's had an education! That's the way girls curtsy when they go to school in a convent in France, the way I did!"

"You have lovely manners, Niece Analix—in more ways than knowing how to curtsy," Elizabeth said.

"Analix was educated by nuns," Ed spoke for the old lady's ears. "She attended Holy Names Academy and Normal School in Spokane."

"The Sisters taught us respect for our elders, but no more than my full-blooded Indian mother taught us," Analix said. "The children of the Sinkaietk all learn right behavior toward a grandmother."

Elizabeth laughed outright. "Even a cranky one! It is a shame that we don't have more time to get acquainted. Thank you for your courtesy to Mama."

Aunt Elizabeth accompanied them to the door. "Could you find it in your heart to write to us once or twice, Analix? Pretending aside, Mama and I are two lonely widows in a great barn. My sister lives in Vancouver and is busy with a large family. Mother's second husband is long gone. Few people have Mother's attitudes. Many British Columbians are proud of their Indian blood today."

"Leschi would be furious if he knew how I accepted their hospitality," Analix said as they drove back to the square. "If it weren't for you, I wouldn't have, Ed! I even promised to write!"

When they boarded the ferry to Seattle, it was dusk. They stood in the stem and observed the wake of the vessel and the seagulls following.

Next morning Ed returned with the brother and sister by train to Olympia.

A letter from Owhi, in Ed's mailbox, awaited them: "Father agrees that our group visit to the legislative session might have some force. He will stay at home because it is calving time. Remember our appetites! We are coming by the next cattle car."

"We need a place where we all can stay and I can cook meals," Analix began planning.

Ed found the place for the Westmore brothers to stay. When he took his shirts to be cleaned at the Chinese laundry, he noticed a sign in the window: "Clean Apartment for Rent."

The rooms were above the laundry itself. The pleasant laundryman took Ed upstairs to inspect them.

"They could easily accommodate a family," the proprietor said. "They are vacant because my brother took his family for a visit to our parents in China."

"My friends are of Indian blood; they will be clean and quiet."

"They would be welcome. Tell them to come to see the rooms."

Analix went to see the apartment as soon as Ed told her of it. It was only four blocks away on a side street.

"The kitchen is spotless, and there are frying pans, coffeepot, and all we need," Analix reported. "There is plenty of room for everyone, too."

"I figured a laundryman would live in clean quarters." Ed said.

"We'll move over there as soon as Leschi turns up," Analix said. "I made a deposit. Leschi is wandering the streets now because he can't stand being cramped up the way we have been here."

An hour afterward, when Analix and Leschi had packed their suitcases and paid their hotel bill, Ed helped Leschi carry their baggage to the new place. Analix found a grocery store, and at supper supplied a kitchen-cooked meal.

Ed telephoned to Senator Handy about the new address. He came for a conference in the evening.

"I've been watching newspapers lately for lawsuits over land sales," the senator reported. "Dozens of them. Also, I've been considering defense tactics.

"Your first move, Westrnores, is to go to the land office to appeal the ruling. You must protest that you failed to receive due legal notice from the local land office when the occupied land was put up for auction. It cannot be sold with a clear title because of your prior occupancy.

"Ed, you will carry a war against land scandals to the floor of the House with some of my notes to refer to."

"You ought to make the speeches," Ed declared. "You have twice the gift of gab that I do. And everyone knows who you are."

"No, thank you," Senator Handy said. "Old men like me can't stand poison drinks as well as young cowpunchers. I won't be surprised if the conflict becomes physical. I'll continue in the role of secret plotter.

"And I have one more ploy," the senator continued. "You all will go with me to visit a friend. He's like me with the same delight in youth slaying the bellowing, fire-breathing dragon with himself in the background."

JUDGE WILLIAM WHITE, retired from the state supreme court, received them at his modest home in the residential district of Olympia. He was a tall, lean man, Senator Handy's age or older. He told his guests that he had begun legal practice in the Okanogan Valley.

"Many a day I watched the horse races at the wintering place east of Oroville. I knew all the children of Chief Tonasket and Susceptkain. Many of them married the Friedlanders, who were my dear friends. I still write to George Friedlander at his home on the old Moses Reservation. I also know Chief Jim James, who is now at Nespelem, and Billie Hill in Spokane."

'We have known them always," Leschi said.

The judge laughed, "You may hear scandal about me, in relation to daughters of chiefs, but they turned me down as a paleface."

Senator Handy snorted, "Quit bragging, Bill; let's get to business."

"Yes, yes, I was bragging," the judge conceded. "Never mind. It does my old eyes good to see another stately princess. What can I do for her?"

He unrolled a surveyor's map on a table in his study.

"I understand you have problems because of the new survey of Okanogan County. Show me."

Analix supplied the legal description of the cache, and together she and the judge found it on the map.

"Here it is—eighty acres, paying no attention to surveyor's lines," Analix said.

"It isn't numbered for entry by anyone," Ed observed.

"It's not numbered, but all the same you see that a good part of it does lie in section 16," the judge cautioned. "The surveyor can't help that even if he liked you people as owners. The decision could go against you."

"Okanogan Smith, our neighbor, kept his squatter's land on the Fifteen Mile Strip," Leschi said. "Papa told us about then court fights. Why can't the

Westmores justify their claim in the same way he did?"

Judge White reached for his visor and put it over his brows as though donning garb to render a decision. He rubbed his chin.

"Courts have been frowning on squatter's rights lately. I had to pass judgment in cases like yours. In the Okanogan Smith case—Hiram Smith, he was—at his death, it wasn't the squatter rights that determined the final disposition of the land. The court did not uphold the claim of the young white woman that Okanogan married in Seattle after splitting up with Mary Manuel."

"Our claim to the cache is that Carr Westmore traded with Chief White Stone Mountain for it. Analix and I, and our brothers and sister, Bethany, are all grandchildren of the chief," Leschi informed the judge.

"Doesn't that make it legal?" Ed argued. 'What else did Governor Stevens do but buy the Washington Territory from the chiefs at Walla Walla?"

"Mr. Westmore wasn't given any bargaining authority by the United States government, like an army general. You're on shifty ground," the judge answered.

"Your father has the privilege of outbidding others at public auction," Senator Handy said.

Leschi shook his head. "Father refuses to outbid anybody for land he's held all his life. We don't have a fence around the cache because the natural barriers make it unnecessary. Calves stay in without fence. But we've done a great deal of improvement and upkeep."

Analix gave examples: "We've built a shack for hands to stay in at calving time; we've built a corral for new calves and improved the springs. We have fulfilled ordinary homestead obligations."

"It's a mistake that the land was ever considered for sale," Ed flared. "Everybody in the country knows that the Westmores have held that cache since the 1880s!"

"You'll never win your case by 'everybody knows' arguments, Mr. McLaren," Judge White said, "but I do believe we have a clue as to how it may be done. In cases in which the state takes land from occupants, it must pay them for improvements on the land. If the bill for improvements is too high, the state won't make any money by selling the land to a third party. That approach to justice will reach the ears of the land officials."

Senator Handy exclaimed, "I wondered how long you would hold out on us for the angle we need, you old bag of bones. Our entire course is clear before us, Leschi. I can take the tiller from here to shore. We're waging righteous war to save taxpayers' money."

ON THE MORNING of the Westmore hearing in the state land office, coast papers published a story from a "reliable source" (Senator Handy) regarding the "outrage over covert sales of state lands to private interests."

Prior to the hearing, at the prodding of Senator Handy, Ed stood for the first time in the House sessions to utter public words. During the opening formalities he said, "Mr. Speaker, I ask that visitors from Okanogan County be recognized."

The redskinned, lean, and handsome sons of Carr Westmore stood up in the gallery and were greeted with hearty spontaneous applause. No legislator could miss the wave of homage, both on the floor and in the visitors' gallery, to the tribe who had come to Olympia to challenge the state land office, which was daring to sell their father's land to speculators on a technicality.

Ed continued, "These young men are part of one of the biggest cattle layouts in the biggest county in the state. Their English grandfather, Arthur Westmore, settled on their present place long before there was any government survey. He bought it from a chief of the Okanogan Indians in the days when the government was buying the Oregon Territory from the Indian chiefs at Walla Walla.

"The English immigrant of noble birth, later an American citizen, had a son, Carr Westmore, who married the daughter of Chief White Stone Mountain. These are their children, bred and born on the land of their fathers and forefathers."

The eloquent tone of the introduction had been provided with the assistance of Senator Handy.

BUT THE LAND office hearing was a closed session. The result of the hearing was that Carr Westmore must vacate the eighty acres that he used for a winter feeding lot so that it could be sold to the highest bidders, Morton and Buford Clements of Okanogan County. The chief clerk of the state land office, Bill Endicott, was to be dispatched at once to give formal notice to Carr Westmore, who had ignored earlier public notice.

Analix and her brothers, silent and formal in bearing, filed out of the office. They told the ruling to the three who waited—Ed, Senator Handy, and a newspaper reporter.

"Is there anything to do after an absolute decree like that?" Leschi wondered.

Senator Handy spluttered, "Everything is yet to do! The hearing is only the first inning of the ball game. Ed McLaren is now going to bat in the second."

Strategy for Ed was outlined by the senator: "I have it arranged with the Speaker for you to be given recognition from the chair when they introduce the bill in the House tomorrow—the memorial asking for the public sale of all lands on the north half of the Colville Reservation. It urges all funds be expended under the Reclamation Service. When they call for discussion, you jump to your feet and start spouting.

"Our friends in the press will be watching for the most unrestrained defiance ever spoken against the mounting evil in the state-selling of state lands to speculators at terms favorable to private interests."

ED, IN CLEAN shirt and pressed suit, picked up his cue properly: "Ever since I've been in the state capital as a freshman legislator, dozens of people have tried to teach me 'politics,' without much effect on my thick skull. They don't want me to cook my political goose by saying things that everybody knows but doesn't dare say.

"I'm opening my mouth as wide as I can: Land sharks are making millions of dollars on sales of public lands; buy low, sell high. The slipshod way they run things at the land office lets them get by with it.

"I've seen this happening for years in Okanogan County. What brings it to my attention today is that some half-Indian friends of mine who've lived all their lives in the Salmon Creek country are having their eighty-acre livestock cache sold out from under them because a new survey places that land on a section 16.

"The citizens of the state are being defrauded of millions of dollars by secret sales to speculators."

Waves of shock went through the room. Was this cowboy trying to ride a thunderbolt?

Ed charged that a land official, eager to do a favor, had been shown one place left off the survey, figured that it must be a section 16, and sold it without further ado. He decided that the land in question was without clear title, though one family had been resident on the land fifty years. Ed asserted that this family had every right to the land according to the prevailing rules governing disbursal of land to the public; that legal provision had been made to protect the interest of those who had settled on land before surveys, and that other lands were regularly given to the state in lieu of lands already occupied. Rats had got into the land office files! Rats had taken a nibble off the wrong piece of cheese; had sold a man's land without giving him warranted notice.

"If the land office stood on its rights to the land in question on the ground that no deed had been recorded, it would face a bill for improvements that would make the sale a farce from the standpoint of a profitable business transaction."

As impressive as any politician from King County, Ed pronounced, "It is imperative that a state land committee be formed to investigate sale of state lands as presently being conducted, and that this committee make a full report to the governor."

The representative from Seattle called out, "Hear! Hear!"

Ed flushed to the response, but it added to his courage. He produced from his vest pocket careful notes he had written on several envelopes, the vocabulary amplified by Senator Handy. "Lands that should be held in trust are being sold to speculators; let us as a state investigate:

1. Heavy purchases of timber by private lumber companies.

2. Dishonest appraisals of timber lands.

3. Insufficient inspection of lands to be included in irrigation districts to be financed by the state.

4. Looseness of land laws under which the state, receiving bribes, politely called influence, may take poor lands as indemnity for school lands.

5. Current instances in which the state is accepting low price section 16 land for school land when it could select, in lieu, land worth twenty to one hundred fifty dollars per acre.

"Newspapers have published reports that the state contemplates sale of five hundred acres of school lands near Conconully; that Seattle capital is trying to buy another five hundred acres near Malott; that Spokane capital proposed to purchase two thousand acres in Stehekin Valley and develop a large irrigation project, to be sold in ten-acre tracts; that an Iowa syndicate is trying to buy five hundred acres near Oroville; and that six thousand acres of state land are going on sale at the courthouse in Conconully, Okanogan County, in July—all isolated instances, all subject to question!

"What are the terms of each sale; what is the report of the land appraiser?"

ED SAT DOWN to a dead silence. His seatmate, Nelson, patted him on the back.

The session adjourned with common consent. People from the east side of the state came to Ed in a body to shake his hand; but from the west side, the coast lumbermen's representatives and the land office representatives vanished from the chambers.

Coast papers, alerted by "reliable source" Senator Handy, carried Ed's speech in full. Awaiting the harvest of news on an issue that they had long been nurturing, other journals picked up the coast reports and displayed them prominently. Ed's constituents in the Okanogan read of his outburst and remarked to one another, "Ed lets you know what side he's on."

Okanogan weeklies, excited that the scoop was developing in their province, reported that the state land office representative had called at the Westmore place with the notice of sale, only to be given a counterstatement consisting of a bill for $250,000 for improvements of springs, corrals, and barns. Twenty-five thousand dollars was quoted in the city papers of Spokane, Portland, and Seattle as a correction of the scoop report.

Regional news editors called for a direct statement from the squatter,

Carr Westmore. Local Okanogan reporters refused to go within a ten-mile radius of the wrath of Carr Westmore.

Meanwhile, Bill Endicott had traveled with notoriety over ruts and logs, through clouds of mosquitoes, from Oroville to Conconully. Old Man Westmore was unavailable for any quotation whatsoever. The invasion of his world withered of its own guilty conscience. The state land office phoned to its clerk at Oroville, "Bend sail back to Olympia and stop letting yourself be photographed. Why in the name of Jumping Jehoshaphat didn't you give the front office due notice before going to the Okanogan?"

A bewildered Bill took the first train out, causing him to miss lunch at Oroville.

Ed, Senator Handy, and a reporter named Joe from the Spokane *Spokesman-Review* awaited the emissary's return. The next morning, they stationed themselves at the land office door and accepted the hard looks of the harried clerk as he arrived at nine o'clock sharp for duty.

Senator Handy bearded him immediately, "Say it without swallowing: 'I didn't give the front office due notice that I was making the trip to the Okanogan.'"

Bill's eyes dropped before the reporter's stare. He swallowed and knew he had given the case away.

"Yeah. The hell with making me the patsy. I did just what they told me, and that's all the thanks I get. They saw off my limb."

"LET'S GO FOR a cup of coffee, Joe," Senator Handy invited the reporter. "Get acquainted with Ed."

"You're fun to have around, Mr. McLaren," Joe said. "You started a landslide. You going to run again?"

"Nope. I don't have time for listening to long-winded speeches and making them myself with other damn fools. I should be with my cows. Calving starts in February."

Page one detailed: "Buckaroo Ed Misses Spread."

The land office closed the Westmore case and stated to the press that the plan for selling the land occupied by the Westmores would be dropped because the size of the payment required for improvements made it unfeasible. Westmore claims to title would be determined in Okanogan County superior court.

Analix, Leschi, Ed, and Senator Handy walked from the capitol grounds.

"Will you come to supper to celebrate?" Analix invited Ed and the senator. "All of the Westmores are going home on the morning train."

Senator Handy said, "I'm sleepy by eight o'clock. Ed can go; but I hope there's a moon out when he walks up the street afterward to his hotel. Ed, stay out in the open, no dark alleys. You're due for worse than a Mickey Finn this time."

"I'm not scared of anybody in a fist fight," Ed said. "I'll come to supper. I'm hungry."

AT HIS HOTEL, Ed was handed a letter from Sammie. His son had written with a scratchy pen: "That Portuguee Joe you left on the place is no good. A lot of calves have been born, but some of them have become separated from their mothers. He can't find them and neither can I, by now.

"The feed is running out. There is not much snow. The cattle could rustle for some of their feed. I told him he is feeding the cattle more than they need each day, but he said they were hungry unless he fed them twice a day. He always fed his sheep twice a day.

"Instead of looking out for our stock, he spends half his time at his own homestead building his cabin.

"The yearlings in the orchard seem to be bloated."

Churning in anger, Ed stalked over to the Westmore quarters. He found no one but Analix.

"Where is everybody? I was gonna ask someone to take a look at my place as soon as they get home."

"You'll have to write," Analix said. "They're already gone."

"Gone!" Ed echoed. "I thought we were all going to have supper."

"Don't worry, I'll fix your supper," Analix said. "They left on short notice to catch the cattle train going from Seattle up the valley tonight."

Analix stood in an array of suitcases half-full of clothing.

"So you're stuck with all the packing. Is that what makes you cranky?" Ed asked.

Analix sighed. "You'll understand. After you went on to your hotel and we came here for lunch, Eddie Brewster, who says he comes from the Okanogan, was waiting to invite us all to a party. Tamma and Kahpat wanted to go."

"To a party to ply the Injuns with a jug?"

"Exactly."

"Don't blame you for herding them out. Won't stay to supper then."

"Of course you will! I made a pie this morning. There won't be a fight for the biggest piece for once. You can eat the whole thing."

"What did you want to talk to the boys about?"

"This letter from Sam, about my hired hand."

He gave her the ink-stained piece of tablet paper.

She went to sit on the cushioned divan that provided the only Oriental suggestion to the austere apartment. Her face grew sober as she read.

When she finished reading, she said, "I'm not surprised. A person can't leave his property without trouble. I'll tell one of the boys to go to your place. It won't be long until the session is over. I'll start boiling potatoes."

She lit the gas burner and set the table. In a few moments, she had the simple supper ready. They ate less heartily than they would have done with all the family.

When she brought the whole pie to the table, Ed shook his head.

"What's the matter? Don't you want any? It's apple."

"Guess not. It looks good, but I've had too much steak and potatoes."

"Dogs always eat more when they're in a pack," she teased. "I'll give the extra food to our Chinese friend downstairs when I leave in the morning."

Analix began rinsing the dishes in the sink. Ed said, "I better get over to my hotel. You have all those clothes to pack, and I have some things to do myself."

She did not urge him to stay as he went to the hall closet. He took out his coat but impulsively threw it on a chair. "I don't want to go. I have no home with anyone but you."

"I'm sorry about your wife, Ed. It's hard to understand why she moved to the flat."

"Eleanor follows her brothers' advice. They have her convinced she can make a million when the new dam comes through. She kicked me off her claim. She wants to grow garden truck on ground that will grow cheatgrass."

"Homesteaders are going to be disappointed," Analix said. "Your wife isn't the only person with hopes built on sand."

Ed wished he had the courage to ask Analix about Gerald Gaston. Except for her statement to Senator Handy that her husband had not come to Olympia because he was ailing, she had said nothing.

As though answering his unspoken question, she said, "I must get home tomorrow. Poor Gerald gets short shrift when I'm not there to help."

Ed shifted his feet. "Nobody has told me what's the matter with him. I wouldn't want to show my face over here again if I was him. When I finish this term, I'm never coming back."

"People from the cow country seem to wind up with red faces," Analix said. "But it isn't only embarrassment that kept Gerald home. The boys say he is lazy and afraid to get dirty with ranch chores, but he has a fever every night. I feel his skin. He complains of pain in his arms and legs."

"Sounds like good old rheumatiz. Isn't he young for it?"

"Yes, he is. But some mornings he can hardly get out of bed."

"I can believe that," Ed remarked. "Your Old Man thinks four o'clock is time to light the fire. Many's the morning I wished he'd get sick and not start the coffee boiling."

"Gerald's stiffness and soreness don't go away as fast as everyone else's by the time they reach the table," Analix said. "No matter. I'll soon be home to help him on with his boots."

She took Ed's coat from the chair and gave it to him.

Her eyes were soft and black. "We were always special friends, Ed. How did we grow up so fast? Remember how you pulled me out of the spring flood? That was all, as the Sinkaietk say, 'Before the Earth turned over.'"

"Yeah, things are different now, and not better. You're the only woman I've known who doesn't hurt me someplace."

"Maybe you let your wife hurt you, Ed. Maybe you should stand up to her more."

"You can tell I love you, can't you?" Ed said. "I always have. I guess I lost my chance thinking of you as the boss's daughter too long. He never doubted that a hired hand would keep his place."

"I hope God will pity me because I have always loved you, too, Ed. When I was a little girl, I thought I already belonged to you because you saved me from drowning."

The coat fell to the floor. They were in each other's arms, the longing between them at last taking over. They were caught again in Nature's whirlpool.

But she pulled away from him. "I wouldn't be doing you a favor by letting you make love to me, Ed."

"I don't know right from wrong, maybe. I think for you and me to have each other would be right. As you say, once in a while the world turns over."

"It won't work, Ed. Father deRouge would say we have responsibilities toward other people."

"Go on home. I have six suitcases to pack."

She opened the door. Scooping up his coat, he went out with no words to express his sadness.

It was still February; the winter night in the side street was pitch dark. Three men walked into Ed's path before he became aware enough to step aside.

"That's him!"

Ed only then remembered Senator Handy's warning. The voice from the dark belonged to Eager Beaver.

"We're looking for you, Ed."

"What you doing in this part of town?"

"Might say the same for you," Eddie snickered. "We're on unfinished, legitimate business with the squaw. Waited till the end of your visit."

"The hearing today settled your business with the Westmores. They're taking the Clements brothers to court in Okanogan."

The oily glad-hander tried to be sinister. "We have a message for you: Keep out of school land sales."

"Who's gonna make me?"

"We'll give you a hint. Let him have it, guys!"

One of the thugs who had let Eager Beaver deliver the spoken message performed his chores now. He landed hard knuckles across Ed's mouth.

"You wallopers!" Ed roared.

His reflexes answered the blow. His sledgehammer fist met the mush of a pudgy face—the right target, Eager Beaver.

Brewster squealed and hopped a safe distance from further physical encounter.

"Take him apart!" he ordered his cohorts.

"That's easier said than done!" Ed rejoined.

His fists, hardened on shovel handles, landed like rocks. For each blow he received, he delivered three. His arms that threw calves and held them to the ground had no trouble with city muscle men.

At a frenzied whistle from Eager Beaver, already in the alley, the two bullies fled from further pain. Their shoes clattered as they retreated over brick.

Ed grabbed a two-by-four that his feet had bumped. He clutched the stick in his hand, cussed, and muttered as he peered after his assailants. He became aware that his nose was bleeding.

"You guys started it, come on and finish it!" he yelled into the darkness.

Then his shoulders were grabbed.

"Stop yelling! You hear me!" Analix was shaking him.

"How'd you know what was happening?" he gasped. "You shouldn't have come out here!"

"I've heard enough yowls in the dark to recognize tomcat fights," she said fiercely.

He tried to hold himself upright. "I'm O.K. I gotta get back to the hotel."

"Not the way you're bleeding." She piloted him back toward the apartment.

"Made a fool of myself, letting them jump me."

"I agree," Analix said. "Come on before they reassemble their forces."

"Wish they would," Ed still bristled. "But they've skedaddled. They told me they were coming to visit you. They know better now."

He dripped blood all the way to her kitchen. She put cold, wet dishtowels to the back of his neck, and soon the nosebleed stopped. She settled him into a chair.

"No real damage," Ed assessed his condition.

He opened his mouth and felt gingerly. "Guess a couple teeth are loose."

"Don't monkey with them," Analix said. "They'll grow back in firm again if you let them alone."

Ed was becoming aware of sore spots on which he had caught blows. Then he noticed that Analix was crying.

"I'm sorry and ashamed we've caused you so much trouble," she snuffled. "We asked more of you than you should have to give. I talk the language of the white people, Ed, but I have already learned the meaning of my Indian blood. I rage at what your friendship for us causes you."

"Now you're the fool!" he told her as he put his arms about her.

"Father deRouge warned me that one day I would feel a hurt that will never go away. He made me promise not to throw a blanket around my shoulders and start grunting and taking drinks from white men. I keep a promise, but my heart has the lead in it of a squaw whose place has gone to a woman with hightopped shoes, a corset, and curly hair."

"Quit talking like that!"

"I'll try."

"Do you want me to go again?"

"No. I'm through sending you into the night to be mugged."

She turned out the gaslight and led him to the bedroom. The love that had never before found a corner in which to express itself now was the reality that should always have been. In the tenderness that took place between them, their hurts went away for a while.

Ed, who had slept uneasily for months, fell sound asleep. Analix would stay beside him forever.

In the morning, he awoke to find that she had already departed with true Indian stealth, all the suitcases with her, even the pie! How had she managed?

He was offended and hurt. He had planned to say by daylight that they would be married as soon as it could be engineered. She should send Gerald packing at once. Everyone knew that her husband had given her nothing but grief. Even her priest might say that because Analix had been married only in a civil ceremony, it was not binding for a Catholic. As for Eleanor, Ed would introduce a bill in the legislature asking for his own divorce.

But Analix had not waited to listen.

16

In the Henhouse

Eleanor McLaren, née Clements, who had gathered up the gumption to shed her shortsighted clod of a husband, sat in her temporarily dusty cabin and waited for irrigation water to come flooding down the hill. Though it was early spring, the threat of a dry summer was already present. She carefully studied the Okanogan newspaper that her brother had left for her to read. Mort, who had given Eleanor the courage to take her independent stand, had intimated that most of the land sales reported in the paper had been accomplished under his auspices.

She could see for herself that canny people who had filed early claims for homesteads could make a fortune merely by resale of their land at double the old prices. The state had just sold a Seattle company four hundred twenty-four acres of school land near Conconully at twenty-one dollars and three cents per acre, and four hundred fifty-one acres on the west bank of the Okanogan for sixty-seven thousand dollars.

The Clements Trust Company had bought from the state at public auction two hundred acres of section 16 land. Mort had entrusted his sister with the secret that the newly purchased land included the cache used by the Westmores. Eleanor had gloated. It was time the high and mighty squaw man and his offspring felt the sting of the law. Analix Westmore would have to adjust herself to being just another half-breed and not queen of all creation in the Okanogan. It was revolting the way she managed her father, her husband, her brothers, and even men who had worked at the Westmore place!

During Eleanor's last visit to the store to buy groceries, Audrey, the store clerk, had given her the gratuitous information that Analix Westmore Gaston and one of her brothers had taken the early morning train to the coast. Audrey, a small-bosomed old maid who had proved up on her homestead with still no luck at catching a husband, guessed that the two were traveling to Olympia to the Land Department.

"Ten to one," she said, "they'll hunt up Ed McLaren, too, and expect him to do something about that land they are losing." She pretended not to know that Eleanor was Ed's estranged wife.

"Do you think it is right to take that land away from the Westmores? After all, they were the first people in the country—here a long time before any land survey," she continued.

"I see no reason why those of us who have filed legitimate claims should be concerned for the welfare of squatters," Eleanor replied, firming her lips against further prying.

Audrey gasped in histrionic embarrassment when Eleanor charged her purchases of beans and prunes to Ed McLaren's account.

"I suppose, after all, that the law is the law," Audrey tittered. "There were notices of the sale in the papers. The Westmores insist they never saw the notices; but they'll have to take the consequences, likely."

Eleanor picked up her load from the counter and walked sedately into the street and back to her homestead.

"Let them go crying to Ed!" she thought now, as she rocked and read the newspaper. She would have preferred to scrub the cabin floor, but there was water in the pipe only for drinking and cooking. "My brothers are within their legal rights. They're big men around here. They have so much land they lease some of it instead of operating ranches themselves. They learned the use of lawyers the hard way from their dealings with the traitorous Good Roads Association and the county commissioners!"

Eleanor was glad to read further that the state legislative committees had given unanimously favorable reports on damming Aeneas and Bonaparte creeks. Locally, the wooden flume was already under construction, through subscriptions of private capital.

"If only I can keep my patience as Mort tells me!" she prayed. "I need to find someone to dig my ditch from the flume. I'll visit the neighbors to find out how much capital is required. I wish Mort or Buford would dig my ditch, but they're much too busy."

For a day or two Eleanor occupied herself with cautious calls. Every tongue had its wisdom. Some pessimists had heard that the flumes should be built with as few curves as possible so that water would not spill. But the construction was proceeding in the quickest and cheapest way—following the natural contours of the land. Any day now, Eleanor was assured, the concrete spillways and outlets would be installed. The graders would be pushing a wall of dirt across the gap between the two hills, Aeneas and Bonaparte. The legislature had earmarked seven hundred fifty thousand dollars for the project. Some of the men had already begun to dig their individual ditches.

Eleanor went to visit some of the women with whom she had attended religious meetings. But each visit left her with the feeling that these women who had been her friends now looked down upon her because she had no husband to dig her ditch.

"They forget the truth of the matter," she soliloquized. "I sent Ed McLaren away. He didn't leave me! Those women certainly all favored my giving Ed his walking papers. Every last one of them agreed at the time that I could do nothing else. Ed McLaren is crude, godless, and profane, and no children should be brought up under his influence!"

The store owner made no comment about Eleanor's continuing to charge groceries to Ed McLaren's account, but she wished that she could escape the necessity. She must find an income of her own.

Finally she decided she would keep chickens and sell the eggs for cash. She regretted having left her chickens at Ed's place but she hesitated to go there or send the boys because of the presence of the hired man. Ten to one, the house was a shambles with no woman to clean it one month to the next. She considered making a tour of inspection.

"I am entitled to as many hens as Ed," she thought. "I'll go for them while Sam and Billie are still at school. The Portugee will be out with the cows. I'll take only a couple old hens, as if they aren't all actually mine! Ed never so much as looked at the Plymouth Rocks that I raised from chicks!"

On a sunny but chilly March day, Eleanor walked up the road to her former dwelling. She had been mistress; she had no reason to feel shame. So why did she? The henhouse was at the rear of the residence, which, she thought, probably could be called a 'house' now because of the addition of three bedrooms and a kitchen.

Hens, with a Plymouth Rock overlord, squawked and lazily pecked at the dirt in the chicken pen. Eleanor opened the gate and went to the shed, heading for the biddies that would be perched in nests doing the chores of the season. The henhouse door creaked noisily on its hinges; she had forgotten the sound. "The door should have been locked," she thought irritably. "No telling who might wander in to help himself to a roasting bird." The hired man likely hadn't ever bothered to use the key which she had hung on a nail on the back porch.

As Eleanor had anticipated, a pair of old hens were sitting quietly. They shifted position over the eggs underneath them and cocked their heads suspiciously but did not fly off the nests.

Maybe they still remembered her. It might be possible to transport hens and eggs without panic ensuing. She reached for a cardboard box that she had placed in a corner months ago. Even then she must have intended it for a temporary nest, for it was stuffed with straw. A second box was also ready.

Deftly, she slid her hand under a hen and one by one extracted the warm eggs. When she had them all arranged in a neat circle on the hay in the box, she lifted the setting hen and placed her over her eggs. The hen crouched to her work in the new location with only a cluck or two.

When Eleanor approached the second hen, she found it not as tame as the first. The bird stood up from the nest with a loud screech, opened her wings, and flew out the door to the yard, alarming the flock with her behavior. The rooster poked his head through the door like a gendarme while the hens outside talked uneasily. But before he could report his findings, the rooster quickly hopped aside as the shadow of a human being fell over him. It was a man holding a rifle; he gaped in surprise at the henhouse intruder.

"A tramp, a coyote, a dog I expected, but not a pretty lady stealing chickens!" he exclaimed with a lilting accent.

Eleanor looked up at the short, slender, handsome man with black hair and a curled mustache. Portugee Joe without a doubt!

"I am your Old Man's wife," Eleanor blushed as she spoke nervously. "I am Mrs. McLaren."

Joe's eyes widened with curiosity and amusement.

"Oh, I heard about you. Yes, I heard about you."

Eleanor seethed at his insulting innuendo.

"Don't mind me, ma' am. Sure. Take a couple hens."

He lowered his rifle and chuckled, "I'll help you catch the one that flew outside."

Eleanor wanted no help. She tapped her foot on the henhouse floor and wished her situation were only a bad dream. The man was already bringing back from the yard the wayward setting hen, which was gamely pecking at his hands.

"We better put this one in a gunnysack," he said.

From a nail on the wall, he unsnagged a woven sack and dumped the old hen into it. The fowl squawked and struggled while Portugee Joe held firm and laughed. When he had tied a knot around the sack with the twine at the top, he offered further, "I'll fetch you some eating eggs from the house. The hens lay a lot more 'n just me can eat. I have a big pile that you can take along."

Eleanor wanted to go through the floor. If only the fellow would quit his familiarity and his chuckles!

"What I have will do," she said. "All I need are the setting hens."

"Oh, no, ma'am."

He went to the house and returned with a large tin can filled with eggs. As he forced the gift upon her, he asked, "You afoot? How can you carry a load of chickens and eggs?"

"I'll manage."

"Maybe. But it's so far to walk to the flat! The team is still hitched. I'll drive you there."

"No! You needn't bother!"

"Please, yes. Get over being scared of me. The ladies all like me. I'm nice. Lots of pretty ladies call me Joe. Portugee Joe, that's me."

Eleanor rationalized. She was silly to think that she must for propriety's sake traipse down the road with her arms full of chickens and eggs when she could be conveniently taken by Ed's hired hand.

"Since you insist, Mr. Joe, I'll thank you if you drive me back. I left my little girl sleeping and should be with her. She doesn't sleep as long in the afternoons as she used to."

"Now you are smart. I'm glad you'll let me take you!" the chivalrous Portugee Joe said happily.

Portugee Joe's voice was soft and melodious. As he smiled at her, his white teeth flashed in his mouth; the sunshine gleamed on his wealth of black hair. He was behaving like a gentleman, and Eleanor could not help thinking, "He's handsome as a highwayman, different and dashing, even a touch romantic. God knows there was never anything romantic in my relation with Ed McLaren."

She shook aside such thoughts as improper and ludicrous. She did need a ride! She let him help her with the boxes and the gunnysack, and even took his hand for a lift to the seat of the buckboard.

"Where has he been with the buckboard?" she wondered uneasily, knowing that he had not been herding cattle.

As they drove down the lane, Joe told her that he had come across the southern border with a band of sheep, but the cattlemen had shot all his sheep when he reached Nevada. He was glad that he had been able to find work when he came penniless to the Northwest.

"I like cattle, too," he said, "but still they are not sheep."

"I guess Ed is lucky to have a man to stay on the place, somebody he can trust when he is gone."

"It is good for me that a man can still file for a homestead in this part of the country. I have made a claim on land this way, near you. When the Old Man comes back from wherever he is, I'll start to dig my ditch for the irrigation. I'm building a cabin now."

"That answers the question about where he has been in the buckboard," Eleanor thought.

For his courtesy in bringing her home, she thought that perhaps she should offer him a cup of coffee, but she decided it would be silly. She could not have Leila wakening to the sight of a strange man in the cabin.

"Thank you for bringing me home," she told him primly.

He helped her carry the hens and the eggs to the lean-to at the back of the cabin, then showed his even, white teeth in a final farewell smile.

After he drove away, Eleanor took the skittish hen from the gunnysack and placed it on its clutch of eggs. She stroked the feathers of the biddy soothingly until it grew calm. When the hens were settled, she took the overflowing can of extra eggs into the cabin. The children would have the surprise of an egg apiece for breakfast. Day after day, they had eaten oatmeal mush.

"Oatmeal mush, same old slush!" Bill had complained this morning.

Inside the reassuring walls of the cabin, Eleanor's unsettled feelings subsided. It was a relief when Leila woke with her usual whimpers.

Eleanor reiterated to herself, "You have to eat. Lots of people even steal cows! I'm certainly in no such class."

She felt for the first time the jolt of being a female unprotected.

"If I'd had the sense I was born with, I'd have gone to Mort and Buford's place and asked for some hens. I started their flocks, too.

"But then," she admitted to herself, "they'd never take that into consideration."

AT THE WATERUSERS' meetings her brothers, who had opened land agent offices in downtown Bonaparte, were always present and always encouraging to homesteaders. Mort and Buford visited her and the children at the cabin. They came at mealtime, seated themselves at the table, and ate until satisfied. They said in jolly tones, "We never had it so good as when you were our cook, Sis."

"Did it never occur to them," she sometimes wondered, "that every mouthful of food had to be paid for by Ed McLaren when he came home from the coast?" Mort and Buford had not brought her so much as a rick of wood for the kitchen stove. She did not know what she would have done if Ed had not bought a winter supply of slabwood from the sawmill just before they quarreled. Eleanor was now ready to admit to herself that although she had been continuously irked by Ed's gregariousness and his determination to follow his own course, he had always been a responsible husband.

Then she reproached herself for disloyal thoughts toward her own blood. She had made her decision to follow her brothers' judgment, and she would stick to it. They had formed a partnership with the man who owned the Eastern Loan and Trust Company of Spokane. With him, they had obtained title to eighteen hundred acres of state land that were to be developed as ten-acre tracts planted with fruit and alfalfa as soon as the land had irrigation. They would succeed in their project despite the obstruction of persons like Ed McLaren.

At the store, Audrey delighted in reporting Ed's involvement with the Westmores' land troubles.

"Did you see it in the *Spokesman-Review* that Old Man Westmore up in the hills is standing off the state timber cruisers with a shotgun? Ed McLaren in the legislature has started a big land war."

"Sounds just like him," Eleanor snapped. "He's always in the midst of some ruckus. He'll come home with his tail between his legs."

"I guess you and him are separated," Audrey fished for information, as she brought out the charge account booklet and inserted the carbon under the statement page.

"We are still legally married," Eleanor said stiffly. "Ed McLaren will pay this bill."

"We aren't worried," Audrey assured her. "He's never written to cut off your credit the way some men do when the family splits up. Some men even advertise that they are no longer responsible for bills run up by their former wives."

17.

Commensurate

At the close of the legislative session in Olympia, Ed took the train home. As he hiked to his place from the Great Northern depot in Bonaparte, the smell of rotting flesh assaulted his senses. Valise in hand, he plunged through the orchard to investigate. In the alfalfa that he had planted among the trees, he found the source of the smell. Ten dead, bloated yearlings!

He burst open the door of his house to find Portugee Joe happily eating a noon meal of fried chicken.

'Why the hell are those critters lyin' there in the orchard?"

Portugee Joe finished his mouthful and shrugged.

"Don't know what killed 'em."

"Any numbskull would know better 'n to leave cattle in a stand of wet alfalfa! You could at least have buried 'em."

"They'll dry out to nothing but hide and bones pretty quick."

"Not ten carcasses. I'm paying you off, you walloper!"

Joe, who had anticipated the termination of his job, finished his lunch and went unconcernedly to the bedroom for his pack.

Ed cursed the whole countryside as he matched his cows with their strayed calves.

"Seems like somebody could have let me know sooner that my place was goin' to the devil!" he railed at Sven Linstrom when he met him at the post office.

"Sorry, pal. I shoulda paid more attention. Thought you had somebody hired. That Portugee was gone from your feedlot days at a time just when the calves were cornin'. He was lettin' the cows eat orchard grass 'stead of havin' to feed them with a pitchfork."

"I'll never run for the legislature again. I was a damn fool stayin' over there at calving time."

Sven grinned as he said with the candor of long friendship, "Maybe everybody thought you were too busy to be bothered."

"Whaddaya mean?"

308

"From what I hear, you weren't lettin' any grass grow under your feet. I'd take your troubles any day in the week."

"What you driving at? I got troubles, that's for sure. All my own fault, I guess."

"Innocent as a newborn babe, ain't you? Half the county is gigglin' about you carrying on since Eleanor turned you out. Why shouldn't you carry on? You're footloose and fancy free! But I always was told politicians were supposed to be discreet."

"Where'd you learn a big word like 'discreet'?"

His skin prickled at the thought that someone might have seen him leaving the Chinese laundry apartment after all the Westmores but Analix had gone home.

"Yep," Sven continued, "makin' a jackass of yourself over that bank president's daughter. Forgot all about your stand against a dam you know won't hold water."

The floor steadied under Ed. He could endure being heckled about that fool Nancy Robinson. "Oh, yeah! I remember those guys peekin' in the window."

"Accordin' to Mort, you were sparkin' a hot little number. She had to slap your face."

"I don't know what cock-and-bull story is going around, and I couldn't care less!"

He went home to his cheerless bachelor's hovel.

EVEN THOUGH ELEANOR would no longer be around to complain of the proximity of the cattle to the house in winter, Ed completed a transaction that he had begun last fall to please her. He had planned to keep cows beyond the range of her nose if she hated their smell so much. From Art and Tom Johnston, who had learned the hard way that Okanogan soil could not produce a mature wheat crop within the growing season, he bought forty acres of meadow ten miles up the river. The sellers were moving south to the loam of the Big Bend of the Columbia. Because the Johnstons needed capital for wheat seed, they sold to Ed at a low price for cash—ten dollars per acre. Far enough away to keep the town air clear of odor, the layout still was not too far for Ed to make a daily round trip.

Even though Eleanor was no longer interested in his cattle growing, Ed was pleased to have a new watering area. Recent settlement higher up the creeks was reducing the amount of water that emptied into the Okanogan River at Ed's original base. The riverbank, his west border, had always been steep for cows heavy with unborn calves, and the rank growth of poplars over a period of years had added to the problem.

To register his deed for the Johnston place, Ed went to the county auditor's office early in the summer. The county seat was now in Okanogan; Conconully, no longer the population center, had been forced to abdicate. The town in the south end was victor in a dispute that had entailed years of political maneuvering. Riverside had at one time aspired to the title. The final contest was between Okanogan and Omak, four miles apart. The Okanogan Commercial Club, as a lure, had pledged the town to build an imposing three-story brick building with a bell tower. This edifice was now under construction. County business was temporarily being conducted in a one-story, falsefront complex that also housed the Okanogan Valley Bank.

ED FIRST RECOGNIZED Analix by the familiar gold nugget earrings. She was standing several persons ahead of him in the line to the clerk's window. Even before she turned at the end of her business, Ed could see that her body held a child. She surely saw him as she passed by, but she went into the hallway without speaking. He followed her.

"Analix!"

"I didn't expect to meet you here, Ed."

"You won't let me come near you, will you?"

She ignored his question and said, "You'll be glad to know we have our cache. I brought the deed just now to be recorded. Judge Bill Brown, who knows how long the Westmores have had a possession, awarded the grandchildren of White Stone Mountain a clear title. We're grateful to you, too, for all your help in Olympia."

"I didn't do anything."

"We know better."

"You are going …" Ed hesitated, afraid to finish his sentence.

"To have a baby. Yes."

"It's my child, isn't it?"

"Gerald isn't enough of a cattleman to count the days of gestation. We both know it can be yours."

"But you are going ahead and having it?"

"Of course. I am a half-breed, not a white woman to go galloping a horse."

"I didn't mean that! I don't know what I meant."

"It's all right, Ed. I shouldn't have said that."

"For you and me to be together would be right. I'd like to work it out so we could be married."

Analix shook her head. "I would feel irresponsible to many people."

"I guess it's too late for talking. Can I do anything for you?"

His spirit sank at the retreat in her dark eyes, a look that he had never seen before.

"All I ask is that you leave me alone, Ed. Don't think that I have quit caring about you, but the sight of you makes me hurt like a savage who wants what I cannot have. I have confessed, and that must be the end. Bearing the child is my penance. It will be a bright child, a happy one with my other three."

"I can't be sure of anything just because a priest forgives me."

"I won't break the heart of Father deRouge, Ed. He is getting old. He has given his life for the mission. He goes without food, travels in all kinds of weather. He coughs blood."

"He asks for your whole life with his strict rules."

"Nothing for himself. He saw to it that I was educated because the Sinkaietk need *skumalt* leaders. He says that because of the displacement and bewilderment of my mother's People, a granddaughter of an English earl and Chief White Stone Mountain must help to preserve law."

"Are you the only one responsible?"

"I am the oldest of the grandchildren. Marna, who used to speak for *N'Chi-lix-czin* to the *Suyapichs*, is dead."

"But there are the grandsons."

"Perhaps it is better now that the People have a *skumalt*, a wise woman leader. There is calamity among the men. When Chief Susceptkain's family finished a haying job last month, they had money to get drunk. Alec shoved his father over a cliff into Fish Lake, then killed his own wife. Alec wanted to replace his father as chief, but the Old Man felt that Alec would not make a good head of the tribe."

"God Almighty!"

"Now you can understand why I stay with the Sinkaietk. I care about them. You care about the needs of all the settlers the way I care about Marna's relatives. People depend on you."

"I doubt that."

"Your wife and your children are withering on that driedout garden patch on the flat. Make her take you back. Your separation was foolish. I could never feel that I would have a clear title to you."

A heavyset man came from the auditor's office and glanced at them with curiosity. Graceful and free as a forest creature that he could not catch without killing, Analix moved away from Ed.

A MONTH LATER, Father Etienne deRouge was found dead at his desk of a hemorrhage.

Ed stayed away from the Mass because Analix would be there. He had simply lost her to another man of greater charm and strength—to the son of a French count.

ELEANOR TOLD HERSELF that the only thing that worried her was how to get her private irrigation ditch dug to connect with the water that would soon come down the flume. She noticed Portugee Joe frequently at his shanty only a mile from her own cabin. She was told that he had plans for setting out an orchard. She wondered how he could work on his own claim all the time. Apparently he no longer worked for Ed. She refused to believe the gossip that she heard at the store about women who visited Portugee Joe in his dwelling.

One morning she strolled in the direction of Joe's cabin, which was at the edge of the winter wheat field that Ed had planted last fall. She told herself that her main objective was to judge how long it would be before the Jones' Fife should be harvested, but she also might make a tentative approach to Joe about pick and shovel work on her irrigation ditch. She hopefully inspected the crop, which was now, in June, in the form of bright green grass. At the time he planted the seed, Ed had said, "It probably won't make wheat, but it'll at least make a grass crop that we can use for hay."

She had resented his negative attitude with fury. The crop must be harvested as wheat! Wheat had made her parents wellto-do in the Walla Walla country. She would manage at harvest time. A crew went about with a reaper, thresher, and four-horse team. They would even transport the grain to Riverside to be stored at the warehouse until the boat came up the river in high water—for half the profits.

As she decided that the crop was doing well for the time of year, she came upon Portugee Joe digging his irrigation ditch. She greeted him as casually as possible despite her inexplicable shortness of breath. Joe swept off his hat and leaned on his shovel.

"Hello, pretty lady! Haven't seen you since you came for the hens. How did the setting eggs turn out?"

Eleanor informed him that the hens had taken to their new nests easily. She was relieved that he remembered her.

"They hatched three dozen chicks that will be fryers or pullets before long. I was just out inspecting my wheat crop. I'm one of the lucky homesteaders who'll have a crop even if the water doesn't come from the dam this summer," she said.

Joe glanced at the growing stalks. "You'll have some kind of crop," he said, to Eleanor's annoyance.

"I see you have your ditch started on the way to the flume."

"I've been working quite a bit," he said, "so that I can have more free time later. I go next week to the Scott brothers, to help in their irrigation system that comes from the Pogue River. I learn the orchard business."

"Will you be going away long? I would like to know how much you would charge to dig my ditch for me. If you have other plans, I can find someone else."

Joe was quick with his sympathy. "Nice lady like you shouldn't have to worry how to get her ditch ready. shouldn't have to pay for it, either."

"I would want to pay for it," Eleanor said.

His white teeth flashing in a dazzling smile, Portugee Joe came closer. They were in a gully, where—Eleanor hoped—they could not be seen from the road. He suddenly grasped her in his arms, and before she could imagine what was happening, he kissed her hotly on the mouth and held her body so close to his that she could not struggle.

"One way a woman pays her bills," Portugee Joe whispered, his breath in her ear. "For that kind of pay, I dig your ditch."

Eleanor wrenched herself loose, scrambled up the bank, and ran crying to the cabin.

"You think it over and come to see me sometime," Portugee Joe called after her. "I'm not going anywhere for a while."

Eleanor's fancy persisted, despite herself, as to what it would be like in Portugee Joe's cabin. He had strong arms and a smile that was like the sun coming from behind a cloud. Gossips said that he played the guitar and sang songs, including "Home on the Range," to his lady callers. Tales traveled from the store to Sunday services, to schoolchildren, to Eleanor. She could not fasten on any one woman who had surely gone to visit Portugee Joe, but she numbered the possibilities: Mrs. Campbell, whose husband beat her every time he drank; Mrs. Comstock, who worked in the kitchen of the restaurant for meals; Mrs. Endicott, who ran her husband off for whipping the children. She shuddered. It was unthinkable that the group should ever include the woman who had run off Ed McLaren because … because why?

She was growing fuzzy in the mind, losing her ability to analyze. Nowadays she was never done with the chores that had always been man's work: splitting wood, for example. The boys sawed the cordwood that she had been forced to charge at the mercantile company after her supply of slabwood ran out, but the boys were often truant at the creek when she needed to build a fire, and there were no more sticks of stove size.

She gathered eggs from the two hens—on the days that they laid them— fed the pullets, washed dishes, swept the cabin, and carried buckets of water from the creek. Although Ed had installed a water pipe into the cabin, it no longer supplied water at the tap because the pressure was too low. So many families had settled in cabins along the creek that Eleanor's water supply, lower down, had been seriously crippled. She looked in her hand mirror only rarely, and sometimes she saw the dusty wisps of hair about her face and wept. Sometimes she told herself that she did not care and left the wisps because she was too tired to do anything about them.

Then her mind would go again to the necessity for the irrigation ditch to be dug if she were to take advantage of her water rights—and the inevitability of a woman's need for a man. She would deny her fatigue and pick up the hairbrush for a stroke or two.

AT NIGHT, ELEANOR tossed and turned, unable to let go of her concerns in sleep. But one night, it was an outside disturbance that roused her. She sat up in alarm as she heard voices yelling and screaming not far from her cabin; a glare of light came through the window. In her nightdress, Eleanor ran from the cabin and saw a large group of people gathered in the field adjoining hers—Portugee Joe's field. Joe's cabin was afire! She threw a long knit sweater over her nightgown and joined the crowd. She hoped her children would not waken and come looking for her.

At the door of his cabin, Portugee Joe was hopping around frantically, yelling, pleading, "Come on out, Sweetie, come on out!"

A woman remained inside the blazing shanty! A woman who had been lying with Portugee Joe! Eleanor shook so that she nearly fell over. She steadied herself and asked the woman beside her, "Who is in there?"

The neighbor woman sniffed, "That silly Mrs. Gibbon, of course. Many's the time I've seen her sneaking in. She goes to Joe every time her husband sneaks over to the Brandons' cabin while Old Man Brandon is gone to Oroville for a drunk."

The cabin burned to the ground, but no one crawled out in ultimate animal terror. Everyone knew that Mrs. Gibbon had met a hellish death rather than face the scorn of the neighbors.

Next morning her bones were found, charred black. Mr. Gibbon asked no questions. He dared ask none. Portugee Joe left the community. No one knew whether he had gone for good or to work for the Scott brothers on Pogue River. Every time Eleanor looked out of her cabin, she had to view the rubble and see the dust rise as curious persons kicked the ashes.

As THE HEAT of advancing summer parched the ground on Eleanor's place, she saw that the only crop that would survive was the Jones' Fife wheat that Ed had planted. Even it would not reach maturity, but it would be good for hay, just as Ed had predicted.

Dust blew thick across Eleanor's claim. In her garden the bean vines died because the creek provided no more water than that required for drinking and washing dishes. The brood hens stopped laying. The pullets, too young to lay, kept up an empty-headed "Caw, caw, caw," and ate ravenously of the feed. The boys had outgrown their shoes; their coveralls were faded rags. School was beginning in a few days. How would they have clothes if they were not charged from Blackwell's store?

Sam, Billy, and Leila squatted listlessly on the stoop and waited for their lives to change by miracle. Eleanor, hair falling in straight hanks about her face and wearing an apron that she could not launder, sat with them. She was waiting for the bread to rise in the pans. She scarcely had the desire to put the loaves into the oven. They never came out high and crispy as they had always done at the other place. The stove in the cabin here was a flimsy toy.

A report had circulated for a few days that the dam was almost finished. Eleanor reminded herself dully that she still had no ditch for irrigation even if it came. Then the news was revamped; lack of a ditch made no difference. The flume had to be rebuilt entirely in a straighter line. The water spilled too much when it went around curves. Some people murmured that the water supply might never reach their places.

IN LATE AUGUST, Sam and Billy had come to see Ed and stared at him, not sure that they belonged to him.

"Your mother must be tickled now that the irrigation money is being spent, and the dam is being built," Ed sought with caution for information.

Sam answered, "Wagonloads of dirt for the fill have gone by a long time. Mother watches them. She's worried because she doesn't have anybody to dig our ditch to the flume. Billy and I can't get the shovel through the hard ground."

"She was going to get Portugee Joe to dig it," Billy said.

"I guess that fell through," Ed concluded.

The night Portugee Joe's cabin had burned, Ed had looked around the crowd and seen Eleanor. Her face was streaked with soot, and her hair, down for the night, blew about her head in the wind. She had not seen him, so he left at once.

"What's she going to do about her wheat crop?" Ed asked Sam and Billy.

"The man who came by with the reaper told Mom there was no sense to harvest the grain. There wasn't enough yield."

"Wheat wasn't supposed to be the real crop," he tried to console his sons. "Nobody knows for sure what can be grown until water's been put on the ground. They're still working on the dam. Maybe water will help in spite of all I've said. I don't know everything, kids."

Sam's face was desperate and grave. "People are beginning to be afraid what you said in the first place is true, Dad. It's too far to bedrock. The dam leaks right through the creek gravel. They should have dug to bedrock."

THE WATERUSERS STOOD on the walls of the dam and saw the water sink away. In the early summer it had risen somewhat behind the dirt fill, but now it was vanishing into the ground every which way.

Eleanor and the children sat on the steps for hours. Eleanor's hand went to her throat. Her ears rang with Ed's prophetic, words, "That dam won't hold water. You can't just dam up a creek with dirt and expect it to stay there."

Ed McLaren, serious-faced, sat stiffly on the seat of the buckboard pulled by the team. He drove to the foursome huddled on the cabin steps.

"Come to see if you need anybody to dig your ditch from the flume. I got the cattle sold and the rest are all right at the new Johnston place. I have a couple weeks I could dig."

Eleanor gathered her ragged children about her, tottered toward the wagon, and clutched the brake. She said, "No thanks, Ed. Nobody needs to dig our ditch. Everybody is saying it. The dam is no good."

Ed clambered down from the seat. He was afraid to touch her, but he did anyhow. He held her shoulders to stop her nervous twitching, and soon she was in his arms, leaning tiredly against him, with tears falling on her cheeks. The children were sobbing around them.

They cried together, "Let's go back home."

"Yes, let's go home, Ed," Eleanor said humbly. "I hope you can forgive me for being such a fool."

"O.K.," Ed said with a catch in his throat. "We've been a bunch of fools."

Sam and Billy cornered their stray puppy; Leila went behind the cabin to find her rag doll. Eleanor grasped the double pan of sourdough loaves.

"I was wishing I could put this bread into a good oven."

"I'll build a fire in the cook stove in five seconds," Ed promised. "We'll have fresh bread for supper."

They piled into the buckboard and rolled down the road to the house near the river, the house with the orchard around it. They would fetch their other belongings later.

"Who needs covers in this hot weather?" Sam asked.

"I WANT TO ask one favor," Eleanor said.

"Anything you say," Ed said.

"Never mention this whole business to me again."

"I sure want to forget. The sooner the better," Ed was quick to say.

He chuckled. A flood of life coursed through the old channels. He inadvertently became his true self again, pronouncing right from wrong.

"I never would agree before that irrigation could be anything more than a dreamed-up, get-rich-quick scheme, but a plan could be developed. I've been studying the matter. If there was one irrigation district for the whole valley, Indian lands included, one big one, financed in a businesslike way, irrigation-minded people could still have a chance. Maybe get some federal help for a dam on the Similkameen River—none of this little creek dribble!"

Eleanor nearly jumped from the wagon. "So! Now! Now! After all the talk! He begins to come through with ideas about dams!"

"My main objection was that everybody was in too big a rush."

A cry of rage came from the wagon bed. "Back off, you two! You fight as bad as ever after one hour together," Sam yelled.

Eleanor and Ed opened and shut their mouths in astonishment. Their son's grown-up orders quieted them.

Eleanor was glad to be done with dramatic defiances for the moment. She settled back in the seat. Her thoughts went darting to other things more precious than a mirage of a garden and a house in the desert. The loaves of dough on her lap must be punched down and rolled a second time.

When the rig stopped in the barnyard, the boys jumped out even before Ed could tie the reins of the harness to the brake. Eleanor first handed down the pan of bread, then Leila, wiggling so eagerly to go to her daddy's arms that she nearly fell. Sam and Bill made a beeline for the river, but their father's sharp whistle stopped them.

"How about a load of wood first! One of you take the bow saw and the other the axe."

The boys' faces kept their grins as they resumed their familiar old chores.

As Ed whittled shavings for kindling and made a fire in the cook stove, Eleanor rolled down the loaves and covered them with a limp gray dishtowel that Ed had been using for some time.

"Baking will kill any germs from this thing," she decided.

She went on a tour of inspection of the house.

Ed's overalls lay strewn about the bedroom floor as they had when she had first come to the house as a bride. Dead mice lay behind the couch after they had run there to die. Ed had scattered poison wheat in all the corners.

"Your notion of housekeeping!" she said with a trace of her natural asperity. "I'm not the only one who's been needing someone to take care of him!"

"I admit it," Ed was fast to assure her.

After the loaves had risen sufficiently, Eleanor placed them in the hot oven. Ed went to the store for a gallon of fresh milk and a pound of butter. Eleanor stewed summer apples that the boys picked from a tree in the orchard.

At nine o'clock the children went to bed with no urging. The mattresses were heaven after the straw ticks of the hot cabin on the flat. Eleanor put out of her mind that she was probably to sleep on sheets that had not been changed since she had done it. Even Portugee Joe had probably snored between them.

Ed went at dawn to his new feedlot to continue work on a shed he was constructing for wagons and machinery.

"I'll stay up and start cleaning," Eleanor said as he left the house. She had risen even before Ed to prepare his breakfast: bread and milk, fried eggs, and prunes. It was the same old fare, but to Ed it was infinitely better because of a woman's magic in laying it on the table.

When Ed came home, his hot supper was ready. Eleanor had boldly charged a large order at the grocery store. As she saw the family enjoying the products of her creation, Eleanor wiped a tear from her eye with a corner of her apron.

Their former mode of living easily returned. The boys had been dispatched during the day to the old cabin with suitcases and gunnysacks to fetch all the cooking utensils, clothing, bedding, and towels. Eleanor had scrubbed Leila in the washboiler and put up her hair on rags. The boys had scrubbed themselves in the river. All their clothes had been washed, dried, and patched in one day.

"Everybody's sure cleaned up," Ed noticed, "but we'll have to get some new school clothes. You boys have grown six inches apiece. Knickers ought to be the ticket."

Eleanor had also opened the doors and windows to air the house.

"It smelled musty," she said, avoiding the words "like a barn."

She had scrubbed the kitchen walls and the floors of the whole house on her hands and knees.

"Golly, Eleanor, I wish you'd learn not to knock yourself out," Ed told her.

Eleanor nearly giggled as she confided, "The sight of so much water sent me hog-wild."

After supper Ed shared some news with his wife: "Didn't do so bad with the cattle selling this year, even after losing those yearlings from bloat. That Jones' Fife of yours out there on the flat will make a good crop of hay for winter, too."

"It's your hay, Ed. You know it. You bought the seed."

"It's ours," Ed amended. "Have to harvest it right away."

Eleanor started back to church with the children on Sunday, but she dropped the Ladies' Aid, the Prayer Band, and the Mission Society.

"It's not that I love the Lord the less," she told Ed, "but I found out that those women are not as much my friends as I supposed."

"Now you're talking my language," Ed said and kissed her. "I think we're really married now. What say we stick together? Like a team in harness, both pulling one direction."

She hugged him back. It was as close to romance as they had ever come.

IT SURPRISED ELEANOR that her husband was going to amount to something after all when he purchased outright two thousand acres of additional grazing land on Mount Hull. She clucked over him like a proud hen with a first brood of chicks.

Eleanor was further surprised one afternoon when her brother Buford came to the house to tell her that he was leaving the Okanogan and going back to Walla Walla to manage the home place for their parents.

"For heaven's sake, how will Mort manage alone?" she worried. "Why on earth are you leaving him?"

"It's just got too thick," Buford said. "He'd slit even my throat for a nickel. When his new wife starts to boss me, it's time to pull out."

"New wife!"

She had been so preoccupied with her own household management that she had failed her brothers!

"When did it happen? I thought Mort would never marry!"

"He got himself a little bride after he came back from Olympia. He stayed over there the whole damn time the legislature was in session, trying to get that section 16."

BUFORD WAS STILL at the house when Ed arrived home, hot and dirty, from harvesting the mediocre hay crop on Eleanor's claim.

Eleanor, fluttering, burst out the news about Mort. Ed grunted without enthusiasm, "Who's the lucky girl?"

Buford cleared his throat. "Her first name's Betsey."

Ed and Buford exchanged cautious glances.

"She 'the Colt'? The one who lived with 'the Mare' and 'the Pinto'?"

"What are you talking about?" Eleanor demanded.

"I know her by sight and reputation," Ed remarked.

"You got her pegged," Buford said.

The Colt was the daughter of the Mare, who shared a bungalow among the willows near the bridge with the Pinto. The Mare's and Pinto's husbands, the story went, had taken French leave to the Alaskan gold fields. The abandoned wives had teamed up as a matter of survival. A lonely man could find an evening's entertainment in exchange for a cord of wood or a quarter of beef. The Colt had doggedly gone to school through the years. Bill and Sam knew her.

"She never plays with the other kids," they said. "She's more grown up."

"She's fifteen or sixteen years old," Buford said. "Knows all there is to know."

"The poor child!" Eleanor chose her tack. "I'll call on her at once!"

"They won't thank you, but go ahead," Buford said.

"My feelings are hurt that Mort didn't tell me, but I'll overlook it."

When Eleanor came home from her call, which was brief, she said to Ed,

"It really surprises me that a good-looking young girl like that would choose an older man. She wouldn't be obliged to."

"The way she and her mother have had to live, she knows a good thing when she sees it," Ed guessed. "Mort is gonna be a millionaire."

"To tell the truth, I'm a little miffed at Mort for the first time in my life," she said.

Mort, bringing Betsey, finally came to the McLarens on what Eleanor considered a return of her call. Mort was dressed in a dun-colored tailored jacket and trousers, with a brown tie. Betsey wore a matching dun-colored tailored skirt and a fancy fringed jacket in her role of indulged bride.

"Were you ever sore at me for letting you get stuck on that homestead?" Mort asked his sister in the course of the conversation.

"Of course not, Mort! We all lost out."

"Betsey thinks it would only be fair if I offered you a thousand dollars for a relinquishment on that homestead so you won't be out anything on account of my advice. I guess I'm getting soft in my old age in more ways than one."

"You silly thing!" Betsey cooed. "You're trying to make people think I have some influence over you."

"A thousand dollars! That's too much!" Eleanor was pleased and flustered.

"Take your papers downtown to my office any time; the money's yours," Mort said.

"I'll tell you right now, I'm accepting, Mort. And you folks stay to supper. Ed will be home in less than an hour."

When he returned, Ed managed to be civil throughout their visitors' stay for the evening meal. He had even answered Eleanor's whispered entreaty to put on clean gabardine trousers. The children, feeling awkward, kept quiet.

"We'll be down to your office in the morning to sign the papers, Mort."

"Not my claim," Ed said shortly. "I don't need to sign."

THE NEXT EVENING Eleanor handed the check to Ed.

"Bank this in your account. You see my brother didn't cheat me."

"You keep it."

"This check is perfectly good, and you know it! He didn't have to pay me anything. I just went off and left that land. You should be grateful."

Eleanor thought a thousand dollars for a relinquishment was a fair price. She put it in a savings account, and referred from time to time to her nest egg.

PEOPLE WHO HAD taken up homesteads on the flats drifted away from the community one by one or went to work for cattlemen and orchardists along the river. Some who had bought into the Waterusers' Association at the instigation of the Clements brothers developed a slow simmer of indignation that became a lawsuit or two to recover damages for fraud. The Waterusers' Association directors sold much of the abandoned homestead land to themselves at prices they chose at closed meetings.

Called as a witness at a suit against Mort, Eleanor averred, "No, my brothers did not use undue pressure to make me take out homestead land. They did not rob me, but bought my relinquishment."

Ed had driven her to the civil suit and home again wordlessly. It came sorely to Eleanor's memory that Ed had said, "Those wallopers are just figuring how to get a lot of homestead land cheap. They know the irrigation project will fizzle and people will pull out."

Coast papers and the Spokane *Spokesman-Review* reported that a legislative interim committee had been organized and was investigating sales of state lands to large private interests. Dishonest cruisers were decried in print, and the wholesale release of land to speculators was explored. Ed read the papers but remained silent to Eleanor.

SOME WHO HAD arrived on the new wave of population in the Okanogan decided to tough out the temporary worthlessness of the land and wait for real irrigation. Ed took part in planning an Okanogan-Oroville Irrigation District that would take water from the Sirnilkameen River.

A group of men met in the McLaren living room to discuss a "Report on a Proposed Irrigation System for the East and West Okanogan Valley Irrigation Districts," prepared by the Columbia Engineering and Construction Company of Wenatchee.

Eleanor listened but no longer cared if the Okanogan Valley had a dam that reached to the tops of the highlands or if it had none. She had decided to give way to the facet of Ed's makeup which impelled him to take a leading role in community affairs. He needed to be important to his neighbors, she concluded.

The proposed irrigation district became reality after James J. Hill of the Great Northern Railway supported the project and bought bonds. The wood flumes and open ditches served the district for sixty years.

What converted Eleanor to admiration of the system was that an indoor toilet became possible. Ed installed a bathroom complete with tub, sink, and flushing stool. The water for indoor use was stored in a reservoir that Ed constructed on a knoll above the house.

Having the winter feedlot entirely away from the residence also made life more pleasant for Eleanor. She did not mind so much anymore the way men made messes, but she never gave up starting the day with making her living room too clean for the comfort of some people.

BY THE FIFTEENTH year of their marriage, Ed and Eleanor McLaren had developed a stable pattern—united in a firm partnership to be "commensurate," the term used by the Forest Service to indicate those whose personal property and community stability made them desirable permanent lessees on the national forest.

Ed bought and sold cattle at the Old Union Stockyards in Spokane. The years were a continuum of hard physical labor combined with stringent self-discipline in management. He studied the science of cattle husbandry through the Department of Agriculture Forest Service bulletins. He read the advice of experts on how to determine the class of stock for a particular range, and he learned to estimate grazing capacity according to formulas given by the department. He studied books on managing cattle on the range, including the strategic placement of salt and water holes, and he read the Forest Service theories on multiple uses of the forest.

Eleanor would never travel with him to national and state cattlemen's meetings, but she always sent along a good supply of clean shirts to help Ed maintain his sense of adequacy in any assemblage.

At one meeting of the National Cattlemen, held in the South, an official for the Bureau of Land Management of the Department of the Interior gave an urbane talk about "Uncle Sam's Acres."

The speaker pointed out a current trend of thinking: "There is an increasing feeling that the private ownership of land does not work out to the best interest of the public. The present policy of the government is not to sell land. Uncle Sam is now a permanent landlord, recognized as a protector, no longer as a land agent. There is no longer a policy of placing land in the hands of private individuals, but a policy to retain all land holdings."

Ed pulled his old trick of challenging the speaker on the platform. In a new outfit of clothes designed to make him look like an old-time cattleman and a past president of the state association, he asked slowly and deliberately: "Since when has it become policy to retain public lands? Is there any such law? Last law I remember—Taylor Grazing Act of 1934—reads that the public domain was to be organized into districts 'pending final disposition to the public.' Isn't the Taylor Grazing Act still in effect?"

The man on the platform smiled, "Well, mister—I don't know your name—you've asked the question that takes a lot of answering. It is the policy of the government to keep title to public lands, to safeguard the best interest of all concerned, to recapitulate what I have been saying for the past twenty minutes; but it would take a book to trace the development of that policy."

"You're darn tootin'," somebody yelled. "It would take a book. A mighty long book."

"It so happens that I am writing such a book," the land management official answered with an edge in his voice.

"I'll read that book," Ed promised and sat down.

At the conclusion of the meeting, leaders of the cattle industry of the Southwest approached Ed to shake his hand and say they were glad that someone from the Northwest was present: the states with large areas of federally owned land must band together to fight creeping government domination.

IV.

Homecoming to Fire

18.

Return to Iowa

In University Village, at Ames, Iowa, Ed and Eleanor found their son Samuel a self-confident associate professor of agronomy with a family that included three active children. Andrea, Sam's wife, whom they had never met before, was a Nordic beauty whose curves had grown more ample than they had appeared in wedding pictures sent west. She made Eleanor and Ed welcome and good-humoredly shared household tasks with her mother-in-law, who, Andrea understood, needed a world to set in order. Eleanor picked up newspapers and folded laundry.

At Eleanor's insistence, Ed revisited his birthplace. Sam drove his parents to Boone, where the other two living McLarens of Ed's generation had remained. Eleanor had sent a card to give them fair warning. They had responded that the brother who had gone west many years ago was invited for Sunday dinner, to be preceded by church; also, their brother's wife, son, and family were invited.

Andrea decided to stay at home with the children.

Ed's brother Bob and sister Martha were the same souls that he had left behind him. Neither had married. Martha, who had renounced a beau, had spent most of her life as her mother's domestic servant. Bob had run the farm, played the church organ, and cried at Ma's funeral.

Ed could practically read their minds: "You could have shown the decent respect due your mother by at least attending her funeral. What did you ever do to prove yourself part of the family? You shook off your responsibilities as a wild youth. How can you return now and face those who followed humbly in the Lord's path and were faithful unto death?"

Everyone shook hands politely, but there was no hugging or kissing.

Martha showed the guests the scrubbed house, the bedrooms equipped with washbasins and slop jars, and the beds still covered with spreads that Ma had made.

"We'll have to leave almost at once for church," Martha said. "We were expecting you a little earlier. Bob can get our Ford from the barn, or since your car is already in the drive, it might just be simpler for us to go along with you."

Ed recognized no one at the church. The woman sitting in the adjacent pew could have been the giggly girl who had been smitten with him in his days at Professor Elson's academy, but her name was gone from Ed. She at least behaved like the flirt of yesteryear, rolling her eyes at the strangers and smiling expectantly for an introduction at the close of the service.

Martha said to her, "How do you do, Mrs. Brooks," and moved on.

Back at the farm, while the chicken fried for dinner, Bob conveyed Sam and Ed about the stands of corn, wheat, and oats which would become ensilage for the dairy cows. Sam kicked the soft, black loam underfoot and admitted, "We don't have soil like this anywhere in the Okanogan, do we, Dad?"

"Nope. Most of Okanogan County's Class IV soil. Pity people didn't realize it. Homesteaders went through a terrible time. The land produced wheat a couple years, then gave out. Lincoln County in Washington is different, of course. Good wheat land there."

"We don't complain about the Iowa soil," Bob said. "It's given a steady income for a hundred years."

"How do you work your rotation? Use any grass?" Sam asked.

"Every fourth year, usually. Sometimes with legumes. We plant grass for winter cover and plow it up in the spring."

Ed and Sam observed that Bob was uncomfortable.

When he said, "Let me show you how much feed we still have in the silo, Ed," Sam took the hint.

"I'll wander back to the house and see how they are coming with the chicken."

When Sam had reached the back porch of the house, Ed amusedly confronted his brother, "Well, out with it! What you got to say in private?"

Bob jerked guiltily. "What do you mean?"

"You got ants in your pants about something."

"I didn't intend to bring the matter up, but since you ask about use of the property, I wonder if you've come purely on a social visit."

Ed's little brother was still watching the size of his piece of cake. "You figure I'm gonna contest Ma's will? Don't you feel safe when I haven't done anything after all these years?"

"We couldn't know. I hope you don't think Martha and I were unfair. We decided it was Ma herself and not us who cut you off. We just left it that way because we thought it must have been the way Ma wanted."

"Don't pester yourself. I don't need anything you got. Ma's will didn't faze me."

BOB WAS CORDIAL throughout dinner. He heaped fried chicken on the plates.

Ed moved for adjournment first. "It's time for us to be getting back to Ames. Sam left his wife alone with the kids. She'll be expecting us before dark."

"Now I'm not leaving until the dishes are done!" Eleanor insisted.

Ed knew it was politic not to interfere with his wife's sense of duty, but as soon as she and Martha finished in the kitchen, he stood to go. Everybody shook hands.

As they drove away, Eleanor commented, "You were certainly in a rush. They are very fine people! A person almost wouldn't believe you could be a member of the same family."

Sam chuckled. "You can always know what Mom thinks about you, can't you, Dad?"

"Remember they cut me out of Ma's will," Ed slyly cooled Eleanor's enthusiasm for his siblings.

"Yes, that's right, too," she took his sarcasm at face value. "Oh, well, we live so far apart we don't have to grow too friendly with them. I promised Martha to write, and I will—as I always have."

"And speaking of wills," Eleanor continued a moment later, "have you said anything to Sam?"

As they drove along, Ed outlined his plan to retire. Sam agreed that Bill was the natural person to manage the Lazy Ear. Certainly, let him do it!

SAM TAUGHT CLASSES in the summer session. When he came home in the late afternoon, the whole family was together, the children usually commanding the most attention. Ed, who had thought vaguely of unburdening himself on the unsettling political campaign in Washington State, had few chances for private conversation with his son. When Sam suggested that they attend a Grange meeting without the women, Ed accepted.

"Want to go hear Old Bull DiSalle Friday night? He's running for some new political office or other. He's the speaker at the Grange meeting."

"Sure, I'd like to hear the walloper; heard him once before."

MICHAEL V. DISALLE stood on the platform in the Grange hall, smiled, and shook off the rounds of boos that followed his remarks.

Afterward Sam conducted his father to a neighbor's house. "You've been invited for a drink."

As a man who ran range cattle, Ed could discuss matters of interest to the Iowa feeders. He related the story of the Northwest cattlemen versus DiSalle under the Office of Price Stabilization.

"Newspapers had headlines like Prohibition days: 'Government Inspectors Raid Before Daylight.'

"They'd crow in the papers how many violations they'd netted. Sale of cattle on the legitimate market almost stopped. The eleven meat packing houses in Central Washington temporarily went out of business. Meat retailers had nothing to sell.

"At the Okanogan auction, slaughter cattle sales went down thirty percent in line with the Spokane and Portland auctions." The feeders could scarcely swallow their drinks for indignation.

"Even if the OPS is ended, we aren't rid of DiSalle in the Midwest!"

"Did you fellows read that letter Mollin sent around right after the Korean War?" Ed asked. "He told how Bull acted at the meeting in Washington, D.C., when the cattlemen went to see him."

"I was there in Washington!" a feeder spoke up. "These guys sent me as their representative at my own expense."

"Now, Harv, we offered to pay your expenses. Don't let Ed think we're a bunch of cheapskates."

"I forget who paid. We sure couldn't get anybody to pay attention to us in Washington. We all went to dinner at our own expense with DiSalle and some other bureau people. All anybody talked about was finding homosexuals in the State Department."

"What's that? Homosexual?" a man queried. "Hear that word all the time these days."

The man seated next to him leaned over and talked into his ear.

"One thing you notice about DiSalle," Ed changed the topic, "he gets the headlines."

"Oh, sure. He was a one-man show, all right. He came on time. He didn't stand for any discussion. He said the packer quotas for June were set at eighty percent of the previous June. Period."

"Didn't some newspaper guys call him on that?"

"He said he was talking off the record, and if they were gentlemen of the press, they would respect that."

"Funny how it leaked all over the country, isn't it?" Sam observed.

Ed made a friend of every man in the room. He became involved in an earnest discussion of the present danger of decisions made arbitrarily by administrative usurpation.

"With four million more cattle in the country and with more cattle on feed than ever before, DiSalle had no excuse for the low quotas, except to break the market," Ed averred.

"I told you my Old Man would be a distinguished Hawkeye returned," Sam bragged.

Driving home, he said to his father, "You made a big hit. I knew you would. You don't have a lot of formal education—oh, I guess it's pretty good for your day—but you sure are up on things! You knew more about the hard facts of the OPS than any of those feeders. Besides, you look so dam healthy and active for your age. Good outdoor life. I let 'em know, too, that you served in the early Washington State Legislature."

"You mighta mentioned too that I still have all my own teeth. Why don't you shut up?"

"Yeah, I got carried away," Sam laughed at himself. "Something I want to show you before we go home. Been saving a real surprise for you. Andrea and Mom won't want us back till the liquor goes off our breath anyhow. Have some materials in my office that made me think of you. Let's take a short detour."

"At home, I'm sound asleep in my chair by this time," Ed said, "but tonight I'm wide awake. Let's see what you have. Want to see your office."

ON THE CAMPUS of the Iowa State College of Agriculture, Sam escorted his father through the new Agronomy Hall, a sturdy, traditional brick building common to land grant institutions. Their steps echoed on the gleaming waxed tiles of the empty corridors.

Sam turned his key in the office door and switched on the lights. Lettered on the glass of the door window was: S. E. McLaren, Assoc. Prof. Agronomy.

"Big shot, aren't you? Have you been promoted since your last letter home?"

"They gave me tenure."

"What do you teach mainly?" Ed asked.

"Crop production and utilization—same things you taught me—sunshine, soil, and seeds. Ag. 508 is Biophysical Crop Ecology."

The compact office held a desk, metal files, telephone, and typewriter. The walls were lined with books and bound periodicals.

A young man of slight build, with dark hair and a Roman nose, appeared in Sam's doorway. "Hi, Mike," Sam greeted him.

"Hi, Sam. Came to see who was prowling around so late."

"Meet my father, Ed McLaren. He's visiting us from Washington."

"Pleasure. Mike Manchester."

"He teaches here, too," Sam said.

"I used to know some Manchesters—lived at Boone the same time I did."

"That's us! Did my dad look like me?"

"Sure did. Same build and color. He was kind of a scholar. He didn't approve of me, I guess. I was always showing off."

"Probably he felt the same as you inside. He told me that he felt backward when he was young."

"You must take after him, being a college professor. What's your field?"

"Forage is what I've studied and taught."

"I'll be darned. A specialist in grazing!"

"Dad ranges cattle over five thousand acres of government land—had a Forest Service permit forty-eight years—and has another five thousand acres of his own range. Has fifteen hundred acres of Taylor grazing land that was badly over grazed by wild horses for years. He's turned it nearly into a pasture," Sam put in.

"How much hay do you put up in Washington?" Mike wanted to know.

"Have some pretty hard winters. Generally I like to have a ton per critter. We been running three hundred head of cows on a cow and calf basis."

"See you know more about agriculture than any of us."

"Dad keeps studying. He reads every agriculture bulletin, every range management journal, and every livestock magazine that comes out."

"Not hardly!" Ed objected. "I do other things."

"Which reminds me what we came for. Good! Marty remembered to put them out. I asked her to find this literature especially."

He handed his father three pamphlets that had been lying on the desk: "Memorandum in re: Changes in Forest and Brush Cover and its Effect on Stream Flow," "Watershed Management in the Southeastern States," and "Reseeding Range Lands of the Intermountain Region."

"I can see this is valuable stuff. I'll have something to read while you're with your classes tomorrow. Anything special you want me to notice?"

"Certainly is. It's here in black and white that all the years you've been pushing range reseeding you've been on the right track! I remember how you jawed for years with the Forest Service to get them to burn brush and down timber that are causing deterioration of the range, and then plant grass."

"Researchers agree that range reseeding must become the national land management policy," Mike concurred.

"Never thought I'd see the day two people agreed with me," Ed confided. "The Forest Service spends all its budget preventing forest fires. They let the forest fill up with rotten timber and brush, then wonder why there's a forest fire."

"Top level policy sometimes lags behind the research divisions," Mike said.

Sam broke in, "This other paper makes the point that timber harvesting doesn't jeopardize the soil. It prevents excessive transpiration of moisture into the air from heavy forest and increases total water yield."

"That's what I've always maintained!" Ed declared. "If old timber is cut out, grass will take over and prevent erosion just as well as tree cover does."

The three students talked until midnight. Mike began a detailed interview of Ed on range plants in the Far West. He and Ed worried about the national infestation of Scotch broom.

"Wow! What time is it?" Sam exclaimed. "Andrea will have my hide."

The forage instructor said good night. "I feel some guilt at keeping you so long. I get on my own interests and buttonhole people who'd probably rather be in bed."

Sam chuckled. "Don't worry about buttonholing my dad. He's a great one for that himself."

Ed clutched the literature that Sam handed him.

"Mind if I take this stuff home with me to Bonaparte? I want to show it around. I'll mail it back."

"Keep it. I have other copies."

Shutting off the lights, they left Agronomy Hall and drove toward University Village.

"Mother always wanted you to believe what most people believed," Sam said. "Mostly she wants you to believe what her own brothers do. You were always grubbing for facts. Now that I've seen research, I appreciate what you were always up against."

"Your mother's a good woman. Has many fine qualities."

"Yeah, she's got better. Once she was downright bullheaded combined with stupid. I never have recovered from the year she went homesteading on her own. Us kids had to stay with her."

Ed cleared his throat. "You remember that? I'd think you'd have been too young for it to make much impression."

"God, no, Dad! I was eleven years old. You turned out to be right about the irrigation, remember?"

"I was never against dams. All I ever said was that a dirt-fill dam was no good and they should dig to bedrock and know the soil."

They sneaked into the house in the dark.

"Turn on the lights," Andrea called from the front bedroom. "Nobody's asleep."

In the morning, with a sense of urgency, Ed sat down to the experimental studies that Sam had supplied. He read deaf to Eleanor's and Andrea's clack; forgotten was the discomfort of an unfamiliar chair. After the children came home from school, he read on, undisturbed by whining and roughhousing.

Ed announced at the evening dinner table, "We better start back to Washington in the morning."

Eleanor flung up her hands.

"I was expecting to help Andrea with raspberry jam tomorrow. You haven't even brought out the papers for them to sign!"

"That won't take long," Ed said. "I have the papers in my suitcase. I've had everything appraised. The contracts show the legal descriptions. All we need to do is go to a notary. Somebody will be in his office by nine o'clock."

"I don't have any early classes tomorrow," Sam said, "but what's the rush?"

"Gotta check the mail, for one thing. We've applied for transfer of the leased land to Bill. It'll have to be recorded. Mainly, I want to get home fast to pass along that information you gave me."

"I see I made a strategic error," Sam remarked. "You're out of luck on the raspberry jam, Andrea. My fault! I gave Dad some materials on range management of public lands. He has to wave them under Hal Buck's nose."

"I've been reading all day," Ed said. "Business about the watershed you gave me last night ought to have public airing in the coming campaign. They're talking public land policy. I hate the whole West brushing up the way it is."

"Let's clear the table, Andrea!" Eleanor said, standing up from her place and taking in hand the mashed potatoes and bread. "The men will be sitting here all night! Dad gets worked up over every election. I almost dread going back home. He's picked out a candidate for Congress who'll promote McLaren religion."

"Not my religion, just good policy. Walt Horan is gonna be out of it one of these days; the party has to start grooming somebody to fill his shoes. Young fellow running first time can't beat Horan, of course, but he'll learn something for the next campaign."

"Seems candidates should talk about disposition of the public domain," Sam came to his father's defense.

"Too much government control!" Ed was off and away. "Lately every time you turn around you have to get some kind of permission or permit. You know that land, Sam, at the foot of Mount Aeneas, where we hold the mineral rights—I told Virg Correo he could take some of the nitrogenous material from the dry lakebed.

"Forest Service wrote me that the nitrogenous matter on the bed of the lake didn't come under mineral rights. Said I couldn't give anyone permission to move it. Correo would have to legalize his use of the forest with a special use permit!"

"I can see that would really make you mad," Sam said.

Carrying out a second load of dishes—the dessert plates and coffee cups—Eleanor muttered, "I bet if you fell down and broke your leg sometime I could go to one of your meetings and make the talk for you!"

"Back to Bill," said Sam, diverting his mother's attention, "I think he'll manage just fine. He has a good head."

"Bill will make a wonderful manager!" Eleanor said as she paused in the door to the kitchen. "All he's ever needed is a chance to show what he can do."

"He's gonna make a few mistakes at first," Ed forecast. "But that's how he'll learn. Hope the place hasn't gone to hell in a handbasket already."

19.

Cattle Auction

"**S**o you bought a tractor!" Susan exclaimed, her eyes narrowing. "That settles it! I can at least keep the house plans. They are paid for!"

She found Scotch tape in a kitchen drawer and began to fit the ripped pieces together.

"We're gonna get into trouble, Sue."

"Always into trouble! I wish there'd be just once we could have some fun before we die. Your dad said you could sell cattle," she reminded him.

"I wanted to see if we can't get a better price at the auction."

"Your dad will have a fit if you don't sell to Willis Barker."

"I know. Willis is comin' out to the place tomorrow. Let's see what he'll bid."

Susan spent the rest of the day putting the house and yard in order. She wished her lazy kids had not fled before helping her drag half the house furniture back in. Her head ached; she decided that she would "lay off the sauce" for an indefinite period.

Next morning at the rise of the ten o'clock wind, Willis Barker's pickup truck pulled into the yard at the Johnston place. He was a short, heavyset young towhead. Susan and Bill had known him all their lives. His first job was running the baling machine for his Old Man at Malott. He had grown into a muscular fellow from lifting hundred and sixty-two pound bales of hay from the compactor to the scales, then heaving the bales to the stack. He had saved his wages for years, and now bought and sold real estate with his spare cash.

Willis knocked on the screen door and rattled it for good measure.

"Hi, Susan. Bill around?"

"Didn't you see him at the corral? He must be in the barn."

Susan opened the door and went to the edge of the porch. She gave the sharp whistle that had been producing Bill for years.

Willis had seated himself at the kitchen table.

"Guess you need a cup of coffee," she told Willis, and poured one for him.

"Sure smells good," Willis said. "Did you get Bill?"

"He'll be in right away."

After scraping his boots on the back steps, Bill came into the kitchen.

"Been muckin' out the barn. How come you didn't come out to help, Sue?"

"I was coming in a minute."

Willis hitched his chair closer to the table and took another swig of coffee. "This is good stuff. I was up at the Briscombs just before I came here. Old Lady Briscomb asked me to sit down for a cup of coffee, too. She hadn't cleared off the breakfast yet, and when I put my arm down on the table, it stuck to the oilcloth. It musta been jam. It was sure sticky."

"Lucky you went to her house before you came here, mine doesn't look quite so much of the mess it is."

"Nope, the McLarens always have their dishes washed when I get there. Ma McLaren makes me nervous because it is always so clean at her place. She don't use oilcloth for tablecloths either."

"I know what you mean," Bill said. "We had to wash our faces and hands every time we went to the table."

"It's women like her who kep' us all from turnin' into slobs," Willis said. "Some o' these bachelors in the hills, I don't want to get down wind of' em."

"How's Irene?" Susan asked. "She sure is a cute person. You neatened up yourself when you married her."

"She's fine. Got her mother visiting her today."

Bill brought the subject of the visit into focus. "Aren't you a bit early in the buying season?"

"Maybe. But I was hearing that you are going to do the selling for the Lazy Ear this year. I want to do my groundwork. Your spread always has fat cattle with shiny hides, never a lumpjaw or a banger. Your Old Man and I have done a lot of business over the years."

"There are some steers up on the mountain," Bill said. "I'm darned if the Old Man wasn't right about one thing. That rangeland is sure brushing up. Went up to look over the herd, and seemed to me they were getting thinner instead of fatter. I was thinking maybe we'd leave the cows and calves in there and sell the steers fairly early this year. Not enough grass for all of' em; only don't tell the Forest Service I said so."

"Not a peep out o' me," Willis promised.

"Want to go up there and take a look?" Bill asked. "I'm not doing any more barn cleaning. Where are those damn kids, Susan?"

"Gone swimming. If they turn up, I'll have them finish the barn."

Bill and Willis drove off to the mountain in Willis's pickup. They returned three hours later; Willis let Bill out and drove away without coming into the house.

"You don't look too happy," Susan remarked. "What did he offer?"

"Couldn't get him to go higher than eighteen cents. Offered him twenty-eight steers. That's how many his truck and trailer can handle."

"How much do they weigh?"

'Willis says nine hundred pounds. He was willing to have them put on the scales at Van Wegen, but he's never off more than ten pounds."

"You could round 'em up and take them to the auction to see if you can get more. If not, let him have them."

Bill shook his head. 'Willis got sore. He said when he left the yard, he took his bid with him. Bet I can run those prime steers up to twenty cents.'

On the last Friday in July, Bill, with the grudging assistance of Tom, his college sophomore son, loaded the truck twice and transported twenty-eight steers to the auction yards at Bonaparte. The Lazy Ear steers were the sleekest and fattest on the premises; however, they would normally have weighed another hundred pounds at the fall sale.

Before the auction started, the buyers, poking with their canes, nosed through the livestock for sale in the pans. By one o'clock the tiered wooden seats were filled with buyers and others who just came to see the show. In the top row, an Indian baby suckled at its mother's breast.

Mark Olson, auctioneer, with a red bandanna around his neck and his Stetson on the back of his head, sang out, "Testing, testing, testing, can everybody hear me?" into the new microphone.

"Loud and clear," said the buyers from Spokane, Seattle, and Wenatchee, who sat in the front-row seats close to the ring.

"We got three pens to sell today," Mark said. "Let's go!"

The ringmaster cracked his whip. Three attendants whose job was to conduct animals in and out of the ring drove in four smelly, slobbery, and nervous cows that trotted about the enclosure in bewilderment.

"Four good young feeder cows to ya there. Turn 'em around. Got 'em real young. Boys, these little light cows are cheaper 'n dirt. Whatcha doin' up there? Gimme 24.6."

A buyer raised his right finger.

"Sixteen. Floor's sixteen. Let's build it up. Who'll gimme seventeen?"

"Sixteen and a half," Tim Brainard called. He hoped to double his herd by fall, to take advantage of his fiercely expensive meadows.

"Seventeen," said the auctioneer. He sang out, "Now, now, now, who'll make it seventeen and a half?"

Tim Brainard held up his finger again.

The Swift representative shrugged his shoulders. "Let him have 'em."

"Sold to Brainard!" Mark announced. "Get 'em outta here. See what they weigh."

They were herded out to the new electric weighing pen. Six hundred pounds apiece, Bill knew without listening to the man at the scales. The cows would have to be tested for Bang's disease and tuberculosis before feeding on the Brainard meadows.

The show grew increasingly exciting as the better stock were herded in.

"Now see here! See here!" Mark called. "Lazy Ear steers, off the range this morning! Where do we start? Seventeen?"

The Cranston Packing Plant man signaled at once.

"Seventeen and a half, seventeen and a half, seventeen and a half?"

Truway buyer Judd Thacker lifted his hand to indicate his first bid of the day.

"Eighteen, eighteen, eighteen!" Mark intoned.

At that moment, Tom Miller jumped in his seat. "Eighteen and a half! Eighteen and a half!"

Bill's heart thumped. He had been right not to let Barker have them for eighteen cents.

A man in fancy stockman's clothes, from the Old Union Stockyards clientele, raised his right forefinger.

"Here we go!" Mark exulted. "Lazy Ear steers, choice beef. Do I hear nineteen? Now, now, nineteen."

Old Man Cranston held up his hand.

"Nineteen and a half, nineteen and a half!" The Gibson man from Wenatchee raised the half-cent.

"Twenty, twenty, twenty!" Mark sang.

Old Man Metzger, who had come from Auburn in a threehundred-dollar suit, waved his hat.

"You're just tryin' to run up the bid," Old Man Cranston yelled.

"I said twenty, I mean twenty," Metzger yelled. "And I got money in the bank to pay with a check that isn't rubber!"

"You old son of a bitch," Cranston yelled. He stood up in his seat and began to pummel Metzger, seated next to him.

"Come on, gentlemen! It's gettin' hot in here! Twenty-one, twenty-one, twenty-one?" It was too much fun watching Cranston and Metzger for anyone to bid.

"Sold to Metzger, twenty cents!"

Bill followed his steers to the weighing pen. He glanced up in the bleachers and waved to Susan. She had driven in by herself. She was wearing a blue denim wrap-around skirt and a white cotton top. She looked like a million dollars in anything. Why had she taken a sudden interest in high fashion? And houses designed by architects! She waved happily back at her husband. Twenty cents was a lot better than eighteen!

Bill went back to the seats for the sale of the last half of his steers. This was the moment of glory. Seller of the Lazy Ear! The word had gone around that Bill was the new head of the outfit. Buyers that Bill had never seen before sang out bids that began at twenty cents. A fever raged among Metzger, Cranston, and a stranger.

"Sold to the gentlemen in the blue shirt! What's your name, sir? Donaldson. O.K., Mr. Donaldson. Twenty-one!"

Before everyone's startled eyes, Old Man Metzger in his three- hundred-dollar suit flew end over end into the sales ring. His bidding competitor Cranston had knocked him over the ropes from the buyers' seats into a pile of manure that had been building for hours. He let out such a yell that a White-faced Hereford steer galloped out the exit without being sold.

The audience was roaring at the unexpected entertainment.

To Susan, falling in cow shit was scarcely worth notice. She paid no attention to the roistering at Old Man Metzger's expense. Instead she was doing arithmetic in her head: "Nine hundred times fourteen times twenty-one cents; plus nine hundred times fourteen times twenty cents."

"Five thousand one hundred sixty-six dollars!"

The check to the architect, Weston Sand, would not bounce. Neither would the tractor down payment! She wondered how much she had been charged for beer and wine for the barbecue. She had better pay that charge account before Dad and Mother McLaren came back to town.

She left her seat in the bleachers and drove home.

Bill arrived at dinnertime with two checks: one from Donaldson, who apparently did most of his buying in Spokane, and one from Metzger's Packing Plant, Auburn.

"You better get to town in the morning first thing and put in these checks," Bill told Susan.

As soon as she had bullied Glenna and Deanna into washing the dishes and making the beds the next day, Susan went to town in the Ford and presented the checks at the bank.

The cashier, instead of accepting them for deposit, left her cage and was a long time coming back.

"I'm sorry, Susan," said Joanne, the cashier. "This check from Donaldson can't be verified. Mr. Lund doesn't know the gentleman. His check is probably perfectly good, but we'll have to wait for confirmation from Spokane before adding it to your account."

Susan felt blank. She had never dealt with insufficient funds before. Arthur Lund always covered everyone's check until the smoke settled. Everyone had capital somewhere.

"Metzger's check is good, isn't it?"

"Yes, certainly. But he stopped payment!"

"Stopped payment! Why?"

"He isn't coming to Bonaparte sales anymore. His spill in the cow manure yesterday turned him sour on all of us."

Feeling frozen, Susan went back to the street. She had planned to charge bread, cooking oil, sugar, and pork and beans at Prince's store; but what if they couldn't be paid for? She immediately left town and sped up the highway to the Johnston place. She changed to Levi's and went to the stable, saddled a mount, and rode to the England place to find Bill. He would be at the pool at the bottom of the falls. This morning he had grumbled, "Should have had salt out a week ago at the waterholes. Knocked off to dig your damn barbecue pit."

At noon she found him watching the herd at the drinking spot among the pines. The White-faced Herefords were lying down, chewing their cuds.

Bill's opening remark was, "Three or four critters have lost their calves. Might as well sell them, too. Tomorrow gotta round these up and put 'em in the corral to spray 'em. Got ticks all over 'em. I'd appreciate it … Say! What the hell are you doing here? You were going to town to put those checks in the bank. Wrote some checks this morning for salt and tick spray."

Susan dismounted and pulled the checks fro her Levi's pocket. "I've already been to town. They wouldn't accept either of these at the bank."

Bill's eyes blazed. "What the devil!"

Bill jumped on his paint horse. "Come on! We're goin' to town together. Lund always takes the checks and waits for the dust to settle!"

"He did for Dad!"

By the end of the afternoon Bill and Susan had learned that Donaldson wasn't anybody's representative from Spokane. Arthur Lund had called the Old National Bank in Spokane. He had written thirty-six hundred dollars in checks with insufficient funds to the buyers at the Old Union Stockyards. Donaldson had loaded fourteen Lazy Ear steers at the railroad depot in Bonaparte into a cattle car bound for Chicago; the man had ridden away in the caboose. Whether he would return to make good his checks on his Old National Bank account was unknown. They would run the check through again next week.

"What's the matter with Old Man Metzger's check? He's been at Auburn for as long as I can remember people comin' to the ranch."

"There's nothing wrong with his check," Arthur Lund said. "Only he stopped payment on it."

"What the hell for?"

"Pure cussedness," Lund said. "He didn't enjoy getting knocked into the cow shit in his new brown suit. Says he's never coming back to Bonaparte again."

"I wasn't the one who knocked him into the shit. It was Old Man Cranston."

"I know that," Arthur Lund chuckled. "Maybe he's calmed down a bit by now. Let's give him a call. He hauled off the cattle. You can charge him with theft."

"It wasn't Bill McLaren who messed up your suit," Lund argued into the phone. "Whaddya mean, not coming back to our sales? We have the best cattle in the state!"

At the end of five minutes of listening, Lund began to smile.

"Lettin' him take it out in cussing," he said in an aside to Bill and Susan.

They squirmed in their chairs until Lund hung up the phone and said, "Give me Metzger's check. I'll have Joanne deposit it to the Lazy Ear.

"How come you took the checking account down to three hundred fifty dollars, Bill?"

"Balance is less than that by now," Bill said. "I wrote two more checks this morning."

Lund pursed his lips. "You realize our minimum balance is two hundred dollars. I count interest on overdrafts."

"Yeah, you're well-known for that," Bill said ruefully. "You musta made a mint on covering overdrafts after cattle sales."

Arthur Lund patted his paunch.

"You can see that I eat well. I give a lot to charity, too."

Everyone knew that Arthur Lund had financed the Dominican sisters in their hospital and nursing home projects in the valley.

"Thanks for straightening out that one check," Bill said. "I don't know what to do about the other."

"It'll come through, too," Mr. Lund said. "I just remembered who Donaldson is. I know his uncle in Puyallup. He's good for it. While we're about it, let's make another call."

Mr. Lund had Joanne get George Donaldson in Puyallup.

"I'm holding Don Donaldson's check for twenty-six forty-six for insufficient funds, George. What you want me to do? Pay it at twelve percent?"

"That kid will land me in the poor farm yet! I been pickin' up his checks all over the state. No, you skinflint! No twelve percent. I collect the interest on this one!"

The remainder of the conversation on the other end was inaudible to Susan and Bill, but they heard Mr. Lund finally concede, "All right. I owe you one."

Mr. Lund relayed a message: "Will you be satisfied by a cashier's check from the Puyallup Valley Bank, mailed tomorrow?"

Bill nodded vigorously.

"Thank God!" Susan breathed.

They handed the rubber check over to Arthur Lund.

"Let him get by with that—shouldn't have done it," the banker said. "You have to learn to watch out for these fellows who skin things, Bill. That Donaldson buys up a carload of cattle here and then rides with them to the Chicago market. Depends on his uncle to make his checks good. Makes thirty percent on our local cattle."

Suddenly Mr. Lund had shed his customary role of banker. "So you're takin' over for the Old Man, Bill. You can do it. But you should have sold your cattle to Willis Barker. Van Wegen doesn't write rubber checks."

"Dad told me," Bill said courageously.

"Understand you were showing some house plans around at the barbecue, Susan," Mr. Lund said. "Don't blame you for wanting a new house. Make Bill spring for it."

"Bill has bought a new tractor," Susan sighed.

"Look here, young lady. If he can have a new tractor, you can have a new house. Talk to me about finance later in the fall."

"How'd you like to get on the new hospital board, Bill? Thousand-dollar donation is what your dad sent in every year. You planning to continue?"

Bill's mouth gaped. "Didn't know Dad was that free with his money."

"He's free but he's careful. He's always been civic-minded. Gives to political candidates with proper views, too. You doin' anything?'

Susan laughed, "Bill is strictly a cowman. The other day my neighbor called—wanted me to join the League of Women Voters."

"You should do that, Susan," Mr. Lund said. "I mean seriously. The second generation needs to take hold."

Susan grimaced but yielded, "They want a coffee party for candidates at my house. Guess we can oblige."

"Good girl!"

The banker stood and offered his hand to Bill.

"I shoulda sold those steers to Willis for eighteen cents. Haulin' is worth two cents. Now Willis is snickering at me."

"Nobody has told anything to Willis Barker," Arthur Lund said. "Don't worry, Bill. You're solid. Just new on the end of the rope. Your dad has been my customer since I opened my first branch at Riverside in 1904."

The couple backed out of the office of Ed McLaren's lifelong friend.

"So much for our wild fling at life!" Susan said wryly. "Old Lund was feeling the need to discipline us probably because your dad left him to baby tend."

"More 'n likely."

ON THE WAY back to the Johnston place, they made plans to get the haying under way.

"You don't have Mom to help in the kitchen this year," Bill said. "The girls will have to pitch in. The tractor is being delivered to the place tomorrow morning; got to figure the damn thing out. We'll still need a couple hands: swather and baler.'

Judd Thacker, driving a Buick, called at the Johnston place in the middle of the haying. Susan, rolling pie crust, looked out the kitchen window.

"Dammit!"

One kiss from him at the barbecue had been all she needed to determine that Judd Thacker held no attraction for her. Even though she had been high at the party, she remembered the repulsion she had felt at his slobbery assault.

She hoped that he would look about the premises for Bill, but he came directly up the back porch steps and rattled the screen door. "Anybody home?'

She had washed her floury hands and wiped them on her Levi's. She said, "Hi," and pulled the latch to let him in.

"Hi, yourself! Came by to say I had a wonderful time at the open house, but it was so noisy. Never did get a chance to finish the stories of our lives that we started in Omak."

She pulled out a chair for him to be seated at the kitchen table and handed him coffee. "The story of my life! Some story! 'Hurry up and finish the housework so you can help fix the fence.'"

Judd nodded that he understood what she meant. "Ever read that book, *A Rancher's Wife Leads a Hell of a Life*?"

"Memorized it."

She helped herself to coffee, sat down opposite the Truway salesman, and fished out a cigarette from the pack in her pocket.

Judd flicked on his cigarette lighter and held the flame under her chin. He was so strenuously gallant that Susan was forced to play actress in a moving picture in which men actually lit women's cigarettes.

"Saw you up in the bleachers at the auction a couple weeks ago," Judd said. "Bill got top price for his steers."

"Out-of-town checks were slow clearing the bank," Susan said.

"Truway checks are always good," their representative said. "Only the company puts a lid on what I can pay."

"You made one bid on our steers, I noticed."

"Have to stay out of price wars. I backed off. Wasn't that a riot when Old Man Cranston decked Old Man Metzger! Old Metzger is an ornery bastard."

"Bill probably won't come in till suppertime," Susan said. "They're haying on the mountain now, so I packed lunches."

She meant to hint that she was getting bored with stale gossip, but Judd seemed to think she was hinting something else.

"Guess I can undo my tie then. I'm curious. How come Bill lets you run around loose? Doesn't he know somebody is apt to move in on his range?"

"Bill and I got married at about the age of twelve," Susan responded quickly.

"To all intents and purposes, you mean?"

"Right. He doesn't have to ask me my life story. He could write it if he could spell."

"I was married like that till a year ago," Judd confided. "Then my wife tells me I've been away on buying trips long enough for her to make her own circle of friends. She wants to marry her steady boyfriend."

Susan felt silly and disoriented when Judd plopped his moist hand over hers. "I haven't had any loving for a year, Susan."

"Must be tough," she said. She snuffed out her cigarette, rose from the table, and went to the back door. She had been lying about Bill being on the mountain with the haying crew. Tom was driving the tractor this summer and wouldn't let his Old Man on the seat. Susan had noticed Bill by himself below the house. She whistled sharply.

Bill, ready to be annoyed, came up from the river. "Got a cow down with boxweed. What's the trouble?"

"One more buyer. Fresh guy."

Bill glanced into the kitchen. "Don't get conceited. The White-faced Herefords are still the main attraction."

"I ought to blab about that pass," Susan thought. "Only Bill'd blame me, not Judd."

Bill walked past her into the kitchen to greet Thacker. "See you had a cup of coffee. Want a fill-up?"

"No thanks. If I drink more 'n one cup at each place, I'm swimming in the stuff by nightfall."

"Guess that would be the case, all right."

After he had filled a coffee cup for himself, Bill put the pot back on the burner. "I'm not sellin' any more cattle till they get off the range."

"Not at twenty-one cents, sight unseen?"

"That's what I got the other day."

"We transport 'em, weigh 'em, slaughter 'em, and ship in our refrigerated cars right out of the Okanogan, all expenses paid by Truway."

"Sounds O.K. But I'm holding off another month."

"I'll be back," the buyer said as he stood. "You must be waiting for your Old Man to show up. When's he comin' back?"

20.

A Campaign Rumor

Eleanor fretted over the unseemly suddenness of their leave-taking all evening, but she began at once to schedule her course. She excused herself as soon as the evening dishes were done and went to the bedroom to take her linen suits off the hangers and fold them with tissue paper into her suitcase.

"What time does the train leave?" she asked when Ed came to the bedroom.

"We've got a compartment on the train that pulls out at one o'clock. We can eat in the dining car."

"How did you manage all this?"

"Sam called the station just now. We already had our roundtrip ticket."

"I give up," Eleanor said. "I suppose you have a notary lined up, too."

"No, but Sam is sure somebody will be open for business in Ames. Big town now."

THE WHOLE FAMILY accompanied Grandma and Granddad to town to see them off. The children behaved when their parents were busy in the attorney's office. They sat in the waiting room while the adults went to a conference room to sign the legal papers.

"You're supposed to sign, too," Ed said to Andrea. "Got your name all typed in."

"Dad McLaren, you are one swell guy!" Andrea exclaimed.

STANDING OUTSIDE THE window of the compartment in which the grandparents were to travel, Sam's family waved a cordial farewell.

When they were in their seats, Eleanor remarked, "Andrea is prettier now that she has filled out a little from being a mother. In her pictures, she was so spindly when she and Sam got married."

Eleanor waved one last time.

THEY RODE IN the compartment for two days back to Walla Walla to reclaim the Fairlane.

On the way East, Eleanor had worried about the cost of the trip. "We don't really need this whole sitting room to ourselves."

Ed had decided on a compartment because he knew that Eleanor was inclined to be shy and insecure among strangers. She accepted the arrangements when Ed warned her that if she rode in an open railroad car and only had a berth at night, she would have to show her underdrawers when she climbed up the ladder to her bed.

On the return train trip, Eleanor stayed in the cubbyhole and read copies of *Better Homes and Gardens* that Andrea had given her. Ed roamed from car to car to visit with anyone willing. He came to the compartment at mealtimes to take Eleanor to the dining car. As they ate, he could tell his wife the life histories of half the other passengers.

LEILA, STILL HEAVILY pregnant, met them at the Walla Walla train depot and drove them to the ranch for the night. At early breakfast next morning, Leila's husband Hal chuckled, "Notice your dad's got all the luggage packed into the trunk. He was up before I was. You rarin' to go, Dad?"

"Yeah, had enough travel. Time to see how Bill's doing."

"It's been a long trip," Eleanor acknowledged, "but it was wonderful seeing all of you. When is that baby due, Leila? I ought to stay till it comes, but I'm afraid to let your dad drive so far alone."

Leila replied at once, "I'm fine, Mom. I just pop 'em out right after breakfast, and I'm up cooking dinner by nightfall."

Hal pretended to choke on his coffee. "She's a barefaced liar! I let her sleep in until next morning."

"Us girls do all the cooking and dishwashing for days," the eldest daughter, Madge, was indignant.

When they reached Omak, it was late at night. They were only twenty-five miles from home. Ed, having driven the Fairlane all the way from Walla Walla, suggested to Eleanor, "We could get a room overnight at the Jim Hill Hotel."

"That's just one more expense! I hope that boy you hired hasn't let my garden dry up!"

"If I drive any farther, I might go to sleep at the wheel," Ed had to admit.

The registration clerk at the hotel knew Ed well. "So! How was the trip, folks?"

"Swell," Ed replied. "Mighty tired right now."

"You bet. I understand. Got a real nice room at the head of the stairs. I'll carry up your suitcases."

"Not necessary," Ed said staunchly.

They finished breakfast in the Jim Hill dining room by seven o'clock and were on their way again. The sun was an orange threat in the cloudless dome overhead. The hills were tawny as straw.

"It's gonna be one hot morning," Ed observed. "Bill will likely be haying and glad there's no rain."

Ed unlocked the front door and carried in the suitcases. Eleanor exclaimed, "Whew!" and went to the kitchen and flung open the back door, which had never been locked.

"The air is stale!"

She sped through the house and raised every window.

"I can't understand how so much dust collected," she cried, with eager anticipation of conquering the film on table tops and dressers.

Ed drove the Fairlane into the garage. He was relieved to close the door for the rest of the summer on the fancy touring car.

At eleven o'clock Ed started the pickup, which had been parked for weeks beside the toolshed. He topped off the tank at the pump. "Going downtown to collect the mail."

THE POSTMASTER HANDED over the counter a cardboard box overflowing with a haystack of bills, advertising, magazines, and letters.

As Ed lugged the box along the sidewalk, he was hailed by Hal Buck. "Ed! Good old Ed! Sure glad to see you! Sure did miss my lifelong friend!"

"You want something, lifelong friend?"

"Not a thing! Just glad you're home."

"Well, thanks. Only been in town a couple hours."

"First thing you want is the mail, of course," Buck rattled on, then paused to emphasize the importance of his next remark.

"Remember there's nothing I wouldn't do for old Ed."

"That's good news. For starters, did you take those papers up to Gaston like I asked you to?"

"Nope. I didn't."

"'Nope?' One favor I ask and you muff it!"

Buck splayed his hands. "Dammit, you asked me to take that stuff up there, but I got to thinking maybe I shouldn't."

"What the hell you jabbering about?"

"I was talking with some of the guys. They're not sure they're for Gaston after what he said at the Injun encampment at Omak. He's puttin' it into their heads that maybe the Colvilles should run their own sawmill instead of disbanding."

"You been talkin' to Mort! The hell with you!"

"Don't get sore at me! I'm on your team."

"Shut up! Where are those papers? I'll take 'em up myself. The reason I asked is I have some more dope to add to the pile I gave you already."

"God Almighty! You act like I been puttin' a knife in your back!"

"Where're those papers? Nobody could ever replace some of 'em!"

"Still in my car. It's down at the garage bein' serviced."

"I'll go along with you and get 'em right now! Didn't mean to put you to any trouble."

"Don't do that. I'll bring 'em to your house in the morning and we'll go into a huddle. We can't talk here."

"Suit yourself. I see Mort is pulling another sashay to get his hands on Injun land!"

Ed stalked away from Buck, who called, "See you in the morning. You take it easy!"

HE SPILLED THE boxload of mail on the dining table. Eleanor at once began to sort through the mound to find the letters from Iowa. Ed's eye zeroed in on an official envelope mailed from Spokane from the U.S. Forest Service. He ripped it open and quickly read the letter.

"Bill's in for a shock. Everything has gone to hell in a handbasket, just like I knew it would!"

Letter in hand, he headed for the front door.

"What now! Where are you going?"

Without hearing her question, Ed was gone, banging the screen door and revving the pickup motor.

ELEANOR, SIXTY-SEVEN YEARS of age, gray-haired but still pretty from a lifetime of scrubbing her face fresh each morning with soap and cold water, stood among the midsummer array of her flower garden. Peonies, petunias, cosmos, calla lilies, roses, and Oriental poppies were in a profusion of bloom. It was still early for the fall gladioli and asters, but the plants were thriving. The slow-witted but conscientious neighbor boy whom Ed had hired to water and weed the garden had done his work.

Eleanor's uneasy mind could not concentrate on the beds. She looked to the bare, harsh peak of the mountain to find a settling perspective.

Ed was becoming both upset and irritable in the way he always did over the years when embroiled in public fights. She had endured times when her husband was so unpopular that people threatened to run him out of town on a rail. How Ed got into trouble was by always speaking what he felt to be the truth when nobody wanted to hear it. He had battled over branding laws, increases on freight rates on cattle, and irrigation projects. She acknowledged that he had influence, but it was not easy to be the wife of a man always in a fracas. Each time he swore that he was through, but he seemed to sustain physical blows from sheer disappointment if any of his pet ideas were not eventually accepted.

She must pick the flowers immediately; she would have Ed take them to the Dominican sisters at the new town hospital. Vaguely insecure, she picked bouquets. After storing the flowers in cans on the back porch, she called Prince's store and ordered groceries. They promised to deliver by four o'clock. For her lunch, she went to the basement and selected a jar of green gage plums. She had done no canning this year. Her shelves were full of jars of fruit canned last year and not eaten.

Deciding that it was good to keep busy, Eleanor found stationery to write to Sam and Andrea in reply to the note that had been in the mail.

"Dear Folks," she began in her neat schoolteacher script.

"Thought you might like to hear we got home all right. We certainly enjoyed our visit. Dad was tired from driving the last part of the trip. As far as I can see, he isn't in as much pain as he was, although he won't say. I mean his pain in the arm that I told you about. He doesn't hold it up in the air the way he was doing to ease the pain. Other times he looks sort of fagged out as though he might have the flu. He can't sit still and take it easy the way he should. He does a lot of running around without much reason. He took off just now without saying what he was going to do.

"He never pays attention to anything I say, but you might write to him, Sam, that he should get another medical checkup—not that it will do much good.

"I shouldn't start a letter with a long tale of worry like this. You won't even read it. So enough about Dad.

"Andrea, my roses are really lovely this year; have been every year since we got the sprinkling system for the flower garden. The boy Dad hired to keep down the weeds did all right while we were gone. Dad is much more thoughtful about things than he used to be. The district flower show will be held in Okanogan next week. Some of my new varieties are worthy of competition—if I can get Dad to take me."

Eleanor looked up from her writing when she heard a car in the driveway. Ed would not be coming back yet. Then she recognized her visitors—her brother Mort and Betsey, his wife. She wished that Mort had come alone.

"I've never been able to warm up to that Betsey," she had confessed to Ed.

Betsey waited in the front seat of the Hudson until Mort came around from the driver's side and opened the door for her.

Mort was seventy years and twenty-one days old, Eleanor knew. Betsey was fifty, still playing the child bride. Her ash blonde hair was a tight cluster of curls on top of her head. She wore a pleated white skirt and a white top embroidered with bright peasant figures. On her feet were white patent leather pumps.

She and Mort had never had any children. "Baby" was Betsey herself.

Mort wore neat, dressed-up cattlemen's gabardine pants and a tailored beige shirt. His face, naturally florid, had additional color from a hefty amount of highballs consumed each evening.

But he was Eleanor's brother.

She shoved away the stationery and went to the screen door to let them in.

"My!" she said cordially. "What a surprise! How did you know we were home?"

"Hi, Sis. Didn't know; just thought we'd drop by and find out."

"How nice. Lord knows where Ed is off to."

The visit was unusual. Eleanor and Mort had not been close since his marriage. Mort and Betsey, even though they owned the largest ranch around Bonaparte, were seldom in the country. They had turned over their place to a full-time manager and crew. In Spokane, they kept an apartment year round as their headquarters. They took tourist excursions to Spain, Australia, Alaska, or wherever Betsey wanted to go.

Betsey seemed to have a guiding hand in Mort's affairs, whereas Ed made decisions, such as planning to sell the timber to Biles-Coleman, without mentioning them to Eleanor.

"We can't stay," Betsey said. "We have an appointment at the office downtown to see what the bookkeeper has been up to at Clements Realty while we've been gone."

"Oh, so you've been away, too?" Eleanor queried politely.

"Yeah, Betsey always wanted me to take her to Mexico, so we went down to Acapulco. Ought to see it."

"Glad we're out of there, now, though," Betsey added. "It was getting really hot! Everybody goes to sleep in the middle of the day."

"I couldn't stand that!" Eleanor had to be honest.

"Mort couldn't either," Betsey said. "I didn't mind it much. I can curl up anytime like a cat."

"You sure can, Baby," Mort said fondly.

"I'm at least going to give you a cup of coffee," Eleanor said. "I can't ask you to lunch. We don't have a thing in the house. I cleared out all the bread and crackers so that nothing would be stale."

Mort cleared his throat. "Aw, come on, Sis! Sit down. Everybody drinks too much coffee. Let's just chat a second."

"Well, all right."

She sat down at a hard chair at the dining table. Mort and Betsey took chairs across the table from her.

Eleanor noticed that Betsey twice opened her mouth to lead the conversation, then silenced herself at a shake of Mort's head.

"Do you have some special reason for coming by?" Eleanor asked sharply.

"Not really," Betsey purred. "Only Mort thought maybe he should be a little bird and whisper in your ear before you hear the news from somebody else."

"News? What news?"

"Oh, nothin' personal, Sis."

"What then?"

"Ed McLaren and the messes he gets himself into!"

Eleanor felt a sinking in her stomach. "I don't know of anything particular."

"It's all dirty politics, Eleanor," Betsey confided.

"Ed hasn't been around to talk politics with anybody."

"Talk's going around behind his back," Mort chuckled.

"Talk? What talk?"

"Before he went on his trip, Ed made himself clear that he was supporting Delbert Gaston from Conconully for Fifth District congressman. That guy's come out against tribal termination when everybody in the country is crying for more hay land, and the Omak and Oroville Chambers of Commerce have passed resolutions favoring termination. Them damn Injuns want their one point three million acres for their own hunting and fishing after Gaston talked to them on the Fourth of July. He's a quarter-breed."

"Ed thinks the Indians shouldn't sell their birthright for a mess of pottage, or some such nonsense," Eleanor concluded.

"You hit the nail on the head, Sis. You're the real brains of the McLaren outfit!"

"No, I'm not," Eleanor said firmly. "Ed has a good business head. He's for that Gaston because he's always had a soft spot for the Indians."

Mort smiled. "You're really on track, Sis. More than you know."

'Who is this Gaston anyhow? I thought he was the grandson of Old Man Westmore, who married a squaw. That family has as much land as you do if you put all their allotments together."

"That's the big question," Betsey tittered. "Who is this Gaston anyhow?"

"I don't know what you are talking about," Eleanor said.

"That's the pity of it," Mort worried. "Just ask Ed when he gets home, 'Who is this Gaston anyhow?' He won't have much to say."

Eleanor pushed herself from her chair at the table and stood up. "You're bothering me. Ed isn't too well. I don't want him mixing in any more political campaigns."

"Now we're seeing eye to eye, Sis. I don't want him mixing in the campaign either. He's on the other side of the bed from most of us on account of a candidate born on the wrong side of the blanket."

"Mort, I can't believe you are talking to me like this! Say what you've got to say so I can understand it."

"Hate to be crude—only maybe you better take a hint about the gossip building up."

"What does 'born on the wrong side of the blanket' mean? Fancy word for bastard?"

"'Catch colt' is the real description," Betsey offered with a giggle.

Eleanor was dizzy and outraged. "This is why I don't like politics. The smears!"

"Not me. I'm no state's witness," Mort disclaimed. "Just this rumor somebody started."

"You have to admit it's possible to be true," Betsey strove for frankness. "They say Ed was practically shacked up with her at one time."

"Ed! Shacked up with who?"

"We gotta draw you a picture, Sis, for your own protection. Remember, years ago, when you stayed here to make good on your homestead land, and Ed went to the coast to the legislature? Ed went everyplace with Gaston's mother, born Analix Westmore. Ed was helpin' queer my deal for state school lands I wanted to buy."

"Now I understand, Mort. I don't exactly appreciate your telling me this, especially for the reason that you're doing it. I certainly am not going to say a word to Ed!"

"Don't expect you to. My only thought is for you to do what you can to keep Ed home."

Eleanor trembled as she saw them to the door.

OUTSIDE BILL AND Susan's house, Ed paused. A dozen extra cars were parked in the yard. Feminine voices told him the vehicles were the means of transport for a gang of females.

He heard Susan's voice, "How do you like this dress? I shopped for it in Wenatchee. I haven't had a decent rag for years. If I'm going to be a new member of the League of Women Voters, I have to show some class."

"It's very smart, Susan," a throaty voice said. "Before we get started on planning the reception for the candidates, we're dying to know your version of the story Betsey Clements is telling."

"Oh, that Aunt Betsey cut me into a corner like a calf she was going to have butchered. She made sure I heard it all."

"She's Bill's aunt by marriage, isn't she? Why is she spreading the gossip?"

"She's Bill's aunt by marriage, but the whole family can't stand her. Mort has given her chapter and verse about the catch colt business."

"Oh, nuts," another voice lifted. "Ed McLaren is an inhibited old Presbyterian in spite of his cussing; you pin the old ladies down that are doing so much talking, and not one of them can prove that he ever made a pass at them! Mort is using the Ladies' Aid to help him get the reservation thrown open."

"Mort knows Dad will hear the rumor," Susan said. "He's making sure Dad will stay out of things. You're right, Cora. If Gaston makes too big of an impression on the voters, there goes his chance to buy the Indian reservation for two ponies and a jug of whiskey! Only he'll let the BLM or the U.S. Forest Service buy it, then lease it to him."

"That's dirty pool if ever I heard it! The old landgrabbers must be scared to death of Del. He's somebody who won't just take orders," another voice broke in.

"What of it, even if the rumor is true? Lots of white men lived with squaws in the early days, and everybody knows it!"

Susan was incredulous. "Janie! You believe it! Think how a dirty story like this will hurt Mother McLaren!"

Before Janie could reply, a sweet-voiced demurrer broke in: "Susie, darling, did you ever notice old Ed's lazy ear? It's where he got his idea for his cattle brand."

"You think it looks like Del Gaston's lazy ear? Well, people can put this into their pipes and smoke it! Mrs. Caliente has told me fifteen stories about Mort worse than this one about Dad McLaren. Mrs. Caliente used to work at the tavern before Prohibition. Mort was always picking up the Indian girls who sat on the steps running combs through their red-dyed hair. Then he married Aunt Betsey, who was no angel herself in her long-lost youth!"

Ed had heard every word. He retreated from the porch, returned to his truck in the drive, and gunned away. In the rearview mirror, he saw Susan bursting out the screen door at the sound of the racket he made. He would pretend that he had never been on the porch. What a harpies' nest! Women's suffrage ought to be repealed!

Bill was in the Anderson meadow loading bales of hay with a monolithic tractor pulling a flatbed trailer. Kitty Caliente was acting as his assistant, turning the switch of the conveyor belt on and off.

Ed took a stance on a knoll.

Bill flushed as he said, "Hi. Glad you're back."

"I bet!"

"Kitty dropped by. I was just showing her how to use the hoist."

"'Go away and let Bill manage,' your mother says. You sure as hell do!"

Kitty turned off the conveyor belt. "I'll get along home. Thanks for telling me that, Bill!"

Bill responded lamely in his father's presence, "Sure, Kitty, you're welcome as the flowers in May anytime."

Ed ignored her. She was soon out of sight, hightailing it on foot.

"You struck up quite a friendship there, it looks like."

"She came over to tell me her Old Man beat her up again last night."

"If her Old Man gets too tough, you'll march right over there and knock him flat like Chopaka knocked Nekotea."

"Want to make something of it?"

"Looks to me like her Old Man ought to knock you flat.

You're encouraging her to hang around and you know it!"

"Don't be a jackass, Dad!"

"That's the trouble. I ain't one."

Ed handed Bill the letter that had come from the Forest Service. It contained the permits for grazing rights on Mount Bonaparte, Mount Aeneas, and Mount Hull, transferred to Bill's name.

Bill whistled in dismay as he studied the forms. "Cut the units in half! They can't do that!"

"They can, and they did."

"You'll have to go to Spokane and talk to them."

"Nothing doing! You're the one that's going to Spokane. You wanted to be manager. You manage."

"But you know 'em at the Forest Service."

"Yeah, I sure do know'em, and there's not a bit of use making any trip. You never did listen when I tried to pound it into your thick skull that the government is squeezing the cattlemen off the range, and you've got to fight it. Give you your head, and the first thing you do is buy this fancy tractor and trailer like a kid that can't wait to spend his Christmas money for a toy! Where'd you get the money?"

"Sold some steers. The forest land is too thick with brush for fattening much. Got twenty-one cents for half of' em and twenty for the other half. You can't kick about that."

"Naw, did Willis buy 'em?"

"Sold 'em at the auction; but it isn't worth the hassle. Next load, I guess I'll have Willis truck 'em to the Old Union Stockyards.

"I bet you're not really surprised about the machinery. Cater gave me a two percent discount."

"Up five, down two! What's the use! I know the next damn thing you're gonna do. Buy one of those fancy drills for planting three kinds of seed at once. Go on and do it! Put in your automatic sprinklers. I hope you don't have to learn too hard not to build up the inventory."

"There's more than one way of doing things, Dad. Everybody says you have to be big or go under these days. That's what I think."

"I think with your leases cut in half, you better not try to run more than three hundred cows. That little Caliente heifer makes you feel mighty big on that tractor, doesn't she?"

"You're hitting below the belt, Dad. And you're in no position for remarks. I might make a few myself."

"Such as?"

"I hear stories lately that Delbert Gaston is sort of a relative of mine. If he is, you're out of line about me giving a kid a ride on a trailer bed."

Ed walked away in frozen rage.

At home, when he went into the kitchen, he knew the story had reached Eleanor, too. She was desperately cleaning shelves she had cleaned in anticipation of leaving home. Every item from the cupboards was strewn along the drainboards and tables. As she felt his presence in the doorway, she raised her eyes, lowered them, and continued moving the damp rag.

"The dust has collected so thick that I can't stand it," she said.

Her mouth worked the way it had done during a period that Doc had explained to Ed as an early change of life brought on by the hardships of pioneer existence, the time that Ed always referred to mentally as "when she went off her rocker with dam fever."

"Mort and Betsey stopped by while you've been gone. Mort is really mad about that son of Analix Westmore running for Congress."

"And that's not all they said, is it? I heard the rest already."

"Please, just don't say anything," she said.

As Eleanor wiped dust from the cupboards, she was trying to wipe away the blow to her self-respect. She knew the rumor was true; but she knew more—that she herself had sent Ed into the night to shift for himself. What he had done in Olympia was none of her business. But the breach had been healed and nearly forgotten over the years. They had even reached a new level of reconciliation during their trip East.

Ed felt weighted. He had turned aside long ago from emotion and dreams as weakness and become a man of totally repressed sentimentality. In the Okanogan, it was said that he was like the mountains on either side of the river—as hard to budge and as unanswerable—but within a man of a thousand practical deeds ran a vulnerable current, a stream of pain. Upon him breathed the frost of a long winter coming, a peremptory and paralyzing force. By holding tight to the scruff of his own neck, Ed over the years had built a concrete wall of activity. If people guessed his unsatisfied needs, they kept silent to his face.

WITH RARE TENDERNESS he placed his hands on her shoulders an instant, then left without saying anything. In Omak, Ed spent two hours over one drink at the Peerless Room. His friends and enemies accepted his familiar presence, and discussed with him the hay crop and the probable fall cattle prices.

"Heard Bill did some early sellin'."

"Yeah, he did all right on the price. Gonna let him have the reins, I guess."

"So everybody's heard. Cheers!"

WHEN HE THOUGHT Eleanor had had enough time to compose herself, he drove home. To discuss the past crisis in their lives was beyond their means of communicating with one another. At least he could think of nothing to say to Eleanor to make her feel better.

AT SEVEN O'CLOCK, he walked into a clean and quiet house. Eleanor had finished with the cupboards; every pan and dish was in order and the kitchen curtains washed.

"I was hoping you'd get back in time to take some bouquets down to the patients at the hospital," she greeted him. "Everything has started to bloom like wild since we've been gone."

"Sorry. You shoulda mentioned it."

"They're in cans on the back porch. They'll still be all right in the morning."

"Guess you must be tired," Ed said to her gruffly. "You shouldn't have started all that grubbing until you had a little rest."

Eleanor studied him in grateful astonishment.

"Well, I suppose you haven't had anything to eat," she made her customary remark.

"Oh, I had a bite in Omak, but nothin' for several hours."

"I ordered groceries," she said, "and got some stew meat from the locker."

"You walk to town?"

"Yes, I did, Ed. Just to hold up my head. I have decided that I am fed up with my brother Mort after all these years! You always told me he was mean and selfish. Well, he is! I almost giggled at the looks on faces when I walked through the store to the meat lockers, bold as brass."

"It's good to be eating your cooking again," he said as he devoured stew meat, carrots, potatoes, and onions, simmered three hours.

"I should think you would have had a fill of restaurants and dining cars," she snapped automatically.

Ed overlooked her response. It didn't mean anything.

"Hal Buck is coming by tomorrow with some papers," he told her. "Damn sonofabitch didn't do what I asked him to. Shoulda know better than to expect him to do one simple thing."

"I'll be civil to him, but I do get tired of the way he eats us out of house and home."

"Don't offer him anything for once," Ed suggested.

"Oh, I can't be like that. He's Susan's father."

"Yeah, I guess so."

They went together toward their beds. Ed stopped at the boys' bedroom as usual. Before she went on to the back bedroom, Eleanor paused in Ed's door. "I put fresh sheets on your bed."

"You put fresh sheets on when we left."

"They got stale."

"I give up," Ed said.

AT EIGHT O'CLOCK next morning, in time for a second breakfast, Hal let himself in by the front door and slapped the heavy manila envelope on the writing desk.

"Made good on my word. Here's your stuff. I'd sure have been glad to oblige you, Ed, about goin' up there to Conconully with it; but after ..."

"...you talked it over with Mort," Ed supplied.

"Matter of fact I did. Anything wrong with that?"

"Naw, I guess not. Sit down and have a bite."

"O.K., as long as nobody's sore."

Ed grunted again and passed Hal the bacon and eggs.

After all the toast and jam had disappeared, Buck pushed himself back from the table and fumbled in the pocket of his shirt. He pulled out a folded piece of newspaper.

"This here's what's done all the damage to your fine young candidate," he told Ed. "Look what he said at the meeting of the Colville Confederated Tribes. Saved it for you."

Ed unfolded the clipping and read Del Gaston's political speech on the national tribal termination plan.

"As A TRIBAL member and mostly a friend, I ask you to consider carefully whether we as a People wish to relinquish our homeland with its culture and heritage.

"A large sum, sixty thousand dollars apiece for fifty-five hundred tribal members, is being dangled before us. The white people are urging us to take our place in the present day world and prepare for the future rather than cling to the reservation and the past.

"'Let us think twice. Why are they offering us sixty thousand dollars apiece? Perhaps it is a bargain for land seventy miles from east to west and thirty-five miles wide from north to south, with 826,000 acres of commercial timber resources. Their offer comes from their real business sense.

"'Let me put a daring thought before *N'Chi-lix-czin*. Perhaps we have our own business sense to harvest and market our trees. Perhaps some young person on the reservation, who has an education, has the ability to organize a company called Colville Tribal Enterprises, to find ways of developing the natural resources of the reservation.

"'I ask the adults to look about a while before giving that young person's chances away.'"

"How long do you have to keep reading?" Hal demanded of Ed. "Now see why Mort wants to put the kibosh on that jasper?"

Ed knew that Del Gaston would not win the party nomination while the incumbent, Walt Horan, was still alive; he likely would not win the majority of votes of the tribal council. But he was saying the truth as it came to him.

"Gaston is no jasper," Ed said. "He's a highborn leader. Old Man Westmore was the hardest-headed English gentleman I ever met. You guys are not gonna get the reservation for a few more years, I can see that."

"Let's not get into any more arguments, Ed," Hal said. "Everybody's gonna vote for himself when it gets down to cases."

"I'm gonna take this stuff up the valley myself," Ed stated. "It's my junk. Fact is, I been keepin' the archives of the cattlemen all these years, just so I can dump the issues in some smart kid's lap."

"Bill's a smart kid," Eleanor interjected. "Only he isn't all fired up about politics."

"Oh, Bill!" Even Hal brushed him aside as a student of issues.

Ed conducted Hal outside to his pickup.

"Ed, don't think I'm taking part in the gossip. I tell everybody I only came here in 1929. I don't know any of the old secrets."

"Buck, if you stay three more minutes, you're gonna shut up because you have a busted jaw!"

21.

Through Fire

Ed turned his pickup north toward the border. On the seat beside him lay the manila envelope he had retrieved from Hal. To the material he had originally collected, he had added the agricultural experiment station bulletin that Sam had given him, and also some correspondence from Evan Hall, the Milwaukee Railroad agent who had organized the MizpahPumpkin Creek grazing district in Montana. That grazing district had been the pilot project that sparked the definitive Taylor Grazing Act of 1934. Cattlemen who joined the first district had agreed to stay off the range until the grass roots could take hold in spring; they believed in range reseeding and respected the rights of the multiple users of public land. Ed's correspondence with Hall showed clearly that cattlemen had taken an active, leading role in protection of public land.

Soon the people and the government would have to come to a working agreement. A young man with an inclination to be an arbitrator needed a broad base for his campaign talks, even if his victory were still several elections down the road.

Ed was thoroughly cognizant that he and others in his age group were objects of jealousy and resentment at times. People called on him and treated him like an elder statesman to his face. As they drove away, they told each other, "Of course, the old birds who came in here in the early days think they have the right to the whole hog."

It was a familiar attitude not only of the new cattlemen but of the city dwellers, the government agents, the reporters, and the average politicians—all who lived by their wits instead of the labor of their backs. They seemed to feel that the old-timers of the hills were now wealthy because they had had an unlimited supply of free land in the early days of the West.

Hordes of people with the dream of making easy fortunes had swarmed into the Okanogan Valley; but when their expectations went unfulfilled, and it became clear that they must work hard to survive, the wishful thinkers drifted on again.

Ed's original homestead had been patented in strict accordance with the regulations at a time when the national land policy had been to encourage settlement of the West. He expanded his holdings by buying other homesteads that had been abandoned, or on which the soil had been overworked by the production of farm crops. Most of the land had been badly gullied and filled with erosion scars, never suitable for farm land in the first place. He broke the banks of the gullies and leveled the land. He loosened the plow sole, burned brush and other undesirable vegetation, and engineered the drainage of basins. In his restoration, he avoided moving the topsoil as much as possible. When the tilth was good enough, he planted grass that resisted the hammer blows of spring rains and run-offs. He transported bags of seed from Jacklin Seed Company in Spokane and broadcast them by hand. In a few years of reseeding themselves, entire fields had thick stands of grass.

Ed feared nothing from inquiry into the use of the land that had come into his possession. Perhaps he could even be distinguished in the public mind from the ones who robbed, seized, and defrauded to obtain their holdings. He had fought the crooked people first. He would like the public somehow to be reminded of the difference between him and them.

Now his enemies were passing the word that would stifle the force of his objective contribution to public land policy.

"Did you ever notice how the girls' current dreamboat, Delbert Gaston, resembles old Ed McLaren—that droopy ear and all? Explains a lot about the Old Man's split with his own crowd."

To the Hot Place with them!

In the meadows of the Westmore spread, he would find and talk to Leschi and Owhi. They'd be glad to hand his materials to their nephew. Memories came like swirls of fog around the familiar bends of the road. He had wanted for a long time to talk with the family about the old days—the time when the Indians burned the brush, and the country was like an open park.

He had to run the risk of encountering Analix alone sometime again before they were dead. They had lived in the same valley all their lives. Between them was a son—a positive, self-assertive individual, who cared about the issues that his blood father cared about. His interests and the droop to his ear were indeed a direct inheritance.

The thread of Ed's life moved far from the woman who was like a wild deer in the forest. She was among the hills, never seen. He had gone his natural way, laying up hay for winter as Carr Westmore had counseled. He could take the credit, in part, when the state uniform brand law was adopted, when the Taylor Grazing Act was passed in the United States Congress, when range reseeding became policy. Students of scientific range management visited him at his home to discuss his theories of controlled brush burning and watershed protection, to argue and be convinced.

For his efforts on their behalf, the Okanogan County cattlemen had presented a fancy Stetson hat to him at the annual banquet; all other rewards came from close attention to the cattle business that relied solely on sunshine, soil, and seeds for support.

The Westmores traded at separate stores and voted in different precincts from the people of Bonaparte. Only in fleeting moments could Ed glimpse the course of Analix's days. Sometimes the auctioneer at the Omak sale would announce, "This fat AW calf to the highest bidder. Proceeds go to the children of St. Mary's Mission."

He saw in the *Omak Chronicle* that she participated in affairs of her church parish and tribal council. She was the granddaughter of a chief, *skumalt*. The orphaned or abandoned children that she gathered from the reservation and sent to the mission developed into industrious and successful members of the agricultural community. Some became lawyers and schoolteachers. There was a self-disciplined and abstemious core to the leadership of the Colville Confederated Tribes because of St. Mary's Mission and the Westmore family.

As a member of the tribal business council, Analix had visited Washington congressman Walt Horan in the national capital and had testified before congressional committees on Indian affairs. She had been photographed shaking hands with the representative from Washington state.

There were numerous valid reasons that Ed could give for his trip up the old Conconully road, but what could he tell himself?

As he entered the Okanogan National Forest land, he noted the dried-out brush, fallen timber, and lodgepole thickets. It was forest fire weather.

HE FOUND THE horseback crew working in the cache. The riders, lined up three on each side of a band of cattle, were cutting out steers. To keep from startling the animals, Ed parked his pickup behind a shed and walked to a high point to make his presence plain.

No one yelled or whistled in AW procedures. The silent riders used the Indian method—as though stalking game—that Old Man Westmore, now deceased, had learned from his father in-law, Chief White Stone Mountain. Despite the lack of a hail, Ed knew the crew had seen him.

Smiling broadly with pleasure, Leschi Westmore, now the Old Man himself, cantered over the rise on a black and white pony.

"Hi, Ed McLaren! What you doing up here? Be with you in a minute. Have to get these critters to auction tomorrow. Look fat enough for you?"

"Best I've seen this season."

"Except your own herd, you're thinking."

"Oh, not necessarily. It still beats me how Westmores can handle cattle."

"Go on down to the corral. We're gonna put 'em in there."

The horseback crew came slowly with the steers. Ed opened the gate for the livestock to file in. The steers moved quietly, knowing what to do.

Owhi came to chat with Ed, who took an observer's post on the corral. "Our old hands always come back wanting to work for us again."

"How much you paying these days?"

"For you, no more 'n twenty dollars and keep, same as I offered Nat and Will last week."

"That's more 'n I'm earning now. I'm canned on my own layout."

"Don't say that out loud in the presence of these kids. They're about to sack Leschi and me, too."

Ed, Leschi, and Owhi surveyed one another cautiously for the effects of time and the elements. The Westmore brothers were somewhat younger than Ed, but the few years that had separated them when Ed was first hired at the AW had now lost their former proportion. The trio were of the generation of Old Men together. Nevertheless, they could all sit tall in the saddle, and could joke readily; they shared the look of those who had borne the weights of life gallantly. Leschi and Owhi's appearance reassured Ed. The pain in his arm stopped momentarily.

"You look good, Ed," Leschi told him.

"Husky enough yourselves. How do you keep so husky?"

"Awful meat eaters," Owhi decided. "You know us. Meat, water, and fresh air, and sticking to business."

Leschi had dismounted with the rest of the crew. Owhi, remaining on horseback, had other chores.

"You wouldn't come all the way up here without something special to say, Ed," Owhi apologized. "Leschi can tell me about it. I'd stop, too, except there are still some strays at the north end."

"Sure. I know all about that."

As Owhi rode off, Leschi climbed to the rail beside Ed. His black and white mare, reins dropped over her nose, began cropping grass. The crew, who had taken hammers and nails from the shed, were checking the tightness of the corral.

"Should have introduced everybody, maybe. That grown man is from Osoyoos. Orchardman. Crop went to pieces this year. Needs the wages. The smallest kid is my grandchild. Bigger fellow is Owhi's grandson. Other one belongs to Analix—Delbert's kid. Analix and her family still live in the Old Man's house."

"You train 'em all to stay with the cows, don't you?"

"They all seem to want to."

"That nephew of yours, Delbert, is running for Congress."

Leschi smiled, "Del's different, all right. He likes to work in public and concern himself with public problems. In spite of it, he's a pretty good cowpoke. I worry about him some. In the cow business, you get by if you follow the course that nature dictates. But in politics, what to do is more complicated."

"You're right."

"You make me suspicious, showing up here after all these years. You come talkin' politics? I see your name in the papers often enough."

"I know you like to mind your own business, but Del's your nephew. Doesn't he need help? Real fight over new state leased lands, and the government wanting to buy up what's left of the reservation."

"All the people quarreling over the land ought to remember that the Earth is everybody's mother; that's the Indian viewpoint."

"There's always been the question of who owns the land," Ed said. "I notice Del is talking up a survey of public lands in his campaign. I have some material in the pickup. I started to collect it when they were promoting the Barrett investigation of the Forest Service. You think your nephew wants any of that dope?"

"Sure he does. But I'm not the person to give it to. Take it up to the house to Analix. She'll see it gets to Del. She drives to Conconully nearly every other day, or Del comes over.

"Haven't talked to Analix for years," Ed said hesitantly.

"Settled down since she was young. Good, steady woman. Gerald is up there in a wheelchair. She waits on him like a baby. He's had arthritis for years. Besides taking care of him, she has two grandchildren on her hands most of the time while Mary, Del's wife, teaches school at Oroville. Analix keeps the books for the whole layout and does all the cooking. Busy, but not a complainer."

Ed plunged into his trouble. "Maybe I shouldn't go up to the house and give the stuff to her. I really had something to say to the men up here. It's about Del running for office and not knowing the talk that's going to hit him head on. Maybe he should be given some idea how much he can hurt his mother. In this fight, they've started a rumor."

"Don't they in every campaign?"

"Everybody is saying he—Del—is my kid. The story is that Analix and I started him when I was in the legislature. What am I supposed to say?"

Leschi grinned. "Of course, I'm half Injun. I'd just say nothing."

Ed's face broke into a companion grin. "I'll be danged. I musta lost my common sense."

"You were about to."

"Analix told me to stay away from her one time."

"And you sure minded her. Everybody minds her. We missed you, Ed. Go up to the house and see her. You'll feel better. You won't be afraid of her feelings getting hurt. She's spent her life ignoring what people think."

"Well, I might go up there. You probably got a million things to do. I wanted to ask—I never heard how the Old Man, your father, died."

"He was keeping the fire going for us one day right here. He busted his hip one time and became feeble at the end. When we came to the corral, he was sitting with his back against that post. The fire was built up higher than he usually let it go. He believed in a small fire. We thought he was taking a nap because it seemed he wasn't noticing the blaze. The fire nearly went out before we realized that he'd built his last branding fire. Died peacefully. That was in '42."

"Did you have a funeral? If I'd seen anything in the paper, I'd have come."

"Not here. We took his body to Victoria. His people have a big tomb that was built for his father. I guess he belongs there. Couldn't bury him in the Indian plot with Mama. She was buried by the old chief, so I guess it's all right for the Old Man to sleep beside his father, too."

Ed returned to the pickup and continued on the lane that would lead to the old stucco house. A new addition to the property was a deer fence to protect an orchard of apples, apricots, cherries, and peaches on the brow of the hill above the house.

As Ed stepped out to let himself through the gate, he was reminded again of the dryness of the season. A great cloud of dust had pursued him down the dirt road and overwhelmed him when he stopped.

INSIDE THE FENCE the dust abated; the orchard floor was covered with alfalfa stubble. He saw sprinkler heads throughout the area and surmised that an irrigation dam that had been built on the creek that had always run past the house. Undoubtedly there was inside plumbing now for the residence that was no longer the mansion Ed remembered.

The cottonwoods that stood when he was young still whispered like old people in the yard. They would soon have to be cut down, or they would fall down and cave in the roof of the dwelling.

He knocked on the jamb of the open door.

Analix, now a grandmother as he was a grandfather many times over, stood in the spot in which she had greeted him when he had come seeking a job as a hand at the AW. Her once black hair was in the same halo of braids. The gold nugget earrings, gift from her father, hung in her ears. She recognized Ed at once. Her eyes flashed with surprise but she remained calm.

"Hello, Ed! Come in! It's Ed McLaren after all these years, Gerald!"

She gave him her hand. It was strong, stronger than any woman's hand he had ever taken. His own waning courage returned. He had been a fool to tremble at the door. Speaking now face to face with Analix after a lifetime apart, he had a sense of coming home. She was a seasoned woman. Like him, she had been watching generations of cattle being born and giving their lives in the cycle of eating grass and being eaten without complaint. She was like many other women of the Okanogan, much changed from the age of thirty. But she was also a distinguished presence, a person who had served as a diplomat and a council president.

In the dining room, Gerald Gaston lay on a cot before an open window. A wheelchair stood by the cot. Gerald, gnarled with the typical deformities of rheumatoid arthritis, smiled cheerfully and slowly extended his hand. As Ed took the claw, he was unable to feel that he and Gerald Gaston had a quarrel between them.

"I told Analix she better start figuring out who was driving into the yard. Did she recognize you at the door?"

"I guess. She spoke my name before I did."

"I'd know you were one of the old-timers like the rest of us, but I wouldn't be able to recall you from the last time I saw you. I'd get up to shake hands, but this damned arthritis has laid me up half my life. You still have the stomach for mixing in it? I remember all about you now. You were a real help to the Westmores when the Clements's tried to buy their land from under them."

"Sorry about you being laid up so long. Can't they do anything about your trouble these days? They claim wonder cures for everything."

"Delbert got the specialists in here by helicopter when they first developed cortisone; but the docs say at my age nothing much can be done. Atrophied. All the swelling has gone down, and I haven't been in much pain for a long time. I'm lucky to have such a good nurse."

Analix smiled at her husband, then said, "Excuse me a minute. I left something cooking on the stove."

While she was in the kitchen, Ed said to Gerald, "Hear your son is running for Congress. Wanted to know if there's anything I can do—in our own generation that is. Don't know the boy personally, but I've heard him speak."

When Analix returned, Gerald said, "He's come politicking, Ana. He wants on Delbert's team."

"That's encouraging," she said.

"We've had a whole series of delegations," Gerald went on enthusiastically. "It's given me a little excitement on the sidelines. There's a woman reporter here today already, Thalia Miller. Where are they now, Analix?"

"Del took her up in the hills. She says she wants to see the Okanogan forest so she'll understand the campaign issues."

Ed said disgustedly, "Way she writes, she doesn't have a lick of sense."

"She writes for popular consumption," Analix said. "She seems quite sharp."

"She says she's all for Del, but she teases so," Gerald said. "She makes remarks that can be taken several ways. When Del's wife knew Thalia Miller was coming, she took the girls and went to town. Mary isn't as used to clever-talking women as Delbert is."

"I know city people, too," Ed concurred. "Not half as smart as they think they are. When they come visiting on the range, they all dress for looks and not for protection."

Gaston chuckled. "Del's reporter came this morning in some kind of cotton pants and a handkerchief top. Analix saw that if she rode under any tree limbs on horseback, she'd be a bloody pulp by the time she finished the ride. Ana lent her a long sleeved shirt and a pair of Mary's Levi's. She was wearing flimsy sandals, too."

"She's still wearing those," Analix said. "I didn't have any boots to fit her feet. Del told me I should offer her moccasins, but I didn't. Perhaps we should consider the subject exhausted. Do you have any news for us, Ed?"

"It's pretty good news in itself that he wants to help in the campaign," Gerald observed.

"Nobody would want me to make any talks or anything like that," Ed began. "I'm on the shelf. My son's taking over the ranch. What I had in mind was to give you some old papers I left in the pickup—from the hearings in '47. I won't even bring them in unless you think your son wants them, but there are some figures showing the decline in cattle numbers permitted on the national forests over a period of years. Didn't use any of it. Hearing never came off in Okanogan County."

"It was a real disappointment," Analix said. "They should have taken time. We're the largest cattle shipping area in the state."

"Delbert will want your material, Ed, especially since the tribal termination issue has come up."

"I hoped he would. My stuff demonstrates just how long government has been taking more and more control over the land. The reservation is only one more parcel for the bureaucrats," he said.

Ed went for the envelope.

When they emptied the contents on the table, everything appeared in good order.

"I sorted it out," Ed told them. "Lot of correspondence with Mallin—the Cattleman's Association secretary—and some others."

Analix regathered the papers and fitted them into the envelope. She took them to an adjoining room where the walls were lined with books and ledgers, and laid them on a desk

"This is the office. I do all my bookkeeping here."

"The Colvilles are grateful," Analix said as she returned and sat down, "that Del is urging them to resist tribal termination. They were about to surrender until Gerald explained that any termination bill would have to be written with the stipulation that the tribe cannot be terminated without the consent of the majority of the adult tribal members themselves."

"Hope you have some lawyers in your tribal council."

"Oh, we do. Dr. Paschal Sherman, for one, the pride of the Jesuit fathers at St. Mary's. Paschal is ready with a complete strategy to follow at congressional hearings on termination."

"I've heard about Sherman," Ed remarked. "Graduate of the mission school who went on to be a lawyer. Some bigwig in Washington, D.C., now, isn't he?'

"He's with the Veterans Administration," Analix supplied. "He says if a bill to provide for termination of federal supervision over the Colvilles is written, we should insist that no Indian land be sold for less than the appraised value, the appraisal of three independent experts."

"Also, you should point out that the United States government and the state of Washington already own forty-five percent of the state, and they don't need any more land, " Ed suggested.

"For our tribal attorney, we have Joe Wicks of the Okanogan County superior court," Analix said. "Joe isn't a Colville, but he is an enrolled member of the Cherokee tribe."

"There won't be any ready private buyers at the appraised value," Ed said. "Who gets the land—the Forest Service or the Bureau of Land Management? Put those two in a squabble over who gets what, and the Indians can sneak back to the reservation and forget moving anyplace."

"That's already been mentioned," Analix said. "If the palefaces find out that they can't buy or lease land for a song, they might not be interested in tribal termination."

"I see the Indians have learned how to fight," Ed said. "And you don't lack for leadership."

He stood to leave. He had made gifts to all his children.

After he again shook hands with Gerald, he walked outside accompanied by Analix.

"I'm glad you came, Ed," she said. "I have something to say to you."

He swallowed. "Maybe it's what I didn't have the nerve to say to you."

Analix smiled. "It's like you, Ed, to burst through enemy lines."

"With papers that belong in the wastebasket."

"Not at all! They're what Del needs to lift the campaign from the bog."

"People make me mad the way their minds work. They want that reservation timber and grazing land, so the way to get it is to argue that the person defending them for the Indians is a catch colt."

"You know there are ringleaders."

"Mort and Betsey Clements. Kept their mouths shut about other people's business until blabbing got useful."

"Did you catch it when Gerald remarked that we have had a series of delegations? There's not only been Thalia Miller, but also Mort Clements. He and his henchmen threatened me with blackmail, and I see they are making good on their threats. Gerald didn't know the nature of the Clements's visit."

"Seems like Gerald is mighty proud of his son."

"Yes. He's the only person who could suffer. You and I don't care what things look like to other people. We're the only two with the straight of the story, and there's no reason to apologize to anybody."

"Gerald doesn't get to hear much gossip, likely. No harm done. You'd think old Mort would've fallen over dead of rottenness years ago."

"Most people see through slander spread by those who try to justify their own greediness."

She held her hand to him again, still sure in the conviction that had been hers many years before. She stayed with the People, *N'Chi-lix-czin.*

"Time hasn't changed some things," Ed said impulsively.

"You and I have changed a great deal."

"You're the same to me."

"My hair is like bunchgrass that's been under the snow all winter. I have deep wrinkles—Indian wrinkles."

"I meant inside."

Her face came awake to his message, the secret they shared under the conscious level of their hardworking lives, from the days before the Earth turned over. They had given the painful energy of their love to making the wheels of the world turn.

"We've stood it this long. We can stand it a while longer," she said.

"Sure, sure!"

He went down the steps and toward the pickup.

Inside the house, the phone rang. He was behind the wheel when Analix reappeared in the door.

She motioned to him to come back. "The phone is for you," she called.

"For me! Who the hell knows I'm here!"

"I think it's important that whoever it is gets in touch with you. It's a woman. I think your wife."

ELEANOR SOUNDED THE fire alarm to the McLaren family. She had trudged to town to Prince's store because she felt the urge to make an angel food cake. The concentration required in beating a dozen egg whites always stopped her nervousness. Angel food cake was one of the few cakes that she made with fine cake flour.

As she passed in the street, the U.S. forest ranger came from his office, hailing her. "Mrs. McLaren! I tried to reach your house, but no one answered."

"No, of course not. I've been walking to town. Do you have a message for Ed or Bill?"

"Lightning last night started fires in seven places on the forest. Your men better know where the herds are."

Eleanor forget the angel food cake. "I'll go home and call the Johnston place. Also, I may know where Ed is."

She was able to reach Bill and Susan at once. They were both in the house. She heard Susan cry, "Fire on the mountain!"

Then Bill's voice, "God almighty! Round up the kids. They'll have to help."

Susan hung up without saying goodbye.

ELEANOR KNEW WHERE Ed had gone. She couldn't escape from hearing the conversations between Hal and Ed. She set her mouth in a firm line, looked in the phone book for the Conconully numbers, and dialed.

ED TOOK THE receiver dangling on the end of the cord of the wall phone. "Yeah."

"Ed! Thank goodness! The Forest Service wants me to find you. I saw you taking that envelope of papers. I thought you might be carrying it up there."

"All right. What's the matter? One of the kids dead?"

"No. But there's fire on the forest. Can you see it from where you are? Lightning started fires in seven places last night."

"On our range?"

"The ranger says for you to find out."

"All right! All right! We haven't been able to run many cattle in there all summer, brush so damn thick. I'll go on up there. Probably won't be home till dark."

Ed hung up.

He turned to Analix. "Let's go outside and take a look. Eleanor says there's fire in seven places in the hills."

"I'll get the binoculars."

"I saw all that dry underbrush when I came up the valley. If it gets started right, it'll burn from Chelan to Colville."

He searched the hills with the glasses that Analix handed him. "There it is! Be crownin' in a minute. Smoke in every direction."

Gerald, who had lifted himself from the cot, rolled out in his wheelchair.

"Del is up there in the weeds with that tenderfoot, Ana. Think he'll see it?" he wondered aloud.

"He'll see it. I suppose I better get out the pickup and find Leschi."

"No," Ed interposed. "My pickup's right here. I know where Leschi is. You stay here to answer the phone. The Forest Service ought to call damn quick to give the lookouts' report."

"You're right. Tell Leschi to bring home any firefighters they want to tonight. I'll get food ready for a crew."

"Here comes Delbert now," Gerald exclaimed.

Leading his saddle horse, Delbert Gaston walked up the path with Thalia Miller, also leading her horse, behind him. The young woman was cursing and walking barefoot.

Delbert Gaston's face looked hot, his expression blank. When he reached the porch, he dropped the reins of his horse, sat on the bottom step, and took deep breaths.

"She mad?" Analix asked her son.

The candidate for Congress replied, "It seems that she can neither ride nor walk. Her sandals gave out. I refused to carry her. See the smoke?"

"Yes, we're going to be busy."

Miss Miller, clutching sandal parts, came into port and plumped on the step beside Gaston. Her face dripped sweat.

"Thanks for waiting," she said.

"Sorry. Fire won't wait."

"As they say, 'Where's the fire?' I haven't seen any fire yet."

"You two haven't had anything to eat. You should have let me pack you a lunch," Analix said.

"Miss Miller should have a bite," Del answered. "I won't take time. I'll go and start the tractor. We'll have to get a firebreak around the cache right now. Thank Amtoos most of the cattle are in there."

Del rose from the step and held his hand to Ed. "Recognize you by sight, Mr. McLaren. Never had the pleasure of meeting you before."

"Aw, we don't need any 'meeting'—knew you since you were a pup. I was your grandfather's hired hand once. Known your mother, aunt, and uncles since before you were born."

"They should have told me. Miss Miller, this is Ed McLaren, one of the Okanogan old-timers who helped open the valley to settlement."

"How big is the forest fire going to be, old-timer?" Miss Miller asked.

"No bigger 'n we can help. But if rain doesn't come in the next few hours, it'll burn to natural barriers."

"Mind if I use the phone before I eat?" the city girl asked Analix.

"All right, but perhaps you'd best limit the call. The Forest Service will be phoning."

Thalia ran up the steps and let the screen door bang behind her.

They heard her putting through a collect call to the *Spokesman-Review* in Spokane.

"Holocaust starting on the Okanogan and Colville national forests. Better get me a photographer up here and a whirlybird. Where am I? Some godforsaken ranch—AW, I think they call it—it's our Indian candidate's boyhood home. Ask somebody where it is when you get to Bonaparte. All right! All right! Fast!"

Del went inside. "Just a minute, Thalia. Tell them to meet you in downtown Bonaparte. You can't stay here."

"Hold it! I have to argue a minute for the freedom of the press."

Those outside heard a scuffle.

"What are you doing!" Thalia shrieked. "Give me that phone!"

In a moment they rejoined the group outside, Delbert firmly escorting the reporter.

"Mr. McLaren, you no doubt will have to leave right away," Del said. "Will you be so kind as to give Miss Miller a lift back to town?"

"Sure thing! Just as soon as I tell your men at the cache what's goin' on. I'll tell 'em you're on the way with the tractor."

"O.K. Tell Leschi we better get the pump going on the meadow."

"Pump there, too?"

"Yes. The lake used to flood the meadows every spring, but it hasn't done that for quite a while; need the sprinklers."

Analix volunteered, "Want me to hike down to the lake and try to start the pump, Del? I've never done it, but I could in a pinch."

"No. Leschi will have time. The fire still has to travel several miles. It's running up the hills, but it will slow when it comes toward us. It won't come down the hill from the orchard. It's pretty wet in there already."

A three-quarter-ton truck marked with the insignia of the U.S. Forest Service drove into the yard. The driver, in uniform, got out and advanced.

"Who is the owner of this property? It's contiguous to the national forest."

"You might say I am the owner," Analix responded. "I'm the oldest living member of the family. We have an undivided interest."

"Only one person will be allowed to remain," the ranger said. "The rest of you have twenty minutes to get down the road before it is closed."

"You don't know the law, young man," Analix said. "The stipulation that only one person may remain on land threatened by forest fire is an arbitrary bureaucratic regulation that we are prone to ignore."

The ranger cleared his throat. "I am empowered to use force to evacuate unwilling persons."

'We can't stand here to discuss it with you," Del interrupted. He moved toward the tractor shed at a trot.

"As owner, I am entitled to remain," Analix said. "My husband is sitting there in the wheelchair. How is he to be evacuated by force?"

The ranger eyed Gerald. "I see. Well, he can stay. There are no helicopters available."

"If it gets too hot, I'll come back and pack you down to the canoe, Dad," Delbert called back. "I'll shove you into the lake and you can have a nice ride while you watch the bonfire."

Analix also left the ranger standing. She went into the house and returned with a pair of moccasins, a square of yellow cheese, and a box of crackers, and gave them to Miss Miller.

"Come on, Miss Miller," Ed said. "You'll have to eat your meal on the road."

"But I haven't changed my clothes. I'm in borrowed clothes."

"No time, Thalia," Analix said. "Take the Levi's and welcome. They're better suited to the circumstances."

Ed opened the passenger side of the pickup for her. If she had been Leila, he would have popped her behind and told her, "Get a move on!"

"I'll keep that damn Injun from getting elected if it's the last thing I ever do! Dumping me like this!" she fumed.

Ed started his engine to get ahead of the forest ranger's dust.

At the deer fence, he left the wheel of the pickup and opened the gate himself. He knew better than to ask a city dweller to open a gate.

He trundled the pickup so fast that the dust rose thick about them. With visibility almost nil, he came to an abrupt halt. A large, white automobile, a Cadillac, was mired in dust to the hubs, squarely in the middle of the one-lane track.

A corpulent man dressed in a business suit was mopping his brow at the side of the vehicle. He had lifted the hood.

Ed approached on foot. "What the hell you doing here?"

"How da do! I'm Bill Thompson. As you can see, I'm in a pickle. Folks told me it would be hard on my Caddy to bring it in here. I promised Del Gaston I'd visit him sometime, so here I am."

"You sure picked a bad day for a visit," Ed said curtly.

A Forest Service transport truck barreled up amid dust clouds and stopped behind the Cadillac.

"Remove your vehicle!" the ranger in charge directed his sharp order at Ed. "An emergency situation exists in the forest beyond here."

"Not me blocking traffic," Ed rejoined. "It's Mr. Thompson's car. Mine's the pickup on the other side."

"Hmm, I see," said the ranger.

Sixteen college student volunteer firefighters swarmed from the transport and studied the problem.

"Back your truck off to the side of the road," Ed suggested to the forest ranger. "Then let's see if we can lift the damn Cadillac out of the pothole and turn it around."

"Hm," the forest ranger said again. "Everybody willing to try?"

"Sure!" the young men chorused.

The ranger backed the transport conveyance into the cheatgrass.

"Careful with my Caddy!" Mr. Thompson screamed.

Everyone but the owner of the Cadillac found a hold.

"All together, heave!" Ed yelled.

With a sucking sound the luxury car came loose from the dust. Straining and synchronizing their moves, the boys, men, and reporter turned the car and planted it in the proper ruts so that it could return to pavement.

Thompson gunned his motor, raised a mighty cloud, and bounced away without a thank you.

Ed moved aside his pickup for the Forest Service truck to proceed, then drove around the pothole. Miss Miller climbed into the pickup without assistance.

Ed felt winded.

"How many acres in these two national forests?" Thalia began to interview him again.

"Oh, it's written down someplace. Million acres, maybe. Mind looking in the glove compartment for a small bottle? Some pills in it. Doc told me I'm supposed to take one when I need to catch my breath."

Thalia, who had spied the tongues of fire-dragon licking the dry brush on the hills about them, came to attention. She flipped open the glove compartment without a fumble. "Got it! Here's one. Can you swallow it dry?"

"Don't swallow it. Doc said hold it under the tongue to dissolve."

Ed managed to take the medication between his lips from her fingers and tongue it into place.

"Stop! I'll drive," she offered.

"Can you drive a pickup? Has four speeds forward, stick shift."

"I can drive anything on wheels," she responded sturdily.

She hopped from the passenger seat and ran around the pickup to take the wheel. "Scoot over. You're turning purple."

"Don't doubt it," Ed tried not to gasp. "Can't get my breath after lifting that car."

"I know," Thalia said grimly. "You'd think that big baboon would have helped lift his own car! Shut up! I'll whisk you to town in no time."

"You can't whisk on this road," Ed said.

Because he was unable to do otherwise, Ed laid his head against the back rest and concentrated on keeping the pill under his tongue.

Susan went outside to the nearest vehicle and blasted two shorts and a long on the horn; that meant "Come here, right now!"

Tom appeared from his bedroom; the girls came up from the river in which they were standing to keep cool.

"Tom, fire! Don't know if it'll come down this low, but we gotta be sure. You love that damn tractor; hop on it and start making a firebreak around the whole damn place."

"I'll get out the horse trailer," Bill said. "Girls, get your ponies and saddles and lead them into it. Pronto."

"Why? What for?"

"To round up the cows and calves. We'll need to fan out and drive the cows under the cliff at the falls."

"I don't want to herd cows! I don't know how!" Glenna howled.

"Listen up, stampede princess! What you do is find a cow, stick your horse's nose up against its rump, and keep it there till the cow is down the mountain," Susan snapped.

"I'll drive the truck with a couple more horses," Bill said. "You better go for Hugo and Louie in the car. I'll wait."

Susan rattled off at fifty miles an hour to alert the men who stayed at the cabins on the mountain. She passed Vernie Allen in the lane, stopped, and tooted the horn at him until he turned around to see what the trouble was.

"Bill says get all the cows under the cliff on Bonaparte. The fire won't come over the escarpment."

"Gotcha!" Vernie said. A member of the hay crew, Vernie had just had a couple of weeks off and was coming back to see if there were some miscellaneous fall chores. He took home his flivver and loaded his puddle jumper with bucket and shovel. Fires were part of the routine.

Susan brought Hugo and Louie in half an hour. They loaded four horses into the back of the cattle truck and barreled away. The girls were on their way to the base of the mountain. They were towing the horse trailer with the pickup.

Susan was jammed between her husband's sharp elbow and the shift.

"Where d'you suppose Dad is," Bill worried. "He hasn't been himself since he got back."

"He'd be worse if he ever found out the whole story of the mess we were in," Susan said.

"I'm not admitting anything, Buttercup. Havin' to deal with a rubber check is no calamity compared to what can happen right now. Three hundred cows could be barbecue by nightfall."

"No, they won't," Susan said. "Not while you have a good cowpoke like me herding."

They saw the billowing clouds of smoke over the far side of the mountain.

"There comes the fire," Bill said. "It's crowned. Look, there's one hell of a blaze on Ruby Mountain, too."

The next hours passed in a blur.

AT SEVEN O'CLOCK in the evening, Eleanor received a call from Holy Family Hospital in downtown Bonaparte.

"Dear Mrs. McLaren, who always sends such lovely flowers," said a Sister's quiet voice, "you had better come at once if you can find a way."

"Is it my husband?" Eleanor asked in a shaking voice. "I knew he wouldn't act his age but head out with a bucket and shovel!"

"He hasn't been firefighting," the Sister answered. "He's been telling us to call his son Bill. He feels you will be frightened at his condition. But I think it is best if you prepared yourself and come. He is in the emergency room. We want you and your son to talk with the doctor at once."

DOC, IN THE emergency room that seethed with amateurs with burned hands, was saying to Ed, who was lying on an examining table, "If you have a lick of sense, you'll hold still. Really still!"

Ed felt as though he was coming to pieces.

"We need your permission to move him by ambulance to the intensive care unit at the Valley Clinic at Wenatchee. Probably not so crowded down there," Doc said.

"Sure, go along," Bill took charge. "We'll follow in the car."

Doc ordered the Sister, "Put him under. Get him ready."

Then Ed felt nothing.

He roused to consciousness next morning in the intensive care unit, electric machines blinking and clacking around him, and needles sticking in his veins.

"Now just hold still!" a voice soothed. "You're going to be fine, Grampa. We're happy you're awake!"

Ed struggled upright. "Who the hell is calling me Grampa! I'm not your grampa!"

"Please excuse me, Mr. McLaren. I didn't mean to be fresh. But you have to lie down, or you'll bother your tubes."

"Get this rigging off me!"

The nurse smiled and gently pushed him back to the pillows. "Careful, careful!" she crooned.

When he was settled, still glaring but with emplacements intact, she asked, "You think you might feel well enough to talk to your wife or son a moment?"

"Get Bill in here!"

Ed attacked Bill, "What are you and your mother trying to pull?"

Bill grinned as he answered, "Plenty. Got you where we want you, haven't we? All trussed up. You better simmer down or they won't let Mom come in. You've had a heart attack, in case you don't know it."

Ed remembered riding in the truck, unable to move.

"I tried one of those damn pills Doc gave me. Knew they were no good."

"Probably saved your life, Doc said. Also, that gal reporter can take some credit; brought you in through the blazing brush. Morning paper shows you being lifted from the pickup onto a stretcher. Made you more famous than ever."

Ed, heavily sedated, replied with less bite than expected, "Let her have her picture. She turned out to be pretty good stuff. Wonder if her grandfather is Ollie Miller down at Sprague."

The nurse told Bill that his five minutes were over.

In a moment, Eleanor appeared timidly at Ed's bedside. "Thank goodness! You look so much better!"

She noticed the bedclothes. "They've got your toes all flattened down, haven't they? Want me to loosen the sheets at the bottom?" she asked gently.

"That might be O.K.," Ed gave her permission.

EACH DAY, FOR ten days, Ed announced, "I'm going home tomorrow."

Eleanor came twice a day on the thirty-mile drive from Bonaparte, in the morning with Doc and in the evenings with Bill and Susan.

On the tenth morning, after he had studied Ed's chart and listened with a stethoscope at his chest, Doc said, "I can let you go home if you promise to keep still for six weeks. You'll probably rest better in your own bed. But you had a good coronary; can't fool with it."

"Peaches here taste like cardboard," Ed grumbled.

"I can all my own fruit in Mason jars, Doctor Bevis," Eleanor said. "Ed's not used to peaches out of tin."

"There's a difference," Doc admitted.

"Funny thing," Eleanor continued, "this is the first time in forty years I didn't can a single jar of fruit. I told myself it would be a waste of sugar to put up more. It's as though I knew something like this was going to happen."

"You're just the person to be prepared," Doc said.

He advised Ed, "You be patient one more day. Let Eleanor talk it over with Bill. If Eleanor has to run up and down steps fetching you fruit, maybe you should arrange for her to have some help. Doesn't need to be a nurse."

When Eleanor, Bill, and Susan came at evening visiting hours, Ed, having considered the conditions of his release, agreed to them to the surprise of everyone.

"About a hired girl. Know just the person," he said. "Bill, that Caliente kid seems to be at loose ends. Why don't you have Susan drive over to the Caliente place and find out if her Old Man will let her be hired out. Tell him we'll pay thirty dollars a month. We'll give that much to him and hand the kid another fifty.

"She might as well stay with us until something better turns up. She's gotta get out of her present situation, or she won't amount to much."

Bill flushed, but said gamely, "Good idea. Dumb kid can buy herself some clothes; maybe Tom can take her down to the Omak Stampede to watch her brothers ride next week."

ELEANOR KEPT FROM Ed all newspapers with headlines about the blazing holocaust on the national forests, the millions of dollars in damages, the recriminations and the blame-placing.

Eleanor could not deny his demand for the *Spokesman-Review* the day after the primary election. Ed read with equanimity that Walt Horan survived one more time as the Republican representative in Congress for the Fifth District. As he had predicted, the election had been only a trial run for Delbert Gaston.

WHEN THE WEATHER cooled, Ed was allowed to walk to town each morning for the mail.

"Take care of yourself, and you'll live forever," Doc said.

On his homeward trek from the post office, Ed looked up at the charred Okanogan Highlands and sighed, only in part for the loss of the timber that should have been sold to BilesColernan. He would never mention the loss to Eleanor. He sighed partly for the death of the old torn cougar, who had climbed a tree to escape the blaze; the blaze had pursued him to the crown. Bill told him of finding the scorched body in the grey ashes.

He was bringing home a fat fistful of correspondence, including cards from Sam and Leila. He shuffled the envelopes until a business size letter from the American Society of Range Management came to the top. He paused to lay the rest of the mail on the Bonaparte Creek bridge rail, took out his pocket knife, and slit the end of the envelope open.

"DEAR ED,

"In view of the serious issues raised by recent fires on the Okanogan, Colville, and Wenatchee forests, we have decided to include in our annual conference a discussion of controlled brushburning as a means of preventing major conflagrations. We know you have long been an advocate of such a program, and ask your presence at the Northwest Sectional Meeting of the Society in Vancouver, B.C. next month.

"Please let me know if you will be willing to talk for forty-five minutes at the morning general session on the second day."

ED SNARLED AT the stationery, "I'm damned if I ever open my mouth in public again! Nobody ever listens."

He picked up the mail again and stomped across the plank bridge. The gully made the bridge necessary although no water had flown down the streambed for years.

Over the railing, a flash caught his eye. How could he not have noticed on the way to town! Brilliant spires of fireweed, their normally pink blossoms made purple by the acidity of the burned-over soil, covered the slopes and clustered around the tall, healthy trees that had survived the conflagration. A twofoot-wide stream was running in the draw. Water again came down from the highlands. The forest fire had eliminated the tangle of vegetation that had absorbed water along the choked streams. Nature was sending her message. She went her way regardless of men's rationalizations, burning excess when it blocked her course, and renewing the land with her cycles.

He smiled to himself and started to compose his victory address: "When I came west at the turn of the century, the forest was open, like a park. Bunchgrass grew to a horse's flanks. When the wind came up in the morning, the meadows rippled like water."

About the Author

Nellie, besides being an author, librarian, and newspaper reporter, also lived fully in many other dimensions. She was a wife to Dr. Robert L. Picken, loving mother of Kathy, Jim and Bruce, and grandmother to ten. She was a strong swimmer and first mate sailor with her family on sailboat excursions on lakes Okanogan, Priest, Coeur d'Alene, Lake Chelan and the Strait of Juan de Fuca. Nellie spoke several languages and was a world traveler, touring Europe with her daughter, Kathy, and China with one of her best friends, Janet. She cultivated gardens and canned fruits and vegetables for winter. For many years she was main cook for cherry picking crews at a family owned cherry orchard on the shores of Lake Chelan, picking and savoring many a ripe cherry while perched on the rungs of a ladder. She was secretary/bookkeeper for her son Bruce's gun-smith business. Nellie had physical, intellectual, and creative energy, a quick wit, and good sense of humor, which carried her through 91 years. She had many told and untold stories.